LEE ROY'S HEAVEN

ALPHA TO OMEGA -
A Metaphysical Story of a Young
Dopeman's After-Life Journey

Big Brother Earl Roberts

Order this book online at www.trafford.com
or email orders@trafford.com

Most Trafford titles are also available at major online book retailers.

Printed in the United States of America.

ISBN: 978-1-4251-1734-4 (sc)
ISBN: 978-1-4269-7063-4 (hc)
ISBN: 978-1-4269-7064-1 (e)

Trafford rev. 08/08/2013

 www.trafford.com

North America & international
toll-free: 1 888 232 4444 (USA & Canada)
fax: 812 355 4082

STORY DISCLAIMER

DEDICATION

"Word-up America—Big Brother Earl asked me to dedicate this book to someone special. I'm truly honored to do so, so I've decided to dedicate it to God. I woke up again this morning—to begin a brand new day. Love and gratitude filled my heart. The love was due to the fact, I know God exist—and God is love! The gratitude is due to the fact, I know because he exists—I exist."

"I shall retire tonight with love and gratitude filling my heart. Love because—I know God lives, all around and within all of us. Grateful for this fact, because he lives—we live. Oh Mother—Father God of us all, it is only natural that I dedicate this book to you, with love and gratitude filling my heart."

"I remember reading in the Bible—(just one holy book amongst many I have read), where Peter came to Jesus and asked him, 'Lord, how many times should I forgive my brother when he continues to sin against me?' 'Up to seven times' Jesus answered, 'I tell you Peter not seven times but seventy times seven.' This humble book Lee Roy's Heaven, is all about forgiveness, love, and all that jazza-ma-tazz. I hope it shines through to you dear readers."

"Oh yeah—to my uncle Earl thanks for your precious assistance, player-player. I should have known you could type, I.O.U. Also to aunt Cynthia, thanks so much and god bless you both. I know it's not easy trying to love everyone all the time right?"

"For all the non-believers out there in spirit-space living in this world's spirit-matrix (this world of great illusions), you'd better find God before he finds you, sleep walking like so many souls are doing today . . . You have been warned, judge me not—least you too be judged. Let's leave the judging to God. Peace and love Sarah & Doc, Lue, Lillian, Little-Ed, Letitia, Dan(my brother), Bobby, Vincent, Bonita, Angie, Pam, Buck and Deb, Vaughn, John, Jerry, Lolita, Lilly, Tony, and Mom—Lee Toya

INTRODUCTION TO LEE ROY'S HEAVEN-ALPHA TO OMEGA

The reason I wrote this book. Simply put, there was a story to be told. As a man, I gave my word I would tell it. I'm somewhat old fashioned, old school as the young people say today. I believed if a person (especially men) gives their word for any reason, then they should endeavor with all their strength of character to try and keep their word. To make good on, and be accountable for promises made, or don't bother making them! A young associate of mine who I see often and whom I care a lot about, told me in confidence on more than one occasion—that they had been having these strange dreams every since they could remember. They told me that it was time to share, what they have believed for so long needed to be shared with others. I applauded her courage and innate wisdom at such a young age . . .

I took this young person seriously when they told me that, they knew in their heart that they had lived before. In addition, after they died in this life, they will return—to live again. Until they got it right, life and living it that is. After talking with and working on this book with my young associate I gave her my word the story would be told, exactly as it was given to me. My final conviction and belief in the project was solidified for me, when I was forced to remember a book I once read long ago—by an author who's name was Richard Bach, and his little powerful book entitled 'Jonathan Livingston Seagull.' My young associate had not been born yet when the book was written or read by me.

As I recall the hero of that novel by the same name, a Seagull named Jonathan—had gone though a series of reincarnations that lead him from earth to a heavenly world (or higher-consciousness) and back again, to enlighten the more fearful gulls (our fears) of what lies beyond death's door (altered consciousness). Indeed I was truly touched by that inspiring story. I also recall reading something written by a British poet-laureate, Sir John Masefield dealing with past and future lives. He said—"I hold that when a person dies—his soul returns to earth, arrayed in some new flesh disguise, as another mother gives him birth. With sturdier limbs and brighter brain—the old soul takes to the road again." Personally I feel a deep level of truth in this quote.

Still, I will not now go into what my concept or definition is of what constitutes truth. However, I can say that my young relative has given me their interpretation of 'truth'. She said, "truth is truth—isn't it uncle Earl? Surely, you know that truth is God, and God is within us!" Then she added—

"The desire to think and speak straight forward about things believed in, without intending to falsify or misrepresent the subject thought of or spoken about. Of course we both know and understand that one should not reveal to mad skeptics or prying eyes, or simply inquisitive little minds, all that one knows to be the truth right? What was it the great Master Teacher Christ told us in one of his sermons—'cast not your pearls before swine, for they may consume them all, yet not understand a damn thing?'

I admonished her for her language usage, saying that Christ probably didn't use those exact words. Well I indeed felt I had received enough material to at least write and tell this story (based on her strange dream diary). Thinking to myself maybe—just maybe, there might be enough acceptable truth within the pages of this new novel for most readers. Allowing me to go back to my young associate and recommend she keep on dreaming and shar-ing her dreams, including this provocative collection entitled Lee Roy's Heaven—Alpha to Omega. Truly I've enjoyed writing this story and wonder what truths many of us will discover in our own future lives, that we have yet to recognize as truth in this life. Wouldn't you agree—that our tomorrows are indeed a kind of new life, if we awake each new day to greet them?

Please remember dear readers, the whole world was once believed to be flat, and now it's truly believed to be round and tilted on it's axis. Can we really be so sure of this, as my way of making the point. So what is "truth"? To the curious casual reader of this spiritual-story, please reserve judgment until you have read the whole story. And if you ever meet my lovely, wise, young-niece out on the streets of the City of Detroit, Michigan—please show her the love and respect due all human beings, no-matter how strange she may behave or appear to you . . . Remember, 'Spirit is all, and all is Spirit'—so can we 'live and let live', maybe one day, maybe one way—we all can and will?

Oh yes to the spirit of my last Mother (Super Mom Lillian)—wherever you now reside in this Intelligent Universe. Thank you for guiding me to the path of understanding that—'we are not just human beings expressing a spiritual story on this Earth, but are indeed spiritual-beings expressing a human story.' To all spiritual beings everywhere in America and in the world, live long and prosper spiritually—until we meet again, and again, and yet again, if we have too'.

Enjoy - The Author
Big Brother Earl Roberts

PRESENTED FOR YOUR READING PLEASURE—
A NEW NOVEL UNLIKE ANY OTHER
YOU'VE EVER READ,

ENJOY THIS NEW CLASSIC

LEE ROY'S HEAVEN

ALPHA - OMEGA

A METAPHYSICAL STORY OF A YOUNG DOPEMAN'S
AFTER LIFE JOURNEY—BY BIG BROTHER EARL
ROBERTS OF DETROIT, MICHIGAN ©-2011

Chap. 1   "ALPHA" 1

"Mr. Lee, Lee Roy – my boy! Lee of the big D . . . You the man, yeah, the young Dapper Rapper – cause I love rap music. These are just some of the names they called me back in the hood, back in Motown, City of Detroit. My family and friends and my bad-ass street crew the fellows, yeah all my mellows, the dogs of the Wolf Pack. We made a difference in town whenever we came around. We made the 6:00 news too. We were tight because we had our shit together! We knew it was our turn to shine all over the big "Dee". We were living large in Motown doing the dope game throw-down. North-side, South-side, East and West-side – we were on top, big-ballers and shot-callers, moving kilos of dope – supplying crackheads false hope, fly young honeys, fast cars. Yeah we were bling-blinging because the cash was stacking up and we were slinging, I mean truly stupid loot! Some local hot-shot under cover agent, was heard to say after a half-successful raid – "money, money, money! These young fools are getting paid, big-time. Tax-free is what we all should be!"

I never realized that a street-player, a young thug with brass-balls could come up so fast and live above his ghetto expectations. All the while surviving the mean streets, and cut throat dealings of the notorious drug-dealers and violent street gangs from the dark-side of the big Dee. Well I did, and I came up from nowhere, starting with nothing! Mom was a star from about fourteen to twenty-four, and a real good mom as I remember. Until she found a deadly habit, popping pills to compensate for a broken heart. Her first husband, and her first real love – my dad, was killed in a shoot-out over another women he was seeing. When dad died, my good mom died too. Her pill popping lead to getting high and excessive drinking, which lead to using hard-drugs. Then she started selling herself for rocks of cocaine. She should have known better – damn fool! She showed me and my little brother what mother-love, family love was truly all about. She left us one day, all alone with an older dope-man on the east-side of Detroit – at a rock house off of Bewick and Mack avenue. My brother was only eight years old and I was ten or eleven, shit I can't remember now . . .

The area was known back in the day as Little Saigon – a reference to a place some brothers had visited over in Nam. You know – during the vietnam war days. Mom never returned to get us, we never saw her again. We were struggling to understand why her drug-habit had become more important to her then we were! At least I was trying to understand, while my little brother just fell into some kind of funk or something. Not talking much and just rocking himself all day till he fell off to sleep. About a month later, we were with an aunt who was on welfare, who also had three bad-ass kids. Our lame and spoiled-ass cousins as I remember them. They were always treated better then my brother and me. Before that year was up, we were attending our mom's funeral.

1

Both of us, my brother and I were dressed in these sunday school rags, damn hand-me-downs from our stank-ass cousins. They were allowed to tease us mercilessly I remember. I will never forget how I felt when I over heard my aunt speak so lowly and mean spirited about my mom and the way she died. She said she hated mom for wasting her precious beauty on my dad, who had introduced her to strip dancing and hustling older men soon after they got married. After my pops died, mom got gripped by a cold-blooded pimp called Rev. Silk.

He convinced her he would get her off of the drugs and manage her prostitute career so she could be the real star she used to be. My aunt said that he was the smooth-talking devil himself, even though he looked like a young Danzel Washington. He was a real user and abuser of young women, yet sexy and charming as hell she had said. They said this dude had argued with my mother one cold winter's night and had thrown or either pushed my mom off of the Belle-Island bridge. When she had come up short with his spank, his hoe-money she had collected from so many Johns. Some how, he beat the murder charges against him. He allegedly paid off the judge in his case. Later he killed himself when he realized that he had lost his top-hoe (my moms) and his little stable of addicted bitches was falling apart. Someone had said it was because my mom was the glue that held his pimp business together, and she was no longer in his life, his world of drugs, hoes, sex for sale, and easy money! Even today I miss her fine-ass and my little brother missed her more. I remember a few good times for me and my baby brother, when we lived happily as kids in the Jeffrey Projects near the express-way that divided Detroit between the west high-rises and east-side low-rise ghetto apartments. I know mom loved us, I just know it. I never knew my dad, and only vaguely remember his handsome face now.

The dude didn't stay around long enough to see me grow up to blow up, or to teach me anything, or provide a role model for me. So I found what I needed, what all young black boys feel they need in every concrete jungle in America. My chosen male role-models out on the dangerous streets of Detroit, which were the pimps, players, and flashy drug-pushers and dealers. Theirs was the only style I wanted to copy. It was fun to learn how to live off of your wits and street-harden finesse. To survive daily by conning and hustling the other tribes and fools, who never seemed to learn the sweet games or how not to become a victim of the deadly street games we played. By the time I was seventeen, there was no shame in my hustling game. Hustling stolen auto parts, fucking with money-getting hoes and the occasional white-suburbanite (a mark, fool, a rip-off target). Those who braved the dark jungle south of 8-mile road always wanting to be directed to dope or sex-houses in the hood, or looking for a pusher that sold that good jack-smack addict-shit.

There was hell to pay if they ran into my good-looking ass! I learned early on that I was destined to do great things in the streets. I wanted to be the man, that big shit Mr. Lee Roy. The king pin of Jack—the pretty girls mack, with a large tattoo running down my back, I had to live my dreams! The brains with gold chains, the star with the $50,000 car, dope fiend's bet, and hutchie mama's pet. Yeah I wanted it all, and I eventually got it all through the use of blood, sweat, and other people's tears. I had long-ago stopped crying myself to sleep, after my mother's un-timely death. Never to show or shed another tear again—ever! You see, I've always enjoyed writing down my thoughts and rap-tunes and ghetto prose. That's how I trained my mind—my brain to be tight, sharp, and quick—cause I knew where I was going required an education, even though it was only a street education. It served me well you see, I loved getting paid—even more then getting laid. Yeah it's true, I got a damn PhD; in hustling psychology, and a sheep-skin in ghetto-survival!

Of course it didn't hurt that I was carrying a gat (357-revolver) since I was 14 years old, everywhere I went. Once out of Juvie, I promised myself I will never go back to no prison cell hell. Still, I think I've been on the DPD's most wanted list since I led the Detroit Dapper Rappers drug-gang back in the early nineties. Let's see—in one prosperous year, when shit was booming—the gang's stats read something like, "6-8 killings, 5 wounded, 3-4 bank robberies, 4 jewelry heists! All at big homes In Grosse Pointe (a wealthy suburb east of Detroit) that fed the Dapper Rappers bellies for months. Also an assortment of drive-bys and beat-downs throughout the city that was attributed to my bad-ass street crew. You see, as a born leader or gangster in the hood out on the streets of Detroit—you had to circumvent your natural conscience every day, to do what you had to do to survive and enforce your gang laws, to stay the top Dog! Like I know now why it was so easy to pull the trigger on another nigga that looks just like you do. It's called self-hate—so what!

Cause truly if you don't have real love for yourself, you have no real love for your twin look-alike in the hood. So you can easily bust a cap in a fool trying to take what you got! Obviously, I had no real self-love or self-respect yoh! Hell, we were only 20 to 25 young-bloods 16 to 26 years old, controlling the lower west-side, east-side, and most of south-west Detroit. When the King Latin Killers were scared to death to show their faces, or throw up their gangs-signs in their own part of town. When ever we rolled through Mexican town in our Escalades and Yukon's to deliver our Jack and collect our chedder (drug money, protection dues) and respect. Doing this weekly all summer long, made my business one of the biggest underground and illegal enterprises in the State of Michigan—City of Detroit. Cleveland Ohio and South-side Chicago were later added to our territory—according to the Feds.

Yeah, I had successfully created a small criminal business empire back in the big 'D'. Me and Big Ike, my main squeeze who grew up with me, watching my back, and even hitting a couple of pretenders to my throne. When consolidating my power base, setting up many dope spots and recruiting new gang members (runaways) from southern states to build our organization. We actually distributed over 250 kilo's and thousands of pounds of B.C.Vancover weed, over a three state area and grossed over ten-million dollars, give or take a loose million over a period of four to five years. A joint Task Force was created by the Feds and the local Five-o to shut us down—after shit got real crazy! Just what the hell was a young inspiring black entrepreneur with just a G.E.D., was supposed to do to get paid and live his dreams. When the man continues to knock a brother down, to keep him from achieving the American Dream—mostly because of my race I believe! Shit—I had to try, I just had to go for it. It was my handsome-ass destiny to rise any way I could, right? It was like a dream come true—a multimillion dollar investment in madness, a destiny in supply and demand in a wealthy racist land.

All controlled by a smart and dangerous young black man. Hey I'd say, don't hate the player, just hate the game Mr. or Mrs. Lame!' Back then the prisons and jails were full of young brothers who tried to find their way, but hey—that is not the story I want to share—now this one is! So peep this deep story dear readers! I'm only 28 years old I think, seeing myself setting in a jail cell I'v occupied now for over three years, reminiscing on paper. Writing raw-raps, prose, and memories down of how it all started. This is a tale of my life and death, and my strange after-life if we can call it that. This is some deep shit yoh! So sit back, get comfortable and prepare your mind to blow up like mine did—cool? At first I didn't know what to call this story or write anything because for a long time I didn't want anyone to know the shit I'v seen and did in my earthly life. But I know this story must be told, because I feel I owe it to somebody—somewhere. An explanation maybe, some answers, as to what creates a drug-pusher in the first place. An evil person—I'd now define as a truly misguided and reckless soul. Well I'm not one to judge, so I'll just let you the readers of this work in progress decide for yourselves the value or moral contribution of this collection of my souls experiences, my visions, and damned after-life drama.

As well as the weird conversations I've had with strange beings and things called 'living thought forms.' That were truly real to me and maybe, just maybe, real for some others who are now manifest (living) in their physical bodies in the world at present—acting and behaving like idiots. In or out of jail, or in the street games of a real hell back in Detroit—word! Maybe a young pimp, a street player, dope-dealer somewhere, will get his hands on this book—read it and decide for himself to take another path than the one I blazed back in the world.

Because I now believe that there are other worlds, other places, and spirit-dangers undreamed of, and especially dire consequences spiritually for our earthly actions and reactions to living life the wrong way. By creating and contributing nothing but suffering and pain for others from our evil dealings or intentional mayhem — all for false fortune, fame, and a mysteriously unearned respect. Some one back in the day told me as a young player that I had to set some serious priorities, because I had to get my plans for my future straight. These plans, my wants (desires), my goals, would be my guide posts. The signs along life's high-ways and ghetto streets — that told me and showed me what I thought needed to be done? To know what was timely and truly important for turning no real skills into getting paid, getting laid, and getting cash, for a young thug's very survival.

Someone said, "Son — little Lee, money is not the root of all evil — not having money is evil! You got to be like a modern day Robin Hood" — (I had never heard of this dude until then). "To do a lot of good for some in the hood and a lot of bad for those who want to stifle a young gangster's search for meaning and respect! This requires a lot of loot, by any means necessary! So chose your path young-blood then go get paid!" I really started to calm down and adjust to prison life and write more, after three years of the same routines of an incarcerated life-style. I found myself doing time for a Rico indictment, allegedly running an on-going, multi-state criminal enterprise. One in-which I believe the Feds and City Cops allowed me to openly operate for a good while, as long as the body-count stayed low and out of the national media.

I think that they actually feared the prized example I was setting for the other up and coming disenfranchised black males within our cities concrete jungles yoh. Which is all set up and controlled by our government I believe, to keep the black race impoverished and contained within certain zip-codes. So we will be forced to pray on each other, oppress ourselves, and never discover more legal ways to enrich our lives. Then the blame of powerlessness would continue to be on the shoulders of the black-ass citizens living there themselves. Isn't it a fact that blacks don't own or operate one damn gun-factory in the whole country or grow raw dope! Yet even I could at a young age, get any piece (gun) I wanted in the hood for only a few hundred bucks minimum. Prison turned out to be just another microcosm, of the urban prison I fought so hard to get away from back in the so-call civilized world. It was my reputation, my quick temper, and the attitude of taking no shit from anyone. That eventually landed me in a dark and shadowy no mans land — on the other side of a death, or perhaps just a dead man's dream. Somehow awakening in a mystical fog, of being lost and afraid — extremely afraid, until I met him!

A gate-keeper I guess, a teacher, a specter, a strange kind of Guardian Angel so he claimed to be. He showed me things, and told me things, that

I'm still somewhat confused about really. We shared experiences and new knowledge that made me, the soul that I am now. I acquired a new way of looking at life, back on my life, and of a new life I hope for the future of others still doing time back on earth. Yeah even earth itself can be a living hell, or prison for many lost souls. Especially those folks still living in a kind of hell back in the dark neighborhoods of America, mentally deficient, in or out of prison. Those man-made jail cells occupied mostly by young black men, and even worst those jails / prisons of the mind (physical additions and self-defeating beliefs) made by young black men them-selves. So please dear readers bare with me, have patience for this soul—that has some how been allowed to give back something of an enigma, from a story I suppose—of my soul's journey from one kind of hell-a-va life, into a stranger kind of life if you will. A life of consciousness and spirit (or of spirit into consciousness). I'm not perfectly clear of the steps of passing over to the other side, because death and resurrection can be so damn confusing to a novice of things spiritual.

Let me just tell you my story, let me share this thing—this longing to leave behind some kind of message. Let me start with what I call my earthly physical death while in prison, up at the Fed House at Teri-Haunt Indiana. Some how, someway, Big Ike and I had ended up there in the same correctional facility. You see someone had fucked-up the paper work I'm sure, cause we were never supposed to see each other again—once we got sent-up! Whoa, two of Michigan's most wanted in the same joint! When I saw him again for the first time on the con-yard, we embraced like road-dogs screaming—"nigga my nigga", and "what's up Detroit?" After Ike was hooked-up by me with some wine and women and current jail-house info. We got down to serious business, cause doing time was fine, if you still got paid and laid. We were still trying to regulate and run things back on the streets of Detroit from prison. Hoping to maintain our hidden capital supplies and gangster-ass life styles, all the while we were locked down. Together again, we still had our mad contacts out on the streets of the 'D.' So we could still afford to wear fly threads and fresh Jordan's, and eat steaks, lobster tails, and scrimps—brought into the joint for us. Paying well those that fell victim to our smooth-talk, or if necessary, the brute force that Ike brought with him where ever he went.

Ike has always been my main-enforcer, my go to guy back in both worlds. Back in the local joints and out on the streets of the Motor City. He was a real mean bastard that loved me like I was his only family, hell—I think I was. He was as big and strong as he was mean, and loved himself some gambling. We spent a lot of time and money gambling in the joint, if we wasn't on the yard pumping big iron.

It was Ike's need to gamble and his quick temper that caused me to be hurt! Shit—it was just one more stupid affair, a prison yard argument over Ike being accused of cheating by another dangerous inmate. One we called the Great White (cause he had all of his front teeth sharpened to a point like sharks teeth, and for holding records for lifting a lot of cold steel in the joint. Well it was a warm fall day as I recall. The yard in area 4-north was crowded with jail-house joggers and minnows trying to bulk-up. Weight lifters were working the steel-stations three on one. Me and Ike had taken a short rest break to play a friendly round of cards with Great White, who scared everyone else on the yard except me and Ike. We were still waiting our turn on the bench-press when an argument started between Ike and the big-ass white boy with Dracula's teeth! Ike had been winning and talking big-shit since the game had started, and had ignored my repeated suggestions to cut the white boy a little slack but keep taking his money! I could tell that G.W. was getting more and more pissed off, mainly because his eyes and skin-tone was turning more and more red. Still I wasn't too worried, because me and Ike were surrounded by a chosen few of our in-house wrecking crew, several bad-ass Mobite mother-fuckers. A few king-size bloods we knew form back in our hood in the 'D', when we thought we were real big-ballers and shot-callers.

Those niggas was supposed to be about watching our backs on the yard, that's what I was paying them for. They failed the test that day! The inmate Great White had his wannabe skin-head crew and a couple of gay bitches leaning on him, whispering bull-shit Into his head against Ike. Shit like — "Big Papa, why you be letting that black-cherry talk to you like that?" I didn't like what I was feeling, with a $2,500 I.w.p. (I will pay) on the table and things beginning to heat up. The more me and Ike scored on the white boys at the table — the further the pin was being pulled from the con-yard grenade! Ike was pretty hyped and talking even more shit and louder. I noticed after a moment that one of the faggots had casually slid behind and to the left of Ike, and begin fumbling with his pants. Just then my street radar went off and I just reacted! I lunged across the table hoping to push or pull Ike out of the way, to avoid the rushing right-hand swing of a glistening ice-pick! It was long enough to reach across Ike's massive chest — ride through his rib-cage and pierce his heart! I had to save my brother, my truest friend from this treachery! Ike was shocked by my sudden movement, speed, and my scream — "Ike look out!" Ike started falling back chair and all, and I landed stretched out across the table and took the full blow of the pick hand of our enemy, into my left upper arm pit. The homemade weapon pierced my heart in a nasty way — so that my death was almost automatic, almost guaranteed!

As I grasped my chest from the pain and rolled over twice on the warm ground, I heard myself saying — "damn this hurts, Ike is gonna owe me big time — if I, if I survive this shit!" Nope — I didn't survive that con-yard attack that day, only Ike did. Even after he went berserk, and put three of the white boys into intensive care that day, I remember floating outside and above my physical body watching 5 — 6 guards mauling Ike. I mean they were putting a real ass-whipping on my upset brother! Struggling to get him off the yard, while two more guards and a couple of Mobite jail-brothers carried me hurriedly back inside towards the infirmary unit. I saw the duty doctor hit my body with some paddles and electricity, trying to restart my heart as soon as I was laid on a gurney. All the while the long homemade sheave (a sharpened, industrial strength coat hanger) was still embedded under my arm and deep in my heart. They really tried hard to save me—the biggest dope-man, the dapper Black Don from Detroit, but it wasn't to be, it was just to late! The darkness had my bad-ass—and I said ok, ok, come on Mr. Death, or Devil or whatever you are, come and get some from a real baller fool! If I had my burner, my A-K with me now, I'd blast your ass too! Death laughed at me, it was time for me to pay the piper! The whole scene and room grow darker, as I sensed someone or something approaching my space, growling out my name, "Lee Roy—ooh Lee Roy."

Ok—ok I thought, now I get a chance to meet the old Soul-taker who I've sent a lot of other punk-bloods to meet before me. Surely he wants to thank me, for helping to keep his numbers up! I could vaguely here his foot steps, and the strange sound of dragging metal—like heavy chains being pulled across some neighborhood black-top. As the room grew darker I felt pulled away from this life, the material physical world. I felt my spirit, my soul, hell—I don't know which, kind of floating away into the quite and cold darkness towards oblivion I guess. I thought to myself—damn so soon? That dying shit really wasn't so bad a due, crossing over that is. Hell I said, at least I know I'll make a good looking corpse at my funeral. Shit—I felt cold, then I felt hot as hell, then—I smiled as I started to cry (don't repeat this). Then I became scared—as I asked the dark shadows floating all around me, "where am I, what's happening to me?" Boy was I longing for the fading light to stay with me. I also had the thought that even prison was better then this dark-shit I be floating in! At least I knew where I was then—damn! I remember crying out "please, please God—then I felt angry and thought, shit Lee, God never cared for you before player! So I said fuck it—fuck this shit! As I stepped out of that life into nothingness! When my eyes had adjusted somewhat to the dark, I looked all around me into the surrounding darkness and said—'ok ok, come on Mr. Death or Devil who ever you are, I know you're near, cause I can feel ya!

"Come and get some of this from a real player fool, if I had my burner, my A-K with me now, I'd blast your ass too—damn, de-ja-vu! Death laughed out loud and growled something (as I begin to lose even this momentary bit of consciousness). I thought I heard him say, "Damn fool—your young black-ass is on my turf now little boy, chain-em up fool! Lay down little dope-man or bow down and kiss your behind and the world good-by, because your soul belongs to me now young nigga, I am the mighty Grimm Reaper! No—(he said) you don't need to ask why—it is I, or what's going

down. Because here in this place I am king young fool, and you be the
clown! Do you hear me young black-baller?!"

"My job is collecting spirit-trash and other useless disembodied souls
for proper disposal Mr. Roy! So rap what you will fool, write what you
can—real death and darkness reigns in this here land. Here in the after-life
realm—I fear no man! So let's ride little dope-selling nigga!" I said (trying
my best not to sound afraid), "let's ride dark mother-fucker! Let's do this
shit ass-hole, I'm not scared of you!" I was lying like a mother, I was really
scared! Shit, I had already lost my physical-life, what more could I lose?
Still I half-heartedly cried out—"I ain't nobody's punk mother-fucker,
I ain't scared—I'm already dead so bring it, I ain't scared of no ghost
mother-fucker! You'ed better ask somebody about me bitch-ass ghoul, my
claim to fame is in my very name, Mr. Lee Roy cause I'm the Devil's boy!"

Chap. 2   "Exodus"

Let me tell you readers something, it was not a long ride into oblivion. I was having strange visions, crazy flashbacks, and hearing all sorts of screams and things going off in my head. Most of which I recognized as coming from my past dope pushing life-style. I felt like I was dreaming inside a damn dream, and yes, I was a little frighten. Then I woke up fully, I was cold and felt the creepy sensation of knowing that I was not in my real physical body but I still had a body. Now I know what ghosts must feel like. I didn't know where I was, didn't know what the hell to expect, and couldn't make any real sense of this strange place that was still dark and soundless, "shit!" I thought, this could turn out to be the damn twilight-zone my moma used to talk about. I suddenly realized I couldn't move my limbs, and started to shake, when I became aware of a floating sensation. I was floating and sensed that I was lying on my back on some kind of rug or carpet-thing, being pulled in some direction in a straight line I believe. There was no sense of any particular elevation of my body or any resistance to my being pulled or dragged along. All was deathly silent except for a constant incessant growling or grumbling, I felt my mind tripping—somewhat slipping!

I felt I was moving slowly forward by some strange and mysterious force or power. Then I heard something, a muffled growl or groan, like a Darth Vader sounding voice (from star wars) above my head. I also knew I couldn't move or turn my head much, or see any further then a few feet around me up or down. I strained to see just where that voice was coming from. It was trying to sing a song I think, just what in the hell was it?! What in the hell was those horrible sounds coming out of it? I could barely make out the words—like strange lyrics from somewhere in my past, in between the dog-like growls, and deep breathing that was becoming more apparent. It was singing—this big-ass smelly creature was trying to rap, "You could be as good as the best of them, bad as the worst, but don't test me—you'd better move over." Then a scary shrill—"get moneey!" I knew I was probably still in some kind of after-death shock, but the words and tune I heard kind of reminded me of one of my favorite rappers from back on earth—Biggy Smalls, damn! Then I became aware of this horrible smell again, like some musty-old, mildewed rags and rotten eggs. The smell was coming from beneath me, what ever it was I was lying on. The thing I was lying on seemed to be attached to some bigger then life-size creature, like a coat tail or funky cloak that was all tattered and stinky.

What ever this thing was, he or it, smelled like dead bodies after they've been in the sun way to long! I suddenly believed this must be, that damn Grimm Reaper! Trying his damndest to bust a old rap song sarcastically! Then I started to think, damn—I hope he's not still pissed off at what I had told him earlier! I started to pray as best I could, that he wasn't pulling me into some kind of painful hell! I also asked God to please restore movement to my legs, and my body—so I could jump up and run like hell! It didn't matter to me where I ran to, I just wanted to break free from the big-ass chains that held me down and run! I wanted so badly to get away from this dark smelly monster! Let me ask somebody, anybody out there, have you ever experienced fear so great, you felt it would or could stop your heart? Was your breath, your breathing hard to regulate or catch? Well mine was, I knew inwardly that I had died not long ago, but couldn't remember exactly how long ago. Yet due to my current fear and paralyzed state I felt that I was about to die all over again!

I felt within my racing mind that this time it might be worst, much worst then before! I was trapped and chained like a vicious wild animal. I needed help real bad. I cried some, prayed some, asking God to please forgive me and help me! I just kept falling into and out of awareness and nothing had changed, on this slow ride to lord knows where! Not the smells, or the cold and hot flashes tripping through my spirit body. I really felt doomed! Nor the continuous grunting and sorry-ass singing by the reaper—until all movement suddenly stopped. I felt that Grimm had suddenly stopped walking and dragging my ass through space. He was looking all around, you know like from side to side as if looking for something. Then I felt we moved forward a few feet, then noticed we started down some kind of rocky steps. Like off to the right of the path we had been going along, into a darker area of space. Old Grimm pulled, and banged my motionless stiff-ass body over and down, about twenty of these rough steps.

I couldn't see them while still lying on my back, but I felt each one. Bam, thump, bang, damn it, oh God now what?! Upon reaching the bottom of this incline—into some kind of hole I suspected, the creature Grimm stopped and looked up and all around again. He then started sniffing the air as if he smelled something different in the stale and musky space surrounding us. Yeah, I'm still scared as hell to tell you the truth! I didn't know what the hell was going on with the Grimm, but I'm beginning to get pissed off that it's not over yet! I tried to remember what I'd heard, or learned about the stories of the Grimm Reaper when I was a kid. I think his job or duty was to pick-up recently deceased souls and transfer or escort them from the physical world—over some dark lake to some fool place or thing on the other side of death's door. Or was it to the very gates of hell where the Devil supposed to live.

I wondered to myself if the big grayish fool was lost or looking for some kind of dark mystical doorway. One that hid the entrance of hell maybe, damn—just waiting to open up for the spirit remains of a young cold-blooded dope-pusher like me. I felt like screaming—"Hey you old smelly mother-fucker, let me up! Lets get this shit over with fool—hey Grimm, I'm talking to you ass-hole! Are you lost sucker, you got lost like me in this here darkness—huh?" He gave me no answer. He just started to circle around then looked down at me finally with those dark big red eyes of his. They were the eyes of the long-ago dead. Lifeless, glazed over, dead. Yeah I had seen that life-less, long-dead stare before. Once or twice back in the real world, Ike had pulled the big 750 Beamer over to the curb at an abandon house in a run-down part of town. He then walked me back to a burnt-down garage, to show me a dead body he had dispatched a few days earlier on my orders. I saw 2 bullet holes in the head and 2 to the chest—maggots and flies everywhere, shit was gross but didn't faze me, cause it was all in a days work for us big-time drug dealers. "Nothing personal—Ike had told me, just business boss." Yeah, nothing personal just business. Grimm's pinkish lips were thick and wet with drool as he started to growl—"You bad-boy, got a big nasty mouth!" I thought—what the fu—! I thought to myself damn, look who's talking!? His breath smelt like a garbage truck!

He looked like he was sporting a large nappy afro hair-do under that dirty purple hoody attached to his cloak. I swear I saw sharp yellowish teeth in his large mouth, and his breath stank as he began to speak again. "I've said it over a hundred times now, this prize is mine—I won't lose you or give you up Mr. Bad Boy Lee Roy—there is a large bounty on this ass, your little punk-ass! So I got to deliver your evil energy to a special place! It's real, real, hot there young-blood! Hot like you like that nasty stuff—you'll see!" Then he laughed a deep funky laugh and asked me sarcastically if I got any dope on me, did I bring any of that crack-cocaine over from the other side? Saying that must have been some badass shit, cause his death collection numbers went way up when that deadly shit hit the streets of urban and suburban America. Again Grimm looked all around—nervously, as if something was about to happen. He sensed it and so did I. The Reaper got all tensed up, and squatted down next to my prone body. My sight was beginning to adjust to this darken environment, and I thought what I was now partially seeing—his face, which was so damn ugly, to ugly to describe. I turned my head away and looked around me at the ground, which looked something like a moonscape. I could hardly make it out off in the distant, but I thought I saw, what looked like two giant walls of flowing water. On both sides of the area where we stopped, like two giant rivers flowing in opposite directions—one flowing up on an angle and the other flowing down on an angle.

Each one sparkling with tiny metallic flakes as they rushed by silently. Old Grimm was just staring into my face now, and I still couldn't get up to clock his ugly-ass. I wanted so badly to bitch slap his big nasty-ass! I tried but I just couldn't move my arms or legs, but could move my head a little more. I could see Grimm becoming more and more agitated, as he rose and started stomping around like a reckless malfunctioning robot. He was blowing smoke from his large nose and mouth while cursing, at the same time appearing frustrated. I didn't know why—and I didn't have a clue.

Suddenly as I looked up into the darkness, I saw something strange. Several small burst of bright white lights was moving towards us from one of the walls of water above us now, from what I had thought before was flowing rivers. These few lights (3 of them) heading towards us, were growing bigger and brighter, moving real fast now. In every direction Grimm turned—he would stomp and grunt and blow more smoke. Because the bright lights had separated and begin to approach our location from different directions. As if to head us off—searching the area for Grimm I guess. The Grimm Reaper started to speak again, and he sounded mightily pissed off! "Damn, damn! Now what to do, what to do?" He turned around and said to me—"there's a bad electrical storm coming this way young dead-man, we need to hide!" I immediately thought, why did he say hide instead of find shelter? Hell! I didn't want to hide, I wanted to die—or get off of his raggedy-ass dirty coat!

I felt Grimm's big hand grab one of my legs as he flung me down into a deeper hole—which felt like a deep grave. Then he jumped down into it with me, and sat up against one side of the hole pulling his big stinky cloak over and around the both of us. Yep—it felt like we was hiding. Then the big fool had the nerve to schuss me, while placing a smelly black clawed finger against his pinkish lips! Then he said—if I remained quite and very still for a moment, while the storm passed, he would reconsider where he was taking me. Or maybe even let me go free to roam this space, this place at will. I just didn't believe him. I knew in my heart from my street training back in the world, that this animal couldn't be trusted! Just a while ago he was gloating and bragging like I was some kind of soul-trophy or special catch! Now he wanted to negotiate a damn deal with me. What's up with this fool creature I wondered. Then Grimm mumbled something like, "They can't see us if we stay low and under my coat." He was now covering his big red eyes with his arms folded across his big ugly face when he added—"they always trying to disrupt my duties, interfearing with my damn job! Curse them—curse them all!" I couldn't wait to speak, to tell Grimm just how transparent he was, but I still couldn't talk. So I just glared at his obviously frighten big ass. Now I really wanted to know just what was it that he was so obviously scarred of.

It didn't take long for my still somewhat confused mind to start working again like it use to back in the world. My fears were subsiding a little now, while Grimm's fears were growing bigger. All I wanted to do was give away our hiding spot, to whatever it was that was scarring him so badly. Still laying face up, I could see through the small ragged holes in Grimm's cloak. That several balls of bright lights were searching for him or us? Then I heard this crystal clear voice coming down from one of those lights. The image reminded me of the ghetto-birds (police helicopters) that used to chase me and my crew in the dark of night, after a shoot-out or drive by against our rivals back in Detroit. The voice coming from above us was loud and yet comforting in some strange way. Sounding like a man's thundering voice, it said—"Elemental Soul Reaper, we know you are here nearby, and we know what you carry! We respectively request that you reveal yourself and turn over to our care the soul-force you're holding captive. Known to us as Lee Roy!" I must be dreaming, the voice sounded formal like 5-0 back on earth—in the hood talking through a bullhorn!

With his head down under his folded arms, the Grimm Reaper shouted back—"No damn you, go away, and leave me to my business! He's mine, I've already promised to deliver his spirit-ass to my Lord and Master!" The voice from the brightest ball of light responded, "Let him go Grimm Reaper, release him now or we'll scorch this place with cosmic light so bright, that you'll be blinded for all eternity—if not totally annihilated! You well know that without your astral sight, your duties will no longer be needed not even by your God—the Lord of Darkness! We won't ask you again elemental! We give you only three breathes to decide your useless uncertain fate!" Now looking up Grimm spoke or growled, "Call me what you will, a low-life elemental or whatever—I know I am much more then that! I have walked the astral worlds just outside of the many physical worlds sense time was not, an have carried hundreds of millions of lost souls to rest with my Lord and Master! He will be very displeased if I fail in my mission to deliver this bad-ass boy's soul-force to him!"

Grimm was interrupted by the booming voice from above, as well as the growing brightness of their white light. Which was blinding even to me but didn't burn me like it appeared to be burning old Grimm's clothes now. The voice from the biggest ball of light said, "Listen to me you low beast of spirit! Give us the soul-force Lee Roy or give us your life right now!" Grimm snorted little sparks and steam out of his big-flat nose and shouted, "Alright—alright, first turn down your blinding light, it pains my sensitive eyes and I'll release him! Shut it down spirits—I'm hurting, I give you my word he won't be harmed!" As Grimm slowly begin to raise, cloak and all, the bright lights begin to rapidly dim.

I realized immediately Grimm's power or spell over me was rescinding, lessening, getting weaker, "Damn." The forms of the three lights changed into floating human-like beings—that had a strange and eerie white glow (aura) around each of them. Grimm climbed out of the hole and waved his big cloak over me and the heavy chains fell away, as I begin to float up and out of our now exposed hiding place, landing slowly up-right and on my feet. I still couldn't move that much, but felt whole again somehow, but I could now speak. Still I felt tired real tired. Tired of being afraid, tired of not knowing what was what—I felt sick of this limbo shit, with all of these strange creatures! I looked at the gray headed old man standing in front of me now, who looked to be about sixty-eight or seventy. He had a short curly white afro with a snow white beard to match, and was surrounded by a softer white glow as I felt he looked vaguely familiar. He threw some sort of silver sparkling dust in Grimm's direction and told him—"Be gone Lord

Elemental, your work here is done. Return to your Master, your source, and tell him that what is stolen in the dark always comes back to the light!" Old Grimm stumbled awkwardly backwards trying to avoid the sparkling dust. Then pointed a crooked finger over at me while mumbling, "Oh we will see each other again little dope man—I promise you, selling drugs grants you and anyone else a free ticket to Hell—you little demon seed, that is where you belong—you'll see!

As he slowly begin to fade away, he turned towards the old-man spirit in white, and it sounded like he said—"You damn Angels—I'll see each of you one day as well, even flunkies of the white-light don't glow bright forever—you'll see, mark my words mystic slaves of the Godhead!" As old Grimm was vanishing into the surrounding dark space, he glanced back over his shoulder to see me flip him my middle finger. Within seconds the light being had stopped glowing and only a small rim of light was still surrounding his gray-white head and shoulders. Then he introduced himself, as the other two light beings—Angels I guess, moved up and out into space in the same direction. "Welcome my little brother Lee Roy. I am so pleased to finally meet you again—it's been way to long young half-soul." Damn—his voice sounded just like mine, but deeper some how. He softly spoke again but with more authority in his voice this time. "Sit down right where you are and rest for a minute. Do you recognize me? Do you know who I am?" I'm speechless—yet I know I can speak now, somebody has got to be making a movie out of this shit! Absolutely no words were coming out of my mouth, but my lips were moving, damn! "A little tongue tied, aye? Had a shaky transition did we? My friends and I tried to get to you sooner but we wasn't sure where your little soul-force would materialize within these astral ethers. Sorry about that Grimm Reaper experience. I hope he didn't scare you to much?"

"Well anyway my friends call me Urge—Lord Urge to most, or Master Urge. You can just call me Urge ok. Yes, I am an Angel—or more technically a sub-angel, or what some would call your over-soul, your higher-consciousness. We'll talk more about that later" (as he began to walk around me looking me up and down). "I just can't remember the last time I've been this close to you, face to face like this, it's been so long—wow! Did we pick this male body form again that you are inhabiting right now?" I'm like what?! I felt like a hoe on the stroll for sale, the way he was eyeing me. "It's been so long since I was able to touch you—I could only follow your vibrations, and communicate with you from a distance through astral vibrations. I've observed your life from this dimension with the cosmic-window we Angels use regularly!" Suddenly I found my tongue—"I think I know who you are (taking a gamble), but I'm not really sure of what you are, I feel like I've met you before—I do! Master Urge, huh? I feel like I should trust you, cause you look like an older version of me, just much older!" "Good", he said—"that's good, you really need to trust me now Lee

Roy." "So tell me Mr. Urge—what was all that shit about bright lights and scorching old Grimm's ass out of existence. Yoh Angel-dude, could you really have done that?" As I thought about his name, Master and Urge came to mind? That's got to be some kind of puzzle or secret code for something associated with my past physical life, it's just got to be. Let's see Master and Urge, Master-Urge, huumm? My thinking was cut short, as I awaited an answer to my earlier question, which would occur a lot more in the times ahead with Master Urge (I later learned why).

My Angelic rescuer who saved me from the dirty-clutches of the Grimm Reaper, sat down across from me and said—"Lee Roy my little brother, all of your questions will be answered soon, but right now it's not safe for us here in this space—on this transitional plane of passage." "We must retreat to higher grounds ok? Like I said, you need to trust me now—I mean really trust me! More then you've ever trusted any other person or being!" I thought about only trusting my moms and Big Ike back in my recent past life, back on the streets of Detroit. Still I said "ok, so what's next old dude besides trusting you?" "Well—he said, first things first young soul, you need to address me properly, and secondly you need to bow down and pray with me. Not to me personally, just cooperate with me—and say what I say ok. So your heart and astral mind, your present consciousness can get used to our nearness—one to the other now, ok. Doing this will perhaps make all things here in this place, a lot clearer and easier for you to understand. Your part of our soul's expression on this plane of existence needs to be made more aware—more heighten, to grow and expand itself, to remember things learned here and carry them forward."

Whoa—I thought to myself, this Lord Urge be tripping me out with this mind and spirit shit. I really do think I'm caught up in some kind of mad-ass dream. I think I'm gonna need some Dom Perigon, or smoking a fat-blunt right about now was definitely in order. If this shit keeps up I'm gonna need a spirit interpreter. Urge chimed in as he began to rise—"Oh yes, by the way son—I can read your mind, your every thought Lee Roy, even after your past life just ended and this one begun." ("What?") "I've always thought it was a good mind, still I'm not so sure yet—so you don't have to move your lips to speak words or make any sounds for me to hear you young soul. Just think your own thoughts and I'll hear you ok!" So I did, I thought to myself—oh shit another surprise, what next! "Lee, I guess you didn't here what I just said huh? Well hear this little brother. We must prepare our selves, because we have a long way to travel, through different areas of space, and on different levels of awareness to be about our spiritual business. Our mission now is a serious one, I mean your mission. Your job Lee is to stay close to me and truly listen to and do everything I tell you to do—ok?!" "You must obey each and every direction or instruction I give to you—understood? This is crucial if you want to stay safe and alive in spirit longer! You can and will learn all you need—to make our time together profitable and a blessed reunion, ok—ok? Have you noticed I've toned down my emanation of angel-light, my aura now? Why have I done this?"

"Because it can attract undesirable creatures here, making it far too easy for them to spot us or track us and hinder our progress—so . . ." (Now I cut him off)—"Creatures huh, now you listen old dude—I'm sorry, Mister Urge—Lord Angel whatever. Are you really an Angel or Devil in disguise by chance, intent on messing with my head? I'd really like to know what the hell is going on. Even better, where are we going—what mission, and what's the real deal holyfield? What do you want from me or with me?" "No my little misguided soul-force—I am not the great way-shower, the Brightstar Jesus the Christ or the Devil. Pray with me Lee Roy—let us give thanks for this unexpected miracle from the Universal God of Host!" "What?!" I said, as some strange force pulled me quickly down to my knees—inwardly I knew it came from this old man. "Ok—ok", I thought I should pray—even though it's been years and I'm not sure if I remember how. I was struggling to appear thankful, so I prayed with this Urge character. My smart-ass started first—"now I lay me down to sleep, I pray the Lord my soul he might want to keep." "Lee!—(Urge was not amused I could tell), you must fight it little brother—fight your ego-ignorance! You must not let your earthly stupidity hinder you—or us, here in this realm!"

"This is not a game my friend—ok?" "What, ok—ok, you da-boss Mr. Urge" I said. He said, "You have no idea of how precious this moment is, or how necessary our reunion and soul-bonding is in order for us to prevail from this moment on-ward and up-wards, do you?" I said somewhat sheepishly now—"No, Mister Urge, all I know is that I'm lost, confused, scarred a little, and tired my friend, very tired!" He responded with, "I hear you little brother, so I'll try to take it easy on you—what's that bonding word you used back on earth? Oh yes, cool, it's cool." Then he said, "Yes—you do look a lot like I did three-hundred years ago." I was too tired to pay any mind at this point in this damn after-life drama.

Urge looked and sounded more familiar to me now, I'm not sure why. Looking like an old white headed wise man with a strange kind of glow around his face. Although I saw no evidence of angel wings, his silver robe looked cool as it shimmered in the twilight of this space where we walked. I noticed a strange and new sensation in my body when I started to pray outwardly—repeating what Urge was teaching me daily to say. I was also surprised to feel the many thoughts my new friend was easily generating inside my head, like some form of unseen magic, as we floated slowly upward and into the still dark space all around us. Which was only partially illuminated by the distant star-light. Let me tell you readers, I felt that he was indeed smarter and stronger then me, and truly incapable of lying to me—and even stranger, I'm sure he could read my thoughts even if I didn't want him too. This whole experience with the Grimm Reaper, and now this look alike older entity, who referred to himself as an over-soul—or Angel is more then I can explain right now. Some how I feel I will never forget this day or night—whichever time it is, in this moment. When I first met my higher-self on the other side of death's door, in the grotesque hands of a monster called the Grimm Reaper, a dark elemental something. Lord Urge appeared to me as an exact robed copy of me, just older—as I might have grown to be, if I had lived longer back in the joint. He appeared agile, robust, even in his advanced years. Obviously healthy and spiritual, very spiritual, I mean like holy-moly.

I was beginning to be intrigued to see how this after-death journey or dream was to play itself out. So we prayed, then prayed some more. We would be in motion, traveling for awhile then stop and meditate, then meditate some more. When one day part of his praying really got my attention. Urge was softly speaking as he reached across from where he was kneeling and grabbed my hand while resting his other palm on top of my head. I didn't dare move, while he said—"Oh great God of this Universe, oh sweet and sublime Intelligence, what grace." "Please shine your cosmic light down and all around us, yea—even through us now. Have mercy on this soul here, and guide us both through the dark valley's, troubled spaces, and evil places to come." Brother knew he was long-winded so I thought, (but I didn't quite know how long-winded yet). "Oh great and evolving center of love—continue to bless us and protect us, as we attempt to complete this reunification with each other, to become one whole and complete soul again. So we may one day return home to reunite with thee—our very source of spiritual power and ever-lasting existence. We truly thank you oh Mother-Father God, for this miracle amongst many past and those to come. Also for this complex soul experience unfolding now, this reuniting of young Mister Lee Roy and I, his Guardian-Angel, the light of this way-ward child" . . .

"In gratitude and with praise, we say please oh God, bring us into harmony once again with thee through your love—our one spirit, our resolve to equal again one mind, one body. Allow us to be found increasingly worthy to complete our journey home, so that we may arrive alive into your great City of Light. There-in to find forgiveness and spiritual justice, and a blissful rest—so be it, it is done. In the mighty name of the first Light-bearer Jesus the Christos, we pray this prayer. Glory-be to all the Gods, on every level of consciousness, on every plane of spiritual expression. In every heart that beats with the force of divine energy—divine love, together we say amen." Urge paused his praying and looked me in the eyes and smiled slightly and said—"It is so and so it is Lee Roy, let us go and let us grow". I was no longer afraid. The fear I'd been feeling had subsided quickly as we begin to rise, higher up off the gray and musty moonscape (where we first discovered each other), and which I had been dragged on by Big Ugly, for what seemed like many nights. I noticed the small white aura around Lord Urge growing slightly brighter as his hand, now on my shoulder lifted both of us up and away from this strange, dark, scary place. Master Urge whispered across my shoulder, "Lee Roy my boy I know that all of this is still a little confusing to you right now, but I do believe you'll share the light of understanding soon—real soon son. I just hope you're ready for this, and for what's to come. In the mean time, let us be truly grateful for any and all opportunities to get this right."

"It's so important to all souls and creatures of the light to get it right Lee, we must be about that business in all life, the true purpose of all existence—to get our spiritual lives right before earth-time itself runs out. Oh and by the way, I'd appreciate it if while we be walking and talking you'd be kind enough to keep your pants pulled up over your butt and your hands off of your crotch area—I truly don't condone that kind of behavior around me, truly it's gross—not cool, not cool." I said—"My bad, ok—ok, I'll try, you-da-man, you-da-man old spirit." I am never sure of the passage of time, or how much, or how long we've been traveling. I know only that Urge has not left my side for long, nor I his for any real length of time. Occasionally he would move off always and meditate alone, saying that he had a few private Angel rituals he had to perform every so often. I felt he didn't understand baggy pants, mine that is. I knew that I had fallen off to sleep a little again and again. The moments of silence lingered, when-ever Lord Urge stopped speaking or sharing his ancient wisdom directly into my head. He once mentioned that he knew I couldn't guess his age. I tried but failed many times, and he would only say, I couldn't guess it because I didn't know how old I was, cosmically speaking that is. So many damn spirit riddles for this player—me. After he had awaken me each time I nodded off, he would reiterate that for recent souls coming over, it was not unusual for them (recently released from their physical bodies) to experience mind fatigue or slipping-ego as he called it.

This was do partly to becoming conscious of real consciousness again (don't ask), he said—after having been spiritually asleep in their material forms (flesh I guess) for a long period of time. Still I felt a growing union of mind between us, a reunion of a soul re-discovering it's Guardian-self or Higher-self (our true oneness), and sharing a deeper understanding some how. I was now embracing new perceptions, new spiritual ideas, and seeing in a whole new way, so I begin to believe. I saw strange things floating by us (Urge called most of them simple thought forms), generated by other nearby spirits. Now using my newly discovered astral sight, we watched various colored flashes of light and spirit—forms passing around us at great speeds, energized by their own momentum, or from our movements when we were in concentrated thought motion—wheew! Sooo—I'm, doing my best to keep up with the old boy, damn I hope he didn't here that (he's said already I don't know what old is). I knew that Urge walked fast, because he was quick in his movements. We traveled quickly wherever we went, because I could see Urge's silver blue robe fluttering behind him on occasion, and I felt it. Urge said to me in one moment of speed walking, "Lee—to get from where you've been to where you are, then to where you want to go, is truly only a matter of focused thought. So it is on all physical planes of existence as it is here within the astral and etheral dimensions of soul existence. All movement, all activity, are only varied manifestations of God's creative spirit expressing itself as life energy." I was like, "Yeah Urge I gotcha", then I thought to myself—"not!"

Once while we were speed-walking or floating fast, whatever the hell we were doing, often I couldn't tell. Urge said—"If a soul has no personal sense of direction-development little brother, then that soul has no true destination-growth to arrive at. Having no goal or desire to be somewhere other then where it is. Then anywhere becomes good enough, even though it may not be where the soul needs to be or is supposed to be within divine order, you know what I mean little half-soul?" Then I would just think my response—without speaking it, and Urge would hear It. "I think I do Urge, I'm still digesting a lot of shit oopss, you've already shared with me old dude. I meant stuff, and yes I'm still trying to catch up, mentally, trying to understand a lot of what I'm learning from you purge, I mean Lord Urge." "Great, see—as I've already said, I knew one day the time would come where we would be so blessed to again communicate face to face. Our long distance communication of mind, where my half-soul was looking in on you—through my looking glass window was often disheartening and ineffectual to say the least. We were lost to each other many times, see? Almost daily watching you grow up, going through all those negative and frightening challenges was hard for me too. I tried like heck many a times to get your attention, but it wasn't always easy."

"You see transmitting spirit or mental energy through varying levels of matter isn't as easy in practice as they taught us in guardian Angel school.

Over the years I've sent you greetings, spiritual advice, many warnings, which obviously went unheard or ignored by you in your past life! Now I'm truly afraid because of your many sinful choices made back then, we may still face on this plane of thought—some form of serious retribution or dire spiritual consequences, may the Godhead help us! Still I think we'll be alright if we exercise care and continue to pray and give thanks for this blessed opportunity—do you understand me? We need to achieve as much unity as we can now, because I've got very little time to prepare you—to raise up your spiritual consciousness, and to sanitize your energy-matrix. Your union with me and mine to you, must be strengthen much more before we arrive at our final destination. Oh yes, if I've told you once I've told you at least a thousand times since we began this journey. You my younger soul, need to cleanse your speech, your language usage is truly obtrusive!

Where we are going and hope to arrive alive—is no place for such continued vulgar and crude speech, you dig pretty boy?" "Urge please, don't call me that!" He ignored my request—"You know pretty boy that I know, just how hard-headed you can be, or is it you're just not trying hard enough?" "What? Yoh, old dude, I'm not cursing nearly as much as I did when I first got here, and I'm keeping up with you right? Maybe you need to show me a little more patience and respect Mister Urge—please, my older brother!" "Lee Roy" he said—"News flash little dope man, it's already been over 350 years since we first parted and formed a split-soul energy matrix, what a big mistake!"

"Truly I've been just as lost as you have, without you. Were you really trying to avoid me, your higher-self all these years? I recall telling you way back then, that we had many life times yet to live. And our spiritual progress home, back to the Godhead would be much quicker if we stayed together as one whole soul force! But nooo, because of your strong feeling and desire mind, after hearing stories and rumors of material paradise—that other head strong and temporary lost souls had experienced back on earth, you just had to see it for yourself! That's what started this mess we find our selves in today!" What mess I was thinking? "It's true Lee, the magnetic material nature-forces that operate in and around most matter worlds like earth, have trapped many a wayward and curious soul—always have and always will. Such is the nature of great illusions." I said in my mind, I don't remember any of this stuff, and out loud—"Mr. Urge, I don't remember meeting you before this crazy scene or either separating from you before now. And news flash to you old-soul, I'm not three-hundred years old—I think I haven't even turned thirty yet!" I couldn't wait to interrupt him again and ask him, "Master Urge what the heck are you smoking old man, and can I please have some, just one or two drags ok!" He said, "See what I mean—poor little misguided spirit?"

"See what I mean, you always thinking with your old ego-mind right slick! You need to stop asking a thousand and one questions of me Lee, and start concentrating more on the concepts and lessons that I'm trying to impart into your thick skull boy" I think Urge was getting a little peeved at me at this point. "You need to listen to your heart-seed a little more Lee. That is where God answers most of 'your crazy questions about spiritual concerns. Oh I forgot again—you don't talk to God to often do you my little dapper prodigal son? If I were to take the time to explain everything in great detail to most of your questions, like—where exactly have I been all these years apart from you? Why we were once united as one soul, and why or how were we split apart? Why didn't I show up on the earth to guide you more directly? Those questions would probably take me as long to answer as it took God Almighty to create the Universe and the many worlds and dimensions within it. Lee, I am so sorry to say to you my young charge, we just don't have that kind of time luxury." I said "Urge, I'm still confused." "Do you really understand the real concept of time anyway little brother?" I thought—no! And he heard me, my lips never moved—I swear it's the truth. It took only a glance between us as usually now to communicate with each other mentally. "Time, Lee Roy as you've known it or know of it, is only a man made concept of measurement of what appears to souls in physical bodies as the passage of life-force energy from one form, or place, to another—moving, changing, or expressing itself in different moments of material exsistence."

"There are many great and small cycles in the Universe that are driven by the creative energy of God for his purposes of self expression and spiritual law. You don't get it do you Lee Roy?" Again I thought—no! "Well let's just say that time is a great illusion. It's just a concept that is used by human beings to interpret earthly nature phenomenon, to mark the seasons of the world, of life, for ground-walkers to understand cosmic-waves or spiritual-cycles inherent in physical matter worlds." Then I mentally projected into Urge's mind—"Urge, if I've told you once I've told you a thousand times (being a little sarcastic), you've got to keep it simple dude. You've gotta make all this spiritual stuff easier for me to comprehend, to retain and elevate my mind—our one-mind as you call it. Look, you've said before—that our mind is only one small part of the one Universal mind of the Godhead. Then why should we be concerned with just one little piece of it, like my little piece you dig?" "Lee, I know that you know, that the great whole cannot be the whole, if even one small part of itself is missing or under-developed." "Nope, Urge I've never given that stuff any thought dude, I'm a money-getting player or I used to be." "I know mister man, it's true Lee, if I fail in this my duty to you this time around. If I cannot transform (you) my lower-self into the shining light of a spiritual Triune-self, the true potential of all human beings. Then I myself would wish to exist no longer."

"A Triune-self would be you—your body physical, your innate spirit mind, and me your higher-self or Guardian consciousness. Hence our struggles to reach reunification, which some call the state of perfection—to become a whole soul again. So we may return to our source and complete the greater whole, you copy young-blood?" I said, "Well brother Urge, I'm just struggling to keep up right now, but I am focused on what I'm hearing and learning—ok! I'm concentrating as best I can on all this new spiritual, metaphysical bull-shit you've been feeding me since I met you! I still don't know if all of this is really real, or if this mind trip is really happening at all! Or if it's only just a damn dream, a dead dope man's crazy-ass dream! My mind and spirit is like . . ."(Urge cut me off). "Number one Lee, this bull-crap as you've called it just might save your partial-soul Sir Foolish. Maybe you're right, maybe I've been a little pushy lately my little brother. If so—truly it's a push of love. No this is not a blanky-blank dream! You need to know that while you were strutting around like a peacock in paradise lost, I've been studying our great Universe and deeper spiritual matters on this side of egotism. Unless I was trying my best to find and catch up with you—to reunite with you, to enhance your consciousness more. Because I knew one day we would get a new opportunity to return to our true state, the first form of our birth into life together—that of small cosmic pieces of spiritual energy from the Godhead!"

"I know you don't remember way back when or feel it yet, but hopefully—together as one whole soul again, we can both feel the joy, the utter bliss of our true state of being. To start sharing again the creative energies we poses with other separated individualized spirit emanations of Universal Love. So we may once again feel the power and the absolute beauty of rejoining with the Godhead. The first cause, that which is truly the most holy of holies, indeed the Alpha and Omega of all life and creation itself. So you see Mr. Lee, I'm a little biased, because there is so much more that I wish to share and give back to you now. You, who are my life's purpose as I am yours. You are a vital part of the consciousness of my own existence. Together we could truly approach the next step of accepting the indwelling or influx of the great Christ-consciousness. If and when we can reach this level of spiritual perfection, then we will become truly complete and immortal energy again, ok—ok?" "Whew, Urge my head is spinning, trying to keep up with all these lessons, new thoughts, and spiritual concepts you be teaching me. I know you're trying—how did you put it, to reintergrate our energies (our life-force), for us to attain some higher-state or level. But truthfully, I've been away from you a long time from what you tell me, and I've done some bad things back in the world Urge! So I hope I don't fail you, as I'm truly beginning to feel unworthy of all this attention you've been showing me my brother. I even killed a man who was trying to jack me for my jewelry, and even ordered other human-beings to be killed in the drug game back in the hood"!

"Yes Lee Roy I know, since you feel like confessing—you even poisoned about one-tenth of a city with your successful drug dealings! I know of your hidden guilt, occasional shame, and the rare but few good things you did back in the world also. Like feeding the homeless and giving money to a few of the bag people you met on the streets of Detroit back when. One of which was a high-level Angel in disguise, doing research on humans beings in the hood. That's why a great black man of God in Africa once said, 'since there's so much good in the worst of us and so much bad in the best of us, it hardly behooves any of us to talk negatively about the rest of us!' I believe you knew him as his Holiness Bishop Desmond Tutu. Do you feel me little man?" "I feel you Urge—I really do, although I've never been to Africa, I don't know no bishop Tutu. But I have been to the Bahamas twice." "Know this little brother, our creator who created the world and all things in it. Never meant for wayward souls or those that become earthbound, to take his great spiritual, material natural gifts and turn them into evil doings or destructive poisons like you had done. But that is just one of the many hazards of blinded, uncontrolled, undisciplined, spiritual children given the enormous spiritual power of creative thought-energy. You see Lee Roy—the great fall of man into matter-worlds, was caused a long time ago in eons past. When young inexperienced souls first discovered the power of the one source individualized within them, giving them the abilities to actually manipulate matter and minor nature-units into solid objects and strange material things from their own creative imaginations. Then having gotten carried away with their Godly powers, they ended up creating the very soul traps that keeps coming back to haunt them and retard their growth."

"Over time, causing themselves, and other souls like them to become lost in various material spheres of our Universe. Mostly as a result of misplaced soul choices. Then struggling through repeated incarnations and flawed levels of consciousness in attempting to find their way back home again." Again I interrupted my teacher, "Lord Urge, forgive me oh light of my life, but I need to ask you another favor—please?" "Well what is it this time Lee—and you can dispense with the sweet talk of light of my life little brother, you have yet to see the great light, and I doubt you or I ever will at the present pace of our traveling and your learning!" "Ok—ok Urge, could you use some of your silver cosmic dust I noticed you be carrying to conjure me up a bigger notebook and pen. So I can write down a lot of what you're teaching me—you know I like to write. You said you saw that on many occasions looking in on me through your looking glass windows. While you were baby-sitting me and my hard empty-head as you called it. Could you do this for me?" "Well—listen Lee, it's not cosmic dust or silver pixie flakes, it's cosmic angel powder—and it's extremely potent particles are dangerous in the wrong or inexperienced hands! Never forget that, please! Is this understood little man!?"

"This little bag of Universal-essence is only given to all Guardian Angels and Over-souls in this Universe, to aid and assist them as they go about their assigned duties in the fulfillment of God's great plans and spiritual works. With a pinch amount of this precious powder, I can instantly create whatever I will, or defend myself from the dark shadow forces that exist all around us. Do you recall that I told you that all matter in truth is a great illusion, along with time, empty-space, and simple nature-units, those lower classes of consciousness dwellers we refer to as elementals. Like yourself, they can never possess this gift of matter-starter dust. For it is given only to the enlighten ones who can be trusted to use it wisely, and only for the greater good and glory to the Godhead. So what pray tell will you write about first little brother? Just what great lesson or sermons of mine as you've secretly called them will you scribble down first?" I wasn't sure how to answer his question—so I gently said to him, "Yoh Urge now don't get mad or angry with me but" (he interjected)—"I don't get mad or angry at anything Lee. There are no hateful or harmful thoughts in anyone's Guardian Angel consciousness—you should know this by now young fool!" "Well sir, (sir—now where did that come from?) I feel like I'd like to write a rap-song or some street-prose, about all this stuff that's been happening, and about you guiding me, teaching me, taking me some place special—yoh?"

"Oh my Lord, my great God of host, Lee Roy wants to write down, of all things, a—a rap song about our meeting—our journey!" Lord Urge was actually turning a purple color-tone, while turning around in several little circles now. I'm not quite sure why—so don't nobody ask! After he stopped circling me he asked, "Are you sure, are you serious? I mean can you do that? Can you turn our adventure, this journey we're on into some kind of rap-prose? Whoa now this I gotta see son, so go for it young dapper rapper. Write that good stuff—just make sure you tell our truth, or maybe some of God's truths ok!" "Ok—ok".

"So be it Lee Roy, here's your tools—your pad and pen. You know youngblood these just may come in handy, cause your astral-mind's recall, and soul's mental short-term memory really stinks! You know you didn't need any of this here cosmic powder to create those writing tools—I've told you and warned you that your very thoughts on the astral plane, are powerful in creating whatever you truly need, to grow or expand your consciousness. Yet a soul alone still needs guidance, and practice in handling focused thought energy. The mind itself is a very powerful and creative force-field, on this plane as in physical worlds like earth. Today right now—if you were to truly focus on a thought, any thought, seeing the very thing in mind, and expecting it to be, to exist—it would be. It would immediately exist in this dimension! By the way, can you really rap or just write such nonsense? Just kidding little brother don't show me, just write it down and we'll get to it a little later, cool—cool?" Damn—I mean darn, Urge can be a little hard, even though I now know inwardly that he's a softie at heart. "Yeah Urge I'll remember to guard my focused thoughts as best as I can, and be more aware of this great gift from God—as a living spiritual being, to create what I will to create, as long as it's good, like to the glory—I gotcha!" "Ok Lee, keep in mind that your unfocused thoughts can also be dangerous and even deadly, especially in the higher realms of spiritual existence, as well as on earth, where it takes them a little longer to manifest into your physcial-reality, your material life, do you feel me son?"

"I'll write that down now Urge ok? I mean right—right! So you do promise to listen to my stuff later on—right Urge?" "Yes young-blood I do, and now it's time for us to pause again, for our regular prayer session and rest period." "Yeah we got to, I mean I got to clean the old spirit, my astral-mind of a lifetime of negative feelings and desires from my gross earthly past life—as you've often emphasized. Which may still be hanging around me, according to your teachings. Ok let's do this Master Urge, let's get down to some serious prayer and rest." "What about the cleansing part Lee Roy?" "Oh yeah—that also my brother!" So we did—we stopped our upward forward motion, stopped our unspoken conversations, where my mind had a rare chance to rest. And just sat there in space, praying again and contemplating things like Universal love, spirit life, soul-energy, and the power of forgiveness. "Karma is really (Urge said this was the root of the first law) the Universal law of cause and effect, stated another way as 'we shall reap (from creative-mind) what is sown'—'or as it will be in heaven—so it will be on earth, and what will be—must be." Also, 'as it is above ground (matter-bound life)—so it will be below ground'—whatever the heck that was supposed to mean—dead I guess.

Things like that—and yeah the true nature of God, counting our blessings, and focusing on the new ones we hoped would come. "Well little brother Lee, would you please define the word carnal for me, to me — this is a little spirit-test ok? I need to see if our last lesson on the difference between physical sex and real love went into your heart or head or some place else?! You did write it down didn't you? So tell me what does the word carnal conjures up for you partner?" Urge seemed impatient waiting on my answer. "Well lets see, that's like having a sexual nature, right? Being in a material body, in physical matter, lusting after women, or doing the do — right? I mean carnal is of the flesh right?" "Oh my Lord — Lee, forget the spiritual definition like you forgot the lesson, and just introduce me to your friend standing behind you there. I think she's been following us for a while little brother!" Urge caught me off guard with that one. Surprised I said, "What — who?!" I sat straight up and turned around to see who or what he was pointing at. Then I saw her, damn!! A beautiful shapely carmel skinned Goddess, and — and damn she was half-naked, smooth brown skin showing everywhere, in a shimmering see through sundress I believe! She was also wearing spiked heels at least 4 inches high, which seemed a little strange in this place. With painted nails top and bottom, a silk scarf was wrapped around her perfectly shaped head and face. As she approached us with a wide-legged stride, her sexy form was being exposed by the gentle caress of her see-through outfit.

I could tell from a distance she had to be wearing a thong or nothing underneath at all! As she snaked her way towards us, she seemed to be so tall, very shapely, seriously sexual or sensual, and as graceful as a big cat. Boy was she hot — I mean this eye candy was the bomb toosie-roll pop — wow! Then she started to approach me, I mean us, Lord Urge and me. I didn't recognize this Cleopatra diva from my past life, all I saw was bits and pieces of the physical virtues of all the women I'd chosen to sleep with back in my life on earth — and there were many! She was a true brick house — for real doe! This strangely appearing sexy fox had it all, fine legs, full delicate lips, curves and ass for days, etc . . . This chick, this choice-lay, oops, I mean lady, was indeed a lotta-hottie, or at least a tall sexy one. As she got closer to us, Lord Urge stood up quickly and tried to introduce himself with authority. I was surprised at his demeanor towards this fine-ass red-bone, creole looking vixen. Urge was mumbling something like — "beware oh beautiful complex being, you are in the celestial presence of a true Guardian Angel. So I command you to state your name and spirit-claim!" I said — "Yeah Urge, get her name man!" (as I thought through my mind to his) this women's fame has got to be in her name — sweet Jesus! Still — I could feel Urge's apprehension and caution growing. Damn suspicious-ass old folks! Then she spoke, "My apologies oh Master Guardian — I meant not to startle you and your young freind here Master Lee Roy I presume?"

Damn, I thought to myself, this bad-ass voluptuous hammer just called me Master Lee Roy! Her voice was like the hypnotic fumes of a junkie's crack pipe sensually lingering in the air. "Yoh, big Urge!" "Quite

Lee Roy—quite please!" I looked at Urge, then back again at her, then back again at Urge like I couldn't understand his apparent rudeness with our lovely sister! It was so obvious to me that this freaky, sexy, floating orgasm was ripe for me and desired me! I am high from the anticipation of some immediate sexual gratification. I wanted to become her g-spot! Urge said a little louder now—"And your name is?" She spoke softly and so sweetly while kneeling down on one bare knee, showing off some sweet caramel inner thigh. "My name is Lady Climaxamus, and all spirits simply call me Climax." As I thought to myself, I know damn well they do! Almost shouting it at her, with her super-fine ass. I hurried to ask Urge—"Yoh Urge, ask the lady to join us and have a seat old man—please hurry!" She spoke again as she rose to her feet—"I had heard that there was a very fine—pardon me, I mean a handsome pair of souls nearby, a pair of choice-lays to be found." Whoa—did she say 'choice lays'? "Passing along these here walking trails not to far from my village. I just had to come out of my home to see if I could find them, and I know now that I have. Wow—you both look so good to me." I could see her licking her lips and gently swaying from side to side as she glided even closer to us, especially towards me. I felt my nature rise and realized I just couldn't resist the unseen pull of this luscious, obviously volumptous-spirit, who was truly magnificent and magnetic. Who had appeared out of nowhere looking like a living desert to me! "Urge, get me some rubbers!"

I wanted to scream and did—"Urge I got this, let me show you what a real bonafide player, shot-caller, big-baller can do with a lady. Especially when he's truly inspired my brother like I am right now!" Hell my loins were heating up the moment I first saw her, and yes I wanted her bad—real bad! So I started to walk coolly towards her unconsciously, readjusting my crotch again like all real players do. I noticed she gave off a warm grayish aura all around her sexy Goddess form. Which could melt the coldness of the strongest pimp or player back in my old world. The shadow light surrounding her made her curves very visible, very desirable—so I believed! I thought I saw Urge smiling a crooked little smile as he projected into my mind—"Boy would I enjoy watching you player, handle this obvious succubus shade on your own. Lee Roy, she is truly only a collection of sexually latent thought-forms you've had since you got here, pertaining to your excessive carnal life-style back on earth!" "What Urge, what the hell are you saying?" "Lee Roy she's only a false-specter that your uncensored, unfocused carnal-mind brought over from the physical world, which you have yet to deal with here. Therefore, on this level of thought, in this world of spirit-existence, I must emphasize—wicked and burning thought-forms of all sorts, can be quite dangerous here little brother! Truly deadly son!"

"Are you reading me Lee, or have your re-awakened carnal appetites took over what little mind you have left? See Lee, her slow ability to speak to us and her generating a low-luminous aura is indicative of an astral thought-form that has only recently become conscious of life itself, and is now looking for life-force energy to sustain it's brief existence, like our life-force energy or yours son! At some point she, or it—must have became aware of your passing in death, and grabbed a hold of some of your creative carnal memories to give herself life. Even if it's just an artificial life, a sort of temporary existence. Can you yet see why all life, any life-energy is so precious Lee? I bet she was somewhere near you when old Grimm had you on his cloak on your back." She spoke to me again—"Come to me Master Lee, let me make nasty-hot love with you, please, oh please?" Lady Climaxamus was inviting me into her out-stretched arms now. I can't speak, I can't resist her sweet charms, I just want to throw her down and have my way with her (even in front of Lord Urge, it just didn't matter! Damn she was fine, hot, oh yeah lust and temptation had my young astral-ass. I was totally rock hard! I just know she's the biggest freak I'd ever have the pleasure of mashing! "Lee—I think she has other plans for you fool, other intentions then the ones you're hoping she has. But we best make sure she's not just here to drink her fill of our astral-blood—you know, like a sort of astral-vampire! I believe she's hungry for your new strengthen life-force energy, so she can continue to exists a while longer on this plane. Personally, I think she's running on empty Lee Roy—would you like for her to kiss you now son?"

Hearing what Lord Urge had just said, I hit my soul brakes hard—stopping within a foot of her outstretched arms! With my mouth hanging open, because of what I thought Urge had reluctantly and slowly just shared—was not funny! She said for me to ignore the old guy, cause he's just jealous of me being the sole focus of her love intentions right now. She begged me again to come into her love zone. She did however—I noticed, avoid getting too close to Lord Urge. She repeated that she had saved herself just for me for a very long time, as she started slowly stripping off her few clothes. Hell yeah—I'm in excited mode! She recounted a few wild and delicious sex-acts that we supposedly shared back in the world in my earlier horney-assed days. How freaky good those times were for her and me! Hell I remembered the freaky acts she alluded to but not with her. I now felt Urge strongly in my mind screaming, "Lee Roy you'd better listen young fool. Don't you know—haven't you been told, that a mind is a terrible thing to waste! That shadest is truly a wicked creature, of your own making! Do you recall when you were on top of your little dope game, you took immense pleasure in pushing the sexual envelope on young cute female crack addicts. Just to see how far they would go, or what they were willing to do to feed their addictive drug habits!"

"How did you put it back in those evil days, 'dope-head witches become instantly horney and freaky—just to get the left-over vapors off of someone's crack pipe when they were feinning!' Right Lee, well do you—I say, do you remember now boy?! Yes, you created this evil booty-trap Lee!" I was like what!? "No Urge, you mean booby-trap I think?" He said, "No Lee—I meant what I said, she's a booty-trap young fool, and a very deadly one too!" "Urge!"—I suddenly screamed, "She's changing man—her, her skin is now looking like snake-lizard skin! Ok—ok, I remember, I remember! But I can't move away, I'm iced over again! Urge help me please—sister big-chest is beginning to turn green, and oh damn! Urge, she's trying to bite me with her sharp yellow teeth dude! I mean she's got fangs man, long nasty fangs! Urge shes turning into a gaint snake woman!" I shouted over my back cause I couldn't see where Urge was. Now I'm really scared! "Urge, Master Urge—please help me, quick—I'm being man-handled dude! She's touching my thighs, my groin area—oh shit, Urge! Please do something, where are you old man?!" I had a sneaky suspicison Urge was rolling around on astral ground laughing his ass off at my impending doom! I don't know why, I just did. Then I saw some silver cosmic dust I believe, falling all over me and this life-sucking ghoul! She, I mean it—it started shaking like some kind of seizure had struck her now ugly-ass. She begin loosening her grip on me and fading fast into nothingness! My breathing was still erratic, as I heard Lord Urge say (while half-laughing) from a few feet behind me and to my left. "Hah-hah-haaa-ha-ha", then he said to her. "Be gone oh evil-shade, back to the mental hell that created you! Christ be praised!"

"Boy oh boy Lee Roy, I sure wanted to see you treat her like a lady—the way you did other souls expressing themselves as females back in the day. You know what I mean player-player?" I was still kneeling over with my face in my hands shaking and praying—a prayer for a player who came so close to getting played for real doe. I was trying to get a grip after coming so close to spiritual-death again, while Urge continued his little sarcastic chatter. "Like that time I looked in on you and you were sleeping with your latest so-called gold digging sack-chaser, what was it you told her that night? 'Yoh Betty Boo'—(imitating my younger voice with his) 'you know shorty you be my main-flame, the Dapper Don's dame—its you and me against the world Ms.Sexy. Me and slick Rick wrote a song just for you called Super-freak, ah-yeah-yeah.' Yes that's it, that's the word, super-freak. Well—do you remember? Hey Lee, please tell me just what the heck were you doing to yourself as she was made to suck on your big toe? Really now, just what the heck was that scene all about player? Why were you treating her like that? And those strange noises you were making—wow. Just like the sounds you were just making a moment ago lover-man, oh horny and smooth Don Juan!" I couldn't answer him, I just felt ashamed, so foolish—and definitely embarrassed by all this shit!

Damn—what was I thinking, I call myself a player! Right after being mauled, almost bitten, and frighten to death, then being rescued again by my main man Urge (a real peeping-tom I think). Still a real Guardian Angel, one with a wicked sense of humor I now know. Somehow I realized that my disguised (now dead) Cleopatra was indeed something cruel, something evil, that I had created—all because of my negative and disrespectful behavior towards my sister-souls in my past life. Oh yeah, and because of the shabby way I had mistreated all women back on earth. At some point in growing up, I guess I had lost all respect for women (something to do with my own mom's I'm sure). So I used them up and threw them away like old bags of White Castle trash. I had often claimed and often bragged to my street crew—'I didn't love them hoes!' When in actuality I just didn't know what real love was, or how to show it, or even worst how to receive it—damn! I had even sent a few young gold-diggers to jail in my place, when I made them hold my drug stashes, or my heater (my burner, you know—my guns). Whenever 5-0 pulled me over dirty, during those turbulent and chaotic times of playing real cops and robbers back in the old world. By now, Urge had regained his calm angelic demeanor. His angel composure now intact he smiled a crooked smile at me and whispered in my mind. "Sir Foolish, you were so asleep back then Lee, so full of yourself—all lustful—selfish ego, nothing but a false super ego!"

As we walked along the remaining winding road, I knew inwardly he was right, right on point about me, damn it. I automatically recalled some neighborhood trash-talk from those cruel days of my old life as a fake-ass ghetto player. I was fond of saying, "bitches and flies I do despise, the more I meet bitches the more I liked flies"—damn I was so stupid then! I'm still wondering whose wearing my many blinging diamonds and imported silk suits—I know I'm not. Urge was right, the only treasure and riches we get to keep is our own soul memories and I'm not to sure of that these days—damn I was so stupid!

I saw my surroundings a lot clearer now—the darkness was giving way to the lighter shades of blue-grays, to pale earth tones. I was beginning to see some shades of color again, astral colors—I guess. Urge then repeated—that this path, this journey, we were on and his guiding me at this stage of my development was turning out to be a much different story for us. Different then the many romantic stories told by other traveling souls he had come in contact with throughout his spiritual travels. He said he had met lots of spirit-beings passing in and out of the many spirit and matter worlds, with each one having different experiences or types of after-death trials and tribulations. This was due in part to what each soul crossing over had held in mind at the time of their death, as their major theological beliefs or spiritual training dictated. Rather or not any valuable real psychic or spiritual-lessons were embraced by them during their incarnations in their respective past physical lives. He said their (souls) final accepted belief systems were solely responsible for what they experienced right after dying, transitioning from a physical life back into spiritual life. Thereby re-awakening to touch the one truth of the great spirit of the living-Universe, the truth that, 'all is spirit and spirit is all that truly is.'

I've also learned that many disincarnate souls re-awake surprised on the other side of midnight. This is the time in which they experience their personal imagined Heavens or Hells. Various levels of purgatory, or their strongest fears—brought over as so much mental-ego baggage. Just like the truly lifeless non-intelligent forces that had formed my sexy deadly vampire. Lord Urge called her a shadest-succubus, a half-alive, half-dead dangerous astral-shell. She was attracted to our life-force like a giant mosquito looking for real soul-food. I don't remember the exact number of times I had asked Lord Urge—just where were we headed, where was he taking me, what would be our end game? He responded usually in mystical ways, as was his angelic nature I guess. He told me about this Heavenly great city of light that looked to most as if it was Heaven itself but it was not. It was located on top of a celestial mountain called Mt. Edon, a metaphor (this mountain) I guess, for another level of consciousness. I naively wondered if Lord Jesus lived there.

In truth I really didn't know Jesus, but found myself calling his name a lot lately, especially in my new prayers. Urge called the Son of God the true Logos, and the Brightstar, saying also that 'his' was all the light we needed to complete our journey. I asked him how many levels of consciousness, or spirit-worlds truly existed in this Universe. Was it necessary for all souls to pass through all of them in order to reach perfection and return to the Godhead, this living Intelligent Universe, or perfection, or what?

He said he liked the new way I was beginning to talk and think, and that our time together was indeed paying off. But we still had a long ways to go and still much mental and spiritual work to do. He did tell me—"Lee, each and every soul picks it's own path back to enlightenment. Each and every soul-force is indeed responsible for it's own salvation from the traps of living in matter-worlds. Even today many souls have yet to discover this simple yet profound cosmic truth, that there is always help available—because God's light is unstoppable, invincible and bright. It shines through even the darkest of worlds, yes—everywhere and eternally. But a soul dictates at any given moment at or after its initial birth into spirit, how much light it is willing to embrace. It chooses life after life, after life (completing varied cycles of reincarnations) to learn many spiritual lessons if needed. During each school of life, it seeks to progress homeward—upwards towards perfection again. During the course of its multi-faceted soul experiences within this our intelligent universe. From the seven cosmic days (it took to create this Universe), approximately seven life-expressions must be traversed after a soul has activated its power and corresponding understanding of the true force of free-will. Which means it has awaken to higher levels of self-consciousness (seven ascending levels of consciousness expansion)—whoa? Urge taught—that 'there are three more levels of mind / ego inter-actional experiences, during and after several hundred years, in and out of physical bodies or incarnations into matter worlds most souls go through.'

Urge added, "before a soul truly comes to know it's true spiritual-self (it's Triune-Self) as a whole and complete trinity unto itself—a ramification of spiritual essence, it must reincarnate through several life forms . . ." Whoa Urge could preach! "Then it knows it is truly one with the Godhead directly, and at the same time a mini-God unto itself in-directly. No matter the distance strayed, or how far they may have fallen from grace—moving away from their true source. They forever carry within themselves the God-seed with all the attributes and sublime characteristics of God himself." I was like, "Yoh Master Urge—please forgive me if I don't ask any more questions like the last one again, I mean ever!" He just kept right on talking, "It is very rare Lee Roy, yet possible and not unusual for a soul to move from its first creation into existence, directly back into the Godhead see? This God-choice has been a debated issue for a long time among Angels and higher entities. You see the matrix for all life and living things has been set long, long ago by the creative thoughts of God. Especially for that God-essence created as individualized souls, to work through the necessary and challenging unfolding of the cosmic spirit-matrix of all life in all dimensions of existence. Or simply stated, spirit-life is forever working (struggling) to return to the original thought-maker God—the first cause, itself causeless. Some Angels call this the seven levels of spirit-elevation. For again as I've told you, all is spirit. Anything else and everything material is truly only illusions of mind, and limiting beliefs of the false ego"

"Damn!" I wanted to scream — "Urge please, can we pray — I like to pray Urge, prayer is good, so let us pray." My head was spinning from to much information, to soon I guess. "Urge how can I lose this astral headache I've thought into existence now?" Lord Urge looked at me intently then slowly bowed his head and said — "Pray with me little brother, I believe there's hope for you yet. Oh great and glorious source of all miracles — make Lee Roy's headache pass away, as we pray this simple prayer of healing. May the light of God surround us — may the love of God enfold us, and may the power of God protect us. May the presence of God watch over us — so wherever we are God is, and all is in divine-order." We sat quietly and still for what seemed like a good hour and a half. By then I had completed my soul-strengthening exercises (mostly breathing and meditation techniques) and felt ready to march on. Yeah, to march on to what — your guess is as good as mine mellow readers. I took a moment to tell Urge how glad I was to know that he was there with me and for me, and that I appreciated him. Again I thought to myself, how I really had wasted my recent past-life opportunity. By not getting to know more about Godly-things, spirituality, and my truest potential as a spirit-being. Urge had told me some time ago that 'most humans trapped in material-matter worlds had no idea they were indeed little Gods masquerading as fools, acting out their lives as powerless, helpless, victims, and angry little materialistic human-beings.' This he said was all due to the corruptive, deceptive power of 'I-ness', which desolves in the face of true spiritual oneness (a soul's gift of enlightenment).

This troubling state is created by the false yet over powering ego-mind of consciousness trapped in matter. A lower level stage of consciousness or spirit-growth, where the personal-ego tries to become its own God. Mostly while spirit is manifesting within a physical-body or matter-world. This is indeed a very dangerous time for all souls, because they become more and more selfish and self-centered. I told Urge again while we were walking, how sorry I was beginning to feel — that I had not been more opened to him, his Guardian Angel's influences (his voice), back on earth during my life there. Yeah — missing his light of understanding of right and wrong choices for me, choices I made alone. He just kept quiet — I kept listening, not saying anything else for a brief moment. So then I offered up my new writings from my astral notebook. My poetry in rap — my kind of word prose for his consideration, it seemed like a good time. "Yoh my elder brother Urge — you just gotta peep this material out I've been composing all along in my head. I've written most of it down, still it's not finished yet — but tell me what you think of it so far ok? Like I said, I call it — Lee Roy's Heaven, Alpha to Omega, cause I didn't want to use the word hell you know — I didn't won't to plant no more bad seeds." Lord Urge dropped his head down suddenly (still walking), but I picked up on what he was thinking in his mind. 'From a bad seed, who doesn't desire to plant a bad seed, go figure?'

"I guess that's some kind of progress aahy?" I didn't wish to respond to his little sarcasm, so I started to read to him my rap-prose from the notes I had written down earlier. "Okay let's do this, lets see page 28 — here we go! 'You know in life you gotta get it right — to get through the pearly-gates, if its not to late then you'll get sent back till it's truly straight. You all know the trinities of life — that mind, body, and soul. It's just the number one life goal, to get it right and that's how it goes.' 'Oh yeah, my claim to fame was all in my name. Y'all know me, they call me Mr. Lee, the big time O.G. Out on the streets, yeah I caused havoc, even let some ghetto-dudes have it. Bagging a cash-dope package, I had it sold in different area codes. I drove a big Benz and kept close, 2-chrome 44's . . . and oh the young divas, it wasn't hard for me you see — to get to them either. I'd just whip out a fat-knot, or come through with a gold-drop! I be running my spots like a Fortune 500 business — running different shifts every eight, with a brand named face. I was dealing in weight. From time to time I'd go out of state — to relax or party, then re-up, or cut-up lobster or steaks. While my young Detroit runners kept busy — working the business, from spring-dust to Christmas. Usually when I got home, that's when I started chilling — tempts below zero, neighborhood hero. I'm feeling like Nero. Now laying down with two honeys, gangster style-illing.'

'Then one day some bad rival dudes, shot at the kid with a bum 38. I made a quick retreat, so sweet, and came back around and sprayed their crew with my own A-K, in broad day. I mean you should have seen their faces, when they headed for the races. Totally mesmerized, they were caught by surprise — while I attempted to end their lives! That's when the feds were enlighten, they watched me for 13 months, then came with my indictment. They left me and Ike and those deadly twins feeling all pent-up. After our first trial no witnesses showed up. Then a new trial, where they repeated our sins in front of white folks — oh rising fears, a damn suburban joke, this a jury of my peers? So we all got sent up! Life behind bars is like a secret society — beds that stack, with killers, pushers, and fake-ass macks. Got me a new number and new bunky, a bank-robbing niggar named Coke-head Jack. Who came up from off of the lower east-side near Bewick and Mack. In fact — I knew his peeps because I sold them smack, now we all be walking the prison track. It's like a damn family reunion I fear, with cousins and uncles and brothers all here — and all that's missing is real mothers and old muh-dears. Most of us locked down truly suffering inside. With the lower classes living like rats, cause they be institutionalized, trying to get prison wise. Doing their time on one thin dime. So they go and make some home-made bats, and some deadly knives, for the weaker boys to get the point. That's life as it is up in this joint. The big house of glass and steel-bars, populated with illiterate fools, and a few ghetto super-stars. Here we all want to survive, this slick-ass American nightmare, where you have to be warrior fit — you know the theory of Charles Darwin's American lit.'

'Now tell the truth dear listeners, ain't this some shit. Soon time is flying by in years, you know why—a evil instinct takes hold of you and that's no lie. With growing confidence jail-house style, you replace your fears or you die!

I'm relocated now to the upper wilderness, where it's cold as hell. Still I'm doing swell, where-ever I'm incarcerated. Because I stay sacked-up, body rock hard and most days pissed! Heart of a lion—I take it to hyenas and street-gang tigers, jailhouse snitches and of course fag-liers. Everywhere I go my name rings bells, never was broke in prison or in jails. That's still living right—my attitude so tight, I got hooked up again with my main man Ike. We turned some tissue into jailhouse dice. Cons will gamble on many different levels—out on the felon's yard, day and night some dudes want to fight, challenging this famous young black Ace of cards! A loser white boy thought that Ike wasn't playing right. Then a big fag gave out a loud bark, pulled a long shank and swung it straight at Ike's heart. I pushed him back quickly you see—but instead of going into Ike, it went into me! I remember grabbing my chest, fell down and went straight to my knees—looked like I was praying. Fag-dude #187 was charged with my slaying. That was the first time I asked God please—why me? I felt all warm and disorientated, slept through my death yet still woke up elated. Sounded like God had said 'son do you not yet see, you can't return to your dead body "G", now you know—when death calls, it's no longer a soul's choice. I knew I was hell-bound when I heard the Grimm Reaper's voice.'

I took a deep sigh as I finished my rap, and looked over at Lord Urge and asked, "Well my spiritual mentor what do you think, that was all I've done but later there's more to come," I said proudly. Urge still had his head down, when he spoke with both hands in front of his face, he mumbled—"Thank you Lee, will you pray with me here, please, please?" No, Urge wasn't smiling this time—I could tell he didn't get it. He wasn't feeling it either, sooo—I didn't respond, I just did as he requested. I sat down my pad and pen and put my hands over my face to mock him a little, then we prayed. "Oh father / mother God, Oh cosmic illumination—where fore are thou oh light of understanding. You charged all divine-beings to have patience with others of their kind and indeed even with themselves. To show great love for one another in or near all matter worlds. For it would be our demonstrated love that sets us free, that washes and sustains our very souls. You taught us to spot evil, to know instinctively when a thing is right or wrong for our lives. Heavenly messengers have always come to tell us how to avoid the wicked and misleading worldly-traps on all levels of soul existence, as well as how to overcome them." I thought for a quick moment how prayers could some times sound a lot like a rap, just a special kind of religious speaking for God's ears only I guess—damn. I'm trying my best to understand all this stuff I'm forever learning something, I think maybe, I am—learning?

Urge was still praying out loud, "Either confirm this as my mission or pity me oh God, show me mercy now most Holy of Holies. Is this an after-life puzzle for me or is it my true spiritual destiny I ask? Am I being tested by my lower-self, or am I being used for the greater good of the one true source of all life? Oh Universal Intelligence, please answer me, is this rap-thing a necessary part of this soul's purpose — especially now, for Master Lee and me? Help us to endure this journey oh God. We give thee all the praise and say, as it is above — so is it below, in the Christos, the Universal Logos, we give our total reunited selves. Let us both, Lee Roy and I — say amen." I said, "Amen to that, old Rapping Duke." Lord Urge just looked at me with a puzzled expression, while I tried to hide a small smile from him.

Our walking, talking, resting, and prayerful journey was progressing on schedule to the City of Light according to Urge. We had been moving in a slow winding way up-wards on this holy mountain Urge called Mt. Edon. He had only told me little about what awaited us once we arrived, and would only describe certain aspects of this great and eternal place. Situated just below Heaven itself and this, the astral—ethereal levels we were now expressing on below it. He said this mountain and the great city resting upon it, just hung in a great center of space and was constructed a long time ago from particles of the first astral magnetic molecules. Supposedly as the city's historians tell it—as a way-station and safe haven for young developing souls passing through this solar system. Like all newly created souls, they went in search of simple discovery of a soul's true potentiality and their relationship to our creator. He or it, who is called by many names but is of the same essence, that essence known as cosmic love. The Godhead is love Urge said, and love is God. Urge was obviously feeling no pain as he continued his mental-talking. "A journey that gifted to most their ever expanding God-consciousness and the keys to find their way home again when they became tired or lost, no matter how long it takes them. These things have been confirmed repeatedly by many a Angelic traveler and various spiritual-masters. They who lived oh so long ago and who had gone forth before us, and occasionally returned to that great place on top of Mt. Edon—the great City of Light.

Bringing back with them such fabulous and wonderful stories, of our God's creative greatness and sublime universal beauty. Stories of mercy and blessed forgiveness holding it all together, throughout all Universes and planes of spirit existence. I asked Urge a dumb question, "Do they have any black-top (asphalt), basket-ball courts in this great city of light?" He didn't answer me, just looked over at me as if he was looking right through me. There were many times, many lessons that Urge tried to teach me—where my consciousness (spirit understanding) couldn't or wouldn't take in any more of his innate spirit wisdom or advanced soul knowledge, which to me at least seemed unlimited. Still I always gave it my best, as I always took copious notes (a word I learned from Urge meaning plenty). Many of our astral-spirit experiences along the way were still strange and confusing to me, and on several occasions even quite frightening. But still we (Lord Urge and I) managed to survive so far. Urge even gave me a marvelous opportunity to peer into other dimensions of existence for non-earthly spirits and entities of intelligence. Using his cosmic Angel's dust and looking glass spells—oops, I mean prayers. He would open up a large window at our feet or near the places were we rested.

Then allow me to see things that boggled my mind—new colors, strange shapes, abstract forms, weird creatures—walking, flying, swimming, crawling, some appeared up close then disappeared into smoke like real magic! He made me promise not to tell anyone we may meet in the great City of Light that he had taken such risk with me, showing me these strange things before my time. Just in case it slipped out, I was supposed to say—that I have had some fantastic dreams since I arrived on this level of existence. I thought this was a little-bit like lying, but didn't say so to Urge. Then Urge asked me—"Lee Roy my boy, what is this black-top and basket-ball stuff you asked me about?" I told him it was a game that young-bloods really enjoyed playing back in the day in the neighborhoods and streets in my past life. I told him I felt it would be a good way for me or us to unwind once we reached the great city. He said now he remembered, "The round-ball game the young-ones played during most of their waking hours, as opposed to studying some school book or self-discipline that would help to elevate their minds more. Thereby helping them to achieve their dreams quicker then some game that most of them would never play at a professional level." Yeah, he had seen that all to often back on earth I guess. He said he even witnessed blood spilled on occasion as a result of someone fouling another player or talking about their mother. Then he added—"We don't need any basket-ball time Lee, because I for one don't want to be fouled by you or any being in the great city when we enter in you see?" "Right, I got-cha Lord Urge." "Besides", he added—"Prayer and meditation is the best forms of un-winding little brother, remember that Mr. Basket-ball Head!"

I remember asking Urge about those two look-alike sparkling rivers I recalled seeing soon after I got here. It had seemed that one of the walls of water was calling out to me. This was the darker one with the sad-eerie sounding vibrations coming from it. While the other one flowing in the opposite direction was much brighter and gave off sweet sounding vibrations. At certain intervals in our traveling whenever that sound from the darker wall of what looked to me to be water—would catch my attention, or if Urge felt me focusing on it. He would gently, mentally, more often pull me back to the present moment and place of our spirit expression. Urge said that, 'Those were giant channels of passing souls, the sparkles or little lights (I saw in each wall) were souls themselves—that were in transition and just looked to me like giant rivers turned on their sides. One was of still lost and struggling souls on their way to their personal purgatories or back into matter worlds for more spirit lessons or to spirit rest-spots,' Urge said, 'While the other was the flow of the many souls who had lived good lives and had balanced out their karmic-debts on their way to higher spheres of enlightenment or bliss-filled rest stops. "Honestly now (he asked)—which giant channel of moving souls did you feel drawn to the most? No need to answer me Lee I think I already know."

"Boy you still have no idea of how lucky—I mean how blessed you truly were, that I showed up when I did do you?" He was smiling a little—while I looked over some of my notes, not answering his obvious sarcastic question.

I was always trying to keep them (my notes) in some kind of order in my mind, of what was real, what was not, and of what was to come from my close association with my Guardian-angel Master Urge. This wise old-spirit who is my humble mentor, and trustworthy after-death savior so far. It never was easy though—as on many occasions my mind or my consciousness felt fatigued, and I would slowly mentally drift off into a kind of deep-resting nod. Master Urge, would gently push or pull me back into the moment, and remind me to stay awake. Saying that souls had no need for sleep as long as they (or we) meditated regularly while on their journey (or ours). Ok—ok, he just did it again, damn, a brother can't get his nap on! I would ask him after being abruptly reawakened again, "Yoh Urge, what is it now dude, more spirit-lessons, take some more astral notes, or—ok let us pray." Urge said—"There is no sleep for us now on this journey. Some souls passing over or on their individual astral-spirit paths would choose sleep, or must sleep, as a post condition of their level of growth back in the material world. We on the other hand had been given a miracle," as Urge often stated it. We had been reunited as one whole soul again somehow—he thanked God. Urge said he had thought for only a moment that we may never meet again—after all the chaos and damage I'd caused back on earth, through the misuse of my free-will powers of choice.

He finally shared with me that our split spiritual separation took place over 380 years ago—damn! Where I spent many of those years living through four or five lifetimes disconnected from him—my higher-self. Hence my downward slide into mayhem and evil drug dealings started a long time ago. I truly don't remember those past life-times or our first painful separation over 400 years ago. Truly I didn't know what to make of this past-life stuff. I often wondered if my mentor liked an occassional drink? He reiterated that we had no time to sleep and or discuss these things further, that we needed only to give thanks that we were brought together again. To use our time, this time to share the real true cosmic knowledge he had gathered from centuries of spiritual-study and associating with like-minded higher level Angels and Spiritual-masters. While searching the matter-worlds for me—his lower self, often calling me his bad side of our midnight birth. During the time of the black ethers of deep space before the 'Logos' balanced all with the cosmic light. Again he apologized to me and told me that it had taken him over 300 years to find me within the many matter worlds and dimensions of existence. He said that each time he felt he was near me or getting close again, that I would leave one existence and manifest into another material-plane some place else. As if I didn't want to be found or re-united with him my higher-self.

He said that there were many places in matter worlds a lost or separated soul (or half soul) could hide if it's will was strong enough to do so. He then added that it wasn't always my fault we couldn't connect, mumbling something about his own fears of lowered vibrations. Something about the power of matter worlds to trap even stronger, whole souls, which I could't quite make out. He added, "A lost soul or one that's un-aware of it's Guardian-Angel consciousness, can wonder around for hundreds of years thinking to itself that it is fully alive, or is truly living life as it was meant to be lived. This is the great dream-trap of all physical worlds and material bodies, where the illusions of duality is strongest. Because a soul-force is never truly alive or lives up to its potentiality—unless it stays united within its own first cosmic trinity birth-state." I remember asking Lord Urge to explain the trinity state of a soul, our soul. Then I thought I must have been crazy to do that, and instead I should have faked like I knew what he was talking about, cause I think I've gotten away with it a couple of times. Faking my understanding that is, he went on to explain, damn it!

"The trinity-state of all souls Lee Roy is the Holy, mystical, combined state of a soul where it is in complete harmony with its many manifest sides. All souls are created with three major particles of spirit. These three aspects are, the noetic—(the doer in a body), the intelligence—(the conscious-self or ego-mind), and the spirit monad—(the God seed) or eternal spirit essence of the creator. This God seed is indeed inherent in every soul-force (or soul) ever created. Balanced together they represent the most holy trinity-state of the triune-self proper. Yes it is written into cosmic law that if any part or aspect of the triune-self (our true selves) or soul-trinity, is out of balance or missing from a soul's many lives or forms of expression—then that soul would be held back from or slowed in it's progress home back to the Godhead. Again—as I have said, until it (a soul) brings back into balance it's feeling and desire mind, ego-mind, and spirit-mind. Until then it is free to walk, crawl, fly, or wander the entire spectrum of energy existence for ever—without much spiritual-light to guide it! Keep in mind Lee Roy that spirit-energy once created can never truly die out or be destroyed, because this form of energy itself is indestructible and immortal. It may change shape into and out of different forms of expression on varying levels of existence. But it remains spirit-energy all the same, you copying down what I'm saying young blood?" "Yes Lord Urge—I'm writing as fast as I can sir." I'm now beginning to understand why I may have been on the spirit-lam from Lord Urge for so long. Boy could he talk and preach, and crack a mean teacher's whip. I was trying my damndest to read and review what I had just heard and wrote down, yet the complexities of this whole trinity thing was a bit much for my little mind to fully grasp.

'Yoh my mellows (you readers of this drama), I could use some more prayers from you guys ok?' I suddenly felt a mind-shift or my mind move back towards Urge's now strong mental impulses, now what? I heard him say in our mental exchange, "Lee—we need to pray again, Mt. Edon Is just over that rise over there (pointing east). We need to be ready, we need to up our vibrational rate of consciousness to be able to clearly see what's to come, what may confront or attempt to hinder our ascent up this mountain to get to the great City of Light. So let us pray this powerful little prayer that will refresh us and protect us now. Say with me now Lee—'Oh most holy of spirit energy, oh God of Gods, we beseech thee Father—with the spiritual blood of our one heart, we release and let go of all that is wasteful, all that is negative to our spirit, and all that has been touched by evil." "We now embrace your great and ancient spirit to manage and renew this reunited soul of ours. Right now, our heart is opened wide Father—waiting for your holy-spirit to enter in. Indeed we are here for you oh God, and we know you are here eternally for all your children. Ease our present struggles, and suffer us no more strife oh Father / Mother God—in this soul's journey or any other soul to come. With our faith in thee strong—oh great source, we seek and find your healing light. Now we are free to live—in this form as spirit, solely for your love, we give you our thanks and send out to thee our great gratitude. Knowing full well it is enough. To the great Godhead within us and without, both Lee Roy and I, Master Urge—give praise to thy glory and say, it is so and so it is—amen."

Personally I feel great each time Urge pulls one of those sweet rap prayers out of his heart, as my own spirit-part begins to soar again. I mean man, I feel better then I've ever felt before and most importantly of all, Lord Urge has given me a chance to really hope again. I hope as I pray with him that this spiritual dream will have a happy conclusion for us both. Especially for a young dope-pusher who now wishes he had never sold drugs, or did any of the other evil and mean things I did back in my physical life on earth! I tell Urge it was a great prayer and I thanked him, then I added—"Yoh Sir-nose De-void-of-Funk, my knees hurt from all this kneeling down—and this here praying, and I can't even swim—I hate water." Then I laugh (making reference to some p-funk song I use to sing back in the day). Urge didn't get it, looking at me with a very puzzled look on his face again. "Hey (I mentally said to him) my elder brother, I was just kidding—it was a joke Urge! I guess you've never listened to p-funk music huh?" He responded—"I guess you haven't had enough of jokes yet huh Lee Roy? Ok little brother just you keep on existing, just keep on living and you will—I bet cha!" Now I looked a little puzzled, I wondered what the old dude was implying?

I find myself and Lord Urge now nearing the base of Mt. Edon hanging in space. The picture here is truly beautiful, like a national park back in the world or something. But here everything within sight seemed to have a frosty glow about it or an aura I guess, in different colors and hues. With every blade of grass, thought-form tree, bush, or plant—even the large astral rocks seemed to have their own beautiful luminous glow. I remember feeling breath-less, even though I knew I wasn't truly breathing, cause spirits don't need air to breath on the astral plane, don't ask! I just felt shock and wonder at the sight of this magnificent mountain and some how knew we were meant to be here! Master Urge looked back across his shoulder at me and asked, "Have you composed any more poetry in your note-book, of that thing you call rapping?"

I said, "Well yes sir—I've added a couple of new pages while we rested back aways, would you like to hear them?" He said—"Maybe later, but first I want to show you something from your past life, maybe you'll feel different about the nature and style—I guess we can call it that, about your rap prose, come over here—sit! View with me now one of your more misguided moments back in the day—right? Oh I mean your recent past life as a seller of dope, of poison—cool?" I said, "Yeah right or cool, whatever you say Urge—however you say it Master Urge, its cool my angel friend, you be da man!" Then I added sadly, "Urge—do we have to look back into that life, do you have to go there my brother?" He responded with—"Oh, so you want me to listen to your hard-core brand of poetry, but you can't take another look at your wasted life-energy from your most recent past huh?" Here was my chance to test what I had learned from the old geezer!

So I took a shot—"Urge, I thought you told me that no thought-action or deed from any physical life, no matter how bad, was truly wasteful. That necessary spiritual lessons are gained from all trials and tribulations on earth—even suffering and sin. That each and every problem, negative thought, or evil action carries within it a valuable lesson—for growing the soul and its individual levels of consciousness. Especially when dealing with other souls, other people, or persons like our physical-selves!" "You see Lord Urge I have been paying attention to you and what you've taught me." He only said—"Nice try Lee Roy, real nice." He didn't even look my way, still sprinkling a pinch of his cosmic angel-dust on the ground to form the window. He carried that magical-stuff in a littl pouch hidden in his waist band that was holding his silverish blue robe closed. After he had uttered some strange soft words over the sparkles on the ground, he asked me "What's wrong with what we see here little man, come on look son?" As he pointed to a scene developing in the angel-dust window he'd just created. I saw a table in the corner of a fancy soul-food restaurant back in Detroit called Reggie's Beans and Cornbread, which had appeared in the smooth pool of glass in full color on the ground in front of us, ugh-oh!.

I squatted down to see better and looked intently back into time to this almost forgotten negative memory. The scene was from my younger gangster dope-dealing days back in the "D", damn I thought, not this, not that! Then I said, "No please Urge, pick something else ok—please show me another memory ok?" Within this sad memory shown—there sat me, big Ike, and this bi-sexual chick named China-doll. A fine young red-bone witch with a real bad attitude that worked for us as our in house drug-money accountant. Because she had a head for numbers. Sometimes she even acted as bait for some of Ike's shooting sprees. Yeah some of those killings were even ordered by me, and a few were on G.P.K., or as Ike called them general-purpose killings. China was talking loud, as I was beginning to remember what I didn't want to remember now! The restaurant-scene went something like this. "Yoh—Mr. Lee, we got a small problem boss!" Ike said,

"A real problem nigga, bringing us some weakass crack-head shit, trying to bitch-us over for 2 kilo's of prime! I've warned this lame twice already young-boss about coming up short on fronted merchandise. I don't think he knows yet that we know about that rip-off take-off bullshit he claims he barely survived three months ago—when his boy little Pee-wee got smoked. He be talking about how he left him to watch over our stash! I believe he was the one who capped Pee-wee's little ass—word?" "Yeah Ike, I heard from him—I told him then, nigga don't be scared, just tell me the truth! You know Ike, I never really trusted that nigga Big Easy, I felt then he would one day become so much dead weight for us—yeah that fool is a real business killer. Yoh China-Doll, just how much has he cost us this year any way for dealing with his slick Nu-Orleans ass?"

"All total boss Lee—(China chipped in), about $48,000! So what's up with that shit Mr. Lee Roy (she laughed slightly)? You ain't getting soft on crime are you baby?" Ike drew his hand back as if to bitch-slap China, and I reached over and grabbed his arm stopping him. China looked surprised and angry (it didn't take much to set her gay-ass off). She shouted at Ike—"Go ahead Mr. Bullet-proof nigga, I won't miss yoh big-ass head this close! She had that no-joke look in her eyes and she wasn't smiling (while reaching for her bejeweled purse with her piece inside). Ike pointed a stern finger at her and said dangerously—"click-click." Then he asked me, "What do you want me to do about that snake-skin shoe wearing, country-ass nigga Big Easy Lee, just give me the word?" I told Ike—"Make it look like an accident, he's to close to us so clean it up. And when it goes down, bring me his pinky-finger with that big-ass yellow diamond he's so damn proud of—you got that?" Yes China-doll was in my inner-circle, she was hard core but still a geniuses with the numbers and pulling other fine ass bitches. She was saying, asking me—"Can I have that nigga's eyeballs boss Lee, cause I've never liked the way he looked at me anyhow when I made my drops at his spot!"

Damn I thought as I sat next to Urge—watching this corrupt memory play itself out. Urge was grimacing as if he was watching a horror movie. I was telling Ike to get it done quickly, "Call him first and tell him I need to see him right now over at China's, and for him to leave his bodyguards in check. Tell him we need a private sit-down. Then stop and buy that nigga his favorite forty-oz. Then pick any red light on the way to China's stash house—pull over and put him to sleep! Even better, push his country jambalaya eating ass out into the intersection, prop the 40-oz; down on the yellow strips, then vacate the area discreetly—no rubber smoking, word!" "Use the black Police Marauder Ike, so any witnesses will think 5-0 did the hit. Wait till dark then burn the cruiser near the tracks under the via-duc near Drexal and Nevada." China interrupted me, speaking loudly, "Damn dapper-rapper why does Ike get all the juicy hits?" I raised my Dom-P (champagne) and pointed the glass over at China, as I was thinking to myself—this bitch is totally out of line! Much too loud for me and the half-filled restaurant we be in. Even worst, she was messing up my high and appetite. From that fat blunt of weed we finished earlier. I knew Ike was getting pissed off at her, so I dismissed him with a quick hand wave and I guess I was getting pissed too. So I had to remain strong and represent, get my props from Ms. China-Doll. I told China—"Yoh little butch-girl (insulting her), you need to quite down and sit your ass back down, and apologize to me and my number one pit-bull (referring to Ike)!"

"Not once during this damn dinner did I give you permission to say a damn thing!" Then I slammed my champagne glass down on the table hard. Ike started to smile and mumbled, "Oh shit" getting up from our table as he sneered at China—then over at two of my attack team thuggish body-guards we called Law and Order, (the deadly twins—Lawrence and Odell). They had come in the restaurant behind us to watch our backs and sat at a table near the restaurant's front door. These two nigga-killers, (the twin-terrors) as they were fearfully known around town never allowed me to leave home without them. They each carried an Uzi or Mack-ten apiece, and made me a blood-promise that they would die protecting my young-ass no matter what—as long as the mad cheddar (big money pay-offs) continued to flow in their direction. China said as innocently now and as respectfully as she could, still trying to be hard. "Hey boss lover, I'm sorry I didn't mean no harm!" I looked at Ike leaving and shouted at him to go set that thing off, I wanted it done before the evening was over. Ike moved a little faster and snickered that little cold blooded laugh of his, pointing over at China as he left the table he shouted back—"Yoh Miss Sassy-ass, nice to see you but wouldn't want to be you Lew-ten-nent!" The twins walked him out after I nodded ok. China-Doll reached across the table again in a half-assed attempt to apologize again. I raised both hands in the air like I didn't want her to touch me.

Then—as I leaned back, I said, "You gotta do better then that Lady-Dike, you know you gotta come correct!" She looked me straight in the eyes, and knew what I meant. She knew what I needed. She knew what calms most big-ballers down in the dope game besides getting high and large cheddar (cash money). In any game for that matter, she knew what I wanted most at that moment in time. She then sat back in her seat and paused a moment looking around briefly, took a deep breath, then slowly but showly slid her fine-ass down in the booth. Down she went under the table, while putting her Sig; 9-mm slowly up on the table from her Coach purse. As she proceeded to unzip my Roca Wear pants, one of the twins (Odell I believe) came back in the restaurant. He walked across the room to where me and China was at, and sat down to block the freaky action show China was putting on me under our table and said—"Boss, Ike took my brother with him, and told me to stay close to you—you need another drink or something?" I said while adjusting my hips, "Yeah another glass of Dom-P nigga and shut the fuck up! Just do your job by staying on point, or we both could get blowed away tonight!" My body-guard said, "I understand young-boss, no-prob-lem-mo." At this point Master Urge grumbled something like—"Jesus help us—all before turning 25 years old—darn!" He then proceeded to give me a spiritual third degree. "Lee sit up—look me straight in the eyes boy, and answer me truthfully! What was wrong with you? No better yet—what three sins against your fellow man and women-kind are apparent in this here scene young gangster brother of mine?"

Damn I thought, I feel like shit now—somehow I know I've changed since being with Urge all this time. "What?" With my head held down in shame, I tried to answer him. "Well for one, I guess I ordered a man's life to be taken, and (I stuttered) it was done for all the wrong reasons. As if there is ever a good reason to cause another person's life to be ended. I believe it was a thirst for power and greed, and a need to control others—truly because of my own insecurities and fears! You know Urge, like, lost respect or ego-tripping or something!" Urge said—"Wow, let me help you to keep it real Lee ok? No one should ever intentionally judge then take another's physical-life, except in true self-defense and even then not without considering showing mercy if one can. Way-ward souls need to learn the awesome power of true forgiveness. To forgive others of their slights, mistakes, or hurts against us—guarantees us the great rewards of forgiveness when we need or desire it for ourselves. Sin #1—acting out any evil actions or violent intent towards others of your kind, or being to quick to embrace the destruction of life—is truly bad for a soul. Most importantly of all, sin #2—showing absolutely no respect or compassion for one of the greatest creations and most beautiful forms of spirit-expression in physical matter.

"That of the female gender forms—the women folk, no matter how hard, or ugly their behavior is towards you or other male souls! If you choose to represent yourself as a man, a real man-spirit. Then you should never return a women's misuse or disrespect with more disrespect, or with anger, hate, or incivility towards her period! That little brother is what it means to be a real man on earth." I interrupted Urge with, "So Urge wouldn't it also be true that both men and women are made of the same spiritual-stuff, and women, especially black women, should recognize that a black man is a man who should also be respected?" He ignored me and just stayed focused on counting out some more of my sins from the fading images on the ground. "Must I remind you Sir-foolish, that one's race or sexual gender is only an illusion on matter worlds—wherein the minor law of duality is in effect! Sin #3—your lack of awareness that every action a soul takes or makes while in the physical body has a direct effect on the immediate strengthening or retardation of that soul. Just what the heck did you hope to accomplish with that horrific scene at the table with your friend China? Didn't you know that others were watching you? How was that behavior supposed to enhance your soul development in any way Mister Man? I've always thought one reason I couldn't get through to you down there on earth, was because of your harden heart, or of course your harden-head, but such disrespect toward feminine spirit—wow!"

"Now I know it was probably both. I also suspect it may have had a lot to do with that type of sordid thuggish behavior you were always embracing or expressing in your earthly life! Every since you were big enough to hold and point a dangerous weapon, what did you call them—a gat, a burner, a knife? You always carried something deadly with you that would cause pain or suffering to one of your other brother or sister souls in that city! I guess you were always too afraid to fight your fights with just your fists huh? What's the matter, cat got your tongue player!?" "What—yoh Urge, young folks or people in the hood anywhere, especially back in Detroit don't fight with their fist anymore—that was old-school thinking. Where I came from, every fool carried a gat, a gun old man!" "Boy what a sad life it must have been for you, to daily feel such fear and self-loathing that you had to have a weapon everywhere you went!" "I'm not judging you Lee—that is not my duty to thee, my little brother soul of my soul. That will come later I'm sure. I just truly wish I could have drawn closer to you in your early years of need—I really do! I'm truly sorry for not trying harder Lee Roy, at being a more conscientious and courageous guardian." "Urge—I asked him (trying to shift his focus), you a Guardian Angel man, just what the hell were you afraid of dude?" He didn't answer me—he just looked at me in a sad pitiful kind of way, still I sensed he loved me. He was just disappointed in me (his lower-self) and it seemed in himself as well I guess. No, I don't guess—I knew he was.

It seemed we both had our very own crosses to bear separately, even though I inwardly knew we were truly one soul-force, trying hard to become one whole—soul again—damn! Who would have thought it would be this damn hard! I do remember when I was a kid back on the streets of Detroit, someone singing—'free your mind, and your ass will follow.' I know now that I was that ass, and my mind wasn't smart enough or free from evil enough, to direct my sorry-ass attention upwards towards Lord Urge's spiritual guidance and love for me.

Chap. 7   "Free Will To Choose"

"Well—well—well—if the little big man is through asking me questions—how do you say it, oh yeah—trying to flip the script on me huh? Maybe we can move forward in this here adventure of ours! Let me ask you Mr. Lee Roy, do you still want to see more similar memory incidents like that last one, you know we have a hundred or more to choose from little brother? You do know now that all life stories are made up of a thousand little individual moments of thoughts, decisions, and actions based on those thoughts—right?" "No Lord Urge please, I don't. I can hardly remember that life now, or those twins, or China. Even now it feels like a bad dream, and I don't want to think I was that bad of a person—that stupid and dangerous back in the world!" "Yeah I guess you don't my brother, so tell me Lee—just what did you think would happen to all those lost and confused souls who brought and used your deadly products? You know you willingly supplied them with a deadly poison to destroy themselves, their life-force, and the whole community they lived in—all over three states if I recollect correctly?" "Yoh Urge I've told I did what I did because I truly wasn't thinking! You know my story, my stupid reasons. I've told you what I hoped to accomplish dude. I wanted respect, money, and fame. I now know better, that it was all a waste—a damn big trick I played on myself. Believing that those drug-addicted fools would find away, use anything to gain access to getting high to avoid confronting their percieved problems and personal demons.

So I figured why not be a supplier of their needs, their wants. Hell, I still maintain that I never ever made anyone I sold too, use that shit by force! They wanted it and I—well, never mind!" Urge responded, "I grant you Lee—their self-destructive need was inherent in their misuse of their own free-will, but still. Still any misuse of God created materials or natural medicines taken from the earth and misused, can and does destroy life and degrades the spirit. The evil consequences and painful suffering for any soul is from the misapplication or misuse of God's creative matter and his natural laws governing them. Was it just your need for respect, for money and fame at any cost—that drove you to be so destructive Lee, to value your own life and the lives of others so cheaply?" "Ok old man—yeah that's it (I'm getting a little pissed now), that's all a young brother like me from the hood wanted ok! Some damn respect, you know like niggas and flies can be so irritating—so the more I met selfish, conniving, disrespectful niggas, the more I liked the damn flies ok!? Coming from a background of poverty, with no real skills or training in how to become a real man, with a mom who was addicted and prostituted herself, lying, cheating, stealing, and gun-play all around me since I was little, hell what was I supposed to become?! I got mad and sick of all that shit early on dude.

It was my earliest dream to want to be respected, to grow-up or to blow-up to be somebody! It was all us kids dreamed about growing up in them damn mean-ass streets! You should know all this Urge, don't cha?!" He interrupted me—"Lee, watch your language son ok!" "Urge you claimed you were always nearby somewhere, checking in on me from above. Why didn't you try harder to reach me, to teach me, to tell me what I was doing was all wrong man? Why didn't you show up at least once in person or in any form to stop me from busting a cap in some fool trying to take what I thought was mine? So where in the hell were you dude?!" Master Urge looked hurt and sat back slowly and said—"Lee Roy I'm truly sorry and I've already apologized, I'm sorry that I failed you on so many occasions, sorry that I let my own fears stand in the way of my duties to you little brother—soul of my soul." "Urge!" I asked again, "What the hell would you be so afraid of, you are my over-soul, you got power, you are my Guardian Angel?" "It was your job, your duty to guide me as you keep telling me!" "We of the great League of Guardian Angels are not allowed to force the power or choice of good over evil on our lesser-selves Lee. Especially when a soul finds itself expressing as one-half of a split soul-force on earth or in any matter world. Its purpose is to grow itself in grace, spiritually, by the choices it makes. To embrace intelligence or ignorance, the dark or the light-wisdom of life. When choosing to do good deeds over evil ones, no matter the compelling desires of the physical body-mind."

"I've already confessed to you, my own greatest fear Lee Roy—that of lowering my own vibration-rate to match yours and lose myself to the traps and pitfalls of an earthly existence just like you had done. Yes it was selfish, and yes it may have been cowardly of me, but I honestly thought that I or we had a better chance of reuniting together as one whole soul. If I stayed my distance, working at assisting you from the upper realms on the astral plane, once I found you again." "I'm sorry Lee that, I didn't try harder to intervene more in your troubled life back on earth. All in all I felt it would be ok to do it my way, and eventually we would rise together to succeed as a Triune-self. Then together we would find our way home to Heaven as you know it, or the Godhead as I know it—the spiritual source of our creation, our first and last home of homes. Believe me son, life on matter worlds is notorious for snaring young souls and even some lower-level Angels who back slide because of the many illusions and temptations found there. There are even stories of Arch-angels, the champions of the Holy Spirit's cosmic light, that have fallen from grace whenever they stayed to long, or got caught up in inferior physical bodies and ego-development on matter worlds. Many have found themselves enslaved to the dark creative forces of cosmic laws in their spiritual manipulations of physical matter in attempted God-like ways."

"Again I am so ashamed to tell you now, after seeing the troubles you caused and the trials and tribulations you created for yourself. That sometimes earth is no place to pretend to be somebody—unless a soul or spirit is there to sacrifice it's lower-nature for all the others there to know spiritual bliss. You've heard of the pattern set forth on earth about two thousand years ago by the Brightstar himself—of death and resurrection, right? To give one's life to save that part of humanity that truly needs saving, is the greatest test of saint-hood and God-ship! Even so it was truly hard for me to watch you falling into and out of wickedness and evil temptations over so many life times, while we were split apart. Yeah so I choked, I froze-up as you would say it. Even though I couldn't communicate clearly with you or wasn't brave enough to push deeper into that life—your level of consciousness. Know this little lost soul-force, I never stopped praying for you, never! I never stopped trying to send you more spiritual-light of the wisdom I had gained while we were apart. So that you could make better life choices and even chose to draw nearer to me your higher-self or maybe towards God himself! It's true Lee, it is never to late to change or to repent. I know you now know that spiritual beings themselves can become so misguided, when expressing their imperfect-selves down in worlds of matter."

"Weakened by their own misuse of spirit free-will, especially when this great gift is used in selfish ways or used to harm others. Listen Lee, the powerful creative energy of free-will given to all souls at their birth, has caused untold damage and destruction in many a soul's spiritual journey all across this great Universe. Even while progressing homeward, yes even as co-creators to God's holy expansion through-out the cosmos itself. I've often prayed as I wondered—how God the Intelligent Living Universe could stand to allow us, his off-spring to become so selfish and still continue to exist, my God. His love for all souls must indeed be boundless. Do you feel me little brother, well do you? Can you—I ask, find it in your heart to forgive my failed attempts to reach you before now? Will you pray for me as I've prayed for you for so long?" What could I say to him—with tears rising in his old wise eyes, and my knowing that I was still lost, still needing him now more than ever. In truth I cannot even remember feeling so alive, until I met him, my higher-self, face to face! So I said to Urge, "Lord Urge I love you old man, I know now how much I've missed you. Your strength and strong faith in the God you serve, has convinced me I need you—and hell yeah I forgive you, I do—I really do! Please don't ever withdraw from me again, I mean forgive me for splitting up from you way back when. Never leave me alone again, anywhere ok—ok? Let my life or my soul choices be more like yours, let my astral-mind and spirit draw nearer to yours—so that we can draw nearer to, to our father God ok!?"

Urge smiled a little, as I put my hand on his shoulder and said to him softly—"I won't to read something to you my elder brother ok?" I opened my now thick notebook and prepared to read to Urge my latest addition to my prose written rap, I'm not sure why I wanted to do this—I just did it. I could have sworn I heard him mumble something like, "Oh Christ—help us stay focused, oh Lord please!" Urge interrupted me and asked—"Mr. Lee, could you, would you read back to me some of the spiritual metaphysical lessons or laws of this Universe I've shared with you. What about the spiritual re-unification or our innate powers of mind we've discussed and meditated on over these past many months." "Ok — ok Master Urge I can do that too! But first you gotta peep (look at) these sweet lines of clever rhymes I wrote about us! About you and me and all this crazy stuff we're going through, ok? So continue to be patient with me old dude — you're good at that right? Ok here we go — come on give me a funky lip beat right here!" Urge said, "Give you a-what? Oh alright Lee if you insist, just give me a second." As he turned around facing away from me, he dropped his head a little and said, "Shoot, oops bad choice of words. I think evil is trying to influence my consciousness and wants me to give up my angel-wings for a what-cha call it, a beat box or something? I'm just kidding Lee." I said — "I know Urge, so stop playing with me man, you're not listening and you don't have wings that I know of. You got a bag of silver cosmic dust and a great big old heart. So give me a funky beat ok — 1, 2, 3, hit it!"

I started reading, part 2 — Lee Roy's Heavenly rap, ok — ok here it is. 'When I awoke in this new place feeling some strife — I saw this silver robed dude I'd never seen in life. I wondered were I was at, because he appeared all white — he spoke so nice and said, 'so little brother you thought you had it so good, but you didn't get it right, while on earth player — you misunderstood. You got to get it right, your soul is in a true tug of war between the dark and the light — yes you alone have started this fight. That was it, I didn't want to hear this shit, so I went to walk away, feeling a dead man's blues. Looked down at my feet but I had on no shoes, so I studied my every motion and it seem like I flew — who would-da knew, this body-less boy, Mr. Lee Roy would float on air feeling big despair. I gotta admit I projected I'm hard y'all but really I was scared, and just acted like I just didn't care. Truly I begged, please Lord now hear my prayers. I spoke then with a open heart, not putting on airs, because the fate I was facing was truly dark — so I begin to embark, on a journey in this questionable place. Met a strange being with an ugly face — saw holes in space, a cold and despicable lonely place, with shadowy steps leading nowhere. Seeing spirits, and souls, translucent forms that wasn't really there. A mind full of questions, mystic answers I couldn't tell, was I truly alive or still dreaming in jail?'

'Am I on my way to Heaven or just slipping deeper into hell? 'I counted my blessings as I asked myself who is it I truly served, in the presence of this being who keeps calling himself Master Urge. He said all my sins must be purged — and that he was my higher-consciousness that had only my best interest at heart, and whenever he talks to me he thought I should listen — because I may still wind up in a hell-va hot prison. A true living hell for a very long visit. He said, young gangster that's all I can tell you right now — just be hopeful that all will be fine. 'I felt I had just left that place yet he spoke of eternal death and damnation, and said the fires of Hades was the evil place I didn't want to be facing. I started to shake, then felt a strange kind of lust, these after death thoughts could make the hardest head bust. Another bad dude I would first have to meet, named by the devil himself, was Lord Mayhem—from down on 666 street. The old man-spirit cut me off—"Whoa dapper rapper—now that was cool player. I didn't quite know you were such a word-smith." Urge said, "Now that was nice little brother, but we best be on our way. We got a mountain to climb and we're almost there, you ready?" "Yeah"—I said, obviously a little disappointed with the cold gentle brush off of my lyrical composition by Lord Urge. Then Urge said—"Let us pray out loud while we walk Lee. I want any and all nature units or spirit-shells, (lifeless semi-intelligent thought-forms) floating by us to feel our strong determination, to reach our destination. Which is that City of Light, were spirits both young and old can find rest and rejuvenation to get their souls right. To experience salvation then jubilation, while they seek to get into God's house, right?"

I smiled over at Lord Urge for his spontaneous attempt at lyrical expression. "Hah, I made a short rap I think, huh Lee?" "Right—right" I said. "So keep your pen and pad out Lee Roy, let's—aauhh, how would you say it—let's kick some serious prayers then." Hell I thought—my mind is still begging to understand this place and this old man. I know I needed it—more praying and more of that spiritual knowledge, Urge keeps hyping into my mind. Urge then said, "Word up little brother, (then) word to your mother." I quickly covered my mouth with my free hand, not wishing to enlighten my elder teacher about saying word to my mother! Urge started to pray out loud, and I followed his lead, what else could I do? "Oh most holy of hollies—to you oh living intelligent Universe. We accept that you are God, our true source of life most abundant. We rejoice in this new season of our uniting with thee and we praise this new day. I feel a fresh conscious anointing is flowing our way. This is a new season of hope for your healing mercy—paid for by the blood of the Christos. He who is love—sent to us from above. We pray this prayer in his name, and say that it is so—and so it is. As always, together again—we both say amen." I said amen to that Count Chocolate, and Urge said, "Pardon me—come again?" "Oh nothing"—I said (that just slipped out, honestly it did).

I could see the rocky steps leading up the side of Mount Edon coming into my head or consciousness, as Urge defined spirit-mind. It was crowded with thoughts still spinning a little, trying to mentally digest all the things Urge had spoken of as we traveled along. I did sense a new level of awareness inside of me though, meaning—I felt we were now standing on real holy-ground. The air-space next to Mt. Edon even smelled sweeter, or at least if there was air here, it would have smelt sweeter I'm sure. The light surrounding the top of this very tall mountain was brighter than any I had seen before, and the whole area seemed so inviting to my little lost soul-force. I caught up to Urge where the mountain steps started winding their way up, as he whispered into my mind. "This little brother is truly a sacred place—our climb now is just a pre-requisite to a vision, a vision of a most beautiful place of many spiritual mysteries and truths. A most crucial moment of time in the astral-life of passing souls or Angels, who stop to rest within its hallowed walls. Spiritual entities in search of the great portal of peace—located on the other side of the great City of Light. Resting on top of this living monument to the beauty and grandeur of the creative genius of our father God." Urge said, "Quick Lee write this down." I hesitated and sort of complained—"Yoh Urge, that's all I've been doing since this journey begin—writing stuff down. I really would rather be playing a game of hoops somewhere, or hand-ball with some hot-honies in shorts. Truly I'm not sure if taking more notes is helping me to draw nearer to you, to God, or whatever—or If all of this still isn't just a dream of some kind. Could it be (I asked sarcastically) that I've been imagining all of this all along old man?"

Urge said, "Lee we don't have the time or the spirit-energy to contribute to any of your doubts right now, or whip up a game of dodge'm-shorts, it is way too late for that foolishness. You are just going though what we call here on this spirit-level as soul-fatigue, brought on by old clinging thoughts and lazy thinking. Like your thought just now, that our climb up this here mountain is going to be hard, difficult, and long, ego—still so much ego. Listen up Sir Slim, have you not noticed months ago, even daily now, how the closer we get to our ultimate destination things and events have sped up tremendously. Truly we cannot afford at this stage of the trip to entertain any doubts or waste valuable time playing earthly games—yours or my own, which I refuse to speak into existence and so should you—ok? Please say ok young rapper, just say it for me?" "Okayy, ok Urgy my main man!" "Remember Lee I've told you often—the spoken word and even unspoken thoughts held in mind long enough are very powerful. So learn to speak from love, and always think before you speak, put your mind in gear before your mouth goes into motion ok? Your words are indeed powerful beings—ok? Now mentally release your doubts, your fears like I taught you, and let go of that b-ball thing, once and for all will you? Us spirits don't play sports!"

"Remember that things, events, circumstances here, are not as you remember them in your short-lived sojourn on earth right? Now in this place your shallow concept of time even has no real consequence here—we must only continue to think well. Reason well, and to sincerely pray forth the things we want, and the things we need and those we really wish for will come to pass almost immediately Lee Roy. It has already been through our strong faith and with a little of my angel knowledge, that we have successfully made it this far! Now again, listen to my voice—and follow my directions and instructions without any, I repeat any hesitation!" Urge suddenly sounded serious and slightly worried about something hidden, something new on his mind I guess. I started to write down these lessons, my thoughts, and those complex spiritual instructions Urge was rapidly—mentally sending me again. He was right about one thing, a soul—especially a lost soul, has got a lot of work to do, a lot of new learning, to come to understand how to grow in grace no matter when it reawakens, or how, or where it encounters the higher knowledge of its true-self, whew! Talk about soul-fatigue, maybe this trip—this journey, is to much for my little limited ghetto mind to handle? I use to think my mind was strong, but now I realize how truly weak it was without the input of my Guardian-consciousness, my higher-self Master Urge. Let's see—I've learned to walk, run, pray, meditate, write, and think better all at the time, since I've been here. How long?, don't ask.

I guess this is why—this story, in this diary of mine has grown so large, yet It still weighs the same—how strange? My not so unique after-life experience I'm told, is shared in one form or fashion by many souls of late crossing over. According to Urge—'many earth-bound souls after losing their physical lives to self-hate, drugs, violence, even suicides, giving rise to just to many unnecessary early deaths.' Especially if for only selfish material gains. They can find themselves lost and afraid in empty space for sometime.' Urge said he believed this condition was caused by many young souls opting to take what they thought, was an easy way out of their self-caused miserable, desparate lives back on earth. They (the earthly masses) all crave more love, more light. They need it—they want it, and still they search for it in all the wrong places to find these! I felt I needed to record this strange and mystical if at all truthful diatribe, (whoa—even my own vocabulary has some how grown bigger). I asked Urge reluctantly to tell me what truth is and wrote down his answer quickly. He said—"Keep in mind that my kind—the higher beings of consciousness, Angels and Arch-angels as we are often referred to by earth-bound wise men, or enlightened matter world souls, as they grapple with and attempt to understand their complex and mysterious lives and or spiritual experiences. Such as occasionally manifesting paranormal occurrences, that they sometimes witness or experience within and outside their physical ego-filled lives on earth."

"This then changes their understanding, definitions, and perceptions of truth as it manifests in their lives and the matter-world conditions they are exposed to. Most of which has been created by themselves through their own thinking or lack of same, and free-will to choose. It has always been easy to say that truth is truth, or that truth as represented by the logos is eternal. But distinctions must be accepted based on one's level of understanding consciousness, and of how this Universe truly works—like understanding cosmic spiritual laws etc; you with me on this?" I said honestly—"No, I'm not Urge!" "Pay closer attention Lee and think son—thinking deeper is not illegal yet, on this plane or back on earth I believe! There are basically three-levels or types of truths. There is Universal or cosmic-truth, spiritual-mind truths, and mental / physical truths on the lower levels of all creation and soul existence. An individual's perception of a thing as being, expressed as objective or subjective feeling and desire of what a soul believes to be real, over time becomes true for that soul—see? Truth then exist as an acceptance of established facts for most, or conclusions of agreement as to the validity or non-validity of a thing, with physical manifestations of thought to support those conclusions. Like that of creative changing matter, with that which we can touch or see—within the mind of man or outside the mental mind. For example, any experiential or gut-level intuition or experiencing spiritual gifts of a psychic nature."

"Aauh, excuse me Master Urge." I interrupted him, which he never seemed to like, speaking gruffly at me—"Now what is it Lee?!" "Urge could you—would you slow it down a little, since I know so little about these things—could you break it down, simplify, make more plain—the answers to my simple questions my teacher? You know like keeping things on a basic level for me, I mean . . ." He interrupted me, "Okay Lee.—peep this, truth is that which surrounds us in all areas of our lives, yet it often disguises itself in many ways until we need to see it, feel it, or study it and come to know it as simply put—what is! Even then the truth as seen or felt intuitively by any observer changes depending on the perspective of the observer and the thing observed, like any good enigma of consciousness. Like the position or perspective of that which is being observed being of a particular reality, and at the same time not visually observable, like the thing you remember as air back on earth, understood? There, it is real, a gas—yet it cannot be seen with earthly eyes." I answered him honestly—"No, I don't understand but I'll write down whatever you tell me, I swear!" "I've asked you so many times young man not to swear on anything, especially those things you know very little about. It is like the 'truth', what you know now at this very moment in time on this astral-level as truth is different from what you knew yesterday, and will be less than what you know tomorrow as the truth!" "Jeez Urge!" "Write Lee, just write and follow my lead. Our light is fading fast on this astral level, so we must begin to climb this here mountain again—cool?" "Cool. (I said)—its all good."

So I started to walk with him, then we started to climb those rocky steps again, still I was writing as fast as Urge could talk, and boy was that fast. Hell—talking to, and listening to Angels shouldn't be so much work, but it is—damn I mean! I know I must keep up—I feel I need to. I have a strong feeling I may need this strange knowledge that Urge keeps kicking my way at some point in time within our questionable futrue. I also now believe that I know what dropping (taking) LSD (orange sunshine on a sugar-cube) must be like. I never ever wanted to try that stuff, cause I was told you could stay high for life if you abusedit.

As we climbed higher and higher up the winding path, Urge was right—I felt no fatigue. In fact, I felt a new kind of freedom and new spiritual awareness that all was well. I know it had something to do with this special place, this mountain hanging in space. We climbed for a good while before Lord Urge spoke again—"Lee how about we review the subject of religion, listen up ok?" I said—"ok Urge old man shoot, I mean go head." He gave me that serious look again—then spoke softly. "Religions are a by-product of Universal laws as expressed and understood by lower-level souls or human-kind, trying to understand their place in the greater scheme of things. The spiritual and cosmic laws of Universal Intelligence are real. They do exist and have always existed since its birth, the birth of the Living Universe. Since God's breath (big-bang) brought the activity of life into this sphere, where newly created souls attempted after their creation, to understand their unique existence, and place, within the greater sea of intelligent-spirit and physical-matter surrounding them. Trying to understand the inter-play of cosmic forces and spiritual laws all around them. Then evolving into varying degrees or levels of consciousness, after many of these young souls strayed to far away from their creator's influence. Their true source of eternal life, the Godhead. Hence the biblical story of the Garden of Eden and the first humans. Again this is what is meant in the written records of the 'Book of Life' on the spiritual plane and the Akashic Records (a kind of book) on this the astral plane."

"Both are mentioned within the great pages of the 'Book of the Dead'—copies of which I believe were last seen on earth about 3,000 years ago. Somewhere in a place on earth called Egypt, listing the names and deeds of hundreds of thousands of the first young souls who fell from grace (those desireing to vacation on a new found paradise planet) long ago. Many of these souls have already found their way back home, returning to their source." "Yoh pardon me Urge" I asked him, "What is a ass-kick record?" He gave me that serious look again as if he found himself talking to a stone wall—me I guess. Without taking an angel's breath he kept right on talking, explaining, looking me in the eyes real tight now. "Listen to me with your heart and with what little soul-mind you got left Lee, take more notes. Akashic is a theosophical term referring to a Universal Filing System which records every occurring word, thought, and action of individuated spirit-energy in it's many manifest spirit-forms. This record is impressed on a very subtle substance called Akasha (or somniferous ether). In the far east back on earth, this ancient mysticism, or school of belief—says this Akasha is thought to be the primary principle of nature. The cosmic-nature from which the other four nature principles—fire, air, earth, and water, are created. These five principles also represent the five senses of the spirit or soul as it masquerades in matter".

"Expressing itself and its life as a world-spun human being—see?" "Urge, I'm sorry—the word is Akashic not ass-kick, I got-cha my teacher!" Urge didn't let up, he continued—"It has been taught, that the Askashic Records are indeed similar to a cosmic or collective consciousness. The records have been referred to by different names over eons—including the Cosmic-mind, the Universal-mind, or the Collective Unconscious River of Cosmic Law. There are many who believe the Askshic Records makes available to enlightened individuals the abilities of clairvoyance or psychic perceptions—word? Like other spiritual gifts, psi-abilites, and precognition, etc. Like future seeing or prophetic abilities. You need not concern yourself with these for now, let's just focus on the lesson at hand shall we. Now back to religions." I bowed my head and whispered, "Oh God, why do I keep asking questions, write Lee—just keep writing." Urge kept right on teaching, sharing, schooling me. "They—mankind, human-kind, mostly wayward, disobedient, lost souls needed and created religions from their long dormant spiritual memories. Religions and the organizational structures they've created are nothing more then substitute attempts for half-awake souls to remember that which was imprinted on the God-seed of every soul that has ever existed, upon its original creation and separation from its source—the one source, the Godhead. Religions attempt to guide, some mean to inform, others to rehabilitate or reunite the whole man, with his higher spirit-consciousness (to reconstruct the Triune-self). Based on varying theories and belief-systems (rituals) regarding the creation of all matter-worlds, human-nature, attempting to define the relationship of human-kind to the sublime whole you see?"

"Again Lee, there is an innate need for every soul still separated from it's true source to understand it's purpose for being, and the future destinies of wayward or lost souls as planned by the creator in the expansion of spirit-life and for companionship for God himself. Many are still unaware of who they are, where they are, why they are, and what a personal God of their choosing has in store for their eternal futures. All religions as you know them Lee Roy have a miniscule amount of transcendental knowledge—or truth contained within them. This is what makes them so potent on matter worlds and on many water-worlds. You know that water is the material symbol for religious and spiritual thought right? Anyway—this cosmic truth that mankind or human-kind is indeed a byproduct of the one source. That source being the same God-idea or concept that they all worship and serve individually and collectively. While calling him by many different names and titles—you see little brother? You understanding all this mister man?" "I guess so urge—sort of." Remember I've told you the only truth you'll ever need, to reach perfection, that is—'all is indeed spirit and spirit is all.' God's truth then, is more then religious head-cheese. Like that which is often organized and taught back in the world to the general masses of incarnated souls, see?"

"So it is then, that any religion based on a personal God agenda is primarily created for the purpose, of glorifying one's professed (often misunderstood) relationship (un-aware of the innate God-seed already existing within all creation) to that God as felt in the hearts and minds of men. Usually over the truer freasher new-age theories of God within and alive in us all. Why this has remained such a hidden secret on earth I'm really not sure. It is a spiritual fact that God-spirit, God-essence, truly lives in and surrounds all living things, regardless of the outer garments of flesh-matter or material appearances worn. Yes, for all things living—all plants, all animals, and humankind itself are but different pieces of the same spirit-cloth of God. See Lee, you can never truly separate completely, that which once was created—from it's creator. Our spirit energy-matrix is, and has always have been complete, within the holy-body of God—this truly devine and intelligent Universre see? Some small part of the Great Artist or Master Architect is always felt, seen, or lives in his creations. Many believers of certain religious systems or spirit-schools of thought, collectively agree—on the simple nature of their religions and their traditional doctrines, as set forth by their holy books or their historical spiritual oral-traditions, as sharing one spirit voice of the great Godhead—see?"

"Hence through the collective force of mind, religious dogma is usually imposed upon sleep-walkers (un-conscious souls) by the requirements of their individual forms of worship-rites, and their so called religious leaders. Primarily to maintain discipline and control over their respective groups, congregations, shrines, or temples. Many of which have been built up for mere pomp and pageantry, and often used and maintained for their own religious gains and profits." "Yoh—Urge, Master Urge. I have a question for you." "Hold that thought Lee Roy—lets us review what has been said earlier about the souls of man, keep writing son, and keep climbing." I was utterly amazed at how easy it was to ascend the large winding steps leading up Mt. Edon. Only once or twice had I needed to use my hands to brace or balance myself, or to pull myself up the path. So I was able to climb and write without much hindrance, until we reached a flat out-cropping where Urge wanted to rest and pray. For an older version of myself, he sure could move, appearing always agile and strong, especially after one of our prayer and rest breaks and moments of in-motion meditation. Urge would simply be glowing—with a strange kind of spiritual light, which he said was a celestial aura that all living things, including elevated souls, Angels, and visiting Gods or Goddesses would manifest—according to their level of power or spirit-consciousness. He also said that every soul ever created manifested some form of light or aura due to the life-force energy all living entities generate from within. Now I forgot the question I wanted to ask him a moment ago—word up?!

Urge had shared with me earlier that one of his instructors back at angel school (a very long time ago), was a Vivatar—a powerful spirit entity from the Godhead of the Milky-Way Galaxy. What ever that is? Urge said that this light-being represented divine-intelligence itself, a level of Christ-consciousness reserved for highly advanced soul-entities. He said this God-like being could generate a light force as bright as a small star if need be, and they had enormous powers just like Arch-Angels have. This being had passed quickly through the higher dimensions of learning — where Urge had received some of his training, and had imparted divine wisdom through his very presence — without words spoken or language shared between them. Then he was off to even higher levels of spiritual existence, obviously to walk again amongst the God-class of entities that exist in this our Intelligent-Living Universe. "Now back to the souls of man." Urge was still speaking into my mind — "Are you paying attention young spirit — are you comprehending me (he had to ask again)?" "Yes Master Urge, it ain't easy keeping up with your teachings, I mean considering all that you know, and all that I don't know." Then, I'm not sure if Urge cut me off at that point or if I just lost the mental connection. When I looked over at him he looked a little startled, and looking around wildly now — he suddenly said, "Lee — I feel a strong warning, a negative movement in the field of spirit-emanations around us!

There appears to be some kind of storm approaching this holy mountain, maybe even this very spot I believe!" I said — "Urge if that's your word, then maybe we need to find shelter my elder brother." I could feel his temperament change to one of alertness and caution. I also was wondering what was going on now with my elder-self, as I myself begin to feel a strange tingling sensation throughout my own astral spirit-body. He responded with, "No Lee, I don't mean that kind of storm, besides I am your shelter now — so be not troubled little brother. There rides on the horizon over yonder a dark-shadow moving rather quickly in our direction! Can you feel it or see it yet little brother? I believe it may be just one more astral-test or soul challenge approaching us, so put on a strong fearless face little brother, we will handle this, come what may!" Oh shit I started to say but didn't — instead I said, "Oh no not again Urge — is it that she-demon coming back to sex me up again?" He slightly shrugged his shoulders and said he didn't think so, once a evil soul or entity gets hit with angel dust, they totally evaporate and usually are never seen again! It's to far away to tell exactly what it is!" What ever it was, it was surely heading up the base of Mt. Edon towards our location. I saw what Urge was seeing now. A silverish cloud of astral dust that looked like it was coming out of a prone rocket or ground-jet of some kind, kinda like a rooster's tail, and boy was it moving extremely fast! Still it appeared to be a graceful thing moving effortless over the many small hills and rocky streams near the base of this mountain.

We watched it as it roared up the base of the mountain like a snake on ecstasy. Within seconds it was within our visual sight. Damn — some kind of vehicle I thought, like a rocket-car I believe. I then asked Urge mentally—"Urge do you recognize what it is—should we be ready to fight or run and hide out my brother?" I was fearing for his safety now more so then my own. He didn't answer me—just ruffled his collar with both hands and brushed off his silver blue robe. Then he gently pulled out from under his sash his little silver bag of angel-dust and readjusted it for easy reach I guess be—hind his back I think. I then noticed that I had unconsciously drew nearer to him, and slightly behind him just to play it safe—in case he needed me. "In the spiritual realms of astral-space you never know what or who you may meet Lee—they, the creatures or entities that can show up on this plane, must all be challenged to see if they are indeed of the good-force, light-side or of the bad-force, the dark-side." Then he said—"When you (or any disincarnate soul) just arrive into the ethereal / astral planes, or are close to your spirit-journey's end, or nearing your final destination, you can't always be sure of what mysterious or evil-force will try one more time to keep you or us from the prize! A lone astral soul—in transition traveling must always keep its eyes on the light—it's true goal, or destination. It must always trust in the light that guides it and illuminates the dark passages and dark forces nearby!" As suddenly as it appeared out on the horizon the silver cloud of speeding dust stopped just short of colliding with Mt. Edon—near where we had first started our climb. It then turned upward, towards us!

Before Urge could finish his next statement of—"It's known they always come in three's. The trinity of the dark-forces behave like that of the light-forces, on the etheric / earth planes. All threats, temptations or tests and rewards—comes in threes, so here we go again I guess, are you ready little Lord Lee Roy?" Damn I thought—what a compliment, the old dude called me Lord Lee Roy, and I liked the sound of that. I mentally projected back at him with passion and conviction—"Yoh my brother Urge, hell yeah I'm ready, lets do what we gotta do my Guardian dude!" I thought as we prayed quickly, "Oh God of Gods, could we please be spared any more tests or problems before we get to the Holy City of Light!" Then the fast moving vehicle just shot up the winding path we had just left and skidded to a dusty smoke-bellowing stop about 40 feet in front of us, slightly blocking our path up the next level of this holy mountain. Boy did that car's engine's side-pipes sound deep—and real sweetl! I mean real cool for a ride so fast. Urge now standing tall spoke out loud—"So Lee just remember what I've taught you, remember your valuable spirit lessons, stand fast beside me and fear not—the glory of the prize that awaits us up in the City of Lights is near at hand. Come what may, we shall prevail this day!"

Urge sounded confident but showed signs of a hidden apprehension, as this tall, well dressed, darkly handsome (if I do say so myself) middle-aged stranger exited the flashy rocket car now resting on this small flat out-cropping near us. As he approached our spot, he spoke crisp and clear with a voice full of strength and authority (sounding like a James Earl Jones). "Well—well—well, if it isn't the great Guardian Angel Lord

Urge. May all of God's blessings be upon you two young spirits of God's glorious communities (young spirits?). Hell if he didn't look younger and stronger then Urge, as he continued his rapid speech. "Oh Lord Urge—your reputation for peace making and spiritual-love shared throughout this Universe precedes you. I feel like I know you sir, or rather I've heard a lot about you and I thought—since I was in the neighborhood, now would be a good time to meet you in person. So I had to hurry along to catch up with you fast-moving fellows. Please allow me to introduce myself." This tall dapper dude looked innocent enough to me, as he moved closer extending a friendly handshake towards Lord Urge, as I quickly glanced over to that fly ride of his. I thought at first it appeared much like a silver and red Rolls-Royce or a new Bentley that was dressed out with low-profile tires and some seriously spiked-spinners, as well as air-squirts front and rear—whoa talk about a fly-ass ride, oops.!

Damn I whispered to myself, that ride is phat! It looked truly mean, I mean awesome—sitting back there gleaming and poised to attract all kinds of attention, even Angel attention I'm sure. Surely it must have cost Fly-dude a large fortune at best. It was so damn sweet it looked like it was still in motion while standing still. He spoke to us, "I am Lord Wish Trader—maybe you've heard of me? I am conscious and powerfully aware of my supreme spirit function, to assist and reward the fondest desires or wishes of all my fellow souls, where-ever we sould meet. On their way to any place in this our ever-expanding Universe, or to the great City of Light above us here. I see Lord Urge you are with—a relative of yours I believe?" Master Urge was like, "Thank you Lord Wish-Trader but no thank you, we're doing just fine and will not impose upon your generous offer of assistance at this time my find friend." I felt Urge's silent reluctance to continue this verbal exchange, and still didn't know why? This dude was seriously polite and sharp, looking like a cross between a tall Morgan Freeman and a dapper Samuel L Jackson, yet he had smooth dark-skinned like Wesley Snipes. He was dressed to the hilt like a rich Mack Daddy or black Super Fly guy. I mean he had on diamonds and gold every damn where. He wore the finest five-button suit I'd ever seen, and a bad-ass short brimmed hat that matched his horned tortoise-skin boots, capped with gold tips at the toes! He had a group of brilliant diamonds on both hands, his tie pin, both ears, both wrists, and in his brim, that any one of which could blind an elephant with their fiery-bling!

Hell, his jewelry alone was almost as bright if not brighter then the smooth-silverish aura that surrounded him! Indeed he looked like the grand marshal of pimps and famous cash-money players from back in the world! All rolled into one, I thought—truly an extraordinary street-king or big-baller for real doe! I hadn't seen anyone so clean and stylish since I had attended my first player's ball back on earth—and I thought I was the main event! I was pumped, even sort of glad to meet him I guess. I had some serious pimp-player flashbacks while standing slightly behind Lord Urge. Still Urge seemed extremely cautious and didn't have much else to say. I had to interject—"Yoh Mister Wish my brother, Wish Master or whatever your Lord-ship? Tell me how you got here so fast—what the hell kind of dope-ride you be pushing? I mean, I meant driving? Was that your chariot that caused that giant dust cloud-funnel we observed tearing up the plains down below, just a moment ago?" The tall stranger looked over at me and asked—"And your claim to fame little brother is?" I thought to myself—this sharp-ass brother-man knows my damn name. "I'm called Mr. Lee Roy sir" I said, as I heard Urge in my head mumbling something like—"Oh darn, they've sent us a big gun from the dark-side Lee!" Y'all know I didn't want to hear that shit, what the hell now!? "I think I know what he's here for Lee, I think I know what he wants with us—or more to the point with you! Careful Lee Roy—please don't let your self be deceived!" Urge must have sensed my awe, my growing interest in this guy who reminded me so much of me back in the day. During my (assumed) peak of power and wealth back on earth—back in the hood when I was king of the hill, and untouchable so I thought!

The hip fly-guy spoke—"You know Lord Urge I believe you think to much, and you're much too afraid of enjoying the real benefits of the material-life God has seen fit to give to us spirits in abundance. You need to relax and fear me not. Truly I'm just curious as to rather or not I may be of service to young Mister Lee Roy—in some small or large way?" This dude is skinning and grinning now, as he whips out a real fat knot of thousand-dollar bills from his pocket (Urge never did advance to shake his hand I recall). He starts counting them out loud, "ten thousand, eleven thousand, twelve thousand"—trying to impress me I believe. Hell I'd seen big money like that before. Then Urge started to speak to this obviously rich and powerful being—who was dressed a hell-of-va lot sharper then Urge and was as strong as Urge I'm sure—so I thought. This dapper stranger then waved one of his hands filled with money gently across his throat, while pointing over to where Lord Urge was standing with his hands casually held behind his back. I mentally asked Urge, "What's wrong dude, (feeling now his soul distress, why aren't you moving or saying anything now?" No answer—Urge was frozen, just staring over at me and Mr. Wish Trader, as fly guy stepped up to me and said.

"Well Lee I think your security-guard, Lord Urge is just plain old worn out. Perhaps a wee-bit overwhelmed by my elegant and sudden presence I'm sure—don't panic player he'll be fine in a moment." I had to ask him—"Yoh Richy-Rich, what the hell did you do to Lord Urge when you pointed at him just now?" "Lee stay cool little brother—relax my man. You see, I just wanted to talk to you without being interrupted by Lord Urge little man, that's all. So I put him in stasis, a sort of temporary freeze for a few minutes, he'll be alright, trust me Lee! Now we can talk freely about shit (oh so he curses too) that really matters to players of the same lodge. Maybe even conclude some small business here, you feeling me player?" Urge now looked upset as he stood a few feet away from us still frozen with his hands behind his back. I don't know how I knew, but I felt he was holding on tight to that little silver bag of cosmic dust he carried, even though I couldn't see it from where we stood. I don't think Urge had a chance to use it if he had planned too. I also wondered what he actually meant earlier when he said they do come in three's. I knew one thing for sure, that this guy Mr. Wish Trader was a real slickster. Because he was just too smooth, to cool and non-threatening at first, so he had caught us off guard I think! Still I felt no real fear of him, just a little surprised not to be able to here Lord Urge in my head any longer. "Well listen up now little brother" – Wish was saying, as he slipped his arm over my shoulder. Walking me away from where Urge was standing like a cold life-less stature.

"I see only bright lights and big cities in your future son" – Wish said. I did feel a little helpless and apprehensive, because it seemed like I couldn't resist this tempting force from getting inside my head, inside my spirit-mind, oh damn! I begin to feel the rising pull of great temptations throughout my being for my past life-style I had recently lived, because of what I was now hearing and seeing in these powerful mental visions running through my somewhat reformed astral-mind or consciousness. I was seeing astral-images of fame, power, and wealth undreamed of, while old smooth Wish Trader whispered new dreams into my head even though I now know that a soul (any soul) should never embrace evil or violence to get these transitory things. That the cost to one's soul would be way too great! These were only illusions that the Wish Trader was placing into my somewhat reformed consciousness, my head, my so-called stronger mind. I knew I had to do something quick, or I would fall victim again to my past gangster-ass life-style, I just felt it! To myself I was like – Lee Roy what the hell are you doing – what are you thinking fool, get a grip!

God knows, I should know better by now, then to allow myself to be separated from Master Urge at any distance!

This Mack man, Mr. Wish Trader was smooth talking me now, as he pushed me closer towards his gold-plated twelve-valved chariot of power and beauty. It was then that I noticed a familiar rap song playing on a bad-ass sound system booming from the fly ride. It was Snoop Dogg and his dog pound I think, blasting out one of my favorite raps, singing – 'rolling down the street smoking indoe, sipping on Gin and Juice – laid back, with my mind on my money and my money on my mind.' the song's bass line was booming! Hell yeah that was it, pointing to his fly-ride Wish said – "Lee do you want this bad-ass ride? You can have it along with all the sexy sack-chasers that are drawn to it, like bees to honey. Meditate for a moment on that my friend. What if I were to tell you that all this that you've been going through, is nothing but a cruel after-death dream son (pointing now towards Urge and the mountain behind us), and you only dreamed you died in prison. Then you dreamed of floating out of one body into another one, where you met your childhood bogeyman—old Grimm. Then this shadest figure calling himself Lord Urge showed up and claimed to be your Guardian over-soul and your friend! Hell he just wants you all to himself Lee and I wonder why? Don't you see young good-looking brother of mine, this is all just a dream Lee. Just a damn dream hustler! That's all it will be my man if you just say the words I need to here player! Don't, I repeat—don't think too much on it like that old square over there." Pointing back towards Urge. "Just look at how he dresses—like he was taking you to some damn toga party. Probably to hand you over to some big muscle bound Greek-spirit with a sexual fetish for young men?"

"Here touch the sleeve of this suit I'm wearing, you won't believe the feel, the attention to detail. You wouldn't believe the thread count or the origin of the silk it's made from—hah!" He was boosting, bragging more and more, laying it on thick and fast. He said—"I can make all of this here nightmare go away quick Lee. I am the greatest fixer in the Universe boy! I can set you up in a five-thousand or six-thousand square foot palace Lee, with two or three Hummers, Olympic size pool, full B-ball court, Jacuzzi and twin bar-be-cue grills, the works Lee! And you know what, you can have the biggest, warrior-fit pitbulls in the world to protect you and your empire. I know how much you loved those dogs dude. You know—you were almost there dapper rapper, you were close to becoming the biggest, and the badest, the most powerful dope-man the world has ever seen. Yes, the biggest black Escobar or Scarface! But you lacked my supernatural support little brother. The keys to the nation would have been handed to you young—blood, if one of your chump flunkies hadn't sold you out. Just like most humans do to one another back on earth, always hating on each other—so much damn hate, you remember?! I think it was one of those deadly twins who snitched you out Lee Roy. But don't be shocked now, cause we, members of my own Death-squad, my posse, sent that rat-fool a hell-of-va message!"

"I took care of him and his whole damn family for rating on you! Unfortunately it was after he testified against you and your crew in federal court. Dig Lee, big-cash like stupid money, and young freaky women, jewels, and hot exclusive rides—whatever your heart desires can be yours all over again. Bigger and better—if you'll just sign this little contract with just a drop of your soul-blood to make it binding and sacred on us both. Then and only then can we end this purposeless journey to nowhere—cool, cool?" Foolish me, I thought the bullshit had ended—nope! The soul-trap had been set by Mr. Wish maker with the best of bait for my young-ass to bite on! Someone told me back in the day, 'be very careful of what you wish for Lee—you just might get it', boy was my heart pumping! "Haven't you wondered at all Lee (this fool was still running his game), why old man Urge hasn't really told you anything specific about the so-called great City of Light? Or why he keeps insisting you and him must go there. Do you really know what awaits you on top of this here Mt. Eat-em-up my man? Do you know what the real spiritual punishment is for dealing in illegal drugs, destroying the life of your less fortunate lazy-ass brother and sister souls back on earth? It applies to any life any where in this cold, unloving, unforgiving Universe young gangster? It's total and complete soul-annihilation Lee Roy, with no evidence or any trace of you ever having existed! Did you know this!?"

"Well no, not exactly" — I said as bravely as I could. "I like what I'm hearing except that part about never existing Lord Wish Trader!" He said, "You can call me Mister Big-time, cause I've taken many young souls like yourself and helped them to achieve the big times like you couldn't believe son!" "Well — speaking of old man Urge, no he never did tell me exactly why we had to visit the great City of Light" (I lied). "Or just what was going to happen to me once we got there (I lied again)." "Think about it son" Wish said, "Just what would a place like that hold for a dirty low-down gangster-ass nigga like you, huh? Maybe a Caligula-style party with all the vices and sex which you still desire, nooo! I think the pain and surprises you'd find there would be a real living hell for you dude! Truly it must be a trap, a cruel way of toying with a soul that has already thrown several life chances away — bet! Oh yeah, what if when you got there — all you find is uppity, self-serving, conniving, racist white-folks? Maybe a big Roman-looking white pervert with a sexual appetite for young negro male-souls! Still I can fix this shit real fast little brother, I really can cause — I have the power! I am, the Mighty Wish Trader entity you see before you?" "So tell me the truth Mr. Wish, (I asked him stalling for more time) could you really deliver on all that stuff you just promised me?" "What? You can't feel me young thug for life? Hell yeah I can deliver! That and much, much more my business-man brother!

"Now the real reason the great Lord Wish Trader silenced old man Urge, is because I know he believes he's doing the right thing in this here dream — but he also knows that the choice to dream this here dream, or getting back to the business of stacking dollars and clocking the young honies, is a choice only you can make, right now! So this is your last chance to truly live again, and be all that you can be player. Yes it's true little big-man, I'm only looking for a few good men — just like you son. So please don't mess this up now. You do remember how good it felt back then now don't-cha? Back when you were the shit! The elite on the streets, a young Dapper Rapper known to slap-her! Yes, you can do it all over again little Lee — if you just trade a few drops (oh now it's a few drops — humm?) of your life-force energy, for the noble desire of being on top again! And with my help — oh what a party we will throw little brother! So Lee Roy, what it's gonna be my man? Do we have a deal so we can jet this forsaken place, and leave behind all this childish holy-moly bullshit?" Damn, I said to myself — I know he needs an answer so I said, "Yeah — hell yeah I'll go with you! That big time dope-game and getting paid big time is all I really know anyway!

I'll sign your little contract, but first you gotta let me say so long to old man Urge — cool? I think I've grown kinda fond of him you know even though I always thought he be setting me up for the fires anyway — right?" This fly guy Wish Trader turned slightly to look over his shoulder at Urge again and said, "Ok, I guess that won't take you to long — so hurry it up Lee. Because we gotta set this beautiful wish off my partner, my friend! The people back on earth want what you got player — player, real dope-selling skills!"

I'm G-walking coolly over to my still frozen Guardian statue now, still listening to the bull-shit still coming from Mr. P.H.D. (shit Piled High and Deep). He shouted after me — "You know, the junkies and hoes world-wide be waiting on your return big-baby, aye-carum-ba!" Damn (I thought) nobody has called me big-baby in over ten years! I walked about twenty to thirty feet over to Lord Urge to tell him I was leaving — to say goodbye to him. I kept my back to Wish-man as cover, and with my head bowed I put my arms around Urge as if to give him a brotherly hug good-by. Then I slipped my right hand down quickly into his slightly opened little bag of cosmic angel dust still hidden behind his back. I made sure I spoke loud enough for Wish to here me — "Yoh Urge it's been fun old fool, can't say I've really enjoyed this fucked-up spiritual charade you've been playing with me. But hey, I've got to get it right man. You know I was born to blow up (still reaching behind him faking a long hug), to blow up big you'll see!" I then felt the pull of Mr. Fake-ass fancy-pants Lord Wish Trader as he calls himself, drawing me slowly back to where he was standing next to that sweet-ride of his. He was now leaning all cool-like up against his fast fly-ass low-rider. The closer I got to them, the damn car began to look like that fresh-flamed out, dressed out Dodge Viper I had always wanted back in the day — how strange!

As I rushed back towards both him and the car like I was excited, I spoke loudly — "Yoh Wish, that's got to be the fattest, fastest ride I've ever seen! It's truly one bad motherfu . . . ! The last words from my mouth had hardly finished falling off of my lips, as I flung a handful of Urge's cosmic angel's-dust as hard and as accurately as I could, directly into his face and chest. Then I jumped back and yelled at him — "Be gone you damn beast of treachery and illusions — you black trickster of Satan! Get your punk-ass back to where ever you came from demon! I got you — I got-cha fool," I screamed at him! Lord Wish Trader fell back shocked and then down to one knee, while holding his face and chest. What I saw was terrifying and amazing at the same time! He had immediately burst into blueish-green flames and astral smoke I guess — while squirming and falling down in obvious pain and anger, and boy was he angry at me! He shouted out real loud — "Little dope nigga, mother-fucka, what have you done to me foolish soul, why — why did you @*#!%*?!" He was screaming all kinds of obscenities as he stumbled towards me trying to grab my lean nimble-ass! I side stepped him as he fell down again and started melting into the ground, just like the wicked witch in that story of the 'Wizard of Oz' did. So did his fly dressed out Bently behind him! I said damn not the car—shit!" Then I shouted courageously at his ugly smoldering remains, forgetting most of my new spiritual training—"Yoh ass-hole, that's for what you did to Master Urge fool! You damn demon spawn, good riddance oh fake-ass shell or whatever you are! In the mighty name of Jesus Christ, I'll see ya—wouldn't won't to be ya, old slickass, fakeass temptation!"

"You gets none of my blood today damn devil! Not for all the money, fame, or power in any world!" I'd recovered enough from my fear and shock at what I had just did, and turned to rush back to Urge to see if he was still alive, wiping a tear or two from my eyes. I wondered what I would have done if the angel dust I threw, didn't work on Lord Wish Trader, except just to stain that bad-ass suit he wore. Then it hit me hard like a ton of bricks—Urge was gone! Still shaking I stumbled around, cried a little, then fell to my knees. I didn't see him standing or lying where he was last fast-frozen, wiping the astral-tears from my eyes, my heart truly begin to break! It was at that moment after I had fell down to my knees, that I felt a gentle hand on my shoulder. Yeah of course—I damn near jumped straight up out of my spirit-body! I thought it might have been that beast Wish coming back to jack my dumb-ass up! Suddenly I realized it was Lord Urge standing behind me with a big-ass smile on his face. Laughing a little and crying a little too, and trying to tell me how much he loved me! And how proud he was of me, because I'd passed the great karmic test of desire-temptation. A seriously deadly test created from the many negative effects of my old thinking, ego-dreams, and lusting after power and fame. At the high cost of destroying so many lives and families of human-beings back on planet earth.

Urge said it was one of the worst karmic-test for any soul-force to pass on this plane of existence, because truly it could have been our spiritual end. All just to get a taste once again of those material things just out of my ghetto-reach back on earth—that I temporarily enjoyed, which I thought then was so important. Those things that came with such a huge price and did nothing to help me leave the world better off, then the way I found it at my birth into physical matter. All that material bling-bling, none of which I could have brought over to this side of death if I wanted too! Urge was literally ecstatic with me, he said—"Oh God Lee, feel the glory—feel my joy young soul. You be growing in God's grace big time player! I love you, because you saved me, I mean you actually saved us both this time Lee! We could not have continued to exist a day longer if I had failed you again, or if you had chosen to leave me here—all would truly have been lost son! Whoa my man! Lee Roy you just don't know what you've done here today! Now you are my hero young dude!" Urge had never hugged me like this before it seemed, since we first met again on this side of death's cold and mysterious exit door. His hugs were now tight, real strong, and truly uplifting since my feet were now off the ground! Yeah I know I did good!

Then he suddenly put me down and gently pushed me away from him. He looked me straight in the eyes and said—"Now listen my brother, my friend, I need you to hear me now and understand what I'm about to say to you completely ok!?" His smile turned into a serious scowl when he said, "I need you to feel these words in your heart and then promise me you won't ever break this promise to me ever!" I said, "I got-cha Urge old pal, what's so important now—why you all serious all of a sudden dude?" He put out his hand containing his robe-matching little pouch of Angel dust, and pointing at it with his other hand said in a very stern voice—"Promise me you will never ever touch this pouch again! You must promise me you'll never ever tamper with it no matter what happens ever again! I don't ever want you to touch these very powerful and dangerous particles of dust ever again ok? Do you understand me Lee—do you promise me?! This cosmic powder is just to powerful and would be very dangerous in the wrong hands! There has been many assaults on Angels all over this Universe who were known to be carrying these dust pouches. Also because of what terrible things could be done with this stuff by evil thought-forms or neophyte half-souls playing around with it! The astral repercussions and cosmic backlash if that ever happened, could negatively impact the whole scheme of things spiritually here in this orderly Universe! I'm talking about a cosmic catastrophe!" I don't know why—but I half jokingly said, "Yoh Urge I here you but, I just got to get me a bag of that stuff old man and smoke me a little!"

"No—wait, I was only kidding Urge", as he blew up on me for real doe! "Lee Roy, the amount you used on the Wish Trader was way to much, and could have had a serious backlash on all of us! Instead of exposing and melting him away like it did, if your heart wasn't in the right place—Jesus help us. The smell of massive spiritual death would be sicking! You could have expanded him and his powers of evil a thousand times! Both of us, along with many other spirit-entities here, could have been totally destroyed—lost to existence forever! Are you reading me clearly now little brother?! Truly it would have been the greatest unpardonable sin Lee, do you feel me?!" I said, "Yes my elder brother—I feel you—shit, oops . . . that slipped out . . ." A simple thank you or well done, would have worked for my now crushed bad boy-ego (I thought to myself). Urge turned away and paused, then he turned back and said, "Again I thank you for your example of bravery. Pick up your pad and pen and let's be about our spiritual business. That was a close call, so we need to give big thanks to the Godhead, word-up?" I said, "Word." Urge started to act as if everything was now cool between us, I hoped so. I've never seen him that upset before and didn't want to see it again. We still needed each other I felt, we still had much work to do. "You know Mister Lee, in the beginning of all time and at the birth of all creation there was the Word—and that word was the Logos. That first word was Love and heard only by God himself who spoke this first word. Then came the Living Universe out of empty space, according to his cosmic plan of love, and it too had a sound. You want to know what it (our Universe) sounded like, at the very birth of spirit-consciousness?" I said, "of course I do—let it rip old man."

Lord Urge paused for a split second during our continued climb up Mt. Edon, took in a slow long breath—then forming his lips into a small circle, he begin to exhale just as slowly. Then he suddenly shouted—"Bang!" I was like what the hell?! "Sorry Lee Roy that was a joke son, (ha—ha—ha) let us get it right this time cool, ha ha, check this out." Making a low grumbling sound from deep within his chest cavity now, like a low bass or baritone note, then releasing the sound 'oommaahh', slowly flowing from his mouth on his exhaling breath. "Whoa!" I said, "Hey I felt that—I actually felt the vibrations of that sound flowing all through me. It felt good, yet strange at the same time. Then I tried to make the same sound, it didn't sound as sweet, damn. Urge chuckled a little and said—"It's all in the breathing Lee Roy—in the breath, and if you get it right, over time, producing the sound of the Universe during your prayers can elevate your soul's consciousness. If practiced during daily meditation it will aid you in healing and removing any blockages to your Kudalini or Chakra centers." I was like, "Come again partner—yoh Urge what is this kudalini?" He said, "Some that are yet earth bound, and actively on the spiritual path call it that, when referring to the serpentine fire, the psychic centers based within the physical body-form."

"Or more accurately the spiritual centers that line-up through the spinal system of material-bodies. This is only one path of the many spiritual paths towards enlightenment." "Enlightenment Urge, is that the same as illumination?" "Yes Lee, two terms—describing the same act or level of supreme awareness, a heightened level of consciousness and spirit mental-activity, a bridge to all things spiritual and one's true relationship to access the Godhead, you follow?" "Uuah I guess not, no!" "Don't guess little brother, you can know truth and all things spiritual if you're willing to do the work—the study, see? Remember the great axiom—spoken of back on earth, 'seek and you shall find, knock and the door shall be opened', well it's true here in this place as it is in all physical lives back on earth Lee ok? Ok." I said, "Ok—ok Urge, bet that." We continued to climb higher up the mountain that day and was actually two-thirds of the way up now, before we stopped our vocal meditations using and enjoying this new song of praise to God and his intelligent universe. "Oohhmmaa was it, and it was all oohhmmaa. In my mind, I wondered if I could fit this sweet sound into a rap-song somehow—nawh probably not? Yes we had reached two-thirds of the way up this mountain, when Urge stopped short and turned towards me reading my mind and said softly. "Yes little brother, I know and have known of all the questions that have come and gone from your capable questioning mind."

"Your mind even now is more a part of my mind, as my mind is now more a part of yours. Now we truly understand, feel, and think alike on many levels—and that to feels good to me. Still, I wish we had even more time to bond, to solidify even more our split spirits. We would be well prepared for what's to come on top of this mountain. As it stands, we must face the consequences of the divine law of karma and soul-dispensation that awaits us" (pointing up to the City of Light) on top of Mt. Edon. Boy was I paying attention now, as I asked Lord Urge again—"What's going down when we get there Urge? What will we be actually facing in the City of Light? Was there anything he hadn't shared with me that maybe he should have by now?" He responded, "Well there is no need to panic Lee—there's no need to be afraid of this great old city or it's multi-formed inhabitants. I'll be with you every step of the way, come what may. Which ever way the cards may fall, I'll be there with you through it all—son." Boy, son, Lee, Master Roy, little brother, half-soul,—shit, I wasn't totally sure what my truest relationship with Urge was from all the different names he referred to me as. Yet I never doubted that he was indeed a part of me, the better part of me. He often called us a struggling spiritual work in progress, like many other souls, striving to become a Triune-self. A soul's balanced trinity of it's multiple natures, or the three major aspects of the same jewel, or soul force. You know—the mind (mental self), the body (physical self), and soul (spirit-astral self) something like that.

Urge seemed to be avoiding my questions now, and I became a little apprehensive—maybe even a little freighted. I'm not exactly sure why, so I repeated my earlier question—"Urge why do you hesitate when I ask about my future, our future within the City of Light? So what's ahead for us, talk to me my friend. You know I'm tuff, stronger, and smarter now, so what's up?" Urge stopped climbing and turned and sat down on a flat rock, crossed his legs and arms, then put one hand under his white bearded chin and looked seriously into my eyes. So I sat down near his feet and looked him back in the eyes, waiting for his next word or lecture. "Yoh Lee Roy, you've been asking a lot of questions of me lately about our future together, and what lies ahead in the City of Light. Especially after our run-in with the Wish Trader. Are you beginning to doubt me now and the forces of good that live in the light little—brother? Or are you becoming fearful or anxious as we approach the top of this holy mountain." I responded with, "Yea though I walk through the alley of death, I shall fear no mother . . . ." He said, "Stop that—don't do that, if you're not going to say it right, then don't say it!"

I recalled how Urge had became kinda quite over the last few steps of our climb. Something was weighing heavy on his mind I could feel it. I knew we were close to cresting the mountain top. Even though I wasn't really afraid any longer, I was a little bit concerned however. Personally I couldn't wait to see where all the bright lights was coming from. Because it seemed like we were always climbing into brighter space the closer we came to the top of Mt. Edon.

The starlight grew brighter with each step up-ward. I told Urge no, I'm not fearful or anxious (I lied and I think he knew it). That I was feeling no pain, just curious and maybe a little worried, and wondered if even after a thousand prayers I knew we had prayed throughout this journey, if that would be enough to get us into such a holy place. "So you feel it—do you little brother? You feel the grace, the power of the spirit of this great soul city—huh? I also see you have now become more sensitive to the celestial vibrations that flow out from the city above, and that's good son, real good. So you should remain confident that all is well, and all for us is in divine order. The reason I was so quite and distant a while back is only because I was meditating as we climbed and was truly deep in thought Lee, that's all. Please keep in mind that I love you Lee and so does our God who created us one and all. I took a shot, "Ok Urge—so God can still love a dope man, a young killer, a whack-as . . ." Urge stopped me. "What-cha talking about Willis? God is God, and can love whoever he cares to Sir Foolish!" I was like, what? Who is he calling Willis? "In spite of all our failures and our imperfections over many lifetimes, the living Universe makes away for all soul-energy to belong here, and ultimately to find it's way home again. In spirit, in time, in the great mix of love throughout our Universe, you can never truly remain lost forever, and don't you ever forget that you dig?"

"Yeah" I said, "Check it out—if I had a shovel, I'd dig it in the morning, and I'd dig it in the evening, yeah I'd just be digging my own grave like before"—Urge said, "Shut up Sir-foolish. You've come along way, we be like bonding big time player—it's cool. Did you not understand what I just said to you?" "I think so my brother, my teacher. I just wish I had tried harder to pick up on your signals back while I was still in my physical body back on earth, and maybe" . . . (he interrupted me again). "Stop that, what's up with you lately young soul?" He said—"All worry, all sadness, and especially guilt—viewed in hind-sight is wasted creative energy, truly a sad state for any soul-force! The saddest state of any living souls is to find themselves (or it-self) at the Alpha of a new life or even at the Omega of an old one. Talking about—if I had only known then what I know now, or—if I could have, would have, should have, you ever heard that phrase before son?. What did the old ones tell you growing up back on earth, you remember? Never cry over powdered milk, just get over it and move on." I put my hand over my eyes. "Creative thought energy or the thinking energy of souls can always be used in better forms of magnetic-thought. You should know by now that our thoughts, good or bad will eventually lead to the creation of that which is held in mind or believed in daily thought activity! Like the person in a life who was afraid of everything around him and failed to live his life productively, courageously, until right before his end. He then wisely realized that it was his focused—fears that attracted to him the very things he was afraid of. Eventually becoming expressed into his daily reality, manifesting as illnesses and pain!."

"So be positive Lee, be constructive in your thinking and thought processes at all times—and your outcome will be the same. Again all souls attract that which they think about all day long! Do you feel me little man?" Still looking him in the eyes I said—"Yeah Master Urge I feel you, we will experience those things (the thoughts and ideas) held in our minds that we've mentally created over time, because the mind has power like that—that's why you call it creative mind, right? And if we can't see that, then we must be blind—right old dude?" Urge gave me that look again, and I just said to him—"Thanks my friend, thank you." To myself I mentally thought my astral-mind has turned into some serious head-cheese, so I gotta stay awake—stay alert. Boy I miss my moms, I've often wondered what happened to her fine-ass, I mean spirit-essence? Her valuble soul-force according to Lord Urge, was still at large, at peace—somewhere, on the other side of midnight?

Chap. 9   "Night of The Dope-Dead"

We had completed our daily meditation and prayers and had been walking upward more so then actually climbing. Then we came upon a most beautiful yet distant waterfall, cascading down one side of this mountain. The most beautiful astral waterfalls ever seen by any traveling soul Urge had said. We stopped just long enough to gaze and reflect upon the shimmering colors and silky-flow of the miraculously quite falling waters. Urge said we were getting very close to our final destination. Then I saw it, I saw the bright glow of the City of Light off in the distance. It looked like a distant sunrise off on the horizon of a very large and flat area on top of this mountain. I felt this was a very holy place, one that Urge called God's compassionate jewel. A celestial way-station containing God's very essence. Where souls from this dimension of the Universe would come to judge and be judged, to rest and to find spiritual-healing or gain more soul-knowledge. Many would move on to higher levels of manifest forms from their visits here. He said that quite often within the great Halls of Justice in the middle of the city, souls would even be allowed to judge themselves. Something to do with the karmic spiritual laws he had mentioned earlier. Urge said, after we crested the mountain top always back, that "Now was a good time to pause and meditate and pray." "What — again, ok — ok?" Which we did for several hours I believe. After we rested and meditated for two or three hours, we prayed out loud together once or twice. "Our Father which are in heaven, etc."

Then we talked a little more about the great city off in the distance. I asked my elder brother, "Yoh Urge — how much longer you think it will take us to reach the city proper?" Urge whispered back — "Maybe two days and one astral night by walking." I remember this time well. We had decided to pray again — right after Urge had told me what I had feared all along. Some how in some strange spiritual way, I knew I would be held accountable for the mess I had made of my life — my existence back on earth. So blaming Lord Urge for his absence or anyone else for that matter for the choices I made — wasn't gonna cut it now. I felt I had some real dues to pay, especially for all the other lives I had ruined with my dope-selling and drug-related violence, and its deadly results. I recalled Urge telling me — of the great Halls of Justice located in the City of Light and the Lords of Justice that ran things there. That some souls, that come before the great court in their individual trials of spirit-adjustments and soul-judgments are all alone, or at least they think they are. This was done each time it was deemed necessary for them (individual souls) to determine their own soul-rating in the greater scheme of universal spirit progression and karmic dispensation. Others would be accompanied by their Guardian Angels, as in our case or cause.

It was just before our last prayer this day, with the great city's astral-glow or aura beaming in front of us. Urge was looking me straight in the eyes again, and asked me a very serious question. He said as he promised me—it was a question I would hear again real soon. "Lee Roy, can you now honestly say from your heart of hearts, if you as an evolving soul incarnated within a physical body back in the matter world of earth—left that world better off when you died, then when you first birthed into it?" He continued, "I mean particularly after you had reached the age of awareness, of ascension in that recent past life? Having some knowledge of the principles of good and evil, of right decisions verses wrong choices, resulting in self-willed actions of either love or hate?" I first had my head down—then I looked up at Urge and didn't answer his question, feeling like I didn't need too. He knew my past life as well as I did. He had seen it all I'm sure, what I had to live through growing up poor and most of the time alone. Which led me to try and conquer the mean concrete jungle-life of inner-city Detroit, my way. Now very mindful of the shit I did with my young gang (my street drug-crew), with our guns and bullets blazing in the dark of night. Where another mother's son, some juvenile hanging out way to late, trying to earn some gym-shoe money by being some doper-seller's look-out. But not street-wise, smart, or fast enough to get outta the way of a no-name hallow-point, when a hit or revenge shooting went down in front of his or her now closed eyes, as just another dope-deal gone bad—damn!

It never was cool or heroic catching a bullet in the head meant for some other fool. Yeah I thought I knew what I had to do, to fight my way up to the top of the dope game. A deadly game called by many young bangers and ballers, the shine and survival of a black ghetto diamond! I was still looking back into Urge's eyes and without flinching or showing any sadness at this time I remember saying, "Master Urge—please, let us pray for more peace, and more light back on earth." I think I finally caught him off guard a little, as I started to create my own prayer with the hope that he'll follow my lead. He sat down and whispered, "Go ahead little brother—run it." "Oh Father—Mother Spirit of this living, loving, Universe—we pray to thee this prayer of safety and protection. Oh God as we near the end of our journey, we are as prepared as possible for that which is to come I think. We rejoice in knowing that the power, the love, and the mercy of the Christ Consciousness is nearby and watches over us. We both—Master Urge and myself, have come to know full well that the safety and security of my soul's destiny is held within your loving hands. Yes father any soul's destiny, does not—nor ever has come from attempting to control people and life events that surrounds us. That we are only obliged to respond to life from a position of love and faith that all in life and the Universe is as it should be. I have learned to shift my focus from fear about my spirit-life, or from what is going to happen to me, to my faith in you oh God—come what will."

"I realize now that you God, and our true-selves our higher-selves, are one and the same for all time. We have always been and will always be secure in your love oh God, no matter what level of existence our souls touch down on. I now know and understand that we dwell within God's heart and God dwells within ours—if we allow you to do so. The truth of God's mercy and grace-filled love protects us, and is the source of our security and the justice of universal law. We need only to trust in the safety and protection of the great light of Jesus the Brightstar, to experience the peace of mind of true harmony and justice in our love for others who often appear unlike ourselves, which increases God's love for us all. Amen!" Urge raised his head and showed me the biggest smile on his face and said while clapping his hands together. "Wow Lee! You have been paying attention and growing in your knowledge of prayer and spiritual law – whoa, I'm impressed young man! So its getting a little late and dark out. We should cover a few more miles towards the city before we lose more light – cool? Yoh Lee – truly that was the bomb prayer slick, I'm very proud of the progress you're making son, yoh – you be . . ." He suddenly stopped talking and walking for a moment, and looking around somewhat startled by something.

He shot into my mind a strong – "Damn not again Father" whoah, Urge had just used a curse word!

I knew then it was trouble again! Urge said, "No Father above – not again, we're to close to our journey's end, now what?!" I felt Urge had become quickly agitated from just a moment ago, feeling proud of me and smiling. Urge turned around and looked at me with a very serious look and said, "Yoh young-blood pick up the pace dude, have you noticed our cosmic light (meaning starlight as opposed to the city lights I guess) is fading fast? We gotta move out, darn – darn!" He said, "The astral-light is on the run, it's fading much to fast on top of this holy mountain. We should have hours before the city's lights dim even this far out, hell – something's wrong, quick Lee follow me!" I was like damn, if Urge felt the need to utter the word hell or to use any curse word, then something is seriously wrong! I heard what Urge was saying, but I really wanted to ask him about my up-coming trial in one of those great Halls of Justice we had talked about only briefly. I sensed something wasn't quite right with my Guardian Angel, even while my mind wanted to question him about the future destiny of my half-soul and his half. I wanted to ask him if he, as well as myself – would be judged and or punished for my sins and failures back in the old world. I thought that would be wrong if that was the case, considering he often couldn't get through to me back then. "Damn – oh God not again!" "What's up Urge – I said – what?" Urge just said, "What the hell is this now?!" Urge had cursed again, then Urge said "Forgive me Father God – will the forces of darkness ever give up?!"

Urge had used a real curse word twice, I thought to myself! As I also started looking around, trying to see what had agitated him so since we were so close to the city of light now. I wondered what it was now that caused him to speak a curse word, knowing how strongly he felt about vulgar language. I had a sudden crazy thought in my head, as we stood motionless looking all around into the rapidly approaching darkness. What if Lord Urge had become somehow tainted or corrupted, from being in my evil, sinful presence all this time. What chance in hell would I have if I'm put on some kind of spiritual trial in the great city without his holy help? Could it be that Urge was becoming more like the old gangster me, then I was becoming more like the spiritual him? I stopped asking myself these crazy, perhaps premature questions, when I felt cold fear again. That was being carried on the mental-vibrations coming from Lord Urge's mind into my mind! His voice was loud now as he took my hand and we dashed off into the direction of the city so I thought. "Urge what's up old man, slow down dude (Urge was now dragging my slim-ass with the utmost quickness) — "Tell me what's happening bro.?" "Lee we need to get to safety — some water Lee, hurry — we need to find a divine river or pool of astral water! So move it young-blood!" I truly didn't like what I was now feeling at all ya'll! "I know there is some water nearby so lets go — quickly Lee Roy, there it is over there, hurry up son!" Now I'm really afraid, as I quickly followed Urge's lead. I was right on his heels as I thought to myself, boy could this old man move out when he had too, without hardly any effort or sweat. He just seemed to float across these grassy fields and grounds, almost like flying with me right next to his side.

"Yoh Urge — what's really wrong now old man, slow down will you? You still got your silver pouch of angel's dust don't-cha? We got the power . . ." he interrupted me quickly. "Lee — we need the divine waters now! There isn't enough angel dust or time left to reach the safety of the great walls of the city! It feels like there's a lot of them, there's just too many negative vibrations approaching this spot — and coming from all directions it seems, trying to surround us I think — yes I believe!" We reached this large pool of water and slipped down into what appeared as its middle section. It was about the size of a large public swimming pool, and not very deep either. "Jesus (I said to myself), what the hell is all this about — we damn sho can't hide in here?" With our upper bodies sticking out of this strange water from my chest up, we made good stop-sign targets for whatever! The strange astral water only came up to Urge's waist and didn't seem like water at all! It didn't have any temperature to it and it didn't feel wet at all either, and I couldn't here any splashing sounds coming from where we were standing and moving around in it. Urge spoke again and sounded really serious. "I guess it's true Lee Roy, sometimes when it rains, it pours — troubles that is, and we're not hiding, this is just a temporary shelter." I asked him excitedly "Yoh Urge — shelter?"

Shelter from what?!" He said "Quite Lee — hush up and listen!" I listened but couldn't here anything over his mumbled prayers, as he moved away to sprinkle a hand full of his dangerous cosmic dust around the edges of the pool, while speaking some of his secret angel incantations. Oh yeah, by now I was fully aware of the rapidly encroaching darkness that had cut us off from the distant light of the city. Rolling in on us like a dark storm cloud that was determined to shut out all the astral-light. Urge had moved back closer to me in the center of the pool and spoke softly, cautiously.

"Lee—there must be something very special about you boy, it seems to me that the forces of darkness just don't want us together, or for us to reach the city of light. Perhaps they don't want you to be judged at this time? Or could it be you've made a pact with the Devil himself back on earth that I just didn't know about?" "No, no Lord Urge—I never had the chance to meet him in person, but some folks back in the day in the game actually thought I was him. Especially whenever I arrived on the set with my two nine-m-ms in my hands!" "Well your nines (guns) won't help us now Mr. Bad Boy—I'm feeling, sensing, the sheer magnitude of this here evil approaching us. This amount of negative energy surrounding us is a first for me, and I've been all over this Universe little man!" Now I'm truly frighten, shit! I'm thinking—if Lord Urge is this un-nerved, just what the hell is about to go down?! I'm sure Urge could feel my rising fear and apprehension, because he tried to reassure me. "Lee—we'll be safe for now, but we must stay on guard, stay alert, be ready for what ever comes out of this dark moment!"

"Listen can you here them?!" Damn—I said this must be some seriously evil-shit coming our way, not knowing if Urge heard me curse or not, being much to afraid to care if he did. I could feel Urge's early mental or spiritual warning system going crazy, as he clutched his little bag of cosmic dust real hard to his chest. I wanted to ask him why we were standing in this non-wet astral pool of fake-water, and how was it suppose to protect us, and from what? I felt he thought we were gonna be ambushed or beat down or some-ten like that? Then we heard something truly scary off in the distance! In the surrounding darkness I could see shadows moving, strange broken down ghostly forms. A dark-wave of movement circling the pond, then I heard what I thought was singing, or just a lot of voices all speaking at once. There was shouting, moaning, noises like an angry mob would make. Coming closer and closer towards us, yeah from all directions! I remember telling Urge—"Don't leave me now, don't you dare go anywhere without me!" "Lee Roy I would ask you to get a grip player, but I feel that you have already, do you mind loosening up a little on my robe?" Frantically I asked Urge as I relaxed my hold on his robe a little—"What's happening now old-dude or about to happen!?"

Standing tall next to me with his arms folded in a defiant way, he said—"Yeah it's bad Lee. I don't know if I or even we can fight them all, it sounds like a few hundred of them!" "Them who—or what Urge, what are they—who are them!?" The surrounding darkness was solid now, deep and foreboding. It hid everything that a moment ago was discernable. I—no, I mean we couldn't see anything now, no forms, no images, just dark shadows and barely the edge of our little pool of water. But we could hear them, cause there was growling, painful screams, and loud barking all around us. Sounds like wild lions barking at an unseen enemy off in the darkness! Urge said it once slowly then turned and looked down at me shaking, and said it again—like I didn't hear him the first time. "This is bad Lee—real bad, this must be what's called a night of the Dope-Dead! Souls lost to their material lives, that continue to hold onto their condemned soul-force by sucking up any life-force they can find on their way to their self-created hells! I've heard they've been known also to attack a weary or distracted Angel now and then!" I was like damn Urge! "Are you, I mean is it you they want—are they coming for you, are you their prime feast?" Urge looked at me strangely and said impatiently—"Haven't you been really paying attention at all fool?" I was right about that look—"No it's not me they've come for specifically, it's you Mr. Lunchable! Someone or something told them you were here, and where they could find you or us I'm sure, probably that old useless Grim!."

"Yeah, I bet it was that darn Grimm Reaper, I should have dispatched his behind when I had the chance! But don't worry too much Lee, the Dope-Dead can't stand astral water or bright lights. They won't be able to reach us here. We'll just have to put up with their futile attempts to get at us for their lunch or dinner. The Angel powder and astral water will keep them at bay until I can think of something!" I was thinking—no way God, we've come to far—shit! Forgive me Father God, please honor our prayers of protection! I told Lord Urge, I don't want to be no ghoul's lunch! I was beginning to feel that they were indeed here just for me. Urge was saying—"I wonder where all that barking and growling is coming from, it sounds so menacing? I have never heard of the night of the dope-dead making those kinds of noises before they attacked a soul!" I heard the question and Urge's last strange statement. I had begin to feel real fear again, in spite of believing in Urge's Angel-powers and his ability to protect me. I told Urge "We know that sound, I recognize that growling—that barking! I've heard it before—those exact same sounds back in the day, at out of the way places like darken vacant lots or abandoned buildings or warehouses." I told Urge it sounded a lot like pit-bulls preparing for battle in an illegal dog fight! Preparing themselves to fight another dog to the death, for the pleasure of those who gambled on such unholy-games of chance.

But these barking challenges were so loud and mean, they sounded like the bellowing of raging bull elephants I think! Then one, two, three of them dogs appeared near the edge of the pond. Damn they are big! Urge and I said it at the same time! They were really big Pit-bulls, judging from their ghostly out-lines! Much bigger then the dogs I used to fight and gamble on back in the mean streets of Detroit! They were big (about the size of a hippo) and mean looking animals, with red eyes, smoke or steam coming from their large noses and wet-mouths. Each one had huge jaws full of long dagger like teeth! Urge mumbled—"Oh so you mistreated those animals like you did your women folk—gambling on them too huh, betting on who would win when they fought each other over a small rock of coke?" I ignored his sarcasm, cause I'd never seen such big, bad-ass, dogs like these—I was in shock! They were lurching and pulling forward towards Urge and me, and were only separated from each other by some big-ass link chains. Chains that kept them apart and held in check by six or seven of the double-dead creatures as Urge called them. They were ghouls, long-ago dead, bad, evil, some who had recently passed over, angry souls. Ravaged and ragged from abusing drugs, and showing signs of gun and knife-fights, and other scars of self-destruction. Damn, they all smelled like they aught-to-be-damned, and this ain't no joke! We could just make out a large group of them behind the dogs, moving slowly around and around our little fragile shelter of a pond. Urge called them children of the truly damned! There were all different kinds, males, females, young ones and old ones, white-skinned and black-skinned, and I think a few Hispanic bloods or cracks-heads!

Hundreds of dead people, dead junkies with obviously decayed and infected bodies, sharp teeth, claws, and dead eyes! I thought I recognized a few of them but wasn't sure, and like I said they smelled really—really foul! They looked exactly like those costumed fools (the dancing ghouls) in that Michael Jackson video called Thriller! Some had bullet holes, knife wounds, razor cuts, and most looked like shriveled-up skinny street junkies that just wasted away—showing that life-less stare from to much cocaine smoking! Uh-oh, I just had an eureka moment—cokeheads, crack-smoking junkies, Pit-bulls, oh shit! I'm beginning to see a relationship here. I'm beginning to get the picture. I think they did come for me and not Lord Urge! These things were now screaming in unison from around the edge of the astral water—"Hey Lee Roy, Big Lee, Mr. Dope-man! Give us what we need brother man! We want that good stuff Mr. Ruff-and-tuff, we need those rocks of cocaine Dapper Rapper! Two for twenty baby-boy, sell us that Street Magic, that's the name. A good get-high because the quality is always the same!" One of them yelled from the dark background, "Lee Roy I owe you ass-hole", another one screamed—"I owe you too mother-fu . . . ! You killed my brother cause he stole a couple of eight-balls from you round-da-way, back in da-day!

"Come get your medicine punk-ass dope dealer", and "Still hiding behind your goons huh nigga? We see you Mr. Detroit, it's time big-baller, time to check that fly-ass in friend!" I held on to Urge's sleeve even tighter now, cause the sounds of this group's painful moaning and groaning was really messing with my head. Boy I thought I knew fear, but nothing like what I was feeling now! I started thinking maybe this is it—the end for me, no City of Light, no trial, and no chance at all for redeeming my pitiful soul. Maybe I could cut a deal with these things and somehow give Lord Urge a chance to escape! Somehow I knew that I had caused this sickening shit, or at least contributed to this crazy scary scene! I hated the thought that Urge might get hurt or worst destroyed, because of me and my dope-dealing messed up lifestyle back on earth! Then I had another scary thought—what if one of these double-dead mf's with those bigass pit-bulls, were to let those big chains go on one of those deadly soul-eating dogs. Who would then charge and leap over the cosmic dust barrier and astral water to get to me—to us! It would be bad I'm sure. Urge finally said something, softly yet confidently—"Lee Roy don't even think of doing anything stupid! These creatures are not here to cut any deals, they want us out of existence—they want what's left of our soul's life-force. They also appear to want revenge on you, one of the worst sins there is—revenge! Lee—you know by now or you should know, that thoughts are things of great power and miracleous creative force."

"Thoughts are very magnetic too, so don't even . . ." We both heard it at the same time, a screaming loud voice from the Dope-dead, "Yoh chickenshit, foul bastard, feed us nigga—feed us now!" I hollered back—"Fuck you crackheads!" "Urge thumped me in the back of my head, as the dope-dead hollered back—"Look at you now boy! We really need your energy dope-man, you know you still our little nigga even if you get no bigga! We need what you got Lee" (another voice from behind us said). "Yeah we want that dapper-ass nigga. You killed me and my little sister, with that poison you cooked up and sold us!" Then the base-head chorus kicked in—(a hundred pairs of sunken evil red eyes) swaying back and forth singing—"Yeah you thought you were so tuff when you sold us that addictive stuff. You made lots of blood money off of the young innocent homies and honnies, hell bound, hell bound, we all going down!" And again—"Lee, Lee, hit us up please Master P, which stands for punk-ass Mister Lee, yeah, yeah! It's on—young player, get your evil ass over here, let's do this! You won't exist much longer fool just you wait and see! You the one that got us hooked on that junk, now it's your turn to burn you little punk! Prepare your self dope-man, we be coming for you!" They were singing if we could call it that, "Mister Jack Smack sold us crack—now we want our damned souls back!" One of them screamed—"Give up mother-fuc . . . ! Let go of your nanny's hand—and come on over to this land, where you can again be so fresh and clean-clean! We'll treat you right all day and night, you do know what we mean!"

And, "Ok fool we'll let your cowardly-lion friend Lowly-Urge pass—if you just bring us that young evil gangster-ass!" They were hissing like snakes all around the pond's edge now, all bent over and clawing at the air. I saw their crumpled skinny fist, part flesh—part bones, waving all crazy-like in the darkness! They was stomping their fleshless feet, like they were getting ready to party over our last stand. Urge said for me to just ignore their taunts and don't get angry or show them any fear—they feed off of emotional energy too (talk about old school cool). Urge was it. He knew it was hard for me to do—not to get angry, my still carrying remnants of a bad temper and all. I felt mad, angry, pissed, like when playing that video game Quake! Knowing that there was a time when I would have sprayed their asses with my A.K., for rushing up and surrounding me and my man Urge—like Tony Montana did to his enemies in that cool-ass movie Scarface (if only I had my favorite assault-rifle)! I kept telling myself—I never made any of these low-life suckers smoke that shit! I didn't import it, didn't grow it, just processed it and packed it down and brought it to town! Shit, all I did was market and manage a glamorous street product! A commodity that has always been in demand and available in the ghettos of America it seemed, even before I was born into that hard life! Only fools brought drugs to personally use — the smart street players like me, just sold it to the local junkies to get cheddar — to get paid! So whose really guilty here and for what? I could never find a good-paying job in the hood unless I was a young black female — willing to work in the foreigner's Dollars-stores or Coney Islands, who hired black girls only, not males!

Young black males were anti-thema! Just tips and taunts at the local car washes and fast food spots — that shit was not for a cool-ass big baller like me. Urge squeezed my hand hard as one of the Pit-bulls couldn't wait any longer for his meal, broke away from his chains and jumped into the water! Landing only a few feet from where we stood, and exploded in a big ball of bluish-yellow flames and steam, damn! We fell back and covered our eyes! I couldn't believe how cool Urge was under this pressure, as he said while brushing dog splatter off his robe. "Now that was insane, look Lee I've been thinking while we've been trapped here. I don't know how long they can be held back by the astral water and angel dust. I see your demon processed dogs are not afraid to leap over here now." At that moment there was another big splash behind us and another dog blew up. Ba-boom! Urge said — "Maybe it's not strong enough, the sting of the powder and astral water." I wanted to scream at him but didn't, I was like, "Yoh Urge, the hell with why they all haven't attacked us at once. What are we, I mean you, gonna do to get us out of this mess old man — I mean my soul-gladiator!" "Well like I was saying, I've been thinking — that's what hundreds of thousands of Angels in the League of Guardian Angels are very good at, ok — thinking — so I think I got it!"

So here's the plan Lee, if I go down — I'm going down fighting cause you and me, we be cut like that right?" I wasn't sure of what I was hearing — "So if you survive my spirit-death (he went on to say), I want you to promise me one thing", I was like "Yeah — yeah, ok what?" "No traditional burial ceremony for me, and no tears — I want us to be cremated ok brother spirit! You see fire is a great purifier. It's quick and easy, and liberates the incased soul faster from its material shell." "What?" (I screamed at him sort of) — "What the hell is wrong with you old man"? "Ok Lee just calm down — it was only a joke son. I was only joking boy ok? But that's it Lee, that's exactly what we need right now — a big bright, hot fire!" I am not amused, and my fist are all balled up tightly — I don't know who I'm madder at, myself for somehow having created this mess in some strange way, or at Lord Urge's unsettling sense of humor at a time like this! "Jeesus" — I screamed, "Help us oh Lord — please!" I'm standing there with my arms folded now just looking up at Urge, not knowing what to say — waiting to die. Listening to the continuous screaming of the Dead-dead for my ass, and their evil chanting of my name! And the loud barking and growling of the two left-over vicious Pits, was making my consciousness falter. Twice I thought again about giving up, because my head had become numb from my fear and this new sense of hopelessness. One of the Dope-Dead screamed out something about my mother that got my attention.

"Yoh Lee Roy we got someone here who wants to hug her little boy. It's your mama nigga, look Lee over here, see her cocaine-addicted ass is reaching out to you player?" "She wants to know if you got any more of that top-shelf chronic? Two boulders for fifty dollars to ease her pain nigga?" I held back my strong desire to look in that direction. I knew my real mom wasn't there—so I prayed it was a damn lie. While Urge projected into my head—"Don't even think about it Lee, it's just a lame trick, you know—like the ones you used to play on these same fools back in the hood to get yourself a little cheddar-dough for the weekend. So play it off player like I know you can! Remember those slick mind-games of greed you played back then, like 3-card Monty, the Pigeon-drop, and Stick'em up Roger-Rabbit. So don't even look their way!" Then Urge did it again, he asked me another untimely question I thought—"By the way big baller, help me to understand why souls with black faces seem so content on refering to each other as niggers? Nigger this, nigger that, hey nigger and what's up my nigger? What's up with all that negative name calling, I've often wondered about that? I could never figure that thing out, wasn't that word used not to long ago as a serious insult, put-down for dark skinned people or people of color?" I ignored his question and asked one of my own. "Yoh Lord Urge please—where are we going to get some fire from standing here, shaking in this damn predicament?" Urge kept the jokes coming. "You shaking now bad boy, real scared huh?"

"No (I lied again—damn) I'm not shaking, I'm just thinking Urge. Here we are, surrounded by the astral-shells of dead characters from my past, who want to suck us dry of our spirit-energy and you're not afraid or shaking yourself. But asking me about that word nigger, its not nigger anymore—it's nigga ok, it's just a damn habit Urge—nigga, nigga, nigga?!" "Yeah right son, no need to raise your voice at me like that, cool?" With the calmness of a saint under pressure, Urge looked down into my face and said, "Lee you haven't noticed yet have you, the celestial power, the love, and grace this great living Universe is always willing to send our way—to those who recognize that it, the Universe, is truly a living manifestation of God himself? Help is always available for those souls who have faith in a just and caring Universe. It's true, that all things, every-where at once are held together within divine order—the cosmic matrix of almighty love, so never panic son! Many times in your most recent past life, and yes in my own—on this and other levels and planes of existence, our trials and tribulations have forever demonstrated the love and fortitude of the living Universe" (just then I thought I felt something brush against my foot under the astral water). "You were probably not paying attention to those sort-of-things back in the day I guess huh? Haven't you ever noticed on your own Lee Roy — that whenever a soul finds itself trapped or mired in the darkness of existence, then that is the time that the brightest stars come out to cast forth more protective, illuminating light. To give a soul renewed hope and guidance to find it's way out of the darkness, back into the light — you see?"

I can't speak — I'm just frozen, I feel a tremendous drain on whatever life-force I have left. I just shook my head slowly. Urge was beginning to seem like his earlier calm self, before this crazy evil Dead-Dead assault on our spirit-senses. Now Urge was looking up into the night sky, so I also looked up into the astral night, and saw that the stars above were truly bigger and brighter then I had ever seen them before. Still I didn't see any fire that he said we needed. I was like damn — Angel poetry before death, how ironic! That's when I noticed Urge had a palm full of Angel dust he had just removed from the now empty pouch, which he dropped next to us into the wetless water and said — "A great fire is what we need, so a great fire is what we shall have. Boy am I the smart one — you copy that Lee?" He then hurriedly added — "When I create this big flash-bang to clear out some of these encroaching ghouls all around us. The first three or four rows of them will fall away, then others I'm sure will rush in to take their places — so be on alert, be ready to move out quickly Lee! They want you — I mean us real bad son, they'll think we blew ourselves up to avoid a worse fate at their hands and teeth. They'll be hoping to find straps or pieces of our energy matrix nearby to feed on. So they can hope all they want, but we won't be here!"

"Its time for a direct point-to-point transfer of our soul force! I mean teleportation of our energy-matrix into the Holy City of Light! I do believe we can make the jump from here or come very close to it, if I've calculated the distance and speed needed correctly!" I said, "Urge please just do something will you?" "Lee, get close to me and hold on tight — and don't let go my brother, we've got to get this right. Have faith in me if you can't find it within yourself — or anything else young-blood! No — wait even better Lee, you should cast now what faith you do have into the very heart of God's supreme love. The Christ-consciousness that now and has always surrounded us! Lord Christ always delivers on his promises Lee. I know you forgot that lesson right son? Be not afraid no matter what you see or feel, just hang on to me, do you read me?" I was like — "Yeah, ok, do it, do something quick." Wrapping my arms around his waist, because something just brushed against my legs again, I held on to him tightly. Urge and I started to spin slowly at first, around and around our little pool of astral water. While slinging his cosmic dust out-wardly towards the still growing horde of evil Dope-Dead, demon dogs, and ghouls all around us. I grabbed Urge around his sash tightly, digging my hands and arms into his robe. That's when I saw 'them' clearly for the very first time — whooah! The aura light around

Urge's head and shoulders had become much brighter, and was illuminating a giant pair of feathery, silverish light-blue wings moving out quickly on his back from under his robe—wow! Damn, they looked powerful as they begin to unfold and flap, as they spread out around us. They started flapping faster, and faster in unison as we rose spiraling up-ward very quickly into the darken night space!

Urge mumbled an angel's incantation or prayer as he released the cosmic dust he held in hand, that burst into thousands of little serious flames of fire like a giant fire works display or big rocket blasting off. I could actually feel the heat (I thought) growing all around us as we begun to rise up into the safer darkness, faster and faster! For a moment I thought we was going to be burnt up along with the Dead—Dead from the rapidly spreading fires created by the Angel dust flames. As we rose higher up into the air still spinning, I thought I heard a different kind of screaming now, cursing, and barking from below. The flames from Urge's powerful dust was having its intended effect. The Dope-Dead below were now screaming, "Noo-oh-noo! Stop it—don't do this to us again, don't kill us nigga! Help us Lee Roy, have mercy on us poor hell-bound souls, and "we be family Lee Roy—souls of your soul!" Then, "Damn you Lee Roy, damn you to hell dope man! We'll see you again Player, we promise you—you little black-ass ghetto devil, you'll see—you'll see Lee Roy!" We shot out and up from our little sanctuary pool of fear. Straight up into the night and darkness, like a rocket moving up—up—and away into astral space. On our way to safety I prayed as we picked up speed, into the dark astral night that was only slightly illuminated by the bright stars above our heads.

I remember holding on to Urge's waist for dear life, my dear life—with my still somewhat selfish-ass in tow. I couldn't tell how fast we were moving or flying, so lets just say it was an awesome speed! I sensed only movement, a solid humming, blurred vision, then a strange kind of quietness. I tried to say, "I'm not down with this teleportation shi-stuff!" It was then that I realized that I was being lulled off to sleep, by the gentle hum of Urge's rapidly flapping giant wings near by, beating so fast. Feeling as if I could no longer resist this sudden, strong need to sleep, to close my eyes and rest, I asked Urge one last question—not being sure if he even heard me. "Hey Lord Urge, my hero—my Guardian Angel, are you—are we ok, we safe? "The last thing I could hear Urge saying was "son there is always hope, and it often is enough to overcome . . . any . . . ," then I blacked out—zzzzzzzzz. I was out like a heroin-addict after a sweet overdue fix on a day that was too hot to be getting high (some of you readers know what I mean) tell-the-truth, right? . . . zzzzzzzzzz Urge-whispering "Yes Lee we be ok, we got hope son now sleep tight, if you must."

A city of light — a spiritual court, hell I'm still not sure what lies ahead for me and my old-ass twin Master Urge. Yet I'm really glad to still be here, to still feel somehow alive. I don't remember our touching down, nor did I see those big wings Urge had obviously placed back under his robe. But none of those things mattered right now, because I was truly blinded by all the light — the light of the Great City of Justice as Urge called it. Bright lights big city, were my first impressions towards the vision still off always in the distance — within walking distance that is. I thought I was seeing a great massive crystal city, glittering with sparkling skyscrapers and light-filled buildings, reflecting shimmering beams of light. Light that was both colored and golden, with some structures lit-up with florescent-style lights, and very bright yellow lights. It appeared that the whole city was surrounded by a tall beautifully sculptured glass wall made out of glistening crystal. It was truly inspiring and the most beautiful thing I've ever seen in this or any other life time that I could remember. This vision was more beautiful then that multi-colored, quite waterfall on the down-side of this mountain. Lord Urge was now sitting nearby — just a few feet away looking in the direction of the Holy City. Quietly thanking God I'm sure, that we had made it this far in one — or two pieces. I took a moment to thank God as well. I was captivated by the grandeur of this image. This jewel, this diamond of a city on top of this holy mountain. Sprouting up into space itself, that at first had caused me to think we had traveled to the surface of a small sun due to the brightness.

So I sat down next to Urge, to give my astral sight a chance to adjust to all this luminousness ahead of us. Finally I asked him — "Urge — Urge, where are we, is this place real, what really goes on in this joint? Is this the home of God or what? It's so beautiful! What's really inside it, are there great Angels inside or cosmic spiritual-masters living here or what? Is it truly a city of love for lost or weary souls, cause that's all I feel coming from it right now! Will we find mercy inside it, waiting for us, for me? Will I be able to go in, to step inside those great crystal doors with you?" Oh God I felt like a little child on Christmas morning wanting to open up all my presents at once. Urge spoke directly into my consciousness, my ever expanding spirit-mind. "Yes Lee Roy, this is the great City of Light and justice I've spoken to you about. This has been our true destination all along my young brother. Yes it is for weary souls, souls in transition, both young and old, male or female — some with no sexual gender (a-sexual) forms at all. All coming and going, visiting, resting, and yes it is even for both you and I as a split-soul force. But first we must rest up from our last encounter, you have no idea how mentally draining angel-flying can be for someone as old as I am."

"Although it's much safer, less complicated and less rigous then thought traveling, which is much faster yet more dangerous for an untrained or neophyte spirit-mind." I'm still transfixed on the bright lights and big city—and not real clear on what Urge was saying at this moment (it happens ok). Urge was still speaking when I tuned back into his mind again—"We must pray special prayers Lee, and cleanse ourselves with water and meditational-fasting before entering into the holy gates that bars and protects this great place from outer contaminants. You know like uninvited, unwanted, mischievous nature units or unintelligent elementals, some curious thought-forms or evil astral-entities. Like months that are attracted to any light source, the brilliance of this city can and often attracts negative entities seeking to steal a little unearned light for themselves—for their own continued astral level existence. As opposed to them learning how to generate God's-light from within themselves, because generating internal light requires much work by little spirit-minds. Tell me son, have you ever met folks like that back on earth—you know the kind. Those folks you try to avoid contact visits with, because they always leave you feeling tired and or fatigued? We Angels reluctantly call those types of people or souls psychic-vampires, because they just seem to suck up all your psychic spirit-energy when they come around. Most of them are what's called hypochondriacs back in the physical world I believe. They be always sick with something or another, always complaining."

"Of course they were not always aware of doing this to others. They just need more spiritual-growth and self knowledge, in how to return to their spiritual source to strengthen their own spirit-energy reserves. Then they could receive all the juice (life-force) they need in any existence on any plane of life. Many just needed to read that fantastic book by that doctor, author—what's his name, oh yes—Dr. Wayne Dwyer. His book is called 'The Power of intention' I think. Oh my bad, its not due out for another five years—oh well, anyway. Another good little book that's a classic on the power of one's thoughts to create one's outer circumstances and destiny is—'As A Man (or women) Thinkth'—by a Mr. James Allen. You copy that down young brother twin of mine, maybe one day you'll read these good books?" Boy—how could I forget so quickly how much Urge loves to talk, to teach me, whoa! I don't think Urge knows—I don't like to read no books, yeah its my fault—my bad. I think he felt we had over four-hundred years to catch up on, over the short span of time we've been recently reunited. "Lee, this special place this City of Light for soul judgement and justice, was created for all living souls finding expression anywhere within this Universe. It truly represents many things to many souls who all must pass this way at some point and time in their self-directed soul traveling. Many come here to judge themselves or to be judged, others come to rest in between life-times".

"You see young charge—the Universal Intelligence here has seen fit to include all types of entities and some few consciously awake elementals, on their way towards becoming life-forms. Even those unseen living builders of the physical Universe—the active nature-units. Who are only conscious of their functions—to form the building blocks, to push or pull thought forms into physical existence, moving sub-atomic matter particles into and out of certain cosmic patterns—to be acted upon by the intelligent thought or higher spiritual impulses of higher elevated souls. Or just to aid in the Universe's expressing and expanding of itself as itself, in multi-variate forms of love, creative force, spiritual life, and . . ." "Urge", I shouted a-little, "Can we please get to the city, before anything else happens to us! I feel like we are being pulled to go there brother—to be inside already. Can you feel it too old Angel, we're almost at our journey's end right?" "You know little brother spirit of mine, you have always found away, a quick or slick moment to interrupt my talks or lessons, to keep me from noticing when my discussions or teachings, are becoming a little too complex or confusing for your limited intelligence to comprehend." "Yoh pops—(honestly I was just thinking this thought) no need to be dissing me like that." "Anyway Lee, you see I hope you haven't been fooling yourself by thinking that you were fooling me, whenever you've said—'got-cha-Urge', or 'I feel you Urge', oh yeah—'I copy that Urge' and etc, etc. Because if you've been faking your understanding all along during our journey this past year, you may not live long enough to regret it." Damn I thought—has it been a whole year already?

"You'll surely regret it if and when your turn comes up to stand before the Lords of Justice if need be. To show some growth in understanding cosmic metaphysical concepts or spirit knowledge befitting our age!? That is if you have the heart and courage to stand before them, after being requested in person to stand before them. Know this pee-wee, you then will be judged by them—do you understand now Sir Slick?"

I responded quickly to stall out more of the verbal beat-down I knew was coming. "Hey—hey Lord Urge my brother, slow your roll old man, I haven't been faking anything (I lied)! I've listened and learned a whole lot from you since I arrived on this side of death's door. I couldn't ask for a better teacher then you my mellow. So I just got one important question for you now. Will you be there with me, I mean will you be there 24-7 no matter what? Will you huh Urge?" "Of course I will little brother—if I've told you once, I've told you a thousand times, we have been apart way to long. I've given you my word that I'll always be near you or not to far behind you as your higher soul-force, as your spiritual guardian. That part of your consciousness that had as it's sole purpose in all existence, to reunite with its lower-self (you), to once again create a beautiful whole spark of the most high. Again a total and complete cosmic-seed of the Godhead itself, a real Triune-self. There-in lies the truth of the preciousness of all souls, even those classified as lost, downward expressed, trapped spirits".

"In what appears to them as an eternal hell-sphere, manifesting all forms of suffering and pain. Truly a sad state to be in, solely because they themselves felt the need to feel the burn. I've always prayed for them that were led to believe so foolishly, falsely, that they deserved such cruel and unceasing punishment. No soul ever created deserves such pain and suffering. That's why when and if it occurs to a soul, it only last for a short while, then that soul can uuh—repent and ask for forgiveness. And truly believing in the Brightstar 'Christ Jesus'—it will receive forgiveness for most of it's lessor sins, you copy this Lee? No soul-spirit is ever required to suffer eternally!" I popped in a question—"Yoh Urge what about that soul, that dude called Jeffrey Damer back on earth, he was eating up people—you ever heard of him?" "Yes, unfortunately I have Lee, he too came from the same source of us all—he just chose to embrace the dark-forces to bring about some very painful soul lessons he felt he and others needed to express in that life. I guess to demonstrate to mankind how far they could fall if continuing to make the wrong, evil choices in their expression of spirit-energy see? Combine that with the evil influences from the dark forces that exist, sometimes penetrating a soul's protective ethereal skin—then you have what's known on earth as real human monsters, like that Jeffrey character see?" Urge kept it coming. "As hundreds of thousands of souls and young-Angels have discovered to their spirtual detriment, who being so misguided have done and continue to do. This is due in part to their own self-imposed soul choices of believing in and expecting their power, riches and rewards can only be had and felt while only in the flesh or on physical matter worlds."

"Usually they also believe in an after death-state of eternal damnation or a state of permenate heavenly-bliss. Which they were led to believe or choose to believe, that soul annihilation was all that there was to life and spirit existence. When this is truly not the facts or the wishes of our great Father in Heaven, for any of his living creations of spirit. The entire Universe weeps for forty cosmic days and nights when ever a soul vanishes permanently from any realm of spirit-life. Just to cleanse or relieve itself of various forms of ego-disease (translated—absolute selfishness) and evil tendences. Only to be reborn again in a new age someday to experience their eventual return to the light of all life, the forgiving and healing light of their God, which is the same god as our God—the Universal Godhead. A loving and forgiving God—the celestial source of all creation. Who deemed it so and still insures a way, a path, for all his little life-seeds to find regeneration again and soul-growth on whatever level they find themselves expressing on. Even after cleansing themselves in the purifying fires of a so-called personal Hell. This is why we should always be seeking and thanking the merciful and almighty Godhead." "Yoh Lord Urge, (I asked) does that include the Dead-Dead or Vampire shades that we . . . ?" "Yes Lee"!

Urge knew my questions (all my thoughts) before I could finishing asking them now. "This is also why we pray for them all, to come back into spiritual wisdom and true understanding, which they all will at some point and time in their futures. We know that they, in and of themselves can and often-times create the very hell-fires or faux-heavens, through their own misuse or abuse of spiritual-laws. Like I've said before, usually brought on by the misapplication of their spiritual creative powers and free-will. These must constantly be brought back into cosmic balance before they (lost souls) can come to know lasting peace and or the bliss of their eternal oneness with God. Remember I taught you that in spirit-reality there is no such thing as eternal death, that there was only awareness or non-awareness, like in-active consciousness. The so-called sleep of death is only a state of being unaware of true life or one's soul-existence, ie-'true consciousness.' The old concepts of death or dying is usually still found only on all physical planes or levels of material existence for souls who travel there and may have stayed to long. I showed you once within the cosmic dust windows that there are such places, indeed even within this astral part of our multi-planed Universe."

"Where more enlighten material beings live and experience no death whatever, just constant growth and change through cocooning, like that of the Butterfly people of Budhi in Dimension—7. All you need to remember Lee is that, life-essence, itself is pure-energy and spirit energy cannot ever be destroyed, but only transformed or reshaped into other forms of spirit expression. Remember—all is of God, and God is all there truly is. For example, these astral bodies we now find our split-souls contained within, which gives us certain observable characteristics here. They too will undergo a change whenever our journey is completed. You may not yet understand all these things right now little brother, but in time you will." "No shit—oops!" Secretly I was remembering a kids rhythm we used to say back in the world—don't know why, it just came to mind while Urge was preaching. 'Last night—night before, twenty-four hoochies at my door, I got up and let them in—spanked each one again and again'. "Lee!, I feel a strong need to thump you real hard in the forehead right now, but I abhor violence, so I won't do it this time!" I'm like "What—you what Urge, why? Nawh you don't want to do that, please don't?!" "Listen Lee, this is not our truest form of being (touching his chest gently)—we are spirit now in astral-form only. Only on this astral-spirit plane of existence do we look and move in this way. Our soul's innate energy is that of the spiritual-class of energy sometimes called devine love. This love-life energy was endowed at its very creation so long ago—with various aspects and attributes of the great Universal Godhead."

"Remember back always along this path we've chosen, I told you that—not you nor any power or physical-force on earth could never completely separate that which was created—from its creator, no matter how hard it or you tried. Therefore our souls are indestructible, everlasting, and eternal just like our creator's spiritual essence is—you understand young buck? We are subject only to his love and grace, omniscience and omnipotence. Remember now my earlier question to you Master Lee Roy (Urge called me Master Lee Roy on rare occasions lately)?" I suspected he did that to help elevate my simple-consciousness to a higher level, one more attenitive and receptive of the things he was trying to teach me about true spiritual existence. Or maybe just for me to simply feel better about my hopes of a future spiritual life or continued existence,—damn. I mean, if there was even going to be a future life for me. The only thing I thought I ever came close to mastering was the drug-game. I asked him—"Yoh, what was your earlier question Lord Urge, run it by me again please?" "Well first Lee—that is not the only reason I call you Master Lee (reminding me he could still read my mind—my thoughts)." Hell, I kept forgetting that my mind, was his mind, yet on a spiritual-diminished level. So because of my lingering many ego-attachments that I've brought over with me to this place, this strange mystical world. I still think and feel somewhat, like I exist outside of Lord Urge's Angel's existence. Its taking me a long time to truly let go of this obvious ego baggage, of prior earthly thoughts and carnal desires and beliefs—damn, I'm trying ya'll! Suddenly it dawned on me that I've never run out of astral paper or ink, for my ever growing, ever expanding astral note-book. Which now has grown into the size of a small encyclopedia, wooah!

I had another earthly thought, an ink pen that never runs out of ink—now there's an invention for your-ass! I also suddenly felt Master Urge physically push me (my astral body) and say, "Here's a question Master Foolish! Do you have any idea how long you've fought me, my spiritual influence and desire to reunite with you, in your long mischievous physical existence?" "What?" (I thought, hell no, how long?) "I'm only 28 or 29 years old—I think, but I really can't remember now!" Urge answered in my head, "Yeah right Master Foolish, only 28 earthly years (as he shook his gray head from side to side)." He then asked me telepathically—"Can an Angel finish his question before you interrupt him, pleasee?" I didn't respond to this question, I just looked at him seriously as he proceeded to ask me yet another question. "Lee Roy, do you know what real love is? Have you not felt my love for you, which itself is a form of God's great love for you. Expressed as the greatest necessity of self-love and . . ." (I don't know why, but again I cut him off). "Please excuse me Lord Urge, do you really think that God our Father—can truly love an ex-dope man, a pusher, an abuser of women, a young destroyer of life? My own life and the lives of others, a real killer of men and animals back on earth?"

"Now be for real with me old dude, don't be afraid to tell me the God's honest truth Urge—please?" He just looked at me for a good moment with a sort of sad look on his old weathered face. Then he spoke, talking like an old black-face copy of Yoda from the movie Star Wars—"Boy oh boy thick is your head Lee—I mean hard is your skull young-blood, and your heart still is also! If ask you must this question of God's power and joy to forgive many of his backward off-spring, then surely you know him not. Part of that is my fault, of that I'm sure. Still—you must open up your mind Lee, open it wide boy because you can. All the stuff you've been forever writing down in that diary of yours, Jesus I wonder, I mean I really wonder—will it last?" His voice was getting louder now, "You make me wonder just how much of this opportunity, this true miracle you be getting little brother? Yes I love you, and God still loves you, he always have and always will—my Lord" he added. "I'm positive he didn't approve of your most recent spirit-life expression—and gangster life-style choices like I did not Lee Roy! Yet keep upper most in mind that God our father knows how to separate the wicked behavior from the lost or wayward soul itself. From any soul that causes its own disintegration over many life-time opportunities. God would never throw out his much loved babies with the dirty bath-water foolish Lee. Whenever we recognize and try to reconcile our lower natures, our lower-selves to his mercy, forgiveness, and grace, true miracles do happen. Look what he's already done for us here! We're together again, and are truly blessed beyond reason (louder and louder), we are transformed, and we are a team united again—hallelujah!"

"So we are going to beat this thing come what may. We gonna play our part—fight our fight to the hilt young lost and found soul-brother of mine. Lose you again I will not—to any evil or negative desire vibrations of separation! Do you feel me player—do you!? I know over your past few life-times, perhaps you've forgotten my own and Gods love for you. Maybe that's why you choose to live the kind of life experiences of death and destruction back on earth—in pursuit of illusionary fortune and fame. Truly each moment of life is a life-time opportunity! My brother, your very large ego has peeked, now it's identity of itself as the real you has waned. You now know that you are not your ego, that it was only a part of the illusionary material-body you wore back on earth. And it no longer controls your spirit-reality and perceptions of your old physical-self as the real you. It knows it has lost that fight for now, and you are free to be the true spiritual-self you always were meant to be. Now you truly feel me—right? Let me touch your forehead Lee, (Urge don't thump me, I mentally begged him) and make the mark of the cross inside the holy-pyramid, which represents the trinity of man. Remember the mind, body, spirit connection?"

"So feel my touch Lee. Let my words touch your heart, and listen now and believe!" Boy could Urge preach his message of love, forgiveness, and the oneness of all life. "Peep this Lee Roy—you and I as one, are an eternal creation of God. The God of this, our intelligent, loving, Universe. There is no more valuable substance then God-substance in any visible or invisible form, then that which contains the very breathe of the creator. You cannot yet see Master Lee—no force within known existence or yet to exist, could permanently separate you from the God who created you! Know this as truth little black brother of mine, we are still alive, individualized, and indeed held within his strong capable loving hands. How do you think the black slaves of old in your America back on earth survived such mistreatment, hatred and evil acts over 350 years. It was because God truly lived in them, in you, in me, in all of us! He always has and always will be a part of the consciousness of all humankind and spirit-kind. Can you feel me now little brother, can you just believe?" With my head bowed deeply trying slightly to hide my wet eyes, I said—yeah Urge I mean, yes Lord Urge—thank you bro., boy do I feel you!" He said only—"Good very good, let us pray then rest a little longer, to replenish our spirit reserves. We still got aways to walk, and much spiritual preparation and meditation still ahead of us, ok—ok?" I silently thought, you mean theres more to come?

Chap. 11   "Justice—Just For Us Spirits"

"Look Lee—over there, that's it, the City of Light! Where any and all nearby or passing souls are attracted to the celestial lights given off by this holy place, and the good beings conducting spiritual business inside it's giant glass walls." Urge added—"So now you can let go of my waist sash, which you've been holding onto and have twisted into several knots while you slept through our flight here from down on that mountain flat." "Ok—ok Lord Urge, that last Dope—Dead scene was just too much for me old man. I'm awake, I'm awake—word. I didn't want to lose you in flight, you know you may have needed my help. That Dead-Dead scene was truly horrible and scary so I thought dude." "Why yes, you got it right, cause you thought it, then felt it, then proceeded to act out those images back in your physical life on earth. Which I should remind you, resulted in our having to deal with the more deadlier spiritual ramifications on this astral-plane of existence! Why on earth would you choose to create such a challenge for both of us?" "Ok old man I got-cha-dude. I see the relationship to that which we think and believe becoming real for ourselves down the road of life and also in spirit-life right?" "Didn't you tell me that we reap what we sow mentally, that we often get what we wish for—so be careful of what we wish for, right? I'm reading you Lord Urge loud and clear—I understand even more so now then ever before, the power of thought on our actions in any earthly life experience".

"How it does and will effect a soul's after-life experiences—cool? Wait a minute old man, I gotta question for you. Why didn't you tell me you had massive wings, and where are they hidden now, I can't see them—are they underneath your robe?" "Yes, some what, Lee Roy—I didn't think I had to tell you that Angels, Guardian or otherwise had wings foolish boy. You can't at this moment see them, but they're still there—right where they've always been, attached to my back. They are just hidden to your limited vision and to the sight of other spirits and elementals here on the astral plane. It's a kind of camouflage you see, sometimes we don't want to be recognized as being of the Angelic class during our travels and assignment duties—see? The materialization of my wings quickens and shows forth whenever we Angels experience a state of heighten excitement or concern from our inner warning systems. Do you remember the many types of flying things—airborne creatures back on earth? Now think back, they were called birds I believe—right?" (I'm like duah!) "Well isn't it true that whenever they saw or felt danger approach, they would immediately jump into the air and take flight, right? Well my own extra winged-limbs, a mark of angel status, moves and operates in a similar manner. I guess you didn't notice them when me and my two angel friends, my winged escorts, first located you riding along happily with the Grimm Reaper huh?"

"No sir, I guess I didn't notice—probably due to all that bright light beaming all over the place. Still you never said you had wings!" "Yoh young blood if I recollect correctly, you know you never asked either did you?" I noticed now that Urge's new speech patterns seemed like they were deteriorating somewhat. At first when we met, he was like sounding more aristocratic or formal—now I wondered in my mind what effect my presence or closeness maybe really having on him for real-doe? He's beginning to sound and speak much more like me! It didn't seem to matter though. I seem to under-stand him better and learn more quickly from him now, whenever he speaks my kind of ebonic street slang. Truly I know that I've brought over to this side of life—a lot of self-absorbed baggage, and unreal bullshit in my mind (sins). I know now that there is a real spiritual cost for doing so too! Truly many misconceptions just about everything I thought I knew about the world and life. Like what is really important in life back on earth. Like how to truly live, how to treat niggas we meet, I mean other human-beings and even dogs properly, not to destroy any life, kill anything, or selling drugs to make a living. Or preying on other human beings to make big money only to buy expensive clothes, blinging jewelry, and flashy cars. Shit that I couldn't bring with me here if I wanted too. Chasing material stuff that really was a waste of my earthly time and energy, now that I've come to know better. I took in a deep breath and just thought—damn, staring over at the great glass-like city filled with light.

I wondered what is really waiting for me—for us, inside this strange holy place. That looked like Heaven from the outside to me, but wasn't Heaven according to Lord Urge. I knew I had never seen such a place—any place this beautiful before. Right then I started to apologize to Urge again. "Urge I apologize to you my elder brother, I really don't care what is to come on the other side of those giant glass doors of this city of light. As long as you are with me, I'm ready for it ok—I trust you, I love you, I still need you my friend! I know you love me, your sacrifice, your dedication to keeping me safe, moving me forward, growing my soul more spiritually. Thanks for teaching me new things—yeah I'm beginning to see stuff so much clearer now. You've already given me so much my brother, and I owe you for my continuing life—whatever is left of this pitiful life, one in which I once thought I could have it all. Yeah I had it all it seems now, I had it all wrong! I'm not sure if that life was even worth saving, sharing, or whatever. I just want to say thanks for all your brave efforts over many lifetimes as you've said, trying to reach me, trying to save me from myself—and to bring me home to God again . . . ." Urge interrupted me like there may have been too much praise coming his way from me—his lower self, a real loser I now felt. A self-styled gangster, violent, semi-dead dope pusher like me.

Perhaps he was thinking, how could a part of himself—me, sink so low in what he called a serious chain of mistakes committed on both of our parts. One of my biggest mistakes was the intentional misuse of my God given powers, wasting a very important and valuable life opportunity to live a righteous life, without all the material trappings or fabulous ill-gotten wealth and notoriety! A life where I could have treated others of my kind (black people especially) with more love and respect, for the real rewards that would have come later—after that life experience was over. Now I have a real chance to seek out and to get back to my true source, the source of all happiness and peace—the great God source within us spirits. A real chance to fellowship with the ultimate wealth-giver and source of power in this Universe, the creator of all life everywhere—the great and eternal Godhead as Master Urge calls him. All I needed to do back then (according to Urge's teachings), was to try and bring my feeling and desire minds together as one controlled transcendental mind. Too learn to distinguish between my ego and higher spiritual-self as the real me. To try and put any knowledge gained in life into balance with my perceptions of things, and to discover harmony and more charity within the illusionary duality of an earthly existence. Whew—this then was the process of living a truly meaningful and up-lifting material, or spiritual life in the body physical. In essence to clear away negative or bad energy (karma) surrounding self to once again allow my higher consciousness, my Guardian Angel—a chance to merge and bond with me while I was still in my physical body, see dear readers? Urge had said with some obvious shame at the time, that 'his' greatest mistake was not pushing through his own fears of becoming trapped in materiality like I had become.

This is how we lose our way, our so-called fall from grace. That was how we came to be separated from God in the first place. Back when we first discovered this beautiful matter world called earth, and it's new and captivating sensual delights. I was that part of our split-soul that wanted to push even deeper into matter and take on various shapes and forms, to feel the effects of strange yet magical forces mingling with my half spirit-being. That part of me that was expressing as Master Urge—my higherself, knew better and chose to stay behind expressing itself in the etheral realms. Now I feel truly that he had made the wiser decision between the two of us. This then being my greatest sin, or rather my individualized fall from grace. From the perfected state of the companionship with our Godhead energy, down into the madness of dark matter worlds. My backward growth, moving from a particle of the Divine Universal-mind down into a lost shell of an ego-mind on earth—corrupted! Truly there are no comparisons one to the other. Truly it was only a life-lesson effect of a soul trying to penetrate into, and change gross matter on a malleable physical world in this planetary star system, into something I wanted. Like a true child of God could do, but without messing it up. So I prayed—again, 'father God forgive me of my sins, please.'

Urge once said that, 'spirit-children should not have been allowed by God to play in matter worlds at all—or to stray so far away from their celestial home in the first place. Talk about God's misplaced trust.' He said it'll take him some time to fully understand that one. Truly he said, 'The fault was not with our creator but within us—as divine beings entrusted with too much power and the force of Godly free-will. Yet not enough spirit-knowledge or discipline to advance his will (God's will) above our own at all times.' Urge had called the reverse process—the way of resurrection for lost souls, like being born again, or renewed in the spirit again, or returning to our original source of all creation, the Godhead of this Universe. Urge had taught me that this was one of the primary hurdles that all incarnated souls masquerading in physical bodies would be subjected too. Many trials and tribulations awaited them while stumbling through and learning from multiple existences in material bodies. Which we then had to resurrect by enduring and conquering simple problems of matter consciousness—which wasn't simple to do before returning to the spirit world of thought energy. Whew! What a diary I've written. Urge spoke up, "Hah—yes, so you can read Lee Roy, now that was a good review son, right on little brother you are beginning to know the real truth my man! You have indeed learned a lot", stretching out his arms and yawning big time. "Now that was a good rest break during a good reading of your notes. So you have reviewed from what was—to what is, and from what is—to what shall come. We're now on track, so can we now try to concentrate or focus on our next exercise. Truly an important lesson above all that is now past. So please pay attention young soul, we must finish our journey today."

"First before we can enter this holy-place, we must again pray a special prayer, do a little spirit-fasting, and wash ourselves three times. Washing ourselves, our clothes, then our minds ok? This short ritual is the way we signify the washing of our hearts in thanks and praise to God. We must cleanse ourselves before entering the Holy City of as many of the stains of soul travel as possible. Any and all negative or petty remnants made, any negative thoughts or thinking we've picked up along the way here. As well as any of those we can remember from our many other past lives—while separated or together, as much as possible. Do you understand little brother?" "Urge", I stated slowly—"It's all good my man, I understand the need for more spiritual work, lets get busy dude. I myself would like to be in the city before night falls. Does it ever get real dark enough for nights around this glowing mountain top?" Urge just smiled back at me without answering. We headed towards a small washing pool where several other souls or entities sat, I believe they were cleansing their astral feet and hands, next to the big city and bright lights.

While we were cleaning up in the astral fountain / pool, I asked Urge a question. "Urge, I'm still a little confused about some of your metaphysical teachings and concepts, you know. I could really use a blunt (marijuana) right about now—(Urge shot me a mean-ass look across his shoulder) I didn't think he actually knew what a blunt was. "I'm just kidding old man—I'm just joking, I wouldn't think of smoking no weed near this holy place—really I mean it dude, sorry!" After washing up and more praying, a few mental and spoken spiritual meditations, we would be allowed to enter the city. I became aware of our peaceful, now un-eventful approach to the giant glass doors of the City of Light, I was a little excited. This holy feeling, sweet light giving place of untold beauty had calmed my reservations somehow. Words fail me in my attempts to describe the sheer beauty of this place, or these strange sweet vibrations felt in my head. The very walkways we walked on now seemed to be embedded with diamond-chips! I knew Urge had told me it isn't Heaven, but it's probably the closet I'll ever get to the real Heaven in my old mind. Still, it was truly a Heaven for me, yeah a real holy and mystical place. I feel like I belong here, I want to be inside, I feel like I'm at home for real-doe, my soul's home. Urge had his hand on my shoulder, he looked rested, looked more confident every step we took along the white sparkling walk-way leading into the city, this Great City of Light, love, and spiritual justice. I knew I was privileged to be here, to have made it this far—still alive, still conscious I guess, in spirit.

I kept saying "Wow, whoa, what"—like a little kid at a fire-works display at a Fourth of July celebration! Urge was still whispering encouraging thoughts and little, but powerful prayers into my head, like—"Now don't be surprised by anything you see Lee," and "Control every emotion you still carry, and don't point at any alien-spirits, you may notice it's considered rude manners here." (I was like, manners, shoot)—I hadn't heard that word 'manners' in ages. Just then I knew why Urge had said what he just said! I saw what I thought was a damn Klingon sitting off aways reading something, like that dude called Wharf on Star Treck, and he had big-ass gray wings unwrapped hanging back over his broad shoulders! It just slipped out—I said, "Damn Urge look a real live Gargoyle!" Urge said—"Lee I said don't stare or point fool!" Pushing my pointing hand down quickly with his. "We got enough to worry about son." In my mind I kept saying—'damn, look at him', and then—"thank you Urge for being a part of me, and thank you for your patience, for your lessons, prayers, and protection." Still looking over my shoulders and all around me, I could have sworn I'd just seen a real live Klingon—praying! "Oh by the way Urge, I know what true love is I think." He looked over at me and asked "Well—I got to hear this, so run it Mr. Poet?" I looked back at him and said—"True dat, true dat—true love old man, I mean Master Urge, is what I feel for you."

"Also this new love that I have for the Godhead, and this great love I know he has for us, all of his children. I believe—the good ones and the bad ones also." Urge just said "Right—so you think our God loves all his children huh, wouldn't you love all of yours Sir Foolish?" I slipped my arm around his slim but strong waist, his right arm draped reassuringly over my shoulder. He smiled broadly and telepathically placed in my mind these words, "Lee Roy you need not worry son, I got your back—young player.

You know I was somewhat of a young player myself. I can remember a class we young Angels had to take back in Angel School—called 'Understanding the Laws of Pro-creation and Avoiding Sex Between Species.' Where I had met a female Osirian Angel . . ." I quickly cut him off—don't know exactly why, but I said, "No Lord Urge—please don't go there old man, just don't!" He said—"Ok so I won't go there, so don't worry. Just don't worry about this city or be afraid now at all little brother, we're here, we're almost at the end of our journey." I believed in him totally. I wasn't worried or afraid right now and I didn't remember fear. Still I cast an eye over my shoulder back towards where that Wharf looking entity sat. All I remember feeling was spiritual elation, protection, and being in good company with Lord Urge. I knew I was in good hands but still hesitated, right at the glass doors that were being guarded by two of the biggest white-hoody robed Monks or Angels I'd ever seen, not that I had ever seen a real monk anywhere (or earthly angel) for that matter).

I could see their massive muscular physiques underneath their shimming hook-ups, and they each carried a long sword at their side. Why they needed these I didn't ask. I asked Urge telepathically, would he mind showing me just one more time his Angel wings, could I touch them—please! He lifted up his robe's long sleeve and said, "Here slip your hand inside here, and feel around toward my back." I did and I felt several large smooth feathers. They felt good, strong and silky, mentally reassuring and comforting. "Yeah—I said out loud, this is not a dream—let's do this!" The monk guards smiled at us and nodded their sentry approval for us to enter. Urge whispered—"We got work to do and not a whole lot of time in which to do it Lee, lets roll." We proceeded to enter the city, as I was stunned and stood frozen a moment by what I saw all around me. It was all too indescribable—oh the visions! Urge was walking quickly now and suddenly we approached two elderly gentlemen walking toward us, who also wore light-blue silverish robes very similar to the one Urge had on. Their hands were crossed or folded inside their sleeves as they moved effortless and quickly towards Urge and I. I noticed they were smiling a lot and obviously very glad to see Master Urge. One of them spoke a strange African-sounding language like an Arab dialect, I think!

Sounding like James Earl Jones's deep voice he said—"So our brother, you finally made it in one piece—or is it two pieces this time around?" The other elder individual chimed in sporting a thick mustache and matching beard—looking like a Frankie Beverley twin (a R&B singer back on earth). "We are pleased to see you again brother Urge. We prayed over-time for you and your young charge to arrive safely. We both know how honored you must feel this time around." The African sounding gentlemen asked—"Was your miracle, this reunion with your negative-side, what you imaged it to be, now be honest brother?" I thought I heard a twinge of sarcasm, so I looked over at Urge to confirm my suspicions. Urge responded while placing one of his arms affectionately on each of their separate shoulders saying, "My brothers—I, we, have always appreciated your timely help and prayers. Truly your brotherly love and concern is always returned to you two." He turned towards me and said with pride in his excited voice—"This is my lower-self Lee Roy as he calls himself this time around. It is he who has become my higher-self in my eyes. He has made such progress along the path. Lee Roy's great sacrifice back on earth was indeed the real catalyst that unlocked the cosmic gate that stood between us. That action was the spark that lit the flame of our long sought after reunification as one whole, complete, and happy soul." Urge was showing nothing but teeth.

"We decided to continue to communicate like this, one with the other—as two, so as to facilitate a more gentle and slow transition into wholeness again, and enter into this city of our future hope, where our spiritual-oneness will be recognized. Prayerful that our one-life will continue on forever see?" With obvious pride Urge said, "Lee Roy, meet my crew on the spiritual path, my two compardres, my brothers and friends within the great League of Guardian Angels. We've known each—other for many ages! This one here is Lord Nexus. The grey headed gentleman on my right bowed his head and said—"I'm very pleased to formally meet you young half-spirit Lee, it is indeed a pleasure." Urge continued—"This here bronzed-skinned fellow on your left is Lord Zulu." He looked about seven feet tall, and I swear he was wearing a gold medallion shaped like a map of Africa—what's up with that? Ya'll know, the kind of jewelry the afro-brothers wore back in the late seventies and early-eighties back in the hood. He too was as tall as Urge himself—six and a half to seven feet! "Ahsa-lama-linkem little brother Lee Roy—Abdulah-humda-la." "What did he say Urge—never mind?" Bowing my head in both of their directions with respect I slowly said, "I am the one that is pleased to meet you both." I added, "I wish to thank you both for your earlier assistance and prayers." Urge looked at me and smiled knowing that I knew they were the two friends that he spoke of earlier who had helped him to find me, and rescue my captured ass, oops—I mean soul-force from under the spell of the ugly Grim Reaper.

Urge whispered into my mind—"Good Lee Roy, indeed these are my escorts who helped me to find and retrieve your life-force, your astral-spirit, from old Grim. So you remembered, excellent!" Somehow, someway, I thought their luminous forms and energy vibrations felt familiar. Urge spoke—"Well brothers we have a little time to catch up on big city news, so let us walk and talk! So what have you two been up to with out my wise guidance and company. So tell me are you both still here on soul business or for a much needed Angel's rest? Or are we just standing around taking up space?" Lord Zulu said through a crooked smile (I still couldn't understand his words, his speech yet), without Urge interpreting telepathically for my understanding. It sounded like he said—"Our wise and benevolent brother

Urge, indeed we have soul business here. There is always something new to learn, to praise, and share, now it is both good and bad news! Which would you prefer first, the good news or the bad news?" Then Lord Nexus spoke, I could easily understand his speech. "Lord Zulu—do not play games with our brother Urge. Tell him why we are here and why we have waited around for him. Then let us beseech him to consent to our further assistance and support."

"We feel for his noble attempt at searching for mercy and grace for his young charge here Mister Lee Roy. Within the great Halls of Justice, Urge knows that we know—how the plan goes. When a Guardian Angel seeks to run interference for his lower-self (he means defending me I'm sure), when they enter into this great city as two-halves of one whole spirit. Therefore, we will not take no for an answer to our offer of assistance brother-angel." Lord Zulu chipped in—"And don't make us beg you my brother, you know how I detest begging, unless it is at the feet of the Godhead itself and for the spiritual benefit of some other soul-force and not myself—may Allah the sublime be praised." Urge looked lovingly upon his two comrades and said to them—"So that is the good news, that you two are still here of your on accord—you still desire to assist me and Master Lee in this spiritual quest of ours I see. I do so praise such good and noble friends as you both are, and continue to accept your love and kindness. Now if you please, what's the bad news?" Lord Nexus turned and started walking slightly ahead and to our left, then paused and softly spoke—"You may or may not be aware of the facts at this time Lord Urge. We are together in this—the new era of the 12th House of the Lords of Christ-consciousness, and the entire Universe is ending it's third cycle on this level of spiritual existence. All things spiritual and cosmic are moving into their final stage of cogitoergosum (-Discartes tenent, I think therefore I am) the spiritual-matrix, to await the great advent of the next spiritual order that will unfold the fullness of God's holiest plans!" I was like, "co-g-toe . . . what?" What the hell is this Angel talking about—I'm drawing some serious blanks now, mental blanks that is!

I also wondered if they could read my small mind like Urge could. Master Urge interrupted him, "Thank God—Lord Nexus, could you, would you, please be brief and to the point!" Lord Nexus asked Urge—"Have you informed or enlightened Master Lee Roy of the spiritual challenges to come or even why he's really here?" Urge nodded yes, "To the best of his abilities to understand (somewhat impatiently), yes—he's been briefed that there is no life without great challenges and awesome possibilities. We are prepared within the Christ-consciousness as best we could be, because as you already know we've been apart for so long. Time travel, learning, expanding one's consciousness is truly a non-issue here on the astral plane is it not?" "Well said"—Lord Nexus added, "There's been a recent changing of the Old Guard so to speak. A changing of the Dark Advocate General here within the great Halls of Justice! Urge we have a new prosecutor now who controls the dark forces and dark Angel staff within this great city and it's Halls of Justice! The gossip is—not that we embrace gossip, that he's a mean scoundrel, powerful, impatient with court protocol, and hungry for lost or misguided soul-energy!" Lord Zulu interjected something into the conversation that sounded like—"Yeah and he's twice the size, and has twice the power of his predecessor Lord Mayhem (whoa, did he say Lord Mayhem?). "It's also rumored he's fond of dragons too!" I looked up at Urge and saw a shocked, puzzled expression on his old face. Lord Nexus added, "You won't believe what his name is Urge?" "Go ahead Lord Nexus—run it!" "Pardon me Urge, run what—run where?" "So what is his name and claim to fame my brother?"

Urge had caught his brother Angels off guard I think with his newly acquired ebonics style of speech. Lord Nexus looked over at Urge strangely, seriously, stopped walking, paused and said—"The King of the dark ones sent a new special Emissary a few months ago to replace Lord Mayhem the old dark Advocate General here within the great Halls of Justice. Over the past several weeks we've watched this new beast strut around the court—within the great Halls of Justice. He has presided over three hundred soul-cases so far, and his won / lost record is awesome. Beware these stats brother Urge, 188 for dark passage, 100 for light passage (reincarnation), and just 12 souls for spirit elevation for God's grace to end their spirit recyling—to stand as over-souls or masters. We're not close to the 1,440,000 souls we need by year's end! If we're giving up numbers like these to the dark forces these days, we'd better pray harder for the new Universal Matrix to arrive sooner then later!" Just then Urge put his hands on his hips and coughed towards Lord Nexus impatiently, "Oh yes, the new prosecutor's name is—is, Lord Kokhan! It's said he is the Second Grand Emissary to the throne of him who we dare not speak of here in this holy-place!" Damn! I said, "His name is what, Lord Cocaine!?" That's all I needed to here! I thought I heard the word cocaine, so I started to flip out, I just did!

I almost died again spiritually, right where I stood, damn—damn! I literally broke down right there and cried, as I felt my astral body crumple to the white marble pavement. I felt doomed, tired, and tortured! I cried some more. "This can't be happening! This is it, this is the end—the end of the road Urge!" I'm looking up now into the teary eyes of Lord Urge as he tried to help me up to my feet (whenever I cried Urge cried also it seemed). I'm somewhat ashamed to say I sobbed these words but—"Lord Urge please, my friend save yourself, whatever it takes, please just save yourself! Let me receive what I myself have created for myself ok? I can't take this anymore, I can't, I won't, please just go—save your self dude!" Lord Urge lifted me up with ease and said—"Listen to me little brother, get a grip will you. Not only have you been a brave soul during our journey to this point, but you've also proved your rising soul's ability to prophesize!" I'm like what? "Urge—what you talking about old man?" He said, "Remember your poetry, your story-rap as you called it. In it you gave the clues of our old adversary.

How you knew in advance what his name might be I'll never know. Maybe your poetry-rap contributed to all this in some way—you think? Lee I'm just kidding" "Urge don't play with me now old man. How much more of this foolishness must I endure? I know my crimes against humanity, I know I wasted my life back on earth. So tell me please how much longer will this take before I receive my just rewards for all I've done?" Urge simply said said—"tell me slick, you're not turning into a—a drama queen now are you? Thank God you're not here alone Lee, stand up!"

"Surely you would probably be your own worst enemy, like most young spirits are when just exiting human-form, they seek to judge themselves to harshly." "Yeah Urge I've kinda gotten use to that back on earth—you know, it was always hard for a young blackman to get some earthly justice. It seemed that justice in the hood back then was reserved for just-us, the dark ones with no money. You well know that justice in America was always about the cheddar (the money), we got no money here Urge do we?!" "Honestly Lee you can leave the false illusions of race and monetary justice out of this ok. We're not on earth, we need no money—just faith in God! I don't what to think negatively right now about the past Lee, but I do know this. You and I, and my two friends here will see this thing through. Like I've said a hundred times little brother I got your back—believe it!" We continued slowly now walking toward the heart of this soul-filled city. Still wiping astral tears from my eyes, I apologized to Lord Nexus and Lord Zulu for falling out on them, I'd just never felt these strange deep feelings of fear before. They seemed to understand like they've seen this reaction before, as I watched white, gray, light and dark robed entities floating around and above us moving in all directions.

Some were entering and others exiting many of the gleaming buildings and temple-like structures lining both sides of the streets. Lord Zulu spoke-up, "Brother Urge, this is truly an evil presence you'll be up against, unlike any we've ever faced—and twice as arrogant as his predecessor whom he replaced." Urge slowed his walk and stroked his chin with one hand and said—"Oh Lords of Light, oh Lords of Power and Strength. With these two friends with me here and now, with my soul's earnest and all important other half so close to me—my heart and mind shall prevail when the time is right. I too am willing to suffer God's grace or his punishments, his sorrow if need be. But I tell you both—no, you three, Lee Roy included. I fear no evil, no devil, or dark Angel, for I have fully come to know real peace, real love, real spirit-life from being made whole again, because of being reunited with my lower self Master Lee, even for a moment. He who has grown quickly, stronger and wiser, from the base and vulgar matter world of earth. To shine like a Triune-self, representing our true self—the point of all souls ultimate destiny! I will die for him if I must, then—at least I will die whole!"

Lord Nexus added—"Wow that sounds great, but will the Lords of Justice buy into that speech?" Lord Zulu added—"That's why we're here to assist him Nexus, Urge may try and pull a stunt like that I believe." Urge just kept talking—"Who knows, we just might make spiritual history this time around over centuries long past, if we manage this event properly? Yeah we could present to all the inhabitants of this great City of Light—the greatest plea-bargaining this place has ever seen!" I was dumb-founded (what, plea-bargin), shit never changes. That's why so many brothers back on earth went to prison because of plea-bargaining. Damn, I thought (I'm fu..ed). Urge said, "Win or loose, we will be talked about for the next millennium, right guys?" Both Lord Zulu and Nexus appeared shocked at Urge's dry suggestions and some kind of behavioral change that had come over their dear friend I think. They stood stark-motionless and eyeing each other as if they couldn't believe their eyes and ears. Then Lord Nexus said—"Urge really now, have you forgotten the possible deadly consequences of this trial, oh let us pray, and pray hard, and let us then rest! I say Lord Zulu, our brother Lord Urge could not have heard what we were trying to tell him" (looking over at the Zulu). They then looked over at me in a kind of forlorn way and Nexus said to me—"Master Lee, come what may—now how would you put it? Oh yeah, we be down with you and Lord Urge young-spirit, we will not abandon you or Urge's noble (cough-cough) quest for God's mercy and grace this time around." Now I'm begining to become afraid again. I mentally sensed they're not telling me everything, cause Lord Zulu mumbled something to Lord Nexus like—"Get a load of Urge, you think he'll be alright? I sincerely hope he hasn't become tainted to much by his lessor-self."

Urge interrupted them—"Ok fellows, that's enough—I heard that. You two really don't know the sheer joy of reunification do you. How long has it been for either of you? The sweet taste of nearing spiritual perfection—sense neither of you have ever been that near to it—right?" "What Urge, what of your own spiritual imperfections"—Lord Zulu asked, "Excuse me brother! Oh please, even Angels of our class are a long way from spiritual—perfection." Lord Nexus said—"We have a right to be concerned dear brother, you truly appear to be different somehow and we don't want you to count your chickens before the eggs all hatch, you see? Especially regarding your lower-self Mister Lee Roy here (pointing over at me). Remember what you've told us over the past hundred or so years, about what a handful he was. How stubborn and negatively charged his consciousness was by to many material world experiences and desires—do you recall that conversation with us Lord Urge? Have you really been able to truly bond with him—do you believe it to be a real resurrection of sorts or real soul-reunification?" Urge said, "Oh great and wise pillars of friendship, as Lee Roy would put it himself—I'm his boss dog now and he's my best pit-bull!" I interjected—"Urge I don't think they understand the slang, and could you please stop reminding me of my serious and numerous misdeeds back when I was real stupid, back on earth!"

"You've done that a lot since we first met dude!" I turned to confront Urge's boys and said, "Fellows I know I have sinned against life, against women, and the collective consciousness of the one mind, as you would put it — the Universal mind of God!" "Yeah ok, so does Urge believe he's a dog now", the Zulu asked?! I knew Lord Urge was sticking up for me even as he tried to reassure me, and his angel friends that we'll be all right. Urge looked down at me and said confidently — "Lee you be in my territory now young-blood, this here be my stomping grounds, my hood, my neck of the woods — I got-cha back young player-spirit and that's that. So just chill, and peep how down I really am at saving our behinds from everything and anything, you feel me little wayward spirit? Come hell or high water, we either sink or swim together. Yes together little brother, as one tuff and powerful reunited soul-force!" I had a thought for a moment, that Urge might break into that song Reunited — by Ashford and Simpson my moms used to listen to back in the day, and prayed that he wouldn't. I told Urge, "I feel you cool Angel brother of mine. I feel you dude." Lord Nexus interjected — "Uahh — forgive me Dr. Jekle and Mr.Hyde. What we need to focus on is creating a plan, a strategy, and we have only a few short days to prepare for his trial (pointing again over at me) ok, so tell us how we can be of help Lord Urge?!"

"Lord Nexus, you know full well that I will be on trial as much as young Lee Roy here. Also, I am very familiar with the protocol of the great court." Lord Zulu looking away said to Lord Nexus, "He's definitely not the same old Urge that I'm used too." Lord Nexus nodded in discreet agreement. We had been walking around the city for sometime trying to get a feel for the atmosphere and any gossip surrounding this new emissary Lord Kokhan. "Lee Roy we've got much work to do, so while I commune with these esteemed members of the League of Angels on a plan of action — you need to pray the prayers of protection I've taught you, at least fifthy times cool? I'll join you as soon as I put these old fellows minds at ease, ok — cool." "Cool Lord Urge so where can I sit?" "Sit any where there is space to sit, sit where you stand — the choice has always been yours, and also — try and not disturb or ask questions of any passing souls or entities that are moving about. They may be in a kind of motion-meditation. Some of them doing prayer work and others in transition, most don't appreciate interruptions, ok? So I'll fill you in by morning what the three of us conclude." I thought to myself, morning, noon, night, hell I could no longer tell which was which. Most that has happened up to this point has happened in either slow motion or with the quickness. Mostly in the dark, in shadow light, or in extreme brightness. Hell I couldn't be sure of anything on this level of existence, or in this new place, this strange yet welcoming city I find myself in. I listened to Urge's every word, and reacted now precisely as he instructed or ask me to do. Inwardly I now know how important this is on this spiritual plane of craziness — Damn. I surmised listening well is important in this great City of Light.

Today we are near the heart of the city, there are many large avenues spreading out, like the spokes on chromes rims. In three hundred and sixty degrees in all directions with pedestrian soul-traffic going into and out of the buildings surrounding a large center hub, which I was told contained the great Halls of Justice. Some of the buildings and temple look-a-likes appeared to be at least fifthy stories high. I saw a giant beam of white light with sparkles in it rushing up from the center of the city over the Great Halls of Justice a few blocks away—wow! I remember Urge telling me it was the beam that is called Heaven's Gate that leads into the upper levels of higher consciousness, and other higher dimensions of God's spiritual Universe. When I asked Urge about it, he also told me it is a direct link to our source and added, "In our Father's Mansion—there are many, many rooms. Accordingly in the balance, underneath this great city there is the funnel of grayish murky-light or a portal that glows darkest red, where the lost or negatively self-judged, depressed soul-forces and unwelcome entities are returned to their times and dark places within our Universe and other worlds, though a sort of spiritual black-hole in space."

Lord Urge, Lord Zulu, Lord Nexus—the three Amigo's I called them (there's something very mystical about that number three I've come to learn), moved away off to sit at a little white table with four white chairs, outside of what looked like a small-town café or coffee house. "Jeez I thought I must be illing, spirits and Angels I'm sure don't drink coffee, I don't think that they drink at all. Hell, I haven't had a drink since I died however long ago that was. I find it harder to remember how long ago now. Shoot—I might as well start praying, so I did. I prayed hard and long, and never felt so focused on any other spirit assignment. Boy was I praying, the way Urge had taught me. He had said, 'it was truly easy for a soul to talk to God. At any time, anywhere, it found itself on any level of existence. Talk to God as you would your earthly father, in plain language, the language of your soul, from the heart center of your being.' Naw—I couldn't do that, not the way I cursed out my old man when I first saw him again after I had become a teenager. I was so angry at him then, I know God would not have approved of the things I said that day long ago, or my language I'm sure. I never noticed the dark shadowy figures floating quitely closer and closer to my prayer spot. I was shocked back into full awakeness when I heard Lord Urge (some what shouting) near me—"Move away from me, I mean him you minion spies of darkness! If you've touched him I'll . . ." Lord Nexus had grabbed Urge's arm and said—"Brother have you lost what little soul-mind you have left. It is forbidden for spirits, especially Angels to show anger or malice towards any other entity in this city!"

"Even if they are recognized as a threat, or wicked creatures from the dark-side causing a problem! You would be dismissed from this place without the great opportunity of a hearing!" I moved towards Urge as he hurriedly moved towards me, I asked him—"Urge, what's wrong, what's going down old man?" He responded—"Not to be alarmed Lee—they were just a couple of old shadow vultures lingering around you as you prayed, trying to size you or us up for their Lord and Master! I'm sure they were sent by that new prosecutor over at the Halls of Justice." I then asked—"Yoh, why would you think that Urge?" "Simply because they were trying to tap into your astral-vibrations to observe your spiritual weaknesses, and because they were dirty and smelled of sulfur—darn it! They seemed real curious about you Lee. From now on you'll stay close to us and we'll stay close to you until it is done." "Until what is done Urge (by now I had a thousand and one questions I could've asked him), oh you mean our trial right?" Looking at me as if I was truly a piece of work or a child that needed constant attention—Urge said, "Yes Lee Roy the trial, the last challenge we have yet to face. I hope as I pray that will be enough, yes the trial—our trial, and pray that the Godhead will have mercy on us both little brother."

Chap. 12   "A Gang Of Four"

It seemed we spent the rest of the day and all night sitting, praying, strategizing, at the little white table were earlier Urge and his crew had sat. It was very near the heart of the city right outside this little book store I believe. I had noticed above its entrance, written in what looked like blood to me. The large red words—"A soul's record is forever written and stored within the great Book of Life, which is found within the great heart of the Godhead—no copies available today. For your other spiritual needs—please step inside and read." My eyes then caught a glimpse of a small sign on the main door that read—"Sorry we are out of the popular little book—'The Greatest Miracle in The World by Og Mandino—it's on back order,' and I wondered to myself what that book was about. We finished a beautiful little prayer at the table (I can't remember it now) and Master Urge suggested to his two Amigos's, they should do some more research into Lord Kokhan's background before the hearing commenced. He said, "Come with me Lee Roy, let us walk and talk. We have approximately only half-a-day left." I was like, "What—only one day?" Feeling a little-bit anxious again, I noticed that Lords Zulu and Nexus was still with us, as Urge and I pushed away from our table spot and begin walking toward the heart of the city. Boy could these three Amigos talk and pray, I mean both verbally and telepathically. I felt it, yet couldn't always tell what they were saying—especially when Lord Zulu spoke his Africanese, but I felt that tomorrow was indeed going to be the longest day. "Will you guys pray for me ok", I asked to no one in particular? I honestly knew and felt that I coundn't stand much more of this mind-numbing heavy conversations taking place around me about trial-stuff.

I wanted to get it on and over with. Urge put his hand on my shoulder as he always did to reassure me (after hearing my secret thoughts) telepathically, then said—"Yoh mighty one (speaking directly into my mind—my consciousness), you've managed to come this far on the path to judgment, which in itself is a small miracle. It's said that after you've experienced one miracle in any of your life-times, they come more often and grow even larger. So look up, always hold your head up little brother—always! Just trust in the Godhead, as I do! Thank the Christ-consciousness for his ancient and supreme sacrifices for all of us who now live and know God's love. To have available to us that power within us, from which all miracles spring forth—our simple belief in the Godhead. That secret spark of God within us all, regardless of the name we give to it. Do you feel me youngblood? There-in lies a great spiritual secret Lee. God lives within each and every soul-temple Lee Roy, he lives within you too—believe it."

Yes I had felt him recently, I told my good old over-soul, my true Guardian Angel Master Urge. I don't know why I did it but I started repeating a prayer I once learned, "Now I lay me down to weep—I pray the Lord my soul he'll keep, if I should lie before I wake—I pray that Lord, my soul he'll take." I still don't know why Urge thumped me in the back of my head either? I must have gotten some of the words in the wrong order I guess, while Lord Zulu and Nexus both cracked a smile and softly snickered. Urge asked them why they had continued to tag along behind us. "Gentlemen, I thought you two would be off to do more research?" Lord Nexus acted like he was aiming a finger-thump at Urge's head—saying, "We're going in the same direction brother Urge, the information we seek—that which we need for more life, always lies ahead of us you know and seldom behind us Thumper." Urge just threw his hands up at them, as we collectively headed in the direction of the great Halls of Justice. The closer we got to the very heart of the city, the more crowded the streets and airways got. There were all kinds of light beings, dark entities, Angels with exposed wings—Angels with their wings tucked down, some strange pulsating, little colored forms or figures—each with four legs and four little arms and feet I believe. Looking vaguely like Dorthy's little munchkin-friends in that Wizard of Oz movie, and boy could they move about with the quickness.

Urge described them as positively-charged city keepers. They were advanced elementals that are preoccupied with the cleanliness and sanitation of this great city, and they exsist all over this universe. Not a speck of astral-dust escapes their eyes. He added that most of the time they were actually invisible, unless the light shown just right on them to be seen out of the corner of your vision at times. The fact that I saw one or two of them, meant my astral sight had become much sharper now. That's all he would tell me about them. I also noticed that there was no trace of any animal or plant life-forms to be found any where in this large city. Just spirits, light and dark souls seemingly at peace with one another, and a quite kind of serenity or peacefulness pervading this mystical place. I kept thinking I was hearing sounds, singing or such, somewhere off in the distance. Also there was chanting nearby that I heard—and just one or two blocks over I could see a group of maybe twenty to thirty orange robed individuals turning real fast round and around in tight little circles without bumping into one another—amazing! Urge told me that they were the soul's expression of the earthly Whirling Dervishes. A spiritual group in movement trances, giving tribute and praise to their concept of the Godhead that flows into and all around this holy-place, to replenish and revitalize themselves as other occupants here in the city was doing, and for the other Dervishes on there way here to find each other. It seemed like only a moment had passed when Lords Zulu and Nexus suddenly reappeared in front of our eyes out of curtain of fog.

These two friends of Urge's really seemed to be stuck on this new prosecutor called—well you know. They were telling Lord Urge that he had brought with him a real unruly and impish band of personal flunkies and assistants, from the dark realms here to the city. To Lord Nexus and the Zulu it was no secret from whence they came. They said, to them it looked like a small army of dark and evil robed gargoyles. Lord Nexus started immediately sharing with Urge his thoughts on their strengths and weaknesses—adding something about the very large and fiery red eyes of Lord Kokhan that matched his two short very red horns on top of his bald dark head that looked a lot like chilli peppers. Lord Zulu even mentioned on the up-beat, what he was wearing when they saw him in court on their last drive-by, I mean walk-by. He said that Lord Kokhan wore the most beautiful black and gold trimmed robe a prosecutor has ever shown within the great halls of justice. It had two large deep pockets on each side for his massive clawed paws to fit in. His hands and wrists were each covered with diamond studded rings and large bracelets, that could blind a lower soul or forsaken Angel with their brilliance. If one were to fall into the lost-zone of Lord Kokhan's evil and wicked reach. Even though I was afraid of him simply because of his name, I felt I couldn't wait to see this big bad creature. Urge had informed me that from this day forward, our gang of four must stay closely together because he said the most deadly and dangerous place here was indeed located in the various court rooms of the great Halls of Justice. On rare occasions fights had broken out between the forces of the dark-side and the Grand Guardian Angels protecting the court house, that left many a entity and spirit host damaged or deranged beyond repair.

It has also been said that some judged souls didn't take kindly to their respective judgments by the Lords of Justice, and had to be punished right on the spot were they stood in the court rooms—not often, but it has happened. It was also said that these were the times that God cried and averted his eyes away from his little spiritual children. This is why in seeking to keep the balance of power and spiritual harmony during court proceedings, absolutely no weapons, or potions (not even the cosmic dust that all Angels carry), white or black magic, or spells are allowed in or near the courthouse proper. Those that violated this rule have been known to instantly disintegrate into a ball of blue fire for all to witness. I see why very few spirit-rules are broken here. The three Amigos finally allowed me closer access to their little group meetings, their little hushed discussions and prayer sessions. I sat down in a chair with it's back to the wall facing out into the white and grayish marbled streets. Like I remembered during so often back in the old world, subconsciously thinking to protect myself from someone or something deadly and drug related. Like a rival gang's drive-by or drug hit, inspite of my three angelic bodyguards being present here with me now.

Lord Urge and Lord Zulu appeared to be in deep prayer or meditation, while Lord Nexus kept a vigilant watch. Urge had taught me that true prayer and deep meditation were one and the same, or the two sides of the same spiritual-practice. Two ways in which human-beings, or spirit-beings can communicate with the spiritual essence of the Universe—the one mind of all, the Godhead. It is through keeping the silence and practiced stillness that we find one of the best forms of talking to our personal God. Lord Nexus who was watching me reached over and put his hand on my shoulder and asked—"Are you awake young Master Lee?" I said, "Yes, see my eyes are wide opened dude." He responded with—"There are many in this world and yours past who appear to be awake with their eyes opened wide, yet their actions and behaviors tell a different story Lee! And—please will you explain that word dude? By the way—who is your personal God, have you chosen as Lord Urge has chosen, and do you now believe in the cosmic good verses the lowered vibrations of evil, or the great illusions of duality on matter worlds? Did you miss your higher-self when he was found absent in your material existences?" I was like—"Yoh Lord Nexus, when I say dude—it simply means a male friend, like brother man, or guy, it's just a greeting or slang term for another male person. Now you explain duality to me please, and why it appears to exist only on matter worlds?" He quickly said—"Why yes, take you and Urge for example, two halves of the same soul-force. One higher—one lower, divided poles of the same magnetic spirit—on the consciousness scale a split 7 and 3, with you of course being the 3"

"Then there's the universal expression of duality—such as gravity and anti-gravity, dark-matter and light-matter, and . . ." I interrupted him, "No not that stuff, been there, done that with Lord Urge." He said, "Ok, can you—or we spiritual beings, truly possess only one aspect of the source, our source—without having it's opposite, no. Without duality's twin vibrational expressions existing within us or near us—like the principles of cause and effect, or Godliness or Godlessness, we have nothing see? Our very souls have all been dipped into the multi-faceted aspects of the great Godhead matrix." I said, "Dude, I only got my G.E.D. back on earth you know—a second rate high-school diploma. I barely made it out of high-school! Still I got a college degree in street psychology, and a masters in selling drugs and doing violence back in the world. I'm not sure I understand all this stuff going on around me!? Is that what you wanted to hear?" He said—"No, calm down and tell me just what you think you know about this holy-place we're in now." I relaxed a little and added—"Not nearly enough Lord Nexus, except that which I've learned from Lord Urge. It's taken all of my left-over mental faculties after I died and arrived here, just to keep up with what Urge has been trying to teach me—sir." Lord Nexus interjected, "Here is not the place to place your mental faculties or material-emotive thoughts above the spiritual mind's abilities of creative force."

The strictly mental creations of lost souls is truly limited and are weaker expressions of soul-energy compared to the spiritual powers of true consciousness on any level of existence. For example thoughts are things that can and will manifest much faster into shapes or material forms here on this astral level, so one must practice controlled thought here better then on earth—see? What you now think, believe, then feel—is what you'll soon create here see? Things of spirit, things of creative thoughts or the desires of your will must first exist here on this mental-astral plane even before they can be expressed into a physical reality like that on earth—or like you say 'back in the day or the hood'—see? I'm sure Lord Urge has told you to let go of the false mental, your earthly ego. Let go of the lower-self or the false-base perceptions you still carry of who you think you are. Because your true self, your Triune-self can manifest and operate on this spiritual level far faster and easier then it can locked away in physical matter (a human body) or even in spirit astral-form. Do you understand what I'm saying to you?" "Yes Lord Nexus I think I do, I've heard this all before from Lord Urge, I feel like I understand." "Well that's better Lee Roy—I must say I am truly amazed that you have come this far on the path, good work, very good work son. Sometimes, most times, in a time conceptual context—it takes thousands of earth years for some fallen souls to make it back, to make it this far." I was like—"Ok, what—what, yeah right, and so tell me Lord Nexus—what are the real Bookie's odds on the out-come of my upcoming trial (trying to change the damn subject), you know—my survival chances, my spiritual brother? Urge never talked about that much, so what's the point spread if you've heard dude?"

"What Lee—bookies, odds, spread, what are these?" "Lord Nexus I guess you've never heard of gambling huh?" "Uhh—nope, can't say that I have." Lord Nexus became quite and looked at me like he was puzzled. He then lowered his head without asking any further questions or commenting, as he started praying. I shrugged my shoulders and lowered my head to join the prayer party. Master Urge sent me a mental thump inside my head just then, ouch—and I swear it hurt a little, so I thought. He said telepathically in the ensuing silence at our little table, "Why didn't you ask our brother Nexus if he wanted to here your rapping poetry?" I shot back mentally—"Yoh Urge it's called a rap dude it's street poetry, it was the language of my peeps—yoh! It's my personal perceptions and projections of my life without you being there and with you being here old man—remember? So since you brought it up, I think I will share it with you and your crew (puffing up my chest a little). Let's see what they think of my ghetto skills of lyrical thrills—cool?" For a moment while the silence faded, everyone was now awake at the same time. Urge mumbled—"Oh God of Gods please have mercy on us our father, which art in heaven. Protect your ears oh merciful one, for that which comes to challenge us from the lips of Lee Roy."

"Again Father, on this mission we need all your love, patience, and mercy even more." I was not flattered. I wanted to send him back a mental finger thump—to show Urge how it felt. Because the moment was right, but I thought against doing that, since I really didn't know how to do it anyway. I knew I was now out numbered and didn't want to get my butt kicked by these strong and powerful spirit-beings riding shot-gun for their boy Lord Urge and me. Besides I knew in my heart that to survive much longer on this plane of craziness, I probably would need their help. Shit, I mean shoot—I knew my very soul depended on their help. So I got to stay cool, stay strong, and at least put up a real fearless front. Still I knew I was lost, so I just prayed—and forgot about my rap story, and just prayed hard and long till I found a conscious place of peace in my mind to just chill, like Urge had taught me long ago—waiting for this soul, my soul's next adventure episode to jump off. True-dat, yeah so true to this spirit enigma, still wondering if I'm truly stuck or not in a damn dream. The answer really didn't take long in coming either.

Chap. 13　　　　　　　"A Dragon's Last Breath"

The next weird episode didn't take long in coming. Seems like I just blinked and a new mind-trip was upon me, I mean us. Time had passed as quickly as it could, and I'm not sure of how much. I just felt that shit was heating up quickly — so this had to be the next day. It was now time for some serious focusing, hope, and prayers. The sensation of heighten sound was everywhere, much commotion going on near the entrance to the great court house buildings. Lord Zulu was pointing in that direction (after wandering away earlier) and saying in his strange broken English — some what excitedly now. "My friends — come quickly, look, over here, come quickly and look!" He sounded worried or frightened! So we followed him a short distance and all of us gathered together behind a small group of other souls and spirit-beings (with several floaters above us), trying to see what everyone was pointing at and excited about over on the steps leading up to the giant doors of the great courthouse. There were many spectators or souls quickly walking, running, and floating, headed in the same direction as us. My mind was still in prayer-mode, like coming out of a deep meditation when I heard Lord Nexus say — "Lord have mercy, look at that big fool! Can you believe this mad Emissary? He has actually brought a dwarf dragon here, into this holy city! He's actually trying to take that thing, that animal with him into the Great Halls of Justice — oh my god, is this really happening here?!"

I'm trying my best to climb up on the back of Urge to get a better position to see (Urge has always been a foot taller then me), and Urge didn't seem to mind. "Look brother Urge — look at this unfolding madness!" Lord Nexus asked — "Can this be real, is it alive, I mean is it a real living dragon?!" Urge was looking all wide-eyed, his mouth hung open in shock. The crowd was looking hard, and I was seriously looking hard. Damn I thought to myself — if that was a baby dragon, what the hell must its mother look like!? I had never in my life or any life, seen a real live dragon before! There was a larger and more animated crowd around the many steps going up into the Halls of Justice. I could see him clearly now, finally I saw the one they called Lord Kokhan. I felt a cold chill run down my back. He was dressed in this elegant long flowing, gold trimmed, black-velvet robe, damn sharp! He was a tall man-like creature and had little red horns on his big-ass dark bald head, with short sharp teeth and smoke or steam coming out of his mouth and nose. He looked mean and mad as hell too! Jesus, he had to be every bit of eight feet tall and over four-hundred pounds in weight — damn, I mean darn! He was screaming up at the golden courthouse Guardian Angels while holding a big link-chain attached to a real, live fire-breathing dragon! He — I mean it looked like a cross between a giant lizard and fire spitting baby dinosaur!

It even had huge rubberery looking wings about six to eight feet long folded across its grayish scaly back — woah! It's even got six short legs and feet with long claws! The front two looking like small arms, clawing at the air up towards a big bronze guardian Angel—this scene was ill! The two of them (Lord Kokhan and his pet) both looked tuff, mean, and were both snapping at the silver robed Angel-sentries nearby. Lord Kokhan was obviously arguing with the court Guardian about dissing his pet-dragon. The courthouse Angel was carrying a large silver staff with a glowing light-bulb shaped head on it's top. He was pointing it at Lord Kokhan's chained beast and shouting something at them both! Lord Kokhan was now blowing big time smoke and ashes out of his mouth and nose. Trying his best it seemed to intimidate the equally big court-house Guardian Angels, who it seems was trying to stop the dark horned-one and his obviously pissed off fire-snorting pet—I mean dragon! He was trying hard to keep Kokhan from coming any closer to the court's main entrance! We could tell that the Guardian was losing his patience. As he yelled for back-up, he was also threatening to do something bad to Lord Kokhan's pet if he didn't immediately fall back or send it back to wherever it came from! The four of us, with me riding on Lord Urge's back had moved further up the steps near the corner of the white marbled building with the growing crowd of other curious spirits.

Two giant Angel guards were instructing the crowd of spirits and entities to move back or risk being hurt from the ruckus Kokhan and his pet dragon was causing. Other guardian Angels moved in to help their co-patriots with two backing up the first that encountered Lord Kokhan, and the other two watching over and securing the crowd that gathered near the steps. A fifth Angel was hovering overhead and all of them had massive-silverish flapping wings. "Whoa, check this shit out" I said out loud (opps that slipped—I'm trying Urge). The Guardians seemed strangely cool and somewhat unruffled as if they had a secret weapon or secret knowledge or something. I couldn't believe this mad scene! The first guard shouted to Lord Kokehead in a booming voice like that of James Earl Jones, "You have been warned once Lord Emissary—you will not be allowed to enter these hallowed halls with that creature at your side! Chained or unchained—no animals, no creatures are allowed even inside this Holy City! None ever within this holy-court, you are in serious violations of the great codes Lord Kokhan! I insist you and your minions retreat from this holy place—and do it now!" He loudly ordered the dark demon to stand down, sounding like he really meant what he said! I heard Lord Nexus say—"Father within and above us, please here and now—increase the peace, and cause this unholy madness to cease!" The big second guard backing up the first walked boldly down towards Kokhan—with serious intent on his face! Having lost his patience he appeared not to be afraid, as he pushed his now glowing white-hot staff, throwing off sparks (like a giant child's sparkler) into the face of the dragon—ka-boooom! Snapping the dragon's neck and disintegrating it's body with just one touch of his glowing lance! A large 'whooa' sound arose from the crowd as some souls ran away and jumped for cover while some, unmoved, started softly clapping. Before the Angel had touched the dragon with his staff, all had heard him shout—"God's laws will be obeyed!" Lord Kokhan had fallen back as his pet was instantly incinerated in a cloud of dark smoke, when the Angel-guard's staff had brushed against it's dark gray ugly head. I will never forget the sound of the big bang we all heard, as well as the sickly-whine of that evaporating dragon. Damn if didn't sound like a bull-elephant had just got popped with a high-powered rifle, when this ill scene played itself out right before our eyes! The loud bang echoed all over the city like rolling thunder! In the back of my mind—my consciousness, I still wondered if I might be dreaming this crazy spirit drama! Perhaps I'm already a truly-dead soul, and I'm just too stupid to realize it—maybe? Anyway I remembered when the big bang flashed across the court house steps, we all instinctively moved back a good ways. While more then eight winged-guards from around the city descended on the scene to handle the stunned and shocked crowd of dark and light entities curiously milling around. I recall there were some dark-entites and blacken creatures crawling all over Lord Kokhan pulling him away from the courthouse steps, holding him down, pleading I guess with him not to lose total control. I then sensed three shocked and for the first time ever, three fearless guardian Angels surrounding me tightly. It was Urge and his crew of two. For a brief moment I felt like I was back in the world, and the dangerous twins were shielding me from a drug hit or rival attack.

This devil Kokhan was furious at the loss of his pet. Even as he and his crew quickly retreated backward from the advancing lines of city and courthouse guardian Angels. Walking down the steps flanked on either side by two or three flying Angels above, all carrying those long glowing staffs pointed in the direction of the dark emissary and his evil black-robed associates. They were retreating now with the quickness! The dark group were doing their best to contain Lord Kokehead and make him withdraw from the streets in front of the Halls of Justice. With their Lord and Master securely in tow, they pulled him from the scene. Boy was he pitching a unholy fit, as he went stomping off with his dark minions down the street. He was slinging, pushing, throwing them all over the place with ease as he continued to blow smoke and hot ashes from his big angry face. He was also cursing up a storm, (a city violation Urge had told me) and calling back threats at the bronzed-skinned disciplined guards who had stopped advancing at the corner of the courthouse and went no further. They had done their job and done it well. I remember asking no one in particular, "Hey they're not going to go after him or lock his butt up? What if Lord Kokehead decides to come back for revenge or something?" Urge stated—"No Lee Roy, the Angel-Guards are not allowed to leave the Halls of Justice area or follow and arrest the Supreme Darkside Advocate. Let's not forget he still is the Imperial Emissary of the King of the Dark Forces. Obviously a dangerous and arrogant beast! Much is done and tolerated here in the city of light, to keep an incident like the one we just witnessed from exploding into all out war between the dark-forces and the forces of light.

Here in this great city—Lord Kokhan is like an untouchable, and he knows it. Like the guardian Angels of this holy-place themselves are untouchable. Neither of the two sides can be seriously hurt or negatively impacted by the other. This is why he was putting on such a furious show for the crowd. Not once did he attempt to use any of his black-demonic powers. It is the great balance of the holy-spirit here that must be maintained at all cost, as he was probably testing that balance understood?" Lord Nexus added—"Lord Kokehead as you call him Lee should have known better then to create that little fire-breathing creature (little I thought?), and should never have attempted such a fool hardy stunt against the great and ancient codes of this most holy place!" "Served him right" the Zulu added, "There has never been a pet dragon, animals, or demonic lower-level thought forms allowed inside the walls of this holy place, and never any creature walking on four legs—maybe perhaps on two."

Urge took in a deep breath and continued—"Lord Zulu and Lord Nexus please escort Master Lee back to our rest stop down the street, I'll be with you all shortly. Since I'm here at the court, I will enter in and register ourselves for mandatory attendance for later on this day. I really hope we can get this over with quickly. We need not spend any more time then necessary near this fool Kokhan. He appears much too vile and arrogant. He seems like a lot of trouble—big trouble!" Lord Zulu and Nexus just nodded at Urge and we all turned and left the area. I mentally asked Urge—(as he was beginning to depart) "Oh brother Urge when do you think this thing—I mean our trial will actually jump off?" He sent back, "Worry not Lee—you're in good hands, my own and those of the great Christ-Consciousness we've prayed to for so long—and so it is! Maybe we'll kick this thing off in four to six hours I'm sure. Especially if there are no more surprises or distractions like earlier you dig?" "That's cool brother spirit—bet." "I think old Kokehead knows better now not to try any more evil stunts or stupid moves with the holy ones here. I think he knows he gotta behave and so shall we, right fellows? There is no excuses for spiritual bankruptcy or dark-force chicanery in any spirit's life, no room now for us to project anything but a sincere, positive-mind of great expectations, of drawing nearer to the one source of God himself. Surely his presence will be in the court, to insure our fair hearing. So fear not when the time comes Lee, we'll be back here shortly in one whole piece little brother".

"Now please go and rest your mind son, and reflect on God's great love and mercy." Back at our little rest stop now—I didn't rest much, thinking to myself that Lord Zulu and Lord Nexus were the only support system I felt would stand strong for me and Urge. Maybe that will be all the support we'll need—maybe, we'll soon see? It seemed like I couldn't get the smell of dragon's stench out of my mind, somehow it reminded me of burning cocaine vapors (not that I ever smoked any of that poisin, just recalling how it smelt in a room full of pipe-junkies). I truly didn't want to question now my own growing faith in God—cause I had hardly ever acknowledged his existence anyway in my past life. Even now I wasn't sure if God had a sense of humor, or approved of me, or even rap music. Hell, I just know he would frown on the dope-game. I even wondered why any God would allow that poisonous shit to exist and be brought into neighborhoods to be sold (I know I got nerve to even ask such a question—word)? "Annyy-waayy . . ." God has to know that his people, black people don't grow or manufacture drugs in America. We just don't know how, and the Colombians always refused to do business with state-side niggas. I always had to use a caucasian drug-broker to score my shipments in Florida. Hell yeah, we'll use it and sell that shit and that's a losing proposition as I now well know. Therefore—why would he (God), even care for my lowly drug selling, occasionally violent soul, in spite of what Urge has taught me? He once told me—'Lee take heart in this one simple fact of spirit-life son.'

'Because of the principle of free will, each and every soul ever created will come to find themselves on the path to enlightenment at some point in a soul's multiple-life journeys of soul evolution—to arrive at true spiritual perfection (oneness). When they (all souls) have progressed consciously high enough to understand the immutable, ever lasting, universal laws that apply to all conscious life. Life that could not be truly cognizant of itself as itself, without a spirit that animates the physical-expression of same—you copy son? Then they will come to know that they, in and of themselves condemns or elevates their individualized, locallized soul-force by the very choices they themselves make! And yes—they will receive their just rewards for living a good spiritual-life verses living a bad or evil spiritual-life. Truly the choice has always been ours. Justice will be dispensed within divine order according to the negative or positively charged karmic energy a soul has built up to the time of its next soul dispensation trial, or its final cosmic surrender. Our surrender and eventual return to our immortal source—the great and everlasting Godhead!' I watched Lord Zulu and Nexus as they were constantly communicating, talking some, then mentally—telepathically, discussing Urge's and my situation. They discussed our chances, my history, and my spiritual good points—which they knew I had some, because they knew a lot about me through their friend Master Urge.

I wondered again why they had said that Lord Urge would also be on trial probably more so then me. Yes—I'm confused too. Urge never sold drugs I'm sure of that, and that my lower-life essence's possible destination was a closed book—a done deal, damn! Yeah, even I knew that I had to pay some kind of price for my past actions and sins back in the old world, in my most recent past existence. I have become aware on this side of life just how interrelated all our actions and choices towards other human beings are back on earth. Even our daily thoughts about one another, good or bad has lasting karmic-soul consequences long after they've been thought and expressed outside of our petty little minds. I also realized a real record of sorts was being kept on every soul that has ever existed. I knew they had to know, I could still hear them (the three Amigos) even when I was in prayer mode. They whispered that my possible punishment may be somewhat heated and a slam dunk for Kokhan. Damn—I was shocked a little, these were Urge's boys—his crew and they occasionally spoke as if we may be going to a spirit-funeral, my own and maybe Urge's as well! Yeah I was still a little confused and beginning to get a little scared as well. Thinking about what if, and what may happen to me or Urge over the next few hours.

I had long ago reconciled my possible negative future, even though Urge was always optimistic. Always saying the fat lady hasn't sung her song—yet. He was very hopeful, and supportive of our future fate, that things would work themselves out positively for us both somehow, someway. Damn—my brother was the eternal optimist! Like Urge loves to say—'Things always do work out for the good in the long run, or within the greater scheme of things, all is as it should be.' Whenever he said that or something like it—I was reminded of how we used to say it back in the old world—'Don't sweat it yet, bet—things gonna get greater later.' We were about to find out. Urge had returned about an hour ago, don't know if he heard much of what we had discussed, but he spent a little time again, trying to encourage and reassure his buddies and me that all would go well today. He said his heart felt it. I hope he's right. Together we all spent some more time in prayer and talking strategy. Urge was now laying out a few simple rules I would need to follow once the proceedings started. Things like how I should conduct myself, when to speak or not speak, and where he was going to focus his energy and Angel-skills in our defense. Damn, in 'our' defense? Did he say our's? I inwardly knew what that meant, then I asked him solemnly—"Yoh Urge do you really think we got a defense?" He said, "Lee if I've told you once I've told you a thousand times, never give up your hope, it has great power in it, and how did you put it back in the day—never say never until the fat-lady sings, right? Did you know any singing fat ladies Lee?" I quickly said—"Nope Urge, I was a real selective player back in the day, and only dealt with slim-hochies and little tight-butt gold-diggers!"

He responded, "Little brother please don't lie to me, and again—"and watch your language slick! Well—if you insist you never dated any big girls before young lover, that was truly your lost fool. I know there was some pleasingly thick young ladies around you that would have rocked your world back then, if you had only given them the chance!" "Urge please." "So you didn't miss what you couldn't measure Mr. Square-pants Bob" (Urge was actually laughing now). "Urge, are you trying to call me Sponge Bob Square-pants old-man, that was a silly-ass (oops) cartoon character on T.V., you know?" Urge responded sarcastically—"And your stylish, so-called fly, cold-blooded gangster act wasn't just as silly or cartoonish little brother? Think Lee Roy, that's the primary reason we've gone through all of these things together recently you know? Big Baller, Daddy Cocaine, Sponge Bob—what's really the difference silly boy? Besides it was just a name I heard while over at the court house dude—don't get grim with me here, just listen up!" I was thinking, (he had said in our defense) of a life that even I believed for awhile, may be perceived of by Lord Kokhan as a real slam dunk. Urge had called my recent past life 'a real misuse of a soul's creative powers and abuse of the celestial expression of God's love for all souls, as indicative of free-will'—that you Lee Roy, 'had misused and abused while separated from me, your higher-self understand.'

He had told me in one of our past road lessons, 'that any and all negative choices, including the willingness or the acceptance of evil over good, would have to be purged by fire first if a soul is still allowed to exist and move forward on the spiritual path to salvation or perfection. There-in lies the question of our salvation or our being recycled back onto the wheel of incarnating. Marked as a unenlightened half-soul, or worse, sent to a kind of spiritual reformatory.' I believe I've quoted him correctly, I think. I had no idea what if anything would happen to Master Urge. Urge had mentioned to all of us still sitting at our little rest-stop table, what areas of my life—the negative aspects of all that I'd expressed in my most recent trip into and out of materiality. There were only a few choices and actions on my part in that life, the life I just lived, that were even possibly defensible! He then laid out our positioning and the court set-up for the trial. Telling us all to stay alert and watch the dark side for any under-handed foolishness they've been known to try. Urge suggested that we head back over towards the courthouse, and that there was still time for us to pray. Sincere prayers work miracles he said. One should pray as if their life depends on it because it does. The four of us started to float (there was no longer a sensation of walking any more) towards the entrance to the Halls of Justice building, and we all begin to pray quietly at first then again out loud in unison. I heard Lord Nexus start up a new prayer—one that Urge liked to chant on our way here to this city of bright lights.

Almost at the same time—we all were thinking it, then chanting it—"Oh Intelligent and most Holy Universe, may your holy-light shine down on us forever. May the light of God surround us, and may the love of God enfold us. May the power of God protect us, and may the presence of our God watch over each of us. Where ever we are, we know that God is—and all is well, amen, amen, amen, and I said, "amen". I couldn't help it, what I said next, it just slipped out, out-side of my consciousness. I thought I said it mentally but, "We need to get this shit over with! I'm sick of this damn dream or mind-tripping, its sheer torture ya'll! Hell—I feel like I'm on crack or some 'e' (ecstasy)—word!" Urge just looked at me with that look. He knew I was scared, worried too, so I started crying like a damn sissy, it couldn't be helped as we walked up the steps of the court house (don't tell nobody). I mumbled to no one in particular—I remember telling God years ago when I was a nineteen year old gang-banger, a real gangster by choice by then. 'God (I remember saying), if you be listening, know that I gotta do what I gotta do! I'll make you a deal oh number-one player (never really thought God made deals, especially with no dope dealers) — if you stay out of my houses, my spots — my dope houses. I'll stay out of your dope houses — the neighborhood churches.' Boy was I a fool or what? Since that time I recalled, I'd never seen the inside walls of any church. Urge placed his hand on my back gently pushing me up more stairs, and allowed me to continue mumbling. 'And now I'm here God, in this place I believe is in your neighborhood. I know I'm lost, tell me that I'm dreaming or lost in a nightmare, and being punished by all of this metaphysical (spirit) stuff I truly just don't get! I couldn't stop crying. A man or man spirit shouldn't be crying, but . . .'

'Yeah God I know this mind game or soul game must be played out — right, I feel that, I do . . . and.' Urge answered me under his breath — "Yeah Lee its got to be played out — so let's play it out, cheer up poet." I could feel it — he was in-sync with his boys, as I was once long ago with mine. They all started talking at once — then one at a time rushing my mind, filling my head with their hope, trying to keep me strong and focused I guess. Lord Urge went first, saying — "Lee Roy, I know — why you're crying, and trying to hold back your tears son." Lord Zulu added — "It's ok little brother to cry and even to admit you're scared." Then Lord Nexus (they were ganging up on me to help me) — "And of course you're worried about Master Urge aren't you? Well you shouldn't be, because that old coon has always found away to continue to exist — (Urge said) "What did you just call me Nexus?" "Heck Lee you got to know by now he and you are at least a thousand years old, all three of us are about that old son." Now that got my attention, and I just looked over at Urge as he cut his eyes over at Lord Nexus. He said — "As if we don't have a boatload of things to worry about already Lord Nexus. You and Lord Zulu need not feel sorry for Lee or myself, and attempt to distract him or us from this — our soul's true mission this time around." "A Mission to be judged righteously come what may as one whole soul — ok. You see my brother Angels, me and Mister Lee Roy here — we be down with this our mutual spiritual mission and the resulting soul dispensations — ok! I know you both mean well, but please let me carry this burden my way ok?" He then spoke directly to me, "Lee Roy — the things that have happened and the things still to happen have taken their toll on both of us. Your soul-force and this journey — our journey, is not yet over Mister-man. I'm gonna say this one last time Lee, then I want you to get a grip, and bring back some of that gangster strength to shore up your faith in me and the Godhead, ok young-blood, ok?! If you still can't find your faith in God Almighty, in this our loving and just Universe — then at least have faith in what you've chosen now as your spiritual represenitive — me! I will not allow you to cause me to lose one-I-otta of faith in the real one God who is your God too, or in myself as your guardian Angel this time around — do you feel me young soul? Do you understand me?" I looked up into Urge's serious face and simply said — "Yes, ok Urge I read you, I feel you my elder brother, lets go on in." "Wait Lee" (Urge grabbed my arm just outside the doors to the court). "Lee now repeat after me (his voice loud and firm), "This is not a dream — say it." Again (we both repeated it), "This is not a dream." Lord Nexus had heard us, and Lord Zulu probably felt it — and they both felt the need to interject their thoughts again at the same time.

"The past is past Lee Roy, it is done what's done." Lord Nexus said, "Tomorrow is yet come, as far as time is measured — today, right now this very moment is all we have, it is all you truly have and need with Urge so near to you, so rejoice in this special moment that is most valuable Lee. To live in the very moment, cherishing it, loving it — young soul is how to truly live! So dwell not on your past, that's why it's called the past. Nor dwell not long on your unknown future, because it too is yet unwritten. Because if your future sight is off center, then your future expressions would be more or less off center. For that which your soul truly needs for it's continued development, is indeed a cosmic law — see, the gift of all life is in the moment — that's why its called the present?" Lord Zulu contributed, "You must control your fears young warrior like you once did, when staring dark risk and uncertainty in the face. Yes it's ok to acknowledge your fears, but never allow your fears to control your thinking, which controls your emoting, which motivates your actions. Thereby creating your physical destiny and effecting your spiritual destiny. Remember that your thinking and believing is what controls your future path in any form or soul-phase you find yourself expressing. You've always had the power, the potential to create that which you willed, or the desired outcome — see? Like many a soul-force in their search for peace, happiness, or love and their approach to the Godhead. You are never alone Lee — and you are well along on your path of true self-discovery."

"So young blood, your journey to find reunion and make peace with Lord Urge, your higher-self, to right the wrongs (balancing out karma) of the past is at hand and lies behind these great doors before us." Urge said softly — "Go ahead, enter in and greet the creator's represenitives, the Holy Lords of Justice. One last thing Lee, just be mindful that the closer any of us get to the face of the Godhead, there is always self imposed fear and trepidation, and occasionally a trial or soul's test to see if we are truly worthy of being in such a exalted presence. We've already passed three of these tests little brother, do you not remember? At first exposure to the divine light, we are afraid because we don't remember ever being apart of this light. Like we've been away far to long. We feel like we don't deserve to receive such cosmic attention, a divine transformation then takes place. Now it is our turn to be exposed once again. Know that the greater our fall from grace — our true source of being, the greater will be the trials and tribulations to return to grace. But still most souls have found within their hearts — what it truly takes to accomplish such a feat — see?" Lord Nexus said — "Just be thankful for whatever comes from this adventure — this moment of righteous judgment, ok? See this time as your personal exodus from one realm of spirit-slavery into another of spiritual freedom, for truly all will be judged as it should be—all is in divine order, come what may." Urge chimed in with—"Even now Lee you are blessed beyond measure to have as your guide and guardian here, the one and only Master Urge (pointing into his own chest). I got both of our backs covered son!"

"Your very own capable and wise defender of soul-force energy (I noticed he didn't say brave defender, having confessed to me on several occasions that physical matter worlds or physical life expressions frighten the shit out of him). Who will not let any chance or hope flee from us in order to save ourselves from the clutches of Lord Kokhan and his unholy Master—Luciferious the Third! We'll be alright, of that I'm sure of little brother." Lord Nexus again interrupted with—"Our love and compassion for you Lee and all of God's children both good and bad, including our brother Lord Urge here—is indeed unassailable. Know that we are here for each other 100%, for the better or worse for life, or may God forbid, non-life. We got some backs too, whatever that means! We shall not forsake you or our brother Lord Urge no matter the outcome, ok—understood?" Lord Zulu added—"And you can take that to the spiritual-bank little black buddy." I smiled and said—"Thanks, thanks to you both. You are indeed great friends and I know we'll be alright." Yeah I now felt much better as I looked over at Urge. He had wetness around his old wrinkled eyes, an looked as if he too had been reassured and had his spirit lifted like my own, he said—"Lee I got your soul-back and you got mine right? We're due in court shortly—when this crystal city's chapel's sweet bells ring three times this evening. So let us go inside, wash and pray for victory—oppss, I mean merciful forgiveness of our sins this particular time around."

"Because even with Lee Roy's growing faith—we three, I mean this gang of four, are indeed a force for good, a force to be reckoned with! We'll show old Lord Kokhan what a real butt . . ." I stopped him and said—"Don't you dare curse Urge—I feel your heart and it's beating pretty strong, let's just say together we'll beat him and beat him bad I hope—cool?" All four of us said strongly and with the conviction of Angels on a mission for God—"We're on a mission of hope, a mission of love, yeah indeed a mission of reconciliation and justice! Even for one of God's own dirty, but much loved little children. Mr. Lee we would never let the baby (my left-over little soul-force) go down the drain with the dirty water that has washed its soul somewhat clean." They all said—"Cool, let us prepare to kick some butt!" I said (sort of rapping like) "So let's throw our hands in the air and wave them like we just don't care, cause God is great, and he won't be late—oh yeah, oh yeah!" They all looked somewhat puzzled at me. Lord Nexus and Zulu already knew how things were laid out inside the Great Halls of Justice. A four sided pyramid was the center court building attached to two other pyramid type buildings by two large and long corridors. All three buildings creating a central triangle-shaped courtyard, yet accessible to all three great court rooms. All three pyramid shaped courtrooms were peaked at their top points by a very large opening. Urge said that at the start of a hearing or spiritual cause in either court, several large glowing orbs will descend down through the roof through openings in the ceiling to rest atop a large white-marbled pedestal. Which stood behind the center table where we would be seated, across from the dark-side and the devil's advocate, Lord KoKhan my enemy the Devil's represenative (I call Lord Kokehead).

"These large glowing orbs contains several aspects of God's pure essence. They'll be colored red, to represent the blood of Christ-consciousness. Shared for humankind in all the matter world's he's visited and all those under his cosmic spiritual control. Then there is one that's off-white colored, which represents all that is good in the cosmos and the forces of light. Then the last orb of this holy-trinity would be colored silverish-blue. It represents the force of the holy-spirit of the Godhead, or this living, intelligent, and just Universe. These three floating, vibrating holy-orbs represent the living, breathing essence of God's holy presence. They carry within each, his awesome power of creation and destruction. Together they have the combined power to move, create, or totally disassemble entire Universes." Damn I thought, I was taught it was only one great being called God that did all the creating and destroying. I guess even the greatest force in the Universe needs some helpers once in while. So he sent these powerful shiny colored basketballs to represent himself, cool. Still I couldn't believe that all this pageantry and ceremony was just for me, or my little cut and dried soul hearing? Urge continued — "There will be one great court Angel called the most Holy Facilitator, who the holy orbs will speak through if they desire to communicate directly with any beings in the courtroom."

His words will be their words and they are absolute law. His direction and control of the court proceedings are God's law, and must be obeyed immediately. There is no set length of time for cases to begin or end, and a case could last three minutes or three months depending on several variables. Oh yes Lee — you must stay awake, stay alert at all times! The creatures of the dark-side will be separated on one side of the court room from the beings of light on the other and all eyes will be on us I'm sure." Then pausing to catch his breath Urge added — "Lee I believe our presentation could possibly last about a day or two, then several hours to close and await our verdict. Sometimes it comes quickly, sometimes it takes a little longer." I sort of screamed at Urge — "What? Don't you think that's kinda quick old man, for us to mount a strong case, close, and then be judged — I gotta a lot of explaining I want to do, all within a day or two, I don't think so?!" Urge said — "Lee we're talking spiritual time which you can't measure, and I'm just giving you concepts that your limited grasp of the unlimited can bare, ok! Now pay attention son, you will be seated to my right at the great table, with Lord Zulu and Nexus seated behind us behind the visitors railing, and we are not allowed to touch or talk to anyone out of turn. Definitely not while the great court guardian-Angel the Facilitator is speaking! Lord Kokhan will be allowed to come forward first, given permission to begin. He'll probably give his list of charges against you, I mean us. Then he'll make a short recommendation of what he expects the Lords of Justice will accept and possibly so order."

"After that I'll be allowed to make my petition and request. Then I'll be allowed to question or challenge Lord Kokhan's position. I interrupted Urge – "Lord Urge I have complete trust in you, still I got to let them know I made a big mistake, no correction – a lot of mistakes back when Urge! You know what I'm talking about old friend. Just tell me – will I be called to give testimony, can I apologize for everything if its not to late?" "Lee I don't think . . . , I'm not sure if that would be wise. I've told you I got this son – I can handle this, ok? Yes all souls are given a chance to speak in their own behalf towards the end of the proceedings if the Lords of Justice deems it helpful. I'm hoping that won't be necessary." Just then we all heard them as we stood around outside the great doors to the courtroom in the Halls of Justice. The very loud and somewhat sweet ringing of the court's massive chapel bells, that signaled the start of show time! The after shock of the ringing bells trailed off for a long time, after each bong, seeming to last at least 1 – 2 minutes. Lord Zulu and Lord Nexus said we've been directed to courtroom three, located on the first floor in the south-east corner, across from the corner of the court house where Lord Kokhan had showed out earlier. The four of us proceeded down the long hallway toward court room three, feeling like we were ready for what ever! There was heavy traffic all around us in the large hallways, spirits and entities going into and exiting the court. The key it seemed to me to getting into and out of one room to the next was either chanting, or praying, or singing. All the souls and strange beings in the corridors were doing it – mumbling, chanting, or singing songs of praise I guess. Inside the giant court room, after the guardian Angels outside the doors had scanned us with their golden-yellow eyes. Was the inner sanctuary, truly it was awesome, it was . . . majestic – yeah that's it, majestic! There were fifty rows of seats on two opposite sides of the tri-angular shaped large room, where other visiting souls and their escorts would be waiting their turn at bat, or just observing court room events. Most of them would just be spectators I was told. There was one side of the huge room that was much darker, less inviting, and reserved for the forces of darkness, their escorts, and minions of the Devil's hand-picked Court Advocate – his Imperial Emissary to this holy city Lord Kokhan. Urge said, "Lee this is truly a special place, a real city of hope. Within these walls there is great mercy and justice forever flowing. Rejoice that we are here and in the presence of God Almighty's represenitives (pointing over to the raised pedestal that would bear) the Orbs of the Holy Lords of Justice who have not arrived yet." I know why Urge had called this place the city of hope, the seat of mercy – cause truly I was still feeling that hope was all we had and more mercy is what I prayed so hard for. I really did – ya'll just don't know!

I hesitated again for a moment as Urge pulled me into the room. Lord Nexus and Lord Zulu were given permission to sit right behind us, like two big bad-ass sentinels, watching mine and Urge's back, keeping me updated and informed through whispers on court protocol and etc . . .

They were determined to show us support to the end I guess. An end unknown at present, but an end that would be one hell'va finish I thought for Mr. Lee Roy the once Dapper Rapper. Yeah, soon I'd finally get to see my own hell, Lee Roy's self-created hell. Yeah, still I felt the power and magic all around me as we seated ourselves at the big white marbled table in the center of the room—it was show-time! I felt my knees under the big table doing their own thing, and I tried to settle them down with little success. This big marble table just hung there in space without any legs holding it up! I kept looking under it to see how it just floated there, all on its own. I also felt that all a soul-force like me needed was a little more faith, hope, or maybe one or two shots of Hen-dog (Hennesey), and my three friends. Yes, my three Amigos. I still had a hard time holding my head up feeling a little more fatigued I guess. Then Lord Kokhan arrived in pageant-style, followed by 6—8 large, dark, and gray gargoyle looking creatures. Four of them, dark and muscular body-guards with long twisted poles held in their paw-like hands, dressed in black leather trench coats wearing big dark sunglasses, surrounding Kokehead like he was royalty, or the president, or something really special. Yeah I was scared as hell but still impressed by these fools. They truly looked menacing, deadly or just dead!

I asked Urge, why were those beings wearing sun-glasses in the court-room, was it too bright for them in here?" He whispered—"They don't have eyes Lee, they see differently then we, they see with their heighten sense of smell like some forms of reptiles." They were all lined up behind Lord Kokhan, who was not allowed to enter our space across the massive floating table we all sat at according to Urge. Once Lord Kokehead had seated himself, the entire room fell silent for a brief moment. The lone bronzed-skinned court translator (the Facilitator Lord Urge called him), who had been standing motionless all the while the court room was filling up, suddenly moved and stamped his long silver staff on his elevated step where he stood in front of the higher raised pedestal three times—boom, boom, boom! Then he said in a loud deep, booming voice, that got everyone's attention—"All present must rise, this holy court and its occupiers will come to order for the love of God, cosmic law, and spiritual justice. All souls and entities must obey and now bow their heads!" Everyone there did what they we were told to do except Lord Kokhan. He was laying back in his big chair like he was the shit! Like a king or something, blowing smoke from his nostrils into the air creating little floating circles, while holding a black-marble and gold veined Scepter in one of his massive bejeweled paws. The praying, chanting, and soft-singing all around us suddenly stopped, except for Urge who was finishing a soft prayer.

He whispered—"We believe in Father-Mother Intelligent Universe as the Godhead, creator of both spirit and light; we believe in the Christos as the imbodiment of God, we pray that his presence and that of the Holy-spirit will abide within these holy walls to judge us—the living and the nearly dead, here and now and forever, amen." Then I sneaked a look up towards the ceiling. The ensuing silence was def, with just a small vibrational hum coming from above. What next—what? Then I saw them! Faintly at first, then much clearer, the Orbs called the Lords of Justice were descending slowly—down through the large hole in the roof. First one, then another, then globe three. They all looked like large floating, smooth colored basketballs to me just bigger. One reddish, one white, and one light-blue. Urge muttered to me in slang, "Show time Lee Roy—word to your mother." I was shocked, what the hell did he mean by that? Then I saw her, over by the giant doors, it really was my mother, or the spirit of my moms! Damn I thought—not again! God have mercy on her, please God? Her image was crying and smiling at the same time, slowly waving her little hands at me. I started to get up and run to her, but Urge stopped me hard. "Sit stll Lee!" I know I heard her say something like—"Lee, oh Lee Roy, I'm so sorry, I love you son and I miss you and your little brother. But please rest easy now son for you are in very capable hands. Know that God's mercy is unbounded and he never gives up on any soul—yours or my own. So please don't be afraid, just don't be . . ."

Then she started to slowly fade away, still waving at me. I screamed loudly inside my own head—"Nooo mom, please don't go!" Urge pushed me back down into my seat, and then I noticed the dark one, Lord Kokhan looking over at me smiling I think. Urge said, "chill out Lee Roy, it was only an astral-omen, a good sign that she appeared to us. Now be still and quite boy, calm down". Yeah I had a few choice words for Lord Kokehead's stare, but I did as I was told. I felt Lord Zulu's hand on my shoulder and heard him whisper—"Lee you'd better stay calm and pay attention, we don't want you to miss anything pertinent ok?" I then noticed he too was crying a little for me and Urge I think, but why—why?!

"The Many Leaves of Grass"

Show time was an understatement. Every one was still standing with their heads bowed, while Lord Kokhan laid back in his chair like he was on a damn beach or something, while the last of the holy-orbs descended to the pedestal of law to rest on it. The room was all filled up now as souls and entities took up all the seats in the court room. Shit was, I mean things were moving quickly now. I thought I heard the soft sounds of an organ or harp playing faintly off in the back ground somewhere. Talk about crazy visions, this one was off the hook! There was also low moaning, some growling, and mumbling noises coming from the dark side of the room. The souls and entities on the lighter side of the room were still bowing, lightly clapping, being very happy about the arrival of the Holy Lords of Justice. Those on the other side of the court appeared to be upset or irritable, even a little fearful. We all watched the Orbs as they took their positions on top of the pedestal at the head of the court room. With the one in the middle floating slightly higher then the other ones on each side of it. I thought to myself, this can't be good — something about those colors, lets see ok — ok I got it red, white, and blue, oh yeah I'm in trouble! Why couldn't they have been colored red, black and green? Shit — I mean shoot.

Just like the pictures I saw of black America soldiers returning from foreign wars after fighting for other people's freedom, in coffins wrapped in red, white, and blue flags. Just then Urge pinched my leg under the table! Mentally he projected — "Remember fool, no soul is truly free until all souls are free, and that includes you and me Mr. Blackman!" There was a sudden gasp from the soul-filled room when a small lighting bolt sparked its way from each Orb striking the lone tall translator still standing with his head bowed at the front of the pedestal. He didn't move, as if he had felt nothing. He looked alot like a roman gladiator with his white robe and silver and gold body-armor on. Golden boy knew he was muscled up! He finally moved, floated closer towards the Orbs and said — "Praise God and welcome most Holy Ones, we are greatly honored and pleased with the very presence of God's Universal Essence. This holy court has been called to order and we are prepared to obey all your instructions, decisions, and cosmic judgments. So it has begun — all may be seated." Lord Kokhan mumbled something out loud about his Lord and Master not having a much deserved position up on the pedestal of power, along side these living powerful centers of spiritual law. I was like whoa, as the translator turned and walked boldly over to our table right where Lord Kokhan was seated — within about ten feet of him.

He was still reclining as before and was picking at his tall collar on his robe. The translator stopped and leaned forward and just stared at Lord Kokehead, before speaking to him in a deep bass filled voice — "Please rise oh Grand Prosecutor Lord Kokhan, Advocate Emissary for the forces of darkness. We welcome you here again this day, to this Holy City, on this

Holy Mountain, to this most Holy Tribunal. The Lords of Justice welcome you, as we recognize you are still somewhat new to this place and plane of existence—are you not?" Lord Kokhan stood up and walked slowly towards the big court translator showing no fear of him. Lord Kokehead was even taller up close then I first thought. He stood head and shoulders above everyone present except the translator himself. Still holding his scepter—he paused and folded his giant paws in front of him-self and responded, or rather growled out his answer to the big translator's question. "Well old great ones, it is indeed a holy pleasure and honor (bowing slightly and reluctantly it seemed to me) to come before you today. Here—there is always such power, such creative force and spirit life energy. I, the great Lord Kokhan hope as I pray to my great God and Master, that here on this day we will find true justice and fairness. His righteous and Imperial Emissary, the late great Lord Mayhem has returned to our Master and King for his just rewards of evil glory, royal fire, and rejuvenation. It is I who has been called up to take his honoured place here—and I am so honoured. Shall I forgo my numerous titles and rankings in the Under World? Yes, ok—I think I shall. Now where was I? It is true oh Holy Ones I am well versed in the laws and protocols of this place, and I and my staff will obey and honor same."

He turned around quickly to strut back to his seat. His large red eyes were gleaming with self-importance and occult knowledge of his own evil power and dark rankings. But before he could sit back down, the translator Angel said to him—"You say you are aware oh Great One of our laws—yet your recent antics outside these holy walls speak otherwise, do they not? To attempt to bring any animal into these hallowed halls is a great offense to the sublime spirit that resides herein. Let all be made aware—especially you oh Dark Lord, further offenses of this type will not be tolerated. Any evil-antics, dark-magic, or illegal use of spirit force will be met with the spirit force of God himself!" Lord Kokhan whipped his heavy cloak around and faced the translator, and growled out a nasty "Yes—yes, I understand all that, I am aware! May we please proceed Lord Facilatator?" The big translator turned away seemingly unconcerned with Kokhan's response, and floated back over to the pedestal near his assigned position. Urge reminded me that it wasn't always the great translator who was speaking. Any one of the Holy Orbs could speak through him if they needed or desired too. They were the ones who sat in judgment of every soul that makes it here, as well as running and over-seeing the massive operations of this great city of God. They would be the ones to decide my ultimate fate and his.

The translator spoke—"You may proceed Mr. Prosecutor Lord Kokhan, the court has recognized Lord Urge and his charge as being present, and these proceedings are now being recorded within the great Book of Life—may all praise the Godhead." He stepped to the side of the tall pedestal and said—"Hold, the Lords of Justice commands me to reiterate to all present, that there will not be allowed any use of unsanctioned spiritual powers, magic-spells, or disrespectful disruptions in this hearing today—so it has been given, so it will be obeyed! All shall be forewarned — under the penalty of disintergrational death! Sir, you may proceed (pointing over at Lord Kokhan)." A hush fell over the room, as things seemed more serious now. Even more menacing as everyone had acknowledged that this was going to become a high stakes game of who gets my little badass soul force I believe. Master Urge had just told the translator he understood and give all obedience and respect to this latest court edit. Now Lord Kokhan started to rise and speak, he also had four to six assistants leaning over their area railing passing him what looked like old paper scrolls. And they were whispering things into his pointed ears. He waved them back with his big paws, as he stood and stated, "With all due respect to this honorable court and the most Holies. My record of great deeds on matter worlds and my status as a Universal Medicine man is well known and exalted throughout this humble Universe by my God the Dark One!"

"We need not dwell on the fact that I understand the power and protocol of light beings — here, there, everywhere. It is I who created the winged white horse that gives material souls their gift of escape from the pains that they themselves often create. Every now and then a half-soul like Mr.Lee Roy here comes along to help me in my mission, and we appreciate this. We of the dark realm only wish to reward him for his services rendered in his recent past life on earth!" I'm like "What?" What a jokester, what did he mean I assisted him, no he didn't call himself a medicine man! Urge whispered — "Lee Roy, I kept quite and you need to do so as well youngblood when this demon speaks, let him finish his opening cool?" I said — "Cool Urge, I don't like this fool Kokehead." Urge said, "Well he seems to like you alot!" Lord Kokhan was still talking — "I won't trouble the court with my power level victories and greater dark service credentials, I just want it to be known that I intend to bring added value to my God with the souls that I send back from this court. Those little miscreant souls who may fail to prevail upon the legendary mercy and good name of this most holy place — see? I can tell by today's soul attendance ledgers that we indeed have a full days docket to clear up. So let us all dance the Devil's dance one more time — hah! Yes, over two-hundred cases and hearings to dispatch, I mean to reconcile, a rightious disposition on each."

"It appears to me that this, our Universe is in such a mess (sounds like snickering and some subdued laughter, started coming from his minions) these days and fruitful nights, that all Gods here must be feigned too get to the more important operations (snort — snort) befitting the powers of the Universe and its creative classes of Gods, so let us do this thing." Boy, I thought — can this guy talk and swagger at the same time. Still we can take him I'm sure. Lord Kokehead continued, "I'd first like to apologize for my earlier indiscretions with my little huff and puff behavior outside today, with the able Guardians of this holy place. No harm was intended to them see — I was only testing the fitness of those assigned to such a spiritually valuable position. Also I was still fatigued from my far-away, and long traveled journey here—surely a just cause for forgiveness or at least civil understanding between Gods and oh yes, their esteemed Emissaries." Boy talk about a long winded beast. "So I've projected that this minor spiritual matter shall not consume much of this courts priceless time. So with assumed permission now, it gives me great pleasure to introduce again to this hearing my esteemed protagonist, the half-spirit sub-angel called Lord Urge I believe. Whose not yet on my level of power and prestige. Oh what a beat down he has coming—I pity the little cowardly Angel? Hmuupf—fool!"

"It appears he has chosen to represent himself as the Defense Advocate for his little lost lower-self mister Lee Roy here (pointing at me), whose recent departure from the physical plane of earth has caused my Master such sadness. Please let us again welcome the guardian Angel Master Urge, ahh excuse me, Lord Urge as he is fond of calling himself." Mentally Urge sent us—"hey this guy is a real live clown isn't he? I could careless about his powers or credits to his dark God, he knows the power of light beings, Angels, and this Intelligent Universe—true power comes from the Godhead, his love and only his spirit reigns surpreme!" Urge spoke up mentally to me and his crew of two. "I hope Kokhan's dark soul is still around at the end of times—he'll truly know by then what hell is really like!" Lord Nexus whispered across the visitor's railing, "Yoh, Lord Urge relax guy, and please stay focused on the plan, ok!" Lord Urge stood up very tall and proud, inspired by Lord Kokhan's obvious attempt to play us off as of no real importance to today's hearing—or to him its obvious outcome. Lord Kokhan was allowed to continue—"Before I read this long list of sweet and wicked soul-choices and charges against these humble dirty boys, I'd like to begin by asking Lord Urge a simple question Lord Translator?"

The big golden translator looked in Kokhan's direction and said—"Lord Advocate of the dark side, you will address all of your questions and comments towards the Holy Lords of Justice first, then . . ." Lord Kokhan acted as if he hadn't heard what the great court translator had just told him. He turned towards Urge and just kept speaking. "Yes—ok Lord Urge, I'm curious my little brother Angel. Are you fatigued after your long un-eventful journey here (snort—snort), are you tired, and are you truly prepared to exchange your wings for a priceless sulfur neck-ring of fire this time around old man?" Urge was locked eye to eye with the big brute. "That would indeed be a wise choice you know, for an Angel without courage—oh I meant without his wings, you may need the protection of some spiritual hell-fire—right?" Urge who was still standing didn't answer him, he just looked staunchly at Kokhan just like the translator was doing, both with some serious looks on their faces. Damn, Kokhan would't stop his grand standing. "So tell me Lord Urge, where in this spiritual Universe have you been hiding? I have reports that young mister Lee Roy hardly even knew you existed as his guardian consciousness until a year or so ago—is this not correct?" Lord Urge then asked the court translator for permission to respond, and the court Translator nodded his approval, which also meant for Lord Kokehead to take a seat I believe.

Master Urge responded — "Lord Kokhan I'm sure you know better then most, that the activities and locations of God's Angel host, your Master Satan have yet to taint or corrupt is secretive. And at best forbidden to be known by any from the forces of darkness, including you sir." Urge was in the zone I could tell, cause he spoke confidently and strong as if he had no fear of this fool Lord Kokhan or his claims to fame. "It is a well known spiritual fact sir, that all God created souls are endowed with a higher self — a higher consciousness that takes the form of Guardian Angels for most new souls. This aspect of all embodied souls creates a safe haven for the God seed implanted in the heart of all souls to find ultimate spiritual expression — to one day return to their true source. It forever represents a guidance system for any and all lower-selves to return to grace when they need to, if having fell from God's grace in the first expansion of life-energy. The expression of God's love has shown forth in the fulfillment of companionship and his need to know himself as God. It does not matter the length of time or distance of separation. Each guardian inborn or assigned to a lesser-self is eternally bound and shall rise or fall upon the shared experience and loving bond that exist between the illusionary separated selves or lower levels of consciousness, up into spiritual life — as a whole complete soul!" I'm like "whoa Urge run that sweet metaphysical knowledge on his ass . . ." Lord Nexus poked me in the back form over the visitors railing near where I sat, and schussed me with — "Lee watch your tongue boy, they haven't even got started yet!"

Urge kept up his response to Kokehead's opening, "We are here today in this holy moment to address only the future destiny of my humble lower-self called Lee Roy, and maybe a redress for me for my like-wise inherent stumbles. It is well known amongst all light beings, the significant and valuable status of any life-force energy manifest within this our living and just Universe. It is also a well known fact amongst even the most lowly of souls, that spiritual justice is always near and attainable. Even by those who may be suffering under false spiritual-illusions and religious dogma constraints, while existing and moving within matter and astral worlds. We know that they have so often chosen these gross lives, just to experience these convoluted — often times wicked, and offensive afronts to the Godhead. Sometimes God's little children can be so rebellious — solely for the purpose of their own and the growth of innate spiritual knowledge of the living Universe itself. Because all is one and one is the all. Meaning all that is — truth, love, light, and yes dark evil energy included, is interwoven into the very fabric of God's most holy expressions. Anywhere, at any time, on any level, by the great source of all creation and law, the source of us all — the Godhead!"

"Those that shall stand in judgment at any call against any soul, shall themselves be called to be judged. It has been so since the beginning of time and it shall continue on until time is undone. Lord Kokhan should well know this universal spiritual principle by now, if he is indeed a medicine man of this self-healing Universe! Oh most holies of holy Lords of Justice—surely you know that Master Lee Roy's recent death back on earth has been instigated and awaited on by the dark forces that exist around us, due to the great laws of our universe, specifically pertaining to the just and infallible laws of karma. As well the eternal steps involved in a soul's journey of spiritual progression. Yes, we know a record has been made—changed, affected, by both the negative and positive choices made throughout the life of this soul here on trial today. I have the record too and I am the first witness, of all that may be found wanting, in the life expressions of evil and violent behavior of my lower self. It is no great esoteric secret that Master Lee and I are here today to make no claims of innocence." Damn—I was shocked, "Urge what's up dude?!" Urge ignored my mental lapse and just kept working. "He has not inherited a soul's validation of wholeness because it was I who failed him over several life times, by not being united in spirit with him at all times—during his multiple life-expressions in gross matter worlds, so deeply influenced by the dark shadow of the king of evil himself! I let Lee Roy down, my lesser-self, whom I had sworn to serve and protect from the evil influences of the dark forces. So what ever is charged against Lee Roy is charged against me."

"It is well known that a soul that cannot hear the very voice of it's higher-self, or refuses to listen to same, will fall from grace time and time again. Hence the negative aspects of the free-will law comes into question? It was not solely the fault of Lee Roy's hearing that failed him oh honorable Gods—it was also the lack of courage of his personal guardian and my strong fear of entrapment. Indeed, it was my own fear of matter worlds that caused me to neglect my duties to my lower-self. Therefore my own fears allowed Master Lee Roy to design and choose the wrong paths to follow in his physical lives expressed while we were apart. For this—it is I who now come before you to beg for forgiveness and supreme mercy. From this great and holy Court of Justice and most holy Lords of Justice. I and I alone assume full responsibility and except the consequences, for the deadly and sinful actions and wasted life opportunity of this little backward thinking, misguided, soul-force energy seated next to me, and before you today!" Urge ended his speech with a sad look on his face while pointing at me saying, "Truly I don't deserve my status as a Guardian Angel, as it was I who failed to call upon the heavenly resources available to me to assist me in locating Master Lee, guiding, and protecting him, after our initial separation. Thereby—not reaffirming my courageous love and duty to him. It was a moment I guess of ego—pride, that which I feared the most, in terms of knowing human emotions. By not doing this, I indeed have failed the league of G.A.'s and in truth myself and little Lee Roy here—so be it."

I don't know if Urge was being a great actor or if he truly meant the things he just said. I knew I had to choke back some tears, cause the old man was using the strategy of self-sacrifice to save my pitiful life-force, kinda like what I did back in the world in the joint, when I had made a similar move to save someone I cared a lot for. I was beginning to understand just how much love old-dude had for me, and how brave he really must be to do this! I hadn't even noticed I was crying and shaking my head at the same time, until Lord Nexus put his hand on my shoulder again trying to comfort me. "Listen Lee Roy" he said, "You must know and trust that Master Urge knows what he's doing, and why he's doing it his way. Keep your faith strong and trust in him youngman, now hold your head up and pay attention." Urge had returned to his seat, but before he sat down he said to me, "If it is determined that I or we are judged here today to be unsalvageable this time around or defected, then so be it. If I or we are found to be deserving or un-deserving of future existence, know that I — we, are not afraid to hear and obey this holy court's rulings. Lee you and I, have placed our faith in the Christ consciousness, its unshakable, un-assailable, and undeniable — word! We seek no special considerations here within these holy walls. We only ask for a fair and balanced hearing and a chance to have our say."

"Our life is again already one life, then we have already conquered death!" Lord Urge kept doing his thang — "united once again as a complete soul-force, our lives past, this life being judged — is seeded to the will and final decision of God through the great Lords of Justice — so in advance we both thank you all." Boy did Urge have a powerful opening. Just then as Urge took his seat, a big cloud of nose-smoke rolled across the long table as Lord Kokhan started to rise. He snorted back over towards his staff and dark minions — (speaking out of turn again without permission). "Whew I guess this is going to take a little longer then twenty — thirty minutes, (smiling at his red eyed assistants he added) you think?!" The Facilator stamped his long golden staff upon the marbled floor one time. "Lord Kokhan — you may continue, if you can control your unsolicited remarks and direct your words directly to this holy tribunal!" Urge sat down and smiled at me — why I don't know. I knew he had meant what he just said, still I couldn't understand all of it, or why he said it. I just can't find the words to describe all that I'm feeling right now. Allow me to just keep telling the story. Yeah my heart was racing and my fears were growing, and my amazement at what was happening before my eyes was keeping me frozen to my seat! I again felt Lord Zulu's strong hand on my shoulder, and heard him whisper, "Give your brother a chance player — don't lose your faith in him, he doesn't have smoke coming out of his nose, but he got a great big heart inside of him."

I whispered back across my left shoulder — "Yoh Lord Zulu, why don't you or Nexus just pass him some of that cosmic dust you guys carry around just in case of an emergency like this one." Lord Nexus lightly thumped me in the side of my head and gave me a dirty look. I got the message and turned back around and started saying to myself—"This is not a dream, this is not a dream!" I said a quick prayer, "Oh God please find Urge worthy, please find Urge worthy! I know I'm not worth saving and I feel my impending doom, so let it be so God, save Master Urge and do what you will with me." Oh yeah—I meant it! Lord Kokhan got up and floated slowly across the floor from his seat towards the big translator, showing off his power of levitation I guess. He glanced over at us or Urge, with little rings of smoke flirting from his over-sized nostrils and said—"It is indeed a great time to be alive, yes, life is good, life is good as there are many great rewards in hell—so I've heard even in heaven. Even though its said that a soul's continued existence is the crown jewel of the Godhead is it not? Yes, for one to know, to have known spiritual-life or any life, is indeed the greatest blessing—so much creative fire. The very electricity that powers the batteries of the cosmos, and of course the very heart of the Godhead itself it's said!" He paused a short distance from the translator and pulled out a small can or container out of his over-sized cloak.

He opened it and took out a large pinch of some white-sparkling powder and hurriedly sniffed it straight up his large nose, then put the container back inside his cloak. This really pissed off the big translator, we could tell when he spoke out loudly at Lord Kokehead—"Lord prosecutor you have been warned!" Kokhan just looked at him and gently snarled, "Relax big guy—it was just medicine, a little something for my sulfur addiction and sinusitis." I heard both Lords Nexus and Zulu say to themselves—"Yeah right, he has no respect for this court—none!" Urge said, "Just petty tricks I'm sure, it seems we may have him worried, from all his stalling and theatrics." Kokhan kept talking after apologizing again—"This court has noted I'm sure that Master Urge here, has never truly answered my question—of the great negligence of his duty as a Guardian Angel to his lower-self, the very focus of our attention here today. I asked him if he considered himself a real spiritual coward or not? Did he truly believe he deserves to continue on with his charade of guardianship for any soul-force, since he lacks the one quality that distinguishes all Angels from lesser life-force energy, that of courage and fortitude under pressure?"

Turning to face Urge and floating back to the table to his spot, he picked up a different paper scroll. "Lord Facilatator allow me to read this—to the great Lords here in these hallowed halls. Is it not expected by all concerned parties, entities, spiritual-beings one and all, that fairness and justice is dispensed equally here in this much to bright environment. Especially amongst the dark and light beings of this our mutual universal home, especially here within this great city of light is it not? I understand that it is ordained by the source itself—where it is written, quote and un-quote that, 'one half of a soul cannot truly exist long, or have true life, without it's other half being in close proxcimity. Hence the great defect of life-activity, of duality, on all matter worlds and lower levels of existence.

The dark-shadows love these places, wherein billions of souls now reside (raising his giant paws into the air like a subtle victory sign)." He then pointed over towards where the Lords of Justice floated slightly above their royal pedestal to make his point, by grand-standing. "You three great essences of the Godhead are always together—always! This great translator and his associate Angels are always together, I and my assistants are always together. Yet here today in these holy chambers, we have a split-soul force, its lower-self hardly knowing its higher-self seeking mercy or grace from this holy court. Wasting the precious time of all present—please I say, this is a true waste of this courts and my own valuable time. I Lord Kokhan submit, any soul abandoned by or choosing not to follow its Guardian-self, shall forfeit it's right to continued existence after soooo—many wasted lives I believe! Lets not pretend all is honky-dory here with this, this defective soul here!"

"Especially these disjointed soul forces that claim they couldn't find each other over several lifetimes! What a joke of justice, a mockery of all that is established and sacred, if we see fit to fix or even attempt a remedy of this naturally chosen quark of spiritual life, just to feed our own un-godly personalities, or hell forbid, our own egos!" Urge whispered, "Un-Godly, speak for yourself ignoramus." Mr. Kokehead kept running it—"What of the great three, equality, justice, harmony? The three keys to a peaceful and productive co-existence of good juxtaposed with evil on many levels? All three great concepts are indeed predicated on creative whole life. This being instilled in souls at their birth, the cosmic decree of sovereignty—of independence, and Godly free-will! Low and behold the continued assault and abuse of all life, is truly a matter of a soul's choice, thus you think they would have learned by now. Our little soul-force here Mr. Lee Roy has made his choices, his future bed is made. Let us respect his sovereignty, even as a half-of-soul. His mishandling and misunderstood application of the power of the greatest law—that of free-will must be balanced, paid for, as in my earlier petition request. Reward now my God and Master, his esteemed majesty King Luciferious The Third—the greatest King and God of the underworlds and dark forces of this our humble universe, shall we all bow down with respect?" Just then all of the dark minions and dark robed staff-assistants that came with Lord Kokehead to court, suddenly rose and gave a half bow in unison, as if on cue—before taking their seats again. "Wow!"

No one on the light side of the room moved, not one angel bowed to this beast or his dark God statement. "Remember (he added)—"it is important that we maintain the balance, right?—right!?" Kokhan kept right on talking. "Boy what a joke is being played out on all spirit-kind and man-kind all over this crazy universe today, if we—those of us in charge here, cannot regulate justly the empty and hollow value of half of a soul who has chosen the dark ways over the light. Then all things cosmic are indeed out of balance. Would this honorable court like to see or review with me the results of the Godhead's foolish and unwise abuse of such a universal error in it's charity and judgment?" Floating backwards towards our table now, Lord Kokhan turned dramatically and bent over near me, facing me and said with a smelly breath. "See hear the great experiment gone wrong, look closely upon the ugly face of this half formed soul and his messed up heart, this corrupt spirit of a free-will seed, giving wasted soul energy a name, a shape, a cowardly—defective Guardian Angel to protect it, to guide it—oh pleasee? Say it again for this holy-court Mr. Lee—pimps up, hoes down, (throwing his massive arm up into the air) say it boy!! May we truly think that the Godhead would send Lord Urge, a low level Angel of consciousness to nourish and protect this little black pathetic pimp, I mean dope-fiend!?"

Damn—he called me a pimp, a dope-fiend. Hell I never used that junk, I just sold it, what the hell is going on here! There arose from the light side of the room from all the Angels and bright entities on our side of the room, a slight hissing and booing at what the Dark Lord had just said, so the big translator had to stamp his long staff loudly on the marble floor to quiet everyone down. Boom—boom! Lord Kokehead kept right on talking! "I do so wonder if the so-called great God of Light ever learns from his mistakes, as we would like to believe. Well surely when your God creates garbage, or his little soul creations no longer serve his holy wishes and choose to become like garbage—it is known that garbage must be removed by the garbage man, or it begins to stink up the place. So the Universe has its ways of destroying what it doesn't need to fulfill itself. I am he, and have been called over centuries past much worse—behold the great Garbage Man! So allow me to take out the garbage we find here today—including Mr. Lee Imp, this sweet little dope-pimp!" I was tempted to jump up and run screaming outta there faster then Urge, or Nexus, or the Zulu could fly to catch me. But I was frozen with fear because he had gotten so close. His breath smelled a lot like rotten eggs—damn! I really thought for a moment that this large beast Kokhan was going to eat me right there in court room! The translator moved quickly across the room towards Lord Kokhan and his crew. His gargoyle looking minions had become agitated and became nosier, many of whom were stamping their feet and clapping. After Kokhan had been boo'ed by the light beings (those entities and Angels that had white auras around them) on our side of the court room. The translator stamped his long golden staff once, then twice on the marble floor a few yards from where Kokehead was floating up and down near me and Lord Urge.

The translator shouted out—"Move away from them Dark Advocate, you must stay on your side of the table! If you can not restrain your passion, your thirst for intimidation by you and your minions, this hearing will be nullified and dismissed in favor of Lord Urge's petition and cause, by a spiritual-order of the Lords of Justice!" Urge hadn't moved from his chair, which he did slide in front of me at Lord Kokhan's approach, but I noticed that Lord Nexus and Lord Zulu had stood up and moved closer behind me and Urge. They stood quietly, silently, with their hands still folded into the sleeves of their non-descript robes. I bet they were holding onto their cosmic dust, like I would have been holding on to my gat if I had one. It seemed like everyone with wings were now showing bits and pieces of feathers—even the big translator had exposed his winged limbs briefly as if he expected some trouble. Lord Nexus leaned over to me and whispered—"Even in this protected holy place, no one trusts this new prosecutor from the dark realm. There was this moment of concern that some of us reacted too Lee Roy, not to worry though. The court translator has it all under control. His power here is truly supreme!"

Lord Urge put his hand on mine on the table where I had kept them folded and whispered—"Relax Lee, don't show any fear or worry—we can and will survive this day, trust me little brother." Lord Kokhan retreated back to his side of the long table and begin to unroll another scroll he still held in his massive paws—mumbling, "Hummph, free-will oh what a dumb mistake, considering all the wasted lives and creative force that souls are endowed with—oh what a waste, tis truly pitiful. You'ed think they could make better choices with this amount of Godly power—hummph, some baby-spirits need to be spanked! The very cave-jails and fire-prisons of hell is full of souls who chose so foolishly. Still there's always room for one more. Well, thanks be to the Godhead for it—it truly keeps the Devil and I in business, hah—hah—hah!" Kokehead turned around near his seat to face the Gods of Justice. "Oh great and holy ones, I apologize again—I would like to proceed with the multiple charges against this unworthy little creature." Damn I thought, how could this big ugly mother-fu . . . . , "Lee!" creature call me a creature!" Lord Kokehead started to read from the out-stretched scroll under his paw on the table. Taking his time with his speech slow and forceful, loving to grandstand for his bought and paid for minions and dark staff. Who seemed to worship him and praise his every word. "Let's see, ok—ok, nawh can't be, whoa yes it is all here. A thousand and one years old, various levels of soul consciousness and life exposures. With two lives lived on fire worlds, three separated from his higher self—the cowardly lion Urge while in matter worlds. Two in the astral-realm, and one in a water world. With very little time spent in the higher spiritual realms accept for brief transitional periods—humm, sounds like a no-brainer to me!"

"Let's see, very little spirit evolvement, very little contact with his Guardian Angel—oh I've said that already (snort, snort), and hardly any understanding of religious practices or spirit disciplines. Boy no wonder you're a mess little Nigga-Lee. Let's see, other assorted negative rewards and wicked points for doing nothing constructive for your brother and sister souls over several lifetimes. Whoa—having chosen to become a dope-pusher, snake-charmer, whatever the term is back on earth your last time around huh young player? Well believe me, according to this report you've managed to come close to my neck of the woods on several recent occasions—with your marketing of drugs in three states and violent street crimes young pusher. I see also that you and your crew have smoked so many leaves of grass you could probably piss green for decades, hey bad boy? Surely we don't need to read any more of this report Lord Translator now do we? Talk about neglect and resistance to the light. Lets see, rated a class 'C' soul-force, already flowing near empty, after several turns on the great wheel as a retarded life force. If this isn't a case of a soul falling far from grace I don't know what is! Now just who or what is to blame for this poor definition of a soul and its denigration of itself?"

"Who—I ask of this holy court? Can we hold Master Urge accountable, yes I believe we can, and we should (pointing over the table at Lord Urge)!" Boy did I want to blast this big ape. "I'm sure Lord Urge would tell us again why he just stood by for so long on many occasions of separation and helpless inactivity while his lower-self was self-destructing and destroying life-energy all around him. See, the earth has lost a fool and we have gained one—right? All because—as he tells us, of his own fear of matter world peculiarities and incarnation entrapments for a soul expressing as a physical body. This fear that many a soul before him we know have over-come, on their individualized paths of enlightenment and soul-growth towards what beings of the light call perfection. I for one—don't believe him, there's got to be more to this weak cowardly Angel's excuses of negligence and fear then he's telling us!" Lord Urge stood up quickly from his chair and said in a louder tone of voice now—"Hold your wicked tongue Lord Kokhan, you truly don't know a—a thing about me!" The translator broke in, "On what spirit grounds Lord Urge, do you wish to challenge what the Lords of Justice already know to be the truth?" "Yes oh great translator, well sort of—on the grounds that Lord Kokhan knows that the preceding lives or life-times of my lower-self has no value here—not today, governing the judgment of this round of soul expression and perhaps my own negligence in the matter." Kokehead interrupted again—"Oh so you do admit some culpability in this matter hey little Angel-spirit?"

Urge kept speaking, admitting nothing, "Lord Kokhan has attempted twice already to interject privileged and classified information into these proceedings. Without seeking special permission from the Lords of Host!" Lord Nexus leaned over the railing and whispered in my ear—"Urge is bluffing Lee, he knows that all Dark Advocates try to get into evidence the prior life experiences of a soul on trial here. If they believe it will save them time or sway the Lords of Justice decisions even a little bit." I was like what, come again Lord Nexus—I don't remember any past lives and I'm not a thousand years old!" Lord Zulu whispered, "1000 and 1 Lee." The translator shouted back at Urge—"Lord Urge you shall hold and please sit down!" Lord Kokhan was floating up and down a little on his side of the table and speaking again—"Ok, ok let us just focus on this past life's record,

I thought that's what I was doing. Lets see—at just five years old, observed as spoiled and stubborn, at ten—disobedient and disruptive, diagnosed as hyperactive—damn, excuse me I mean darn it—hummph! Then at twelve—observed cursing, disrespectful towards his elders and female souls, and lets continue—at fifthteen, has violent behavior, prone to gang-banging and drinking, and smoking weeds, and . . . there's more abusive and cruel activities towards others of the same class categories—both males and females! Oh yes we might add least we forget, his extreme cruelty towards animals. It seems he liked fighting dogs back then!"

"Then there were two murders, with his bloody finger prints on the trigger, three alleged rapes, five armed robberies, and last but not least his two prison assaults on other weaker inmates and hard working prison guards—wow! Truly a one man wrecking crew—oh please somebody stop me from reading. Please I can't read anymore" (placing his dark paws up to his forehead like he was going to faint or something)—why then did he keep reading out loud even as he sat down? "I am tired now and think I'll take my seat to rest—hummph! Lets see, oh just five million illegally-gotten blood-stained dollars, acquired selling battery acid, heroin, ecstasy, and that greatly misaligned good stuff called crack cocaine. Five thousand addicted drug users spread out over three states, eight rival hits on his competition, give or take four to six drive-by shootings—one in which a pregnant 18 year old female-spirit was killed!" Then Kokehead screamed with joy it seemed—"Whoa, what a little devil, a real gangster banger, extraordinary dude! It never ceases to amaze me how young souls passing through matter worlds as physical forms of spirit-expression, can so easily embrace evil (stated as if he was proud of my wretched accomplishments), and that's a good thing I believe. All after the tender age of enlightenment at 666 years old!" Lord Kokehead got out of his seat and floated quickly over towards me, stopping at the invisible line of court protocol demarcation so as not to mess shit up again. Then looking down at me he asked in front of the whole damn court sarcastically—"Would Master Lee Roy, you little bad boy you, be interested in a plea-agreement right about now, how about let's make a deal?"

Yeah boy, I was plenty upset with this bad-breath beast, but still to afraid of him to answer him or bitch slap his big ugly ass! Lord Urge had rose and stepped between us and addressed the translator. "With your permission most Holy Translator—we move to accept all the records entered into evidence by Lord Kokhan and waive any further reading of the charges without debate. Due to Lord Kokhan's repeated attempts to condemn my young charge based on some inadmissible and antiquated records, that have not been shared with me or my associates for review of their accuracy or completeness prior to this hearing! In fact this is the only meeting today I've been accorded by Lord Advocate to be formally introduced to him!" I overheard Lord Nexus whisper into Lord Zulu's ear—"Darn is that all our brother Urge has, if so he's in trouble—let us pray even harder!" Lord Kokhan jumped to his feet (if we can call them feet) and shouted out of turn again. "Hold on—what is this!?" He asked, "Didn't this little cowardly winged fool earlier say he had access to all the records?" The great translator stamped his staff once real hard as if he was losing patience, and floated over towards Lord Kokehead asking him—"Is this true Lord Emissary of the darkness? Were your files and petitions kept from the required viewing by Lord Urge, while you had complete access to his life records?"

Lord Kokhan stated slowly and with obvious contempt—"He never came to me in my chambers and requested anything from me or my honorable staff when he was seen registering his presence and petitions yesterday morning. And of course I requested nothing of him cause he had nothing on record of value to us, so I assumed he needed nothing from us! Where is it written in the holy book of court protocol, this code or demand that we had to be formally introduced and share our private files before our meeting here today? Now really—what is this new foolishness all about? We don't have time for these childish spirit-games (raising his voice at the great translator)!" Again every one is on edge when the Facilator's staff strikes the floor again. Lord Kokhan (still standing) started shaking hands with a couple of red eyed members of his staff, and taking a few back slaps from those seated behind him. The big bronze translator was not amused. "Silence in the court!" The Angel-Translator said, "Entrusted by the great and powerful love of the Godhead, we do not play games here Dark Lord! If we decide to engage, we play to win—understood Advocate Emissary!? On behalf of the heavenly host the Lords of Justice, we will take pause to consider this minor inclusion. There will be a decision in a moment. All may stand down but do not leave this room, silence and prayer is ordered. I've been called to recess-council with the Holy Ones." The great translator turned towards the tall pedestal holding the multi-colored Orbs of the Lords of Justice, and in a cloud of white smoke or fog just vanished! I mean ghosted!

He just disappeared to God knows where? I repeated my old mantra to my self—"This is not a dream, this is not a dream." Although I truly wished it was, I do, I really did—I wanted so badly to wake up anywhere else but here. Damn, this room is getting hot I thought to myself! The elevated heat level was all in my mind I believe, damn-darn.!

The great halls and court room was silent again for a brief moment. I asked Lord Urge where did the translator go, and for how long will he be gone? Also if we were close to the end of this thing, this crazy trial? Urge told me it was only a short break in the proceedings and that our chances for some form of survival were good. Considering that Kokhan was continuing to test the patience and power of the Lords of Justice. For a moment I thought I could hear a faint distant humm coming from the Holy-Orbs high up on the judges pedestal. Urge said those faint vibrations was the Gods of Justice's way of discussing his complaint. The vibrations creating the humming sound was the very language of the Universe—remember oommaah? "Lord Kokhan didn't think I would be prepared for his treachery and deceitful ploys, cause he thought I was to afraid to meet with him in his court assigned chambers, he thought wrong. He should have insisted I meet with him, but his arrogance got in the way of court protocol, just like its doing now. We must stand fast and see what becomes of my strategy." Personally I'm stunned, no one discussed with me these new turn of events, hell I really wasn't consulted on anything much anyway. Just told to sit still and listen and pray when given the chance—damn!

I meant darn. I couldn't remember hearing if Lords Zulu and Nexus were praying or not, cause they were now so quite—so solemn and all. Urge and I both leaned our heads over the short railings near our seats to pray with the Zulu and Nexus. We just all started together—"Oh Heavenly Father—oh living Intelligent Universe, we feel your energy, your love, your merciful grace through the holy-spirit that now surrounds us. Let it be upon us—your lesser influences perhaps, unworthy droplets of cosmic conscious beings expressed as the soul-forces kneeling before your blissful presence." Urge and I both heard the mental question Lord Zulu asked of Lord Nexus—"Who is Urge calling unworthy, tell me he didn't?" Just then we all heard what Lord Kokhan whispered across the table into our little prayer session—"Aawwhh do that shit, do that shit! Y'all know the hour is late—so do that shit, go head and do that shit, my Dark King just can't wait. How bout it Urgie my man, you want to cut a deal for your little gangster-ass brother—my Master and I really need him and his dope skills back in Deeetroit?"

We collectively ignored his taunts and kept on praying. 'Father we know we have sinned, time and time again, and we know the damage done—and we know the long-term cost to our spiritual existence. Yet we—both Lee Roy and I Lord Urge, have grown together in grace over many, many months. We have each followed the example—the pattern of salvation laid down on more then one occasion by the Christ-consciousness. The great sacrifice of willingly giving up one's life force for the continuation of the life of another—so we pray this petition not only for our-selves here today, but for all souls that have yet to come this way oh God. Please find us and them all worthy of thy mercy.' The translator's staff sounded again against the floor after he had re-appeared, just as we finished our praying. He was informing all present that court would now resume. The faint humming that came from the floating Orbs (the Lords of Justice) had dissipated and the translator spoke first—"Lord Urge you and Lord Kokhan will rise, the great and infallible Lords of Justice have decided to give you Lord Urge a Mute. A spirit-pass on all petitions that originated before this hearing by you Lord Urge . . ." There was some angry muffled sounds coming from the darken side of the room now. The translator stamped his staff once more for silence and continued with what he had to say—yet louder this time. "This is impart due to non-compliance and non-respect of this court's holy protocol, by the most recently appointed Dark Emissary to this holy place. For continuing disruptive, disrespect directed from Lord Advocate Kokhan towards the accused spirit Lee Roy, and his over-soul Master Urge, and the chosen most Holy Keeper of the peace, I the most high Facilator!"

"Lord Advocate Kokhan—you will not be allowed to enter into this hearing's records the past life records and old arguments of soul dispensations from past soul hearings, regarding this split soul-force before us today, that of Master Urge and Mister Lee Roy—prior to the last advent of soul expression most recent for this life-force Lee Roy proper!" I could tell Lord Kokehead was pissed, I'm not sure why, so please don't nobody ask. Let me finish the story. The translator kept talking—"We have reviewed and placed into the collective consciousness of the One Spirit—this soul's chosen separation from its source and it's inter-actions between its recent matter world life and its higher consciousness in the form of Master Urge, whom the Lords of justice have found refreshingly honest about his fears and derelection of duty to himself and perhaps the great League of Angels. The Lords of Justice further rule that no charges will be considered or heard at this time against this Guardian Angel. His failure to perform certain duties related to his lower-self will be dealt with separately at a later time."

"Therefore all should heed the dictates of this holy panel, and show respect and courtesy to this Advocate Lord Urge, chosen long ago to represent the spirit life-force known as Lee Roy, within these and all spiritual matters—you may all be seated. Is this understood Lord Advocate Kokhan?!" Opps there it is! Lord Kokhan stood up and floated slowly around the table to the center of the great room blowing big-time smoke or steam out of his nostrils. "Oh great God's of Justice—so this then is an example of your style of justice here in this so-called great City of Light?! What is this tying of my hands and binding of my lips, and why am I—who am second to none in the dark regions, being punished by this ruling for just doing my job? I've sought only to enlighten this holy court of what we are truly dealing with here! Behold the many life forms—entities one and all (he looked up into the crowd) visiting here today. Are we showing them a perfect example of a life-force on trial here? One that has chosen freely over many a life units and expressions in time—to live and represent it's independence as a source of pain, of violence, of unspeakable levels of sin and evil!"

"Yes—we are very proud of this youngman, the Forces of Darkness indeed look forward to his return to us as an ally of the dark faith! I now ask of you, does this court refuse to honor the great universal law of free-will? Does it not hold accountable those who have freely chosen the dark-rewards over the psudeo gifts of the light-givers?! Have we recently asserted a new form of justice here in the great City of Light—or are we all, who are witnesses to this great and unfair imbalance just puppets to this spiritual charade now taking place, or to the miscreant desires of those who call themselves the Lords of Justice?!" Urge mumbled softly—"Look whose talking about another being's spiritual misdeeds." Lord Zulu told Urge to "Shut-up brother, Kokhan is already pissed off, and things seem to be turning in our favor so chill out old coon—I mean cool." Kokehead shouted—"Truly then it is a spiritual oversight of enormous magnitude to continue to allow, and make excuses for so many way-ward souls to continue to exist—after they themselves have chosen to fall into the hell-lands of this, our long suffering and balanced Universe. Is it any wonder then that the Lords of Justice and those of the light wonder why my God and Master the Great Luciferious the Third is so dearly needed now!" Damn I thought—that was the second time I've heard that name Lucifer since I got here. Lord Kokhan was upset as he just kept talking out of turn. "It is a well known fact—make no mistake about it. That the great imbalance between good and evil is already on shaky grounds!"

"More so then ever—the dark ones are needed more and more to clean up the messes of matter world conflicts—caused by too many little spoiled and greedy, spiritually endowed souls and lost entities. Always acting and behaving in defiance of the great universal laws and spirit-principles of the Godhead himself! Everywhere they exist they continue to go truly unpunished for their disruptive and destructive actions and behaviors over many life-times of their pathetic and useless soul experiences!" I felt Lord Urge thinking to himself—"I can't just sit here and listen to this fools continuous tirade, he may gain the advantage!" Urge suddenly stood up and interrupted Kokehead's speech. "Please excuse me—permission to speak oh great ones?" "Permission granted—you may speak Lord Urge." "Oh most Holy Translator and Lords of Justice—must we continue to hear and tolerate Lord Kokhan's evil and intentionally misleading remarks with the intent to prescribe all matter worlds and physical existence through the very small focal point of this one small soul-force here today, called Lee Roy? Are we—both Lee Roy and I to be held accountable and perhaps punished for the violations of the many souls that have misjudged the great laws of cause and effect in their own lives?" I'm thinking—you go Urge, I'm singing, it's your birthday—it's your birthday, whatever.

"The great and eternal law of balance and justice, itself entered into our Universe long before we were created, to assist in it's great expression and expansion of God's essence throughout the cosmos? Have we all not accomplished this aim? Lord Kokhan knows full well that we alone — both Lee Roy and I, as one soul-force, are not responsible for any true imbalances or shakiness in the spiritual-fibers, that holds our two different worlds apart, or together for that matter. Our intended contribution to the whole experience of spirit has always been to the glory of God's great experiment!" Lord Kokehead shouted out of turn again, "That's a great big lie — why do you think we're here foolish little Angel?!" Lord Kokhan floated closer towards Master Urge and said — "What the hell have you been smoking behind closed doors foolish old man, you got the gall — the nerve, to wear the robe of an Angel!" He turned to face the large translator and asked him — "Do you see the prideful impetuousness, the disrespect shown here. Has Lord Urge spoken out of turn — God forbid he has, and given to lying as well? He knows that his words now cannot cover up the facts of the records of Lee Roy's and his recent past!"

Again looking all around and up into the higher seats he ask the visiting entities in the courtroom — "Are we seeing a double standard applied here!?" The crowded room started erupting again — first from the dark side we could here shouts of foul, and unfair, grumbling. From the light-side of the room the Angels and other light-beings were shouting sit down demons, and go back to school Dark Lord, and some were booing. The translator quickly glanced over his shoulder up at the glowing — levitating Holy Orbs of the Lords of Justice then turned back towards us and Lord Kokhan. In a big authoritative voice he said, "Lord Advocate from the dark realms, you're the one out of order! Lord Kokhan, you will watch your language and be seated! Lord Urge — please confine your responses and commentary of your perceptions and personal interpretations to the charges at hand, and not the provocative statements or arguments of this respected Dark-side Advocate! You may continue. You have three more minutes to rebut what this courtroom and Lords of Justice have already heard!" Three minutes, damn I thought — I'm gonna be railroaded again, that's not enough time for us to truly plead my weak-ass case, what ever piece of case I had! I didn't want to think it but, Urge seemed to be sleep-walking and sleep-talking a bit!

Thoughts crept back into my mind now of the scarcest thing Urge told me that could happen to a soul-force. Which was the loss of it's eternal life, meaning total soul or spirit-annihilation — being truly lost forever! Urge had taught me things like — for a soul to become lost in eternity or even worse removed from eternity, was truly a sad and horrifying concept to most spirit-entities that now live. Urge also taught me that no individualized-spirit wants not to exist, especially after becoming conscious of itself as spirit. To them, (or us)once having experienced consciousness or I-ness, it was much too much to conceive of non-existence there-after, because all life has so much to offer—so much potentiality. No soul or spirit in its right mind would want to experience the cold and empty darkness of non-existence, or to feel the utter pain of such loneliness and doom. For a soul that is cast back into absolute oblivion, this would be the worst punishment a soul could ever imagine, truly the worst! To be separated from God for good! Urge said that the Godhead gave birth to and breathed the breath of life into billions upon billions of souls over a long period of time, in projecting its very essence out into the cosmos that it also created for himself and them. Ultimately too establish companionship for himself and each individualized spirit. This was a way for God to multiply himself, to expand himself, to continue to come toknow him-self as God, word!

When soul or spirit is truly conscious of itself then chooses to disconnect it-self, or gets lost on its way to again recognizing itself as a part of the Godhead. Then it slowly becomes lost to the great spiritual light of consciousness. It slowly loses its very life from the very source of all life, the electrified blood of God. They, we, feel lost to the creative genesis that guides and operates all life force and soul existence in the Universe. I recall Urge telling me, there have been many who where judged to spend a life time or two, in a state of suspended animation because they had been so wicked and violent towards others of their kind. Or sent to a kind of fiery purgatory of their own making. There to cleanse their adopted wicked or sinful natures of false egos. Then there were those who were strong enough to rally against their very own self-imposed punishments. And over time fight their way back into the light stream. Still other beings (spirits) bought into—or sought refuge within the dark areas controlled by the forces of evil. There-in they became slaves, or servants of the anti-light (Urge called this the anti-Christ model) I remember telling Urge that I had not believed in a real devil or dark being called Lucifer. Urge had responded then that it really didn't matter what I believed or didn't believe. He exsist due to humans creative need for him to exsist.

That there had existed for a very long time, a dark God within the Universal planes of existence, who was hell bent on the total destruction of all human-kind and any spirit-kind that carries the God-seed within them. And any spark of the divine that has yet to be corrupted by the forces of evil, were always at risk of becoming a target for evil. I remember him adding—"Think about it Lee Roy, we know that the spirit forces of light exist and that the law of duality overlaps into the realm of spirit on the lower levels—then there must also exist a counter point, an opposite context to the positive attributes of the Universe. If not, then God could not come to know himself as 'God' see? A balance of sorts, a level of anti-good or evil (empowered mostly by mankind's creative-mind) as men would call it, or as some of my Angel brothers-sisters call it, a collective consciousness of dark negative energy." This court-room reminiscing was only a temporary escape from the moment of my own anticipation of a young mind beginning to collapse, from all this confusing drama and shock of colliding, so-called, spirit realities. I begin to feel again, a need for a fat blunt.

"Lee—Lee Roy? Sit up and pay attention youngman," Lord Urge was saying. "You mustn't doze off on me, you must stay awake son!" I heard what he was saying even as I stared out across the big room full of strange apparitions, Angels, entities. Some called by Urge—intelligent specters or advanced elementals. Hell I don't know which is which—except for the Angels, cause their auras are brighter around their heads and shoulders. "I am paying attention as best I can Urge. Oldman Sleep is after me again in the same way he stalked and over took me back in the day. Like right after I got stabbed to death in the joint. He's here again, in this courtroom somewhere I just know it. "Lee—Lee, shake it off Youngblood, we're almost there my little brother." I remember saying, "Stop pushing me Lord Nexus—I'm a wake old freind!" Yes I realized the destiny of my little half of a soul-force was on the line. Whatever I am, life-force, half-spirit, half-a-consciousness, what-ever? I truly felt I wanted to hold on to it just a little longer. Urge had stopped talking, finishing up something about we know we had no legitimate claims to defend, this is sad, so sad. All I wanted was to sleep again dear readers.

Urge turned toward me while I'm nodding in and out and whispered—"Lee don't give up yet little brother, don't be losing your faith, we just about got old beastie-boy on the ropes now, you know like Mohammed Ali's rope-a-dope strategy against that giant George Foreman back on earth!" The next thing I heard was my head hitting the table—bamm! It knocked me back fully awake into that spiritual moment. It didn't hurt much, but the sound brought snickers and some minor laughter from the dark side of the room near Lord Kokhan's crew. The translator was pointing at Kokhan and saying—"You may proceed Lord Advocate of the Dark Realms. Would you now, can you, please state the true position of the Prosecutor's position and make whatever closing petition or judgmental request you care to make. And to you Lord Urge—would you, could you do the same in the interest of saving all some cosmic time? I also remind you both that you may not speak out of turn again, now you both have been warned as Lord Kokhan has, not following proper court protocols will be held against either of you!" Whoa—so I'm still on trial, this then is not a dream—damn it! Lord Urge stood back up to speak. "Oh Great Translator and most Holy Gods of Justice—we hear and we obey." He bowed and gracefully sat back down.

"Forgive us of our weaknesses, no disrespect was intended by the defense advocate." Looking back across the table at Lord Kokehead Urge added—"Forgive my past interruptions Lord Advocate Kokhan please." Kokehead just threw up one paw in our direction as if to flip Lord Urge and his apology off. I mentally sent to Urge—"Lord Urge, just what in Jesus' name is you—we, apologizing to him for?" He didn't answer me, just gave me that shut up and be still look like the one my moms had mastered back in the hood when I was a kid. Lord Kokhan was now more gruff in his behavior and more arrogant then even before. He had to be every bit of 7-1/2 to 8 feet tall and a good 400 pounds. Blowing more grayish smoke out of his large nostrils, he rose to speak. "With all due respect to this holy court (cough—cough) I won't take up much more of your precious spirit-time. With your permission to continue, let us take this small but important hearing a lot more seriously. So let all who see and all who hear—forget not the great purpose of this most holy (cough—cough) court. Is it not for the noble cause of separating the good from the bad garbage. To keep balanced the eternal laws of our (emphasis on our) Universe. From the madness and the contamination of wayward souls and ill-formed entities that continue to threaten and wreck havoc on the very spiritual-fibers that holds this city, this space itself even—together! It's a fact we both still need each other. Always have and always will!"

"I duly submit that the garbage must be removed from this holy place whenever it arrives, so as not to stink up the very halls of Heaven itself. Again I petition the great Lords, I'm sorry—the great and fair Gods of Justice. And all who are present here this day—to allow me to serve, allow me to take out the trash when I leave this most holy place. Allow me the fulfillment of my Godly duties to my Lord and Master. Give me the remaining soul-force Lee Roy and you can keep his ineffectual Guardian Angel Urge until someone here tires of his useless existence, then I'll return to collect him as well. Hummph—if this then becomes the wishes of the Lords of Justice, in the interest of keeping the balance I'm sure. I now fold my request and end my petitions to await this court's holy-seal. In closing, might I add, waste not—want not! We should always get rid of the waste and definitely increase our wants." Lord Urge immediately got up as Lord Kokehead sat down to mumbled cheering, and dark praises from his side of the room. Urge said, "Rejection, rejection, rejection—permission to speak?" The translator responded—"Permission given, Lord Advocate for the defense, you may speak."

Lord Urge shot up about a foot or two from his chair, showing off his own graceful levitation I think. Moving slowly towards the front of the room, he said—"Is it me, or just my old ears? Can this honorable court and all its honored visitors here today believe what we've heard here so far? Can we all not hear the sham of pretense—regarding Lord's Kokhan's deep concern for the sanitation and spiritual welfare of this Universe? He speaks of waste not want not—mere verbal garbage, unfitting an Emissary from any plane. He knows full well that no soul or spirit ever created by our great Universal Godhead was born of any waste. There is no such creature that was born of spiritual essence given the name or title—if you will, of garbage! Even if my esteemed colleague (hummph) Lord Kokhan, likes to stake a personal claim to the title of Garbage Man!" I said sick'em Urge! Lord Kokehead snorted across the table at Urge, "You'd better watch your tone little Angel!" Urge ignored him and kept speaking. "Now let us demonstrate his true motives or concerns for his style of justice, for he knows righteousness is real. He himself must know that righteousness is patient, forgiving, and Godly love for all life-force! That the sanitary spiritual conditions of life here or anywhere else is not his area of expertise. He has not learned how to truly take the garbage out! If so, he would not dare to bring it into the worlds of matter, of spirit, of any holy place, like he attempted to do yester-eve with that ungodly pet trick of his!"

"Never I say, to any concept of a realm of darkness, or evil forces having to co-exist along side that of righteousness and spirit-life—unless it be God's will, and only his devine will! The glory of the Godhead, its Arch-Angels, Saints, and Light Bearers of the Cosmic Universe—would all be better served if there were no evil forces or wicked beings existing anywhere—word! I close as I fold now by starting out with my petition request, the elimination from the record of Lord Kokhan's whole stinking premise, that no soul-force, not this life (pointing over at me) or my life-force, or for that matter any soul—is deemed garbage! Regardless of mistakes made or decisions and choices gone awry by lost or trapped souls, all are rare and valuable pieces of the great Godhead! Especially those that had to withstand many life expressions and spirit challenges in order to find their way back to their true spiritual home. These continued lies from Lord Kokhan, the flagrant temptations, and evil influences constructed by and sent forth from the garbage bosses of the underworlds, is truly what causes most souls to falter and fall from God's grace in the first place—and we all know this to be the truth!"

"Yes, let us waste not to want not, an once of spirit matter—this coming from an underworld junky-flunky of the King of evil treachery, and sinful temptations, that Lord Kokhan has admitted with pride he works for today!" Oh no he didn't slip Lord Kokehead like that I thought—you go Urge, you still the man! Speak up for us lost souls old dude! Just like Johnny Cochrane, a very righteous black attorney did back in the world on Earth. Who had fought hard to save OJ's (old foot-ball star) a . . . , I mean butt from a murder-rap, when white cops in L.A. were trying to frame his a..-butt! Whoa now, shit was again heating up big time. Lord Kokhan and his crew were on their feet growling, hissing, and spitting sparks and smoke all over the railing seperating them from the light—like they were preparing to storm the very gates of Heaven itself! For the first time, in this place I felt a slight sense of hope! Hope that me and my main Angel-man Urge might see one more day! Never say never big baby—hah!

Lords Zulu and Lord Nexus who had been sitting quietly behind the spectator's railing were now standing and had their hands on each of my shoulders, as they whispered into my mind—"Hold your peace and tongue Lee Roy—we feel what you feel. Urge knows what he's doing, and yes we got your back little brother spirit." I again wanted so badly to jump up right then and slap the fire out of Kokehead's mouth and scream at him—'you big ugly mother-fu . . . I know what it is you're after, you don't scare me. You don't care about me, or just my soul force. You're after Lord Urge's soul force too, yeah that's it—a pair of angel's wings are worth a lot more to the Devil then my puny-ass soul force—right beast?!' No I didn't say this out loud, I just thought it in my mind though! I still wondered if Lord Kokehead could read my mind at that time, cause his whole face and demeanor changed, and boy did he seem angry and agitated—after I had that last thought. Lord Kokhan floated around the table towards our side of the big room. My heart started beating faster and louder I'm sure! Lord Urge floated backwards near where I still sat and fell silent—his eyes intently held on the Dark Advocate. Lord Kokehead kept floating closer and closer towards me—oh darn!

I wanted to go to the bathroom right then so I thought. I wasn't sure why, but I held it in. Kokehead stopped just short of Urge and I, and leaned over a little and looked me straight in the eyes and said—"We are tiring of this foolishness little one, don't you want to end this and come with me—you little blacken package of garbage!?" He knew he was taunting and trying Lord Urge's patience and of course myself-restraint. Then he stood up and floated backwards a ways skinning and grinning like he knew something we didn't know. He had spoke out of turn again—"Lord Urge and you too little Lee know in your heart of hearts that it is justice itself for me to ask you that question—right? To this most holy court and to Lord Urge I ask—just what does a dopeman grave above all else—what? Might it be just simple respect? Yes we can give him that. Hummm, little Lee knows he has earned my own and my Master's respect and admiration, for what he was able to accomplish back on earth, starting with so little, and ending up with so much. Yes it's true, his natural entrepreneurial skills and forceful discipline in his life during his most recent sojourn—was indeed nothing short of miraculous. And I might add containing very little negative influences from the dark realms—contrary to what Lord Urge wants every one here to believe."

"Our little gangster Lee Roy here has made his dope game bed—now it's time for him to rest in it! So we look forward to rewarding this young business-tycoon soon, real soon. Indeed, for his able demonstration of free-will leading from poverty and deep despair to fortune and fame in a single life-time. He rose like the Phoenix, showing all his leadership skills and tenaciousness to prevail and succeed in a world that often times treats his kind—those with blacken faces so unfairly and unequal. Especially when it comes to crime and punishment, and even great success on that ball of dirt called Eros. Yes he was put upon greatly and unjustly by those who constantly use his people—those with nappy-hair, showing them illusionary opportunities of achieving great wealth and success in life, then almost always flipping the script on them. It's not easy trying to live in a racist society, a racist country like America. We all know how this adversely affects any soul force living in an often cold and cruel matter world like that of Earth. Life's a burden being born into black face, as a descendent of black Africans and black slaves. America the great had him doomed from the start! Throw in some man made discrimination, mix in a little self-hatedred and wah-la, you have a home grown ghetto dope man. I mean an honorable business man like Mr. Lee Roy here. Truly we of the dark worlds understood his trials and tribulations and offered to support him, but he didn't need our direct imput—see?"

Looking over at Urge, Lord Kokehead added, "It seemed that no one else in or out of that world truly cared enough for these little dark-skinned souls—fortunately I do! I say shame and blame on those souls with white-faces back on earth!" Urge was like, "what the—this has got to be a slick move on Kokhan's part, some new strategy I'm sure. First he puts Lee Roy down due to his misuse of free-will and my absence of guidance, then builds him up as an example of premier entrepreneurship because of a forceful free-will, then to play up the race card—wow! So what's really going on here?" Lord Kokhan was still smoking, saying—"Lets be honest and all say congratulations, what a run little Lee Roy has had, what a real achievement of chaos and madness! If our little brother Lee Roy was expressing his earthly life as a young white enterprising soul, doing the same dope-slinging game of creating jobs and wealth—he would have been hailed as that city's young business-man of the year and a real hero to many, as opposed to being labeled a menace to his society! Its exactly like little Lee has said over and over again—black folks don't grow drugs, and they don't know how to make weapons of mass destruction!" How did Kokehead know I had said that to Urge many months ago?

"Oh the hypocrisy of mankind, spirits one and all, lusting to have it all. Shall we say the same here within these hollowed walls of this holy place, I truly hope not! This realm must remain a true place of justice and hope. Am I not correct Lord Urge?" Urge didn't respond—he just stared over at Lord Bighead with his arms folded now. LK snorted—"Again I ask you young Angel if you would entertain a good plea with me and this honorable court today, what say you young half-a-prince?" Lord Zulu asked Lord Nexus telepathically—"Oh no he didn't, tell me he didn't just play the race card Nexus?" "I believe he did brother Zulu, and played it well I might add for those who are unaware that race on earth is only a great illusion, created by Earth's enviornment—and has no legitimacy in the spirit world, and shouldn't have any in physical worlds." "Yes, yes I know and agree Lord Nexus! Kokhan knows that there is only two true races of beings—those expressing as the physical-matter race and the spirit-matter race of soul energy!" Master Urge looked over his shoulder at Lord Nexus and Zulu with that shut up and be quite look. The big gold and silver wrapped translator stamped his long staff twice again on the marbled floor—boom—boom! Then said—"We will have order—order in the court—all stand down, be seated and silent so we may bring this matter to a close!"

He sounded serious and confident that he was the one in charge of things as usual. Lord Urge was still standing and levitating near his seat with his arms folded. When it came time for him to speak again, he said—"Oh great translator and most Holy Gods of Justice, need I address my point of contention on this minor issue of race interjected here by my opposing Advocate?" The translator spoke—"I think not Lord Urge, in order to forego any further adjudications of repeated charges and recommendations of soul verdict, by Lord Kokhan—and to keep this hearing short. We now find and agree that great failings of spirit and soul has transpired and caused irreparable harm to many life forms associated with the life-expression of this soul here today known as Lee Roy. So hold Lord Urge would you please proceed to accommodate this court with an answer to this question from the Lords of Justices? Are you prepared to transfer your lower-self's consciousness over to Lord Kokhan upon the direct edit of soul dispensation of the Gods of Justice if they so rule it young Angel Urge?" Now the beings on the light-side of the room gave up a collective shudder, like a wave of intense shock and surprise. I felt it too and I was confused, I wasn't sure if I understood what the court Facilator-translator was asking Lord Urge!

Lord Zulu was telling Lord Nexus to—"Stay seated, and pray again!" I asked them both in mind—"What the hell was being purposed, what was going down, was it me?" I looked into the faces of my escorts—and couldn't believe what I saw in their eyes, or felt from their solemn silent responses to my last question. Lord Nexus finally spoke to me telepathically—"Lee Roy, you didn't know—couldn't have known, what Urge didn't want you to know. Urge had filed his original position-petition to assume full responsibility for all your sins and short comings, don't ask me why?" Lord Zulu inserted—"he also requested that any bad decisions or negative judgments against you today fall fully upon his shoulders." Lord Nexus jumped back in the conversation with—"Didn't I just say that?! He truly feels responsible for your past messed up life back on earth Lee. He shared in your pain, your sorrows with every choice or decision you made that hurt another of your spiritual brothers or sisters back then. He said once he froze up when he saw evil approaching you, your life force, and didn't do anymore then try and warn you on those occasions. He said he was to far from you in vibrational force to fully protect you, and he felt extreme guilt at having been separated from you for so long in the first place".

"Also his not being materially there when you needed him the most. He has in effect sacrificed himself and his second love after you, his Angel wings—even above his deeper love for the Godhead's Christ-consciousness!" I had to ask them—"Did either of them know of this plan before now and when did Urge make this decision without telling me?" Lord Zulu spoke in his africanese style—"Yes, and we were asked not to repeat what we had discussed with him with you, for fear of your not understanding this back up plan of Urge's, and passing out on us again. His sole desire in case the Gods of Justice were leaning towards casting your limited life-force energy over to Kokhan as a lost, unsalvageable soul-force, or banishing you into purification. Which in-itself could cost you, 75—100 years for each spirit-term of suspended activity." Lord Zulu then added, "Urge said he wouldn't allow that—so his petition, his last request for mercy was made at the registration desk several days before today. Lee Roy it was always his option, his will, and it is binding on you both if the Gods rule to accept it." Nexus added, "As opposed to letting Lord Kokhan claim victory and take you to where no soul ever wants to go willingly! Since only a hand-full out of every thousand lost souls ever make it back from there each decade, and only after tremendous sacrifices and much prayed for mercy and grace from the Light-bearers, the Saints, and the Holy-ones with golden wings."

"Do you understand now Lee"(Nexus asked of me).
"Lord Urge must be allowed to do this!" Lord Zulu interrupted with—"He already has, haven't either of you been paying attention—Jesus?" "As I was saying before my shadow interrupted me" (Nexus said)—"Urge must be allowed to accept and endure whatever decision or judgment they reach or demand of him and you! It's obvious to us that this hearing is not going to last much longer Lee, so just try and be prepared—even for the worst if and when it comes little brother." I couldn't believe what I had just heard, and with my face hidden inside my hands I just wept, and cried silently. Lord Zulu added his two cents again—"Yes, there will be a decision soon I believe—real soon. This tension will not last until the new day arrives. You mustn't cry Lee Roy, don't do that—no matter what, keep your head up to show Urge your spiritual courage, cause he needs that example now—more so then ever. Think of how brave he's being for you Lee, he has grown stronger himself since your re-unification with him in this spirit realm." Boy was I hurt and sadden by what my higher-self had proposed. All to save my worthless butt, but wait a minute how could I be worthless!? If Urge was willing to lose himself—his wings to save my pitiful soul-force energy! He must have felt I was worth saving!

I had to get a grip, so I wiped away my astral tears and thumped myself hard in the chest as I slowly stood up and shouted over to where Lord Kokehead was sitting blowing smoke rings from his nose—"I want the deal! I will not stand by and allow this courageous Guardian Angel, my friend and soul-inspiration to take a fall for what ever I've created, caused, or did back in the world! I'm sorry for what I may have done to hurt our collective spirit—or that hurt any others because of my misuse or abuse of my own free-will! I'll be glad to be exiled to fire, or annihilated or what ever, as long as Lord Urge is spared! . . . Please Master Urge take the deal, accept Lord Kokhan's offer!" Urge actually shouted at me for the very first time, and boy oh boy I could tell he was upset with me. "Lee Roy sit down young fool of spirit, sit down and be quiet—just do it! Don't you dare interrupt me or this honorable court again! Lord Nexus and Lord Zulu if you must, you two will restrain my lower-self—for he does not understand all things here, and he must not be allowed to speak unless given permission to do so!" He pointed a stern finger in my face and tried to whisper—"This is my neighborhood dapper rapper, and you will respect that, so for the last time—chill-out, I got this ok!" Boy have I messed up but I didn't care. I kept saying mentally and telepathically to Urge—"please don't do this, don't go there old man, I'm just not worth it!"

Lord Kokhan was talking out of turn again—"Yeah that's the ticket my little mellow fellow, speak up son, tell Urge what to do—what is right, you've done it before player!" The translator was slowly floating over towards our table and he didn't look pleased either. I couldn't help myself and brushed Lord Nexus's hand away from my mouth and spoke up again. "Urge it wasn't your fault, you tried dude—I wouldn't listen to you! I didn't know you, I didn't think of the consequences beyond that life. Yes I knew dope dealing would condemn me, but not you too my brother! Please take the cop—the plea, old man my friend—please!" Lord Zulu whispered into my head—"Lee if you don't shut up and remain seated, I'm going to have to smack you with a pinch of my Angel dust little brother—and you won't like that!" Then I said it, I cursed—"Damn it Urge, listen to me! I called the shots, I made those choices not you! I don't want you to give up your existence for mine. I'll go with Kokehead, I'll do what he wants—so please!" Urge shot back into my mind (after asking the great translator for a brief moment)—"Yeah we all know Lee, that's what we're all afraid of—you doing what Lord Kokhan wants you to do. You've proved that already back on earth. So will you please be cool and stronger now little brother? You must trust me Lee, because I know what I'm doing—and it's going to be good for the both of us you'll see! Please calm down and relax your mind. Let me work this out and you'll see every thing will work out fine."

"I got your back as well as my own young 'G'. This is my time Lee, my duty—you made your great sacrifice back when by sharing a courageous love for a friend, your fiend Ike, remember?! Even if you didn't know it then Lee, you had unselfishly fulfilled the pattern of the Christ-Consciousness, set before us so many times in our many life-times lived. So would I—your higher-self, your Guardian Angel choose to do any less—less than you did, I think not?" I heard Lord Nexus whisper to Lord Zulu—"Oh boy, how touching, you think anyone else is buying this scene—other then Lee

Roy?" Lord Zulu returned—"Oh so we be making jokes now my brother?" I didn't care what they said—I held my head up and looked at Lord Urge now smiling somewhat, I said—"Ok I believe in you Urge, go head and do what-cha gotta do old man, you got the stage master player!" Urge spun back around to face the Gods of Justice and the big translator and spoke with serious intent—"Lord translator and great Gods of Justice, we apoligize and we hear and I obey. I will now make my closing statement, regarding my decision to maintain my earlier petition for transference of all guilt. For sins committed by my spiritual lower-half Lee Roy, on this our collective path to enlightenment and much hoped for soul salvation." I was still like, "Whoa—old man at least tell them I was retarded or something, and that you were not totally responsible for my Willie-Lynch type mentality back on earth!" Lord Zulu put his hand on my shoulder again, and this time it hurt. I swear it felt more painful then . . . , "Lee Roy if I have to tie you to your chair—I will! By the way what or who is this Willie Lynch?" I didn't have time to explain it to him, Urge was speaking again to the court—"Oh great ones, this decision as I close is mine to make, according to the great laws that govern this most Holy Court and the Great League of Angels. If it be the will or decision of this court, for a salutory or auto-default judgment of me then so be it, may God have mercy on me. As to your judgment for or against my young charge Lee Roy here, I respectfully hold to this hearing's decree, whatever it might be. My heart knows it would be the greater evil to grant the request of Lord Kokhan and send Master Lee Roy off to an almost certain doom. So being deprived of the existence of God's most holy-light and any future chance at redemption—would be overkill. For surly Lord Kokhan and his minions would simply put Lee Roy back into his old ways to do even more harm to other souls and himself. Than for me, who admittedly is more conscious and entirely negligent in the performance of my celestial duties to him, for which I am greatly ashamed. Yet I am willing to accept being apart from him again, to accept any imposed period of cosmic cessation or spiritual suspended-animation, if it would please this court and these celestial givers of justice here. My wings are at your mercy oh Lords of Justice."

Lord Kokhan stood up confidently to speak—"Oh Gods of Justice grant me permission to respond—to this pathetic plea for sympathy and mercy!" The translator responded—"So granted Dark Lord." "Oh how truly sad this is, to witness such a display coming from a supposedly exalted creature, this so-called Guardian Angel here. My bad—I meant coming from this incompetent, powerless, cowardly piece of light-consciousness. This is truly sad, what a waste of spirit energy! If this then is the end result of eons of spiritual evolution of light beings, then our great and absolute Godhead indeed has a wicked since of humor, and perhaps needs to go back to the drawing board of soul-creation and start all over with each of us!" Woah, I got a serious thought just now! Lord Kokehead suddenly growled, as he continued to strut around the large marble table like a dark peacock.

"More Angels should be allowed to freely sojourn on the dark planes of existence for awhile—then maybe they won't end up so stiff and lame, such drama-queens like Lord Urge here. We know how to toughen these creatures up in the dark worlds".

"Oh yes Lord Urge—word to your mother (sarcasticly), I can imagine how proud she must be of you today!" Staring at Lord Urge with his big bulging red-eyes, blowing rings of smoke across the table that looked now like a pair of handcuffs to me. I couldn't believe how Kokehead had just slipped my man, my protector. Oh hell yeah—he had gone too far by dissing my man Urge, and therefore dissing me too! The big court translator now shouted over to Lord Kokhan—"Lord Advocate from below—hold your tongue! First you must ask for consent to respond, then wait until consent is given! Once again you've spoken out of turn and with obvious disrespect for these Holy Ones present! Why is it that some Dark Advocates never seem to truly learn the ways of this most holy sanctuary. Hold back my staff oh Lords of Justice!"

Chap. 17   "The Real Rope-A-Dope"

Lord Kokehead spun around to face the big guy and shouted back at him—"It was my turn to speak, so we should dispense with glory formalities and get to the obvious decision of what to do with this young killer! This rascal of spirit who thinks his good looks will save his ass! I know we all want what's best for these two lost and found souls here (pointing again at us), so why not rule on the known facts before us, so we may conclude this matter! We all know that long ago this clown Lee Roy had freely chosen to embrace the dark world and forces of evil—so give him up to my God of power and fire-justice!" Kokhan turned back around to face the table and floated over to our area, pointing a big crooked finger at me. "This little man-spirit has been given the gift of all gifts, the cosmic power and creative force of free-will, sooooo . . . . He has made his bed at a terrible cost to humanity and the spirit world—so now let him sleep in it! Isn't it true Lord Urge and Lee Roy what the light bearers taught us long ago, that we reap that which we have sown?! Go head and say it Mr. Dope Man and you too Mr.Cowardly Angel, 'am I my brothers keeper (laughing now)! Right?, yes righteousness is real fools, it's also very hot—which you'll soon discover!"

He was blowing smoke and ashes all over the place now—it seems he (Kokehead) was in his own private glory or something, like loving his over-blown sense of importance. The translator started to speak, he had seen enough I believe—shit was getting out of control, as Master Urge had planned it I now believe. "Lord Advocate Kokhan—with all due respect, please shut up and return to your seat! You have been warned three times now. Go-be seated, peace be still and know this! You should have conferred with your predecessor Lord Mayhem longer about this holy court and its proper protocals and demeanor! We of this Holy City of Light and Justice—do not allow any entity, Angel, Emissary, or soul-force of creation—to run rampant and roughshod over the rules and protocols of this ancient Holy Court. Regardless of their mission, spiritual-status, or purpose for being here! You sir, will subjugate your own free-will and turn your un-holy powers over to the Gods of Justice now! For safe-keeping Dark Lord, and for the safety of all present, or pay a dear price for your insolence and disrespect, and un-provoked dark behavior. This ugly rope-a-dope strategy of yours is truly juvenile and insulting to this great court!" "Oh my God what now?" Lord Nexus said, as Lord Urge started to rise to speak I guess. There was an ever growing sinister vibration growing stronger and becoming louder from the dark side of the room. What the hell is this I thought!

Lord Kokehead had already stood back up with his red-eyes bulging even further outside of his skull. With his mouth opened wide as he was being grabbed and held tightly by his staff of dark-robed red-eyed demons, who I'm sure were afraid of what he may do next! Every one seemed to feel it, as if things were about to explode here in court—in the heart of this great city of light. I knew there would be much astral or spirit-blood lost, if a fight broke out! Kokehead shouted at the big translator while blowing big-time smoke now. "Lord Emissary Kokhan demands an explanation to this travesty! What in Hell's great name is going on here Lord Translator!? You ask that I would give up my official powers here and now—to stand defenseless against possible attack or harm in or near this place?! What arrogance you beings of light have—humph", (coughing—with small flames shooting out of his nose) all could tell Lord Kokehead was seriously pissed off, after being ordered to give up his evil powers! "Oh Gods of Justice—what have you asked of me to do, that I have not respectfully done? I will never willing give up my official powers to no one except Lord Luciferious himself!" The translator was slowly approaching Lord Kokehead's position, saying—"Darkside Emissary, you will hold your tongue and space and sit down immediately!" Suddenly there was a very loud boom like the sound of a thunder clap that shook the entire room.

The translator's staff had given off a very large lighting bolt that had made the whole room of visitors and spirit-entitles fall back in their seats. Many seemed like they were ready to leave in a hurry, but was too afraid to get up and run. I had gotten up from the floor from slightly under the marble table, to look over where Kokhan was before the explosion. That's when I saw him and his whole crew, his red-eyed assistants surrounded by a shimmering electrified cage, with large bars of white and blue flames enclosing them all. Lord Kokhan and several of his dark-robed shadow goons (his personal body guards), all looked shocked and terrified—especially the big-four bodyguards next to Kokhan. This shit was unbelievable, my mind was spinning again. We could see and hear him growling his protest—he was still talking and now threatening the court. "Oh woow"—he shouted from inside the giant gage. "Finally I see clearly how the light works its treachery on top of this mountain within these so-called holy walls. We come to seek justice and fair treatment, but instead we are given a cheap fire-works display and no respect—damn, now ain't this a bitch! And spirit beings wonder why so many souls are attracted to the dark forces. Would this court's visitors truly like to see some real fire-works?! Pray tell us oh Great Translator, what does the Gods of Justice themselves have to say about all this wanton unearned theatrics?!"

"Am I supposed to be impressed?!" Lord Urge, Nexus, and the Zulu holding his hands over his pointed ears, had not moved an inch from where they had posted themselves in defense of me. My three amigos, boy were they brave or what! Soon every body was resettling themselves in their temporary vacant seats. What ever they thought might have happened, thank God it didn't. Inwardly I knew it would have been very bad. The flaming gage around Lord Kokehead and his crew was slowly dissolving now—after Kokhan reluctantly agreed to deed over his evil powers to the Gods of Justice temporarily. Just to save face I'm sure, or to keep from getting his fancy dressed butt kicked by the muscle bound-translator and the other big Guardian Angels protecting the court. The big translator Angel spoke real loud now, "This court recognizes Lord Urge's continued brave presence and grants him under three minutes for his whole-soul summation. Then Lord Kokhan will have three minutes for his rebuttal and final request for this soul's dispensation judgment." The translator stamped his long staff just once and turned to face the still floating, colored Orbs holding the essence of the great Gods of Justice within each. Lord Urge, still standing, floated closer to the center of the room then looked back at me and his crew, and stated for all to here.

"Most holy ones here and around me, yes I know what I have asked in my petition, and yes I know what I'm doing. I have prepared for this day from the moment of my first experimentation and seperation of self over several life-times past. The need to experience this split and shift in consciousness of my life force energy was solely to experience the great want and need of God himself. Yes even to mimic the God-like quality of creating a life-form similar to my own—a part of me, my lower-self Lee Roy here. Made in my own image and likeness like all of the spirit children of the Godhead are. I meant no disrespect to God nor to the League of Angels who found me at a high point, worthy of their class over 3-hundred years ago. It has taken all this and more learned in spirit worlds and in matter worlds, over several hundred years to understand that only God needs to express himself as the Godhead and the true creator of souls. Truly all of his off-spring including me need only to love themselves as they find themselves, then they can recognize and appreciate the love the Godhead has for them just as they are. Have faith my brothers and friends—it should be felt by all present that all is still in divine order, I truly believe. We of spirit and light have come along way and have faced the Angels of Darkness before and prevailed—with the help and guidance of the Holy-Spirit of the Godhead. So shall we do so once again!"

Urge paused, took a deep breath and while looking at me said—"so just chill my peeps, but keep those prayers flowing upward into the Godhead just in case—cool? Cool." The sounds of grumbling and hissing was growing again on the dark side of the court. Urge smiled back at us then turned to face the great spirit Orbs and said—"Oh great and Holy Gods of Justice, it is now known and often said by the Cosmic Saints that, to err is human—to forgive is divine, we seek only that. Now my lower-self and I ask for your divine forgiveness and your mercy, and grant us the soul-dispensation listed in my petition. I am finished and give deep praise to the Christ-Consciousness, the Holy Spirit, the Godhead, and the most Holy Gods of Justice . . . Thank you, thank you." Urge had sounded so serious—and had spoken so well I thought. I had never seen him so focused, as I knew he was fighting for my continued existence as a seed of his own elevated consciousness. And as well I guess, for his own life-force. I knew my destiny was tied to his, as I reflected on my growing love and admiration of him, my higher-self. Now I fully understood and thanked God almighty—especially for the awesome gift of life that had been given to me so long ago. I thought to myself, if this new challenge to our continued existence didn't turn out right, here in this special City of Light—then I would have been the cause of its loss. No one else was to blame for my earthly choices and actions, no one but me.

I thought about how stupid I had been—how greedy and wasteful of my gift of free-will and creative thought powers given to all souls at their birth. Urge was returning to his seat, when Lord Nexus pushed the back of my head with an mental finger. He said—"Are you paying attention Master Lee Roy? This whole scenario, this trial—this Angel's sacrifice is all apart of your continued learning on this, the real spirit side of life. So we'll just ride this thing out ok (was he asking me)? You still taking notes little brother—you writing all this down huh?" I said—"Yes Lord Nexus, I haven't stopped writing in my note-book diary since I got here. Every since I met Lord Urge, I mean this here beautiful old man—this very special Guardian Angel. He who is my beacon of spiritual-light, my hope for future life, my own higher-self, he is the great Lord Urge." Urge had not held back in his closing, he had laid all he had on the line for me. He had spoken for more then three minutes, yet no one had interrupted him. Neither the big Translator nor that big gorilla Lord Kokehead, said a word. Lord Urge returned to his seat near me, and smiling a confident smile—he paused, turned, and said back towards the court Translator. "Might I add one more thing Lord Translator?" Who nodded his consent.

"It is a well established fact that all present should know, that millions upon millions of lost, confused, embodied souls, must really struggle with Universal Laws that affect all worlds and life-expressions manifesting in lower level type life forms. Yes it's long known—that souls are being trapped not only in physical matter, but being limited also in levels of consciousness and spiritual knowledge, where often they become their own worst enemy. Still—there is this great inner need to experience these soul-evolving journeys for their own personal growth. There-in they often find themselves, quite often standing right next to the very gates of Heaven itself—while some keep trying to live and work through varying kinds of a self-created 'living hell on earth.' These many upon many souls are exposed to great challenges and vicissitudes of worlds grounded in illusionary duality and tri-dimensional challenging existence, especially those worlds yet unaware of the power of the Godhead's love for all life. Is it—I ask this great court and all present, is it any wonder that souls may choose more often then not to be drawn to the dark forces, that lie always near-by and lap at the feet of their limited spiritual understanding. Promising all forms of false hope and escape from their pains of life and living it!"

Lord Nexus whispered to Lord Zulu, "We'd better stop Urge before he kills someone with this eloquent speech, I thought he said he was finished?" Lord Zulu only said—"Right, right?" Lord Kokhan coughed out loud then said—"auhh-excuse me" as Urge looked over at him but kept talking. "The combined effects on souls expressing or exposing their little God-selves in and through matter worlds have always been difficult, even for the advanced souls that occasionally had need to visit there or intercede there, on the direct wishes of the Godhead. Even those masters (Arch-angels) that have achieved cosmic enlightenment, who have achieved the state of bliss-connection, of touching the feet of the Godhead, have occassionaly felt pity and apathy for lost souls, while existing down below—on Earth for example. They too have witnessed the distortions of man's religions, his flawed politics, false material-philosophies of gain and fauxe power, as well as the wickedness of man's own continued inhumanity towards his fellow man. Sometimes even within the same genetic families, as over-powering egos causes negative beliefs to expand." Lord Kokhan suddenly sneezed, and said "excuse me again" then mumbled—"Why must this room be so damn cold, can we please have a little more heat up in here? Great Luciferious this room's temperature is torture!"

Urge along with the big translator looked over at him and both floated closer to the space where the big ugly beast sat. Urge kept right on talking. "The spiritual struggles in matter worlds is even more deceiving and deadlier for wayward souls—trying to perfect their true spiritual selves and find their way home, due to the great self-created temptations and evil influences that act on many to sway their thoughts and desires towards the dark areas of existence and false power. Away from the rewards and love of God, and the guidance and rewards of the forces of light! We know it to be true, that if the dark King Lucifer himself and his minions weren't so busy on earth and many other matter worlds—the tumultious existence of most souls would not be so capricious nor destructive!" Urge returned to his seat near me. I heard Lord Nexus in my head—"Yoh Zulu, try and get Urge's attention and I'll flick him a pinch of my dust and . . ." "Don't you dare Nexus, you'll get us all in trouble!" "Like we're not already—especially if he keeps talking!"

Urge was now pointing over at Lord Kokehead saying—"This great and evil Advocate, knows that Luciferious himself continues to interfere, to interject confusion, to encourage the manifest struggles of all souls to interpret themselves as non-aspects of God. Or to embrace atheistic influences, from their self-deceiving and often destructive egos becoming their focal points, which drags them and their spirits down into vibratory weakness and wickedness—hence the fall of millions from God's grace."

"Their choices often appear to have no dire consequences for their physical lives or spiritual existence—yet often turns out to be spiritually enlightening to those who grow outside of the illusions." Lord Kokhan rose slowly and facing the translator and Gods of Justice still floating above their pedestal and said—"Lord Translator, Gods of Justice—may I please speak now, damn!? Truly it's been over five minutes since this fool started his closure! Can we please dispense with these spiritual history lessons of soul evolvement on matter worlds. Let us keep to the point of the guilt—no doubt, or mercy for little Mister Lee and his newly discovered negligent road-dog, this ghetto talking, pseudo Angel Urgy-purgy. With the permission of this court I'm prepared to use my three minutes to close, with the evidence of direct testimony from all (he paused, and devilishly started grinning) or just part of the 2,500 or so dead and condemned souls that little Lee—oh mighty master of dope-slinging, might know some of them personally! Since he in one way or another helped to bring about their early or untimely deaths and destruction while on earth!" Oh hell no (I thought to myself) now what! When it suddenly dawned on me why I had been hearing this faint old song in the back of my head.

I thought I was leaking some gangster-rap memories into my newly developing spiritual-consciousness. When it actually was low-level muffled singing all alone, coming from one of the big hall-ways outside the court room. Lord Kokehead was still talking—"They are all lined up right now in the great hallway just outside of this court-room, and we should grant them their right to confront their personal devil and earthly acquaintance—Mr. Lee Roy the Dope man over here (pointing over at me)." Then I recognized the song the unseen ghouls out side the court-room were happily singing, and it was a killer-jam back in the world with the soulful Temptations themselves singing back-up for my man Coolio rapping—"The devil is dope, out to steal your soul, yeah-yeah—the devil is dope, he's out of control." Then—"You move your scales from motels to hotels—got merchandise to sell, trying to avoid jail," again—"The devil is dope," damn! Kokhan spoke up—"I am impressed that no one has mentioned that which we all had to smell, their decaying stench from waiting in the hall was becoming more then even I could endure!" Then I heard a strange long forgotten voice calling out to me from the door at the back of the court near where the singing was coming from—it, it sounded like China Doll!

"Lee Roy—Lee Dog, word up my nigga? Where you been Dapper Rapper, what-cha doing here boss lover? You be setting off a new drug deal for these stiff fools up in here? We've been waiting for you to cross over, and lead us once again to cash money and big respect in the dope game Lee—Lee can you here me?" I thought to myself—just like most women, China talked to much and at the wrong damn times. The great translator signaled to the Angel guarding the big doors to close them tightly. Then he spoke—"Lord Kokhan, so you brought all these poor wretched souls here to give their personal testimonies ayh? A little bit of over-kill don't you think Dark Advocate? We, the Lords of Justice are not amused! Their testimony won't be necessary at this hearing Dark Advocate, you should know this! Please send them back immediately to wherever you've summoned them from, the Gods of Justice have spoken—and do it now!" Lord Kokehead acknowledged the translator then threw his hands up and said, "Well if it pleases this court—so be it, they shall be returned to their self-created mental hells!" Coolio's bad voice was now fading out in the halls as I heard the last refrain of one of his sweet raps about living 'life in a gangster's paradise' fade away outside the courtroom. All I could do was shake my head.

I sat up in my seat and thought to myself—damn, damn, they must have followed us here, me and Urge. Nawwh—it had to be the handy work of Lord King Kong! They smelt just like those dead-dead creatures we had encountered earlier in our journey to this place. Lord Zulu touched my shoulder, as if he knew what I was thinking, and how hopeless I suddenly felt again. My faith was quickly fading for some kind of positive out come to all this. I remembered how I felt when Urge had told me, that there were many times when he had looked in on me and was truly sadden by and disgusted with my animus-violent dealings with most of my fellow human beings, especially the souls manifesting as females back on earth! But I was thinking—thank you oh great translator for getting rid of them. Also thinking, what the hell chance would I have had if my old enemies and victims had been allowed to testify against me—damn I think we . . . , I mean I dodged a spiritual bullet just now! Lord Nexus whispered into my mind, "You so foolish Lee Roy (and he wasn't smiling either)—Lord Kokhan has always known where you were, he and his kind probably had designs on your separated soul-force energy from the beginning. Every since you split up from Urge hundreds of years ago son. Evil always chases souls it feels are weakened by outer-physical or inner-mental circumstances. Such as poverty of spirit, or inner spiritual weaknesses, even low morals, no morals, gross physical desires, or mental infirmities. Especially those who build mad desires for ill-gotten fortune or fame back in matter worlds."

"Yes, evil always approaches those whose unevolved awareness of their soul's true capabilities and strenghts is limited somehow. Tempting them to have what ever their hearts and souls think they truly desire—as long as it appears not to hurt, or cause to much pain to other living seeds of the Godhead. Of course more often then not, the very surface appearances of things on earth are false, deceptive, and mis-understood. For most young spirits it is usually difficult, especially down on matter worlds where God expresses his love and light for them to discern the differences between that which is of the light or of the darkness." I'm thinking damn, Lord Nexus has picked a fine time to start teaching me more of their metaphysical concepts. I said in a slow whisper back to Lord Nexus—"I guess you think that information is helping us right now? Do you honestly think I need to be reminded of the pain and hurt I've caused others as a seller of drugs? A blackass young dealer of dope laced with rat poison?" His answer to my question was cut short when the big translator called out to me! "Master Lee Roy—will you stand please?" I could tell Lord Urge wanted to say something right then, but he couldn't speak (he looked surprised). I stood up, trying to appear taller then I was—don't know why.

"Master Urge has told us here today that he would give up his life, his soul-force, indeed his very precious angel's wings in exchange for your own limited soul expression to continue to exist. The Lords of Justice have the power to make this a permanent separation with grave consequences to you both, do you understand young soul-force?" "Yes Sir" I thought without speaking the words. "But we hesitate to impinge in such an un-Godly way just to dispense holy justice in punishing any soul-force or spirit-entity, angel, or human-life expression. Do we really need to bear witness to any individualized testimony of the soul-less shells and disincarnate souls, still lingering within these sacred halls. Waiting to seek sinful revenge because of their own misplaced, misspent soul-choices in the earth plane? "I thought all the junkie ghouls had been dispatched as I turned slightly and glanced over at Lord Urge, back towards Lords Zulu and Nexus—then back towards the golden translator before I responded to his question. "No Mr. translator sir—(I answered) we don't, I mean, I truly don't want for myself what Master Urge has proposed as his great sacrifice. Please let him continue to exist and keep his wings—please!" "Well stated young soul, you may be seated—we will defer to Lord Kokhan, if Master Urge has no more to say (looking down at Urge like he'd better not have more to say)." Urge said boldly, "I do!" Damn—this ain't over till it's over!

Urge spoke again—"I also offer up no contest or challenges to any soul testimony, nor do I dispute the obvious sin-charges of creation within and on the lives of the many, who may have been in contact with Master Lee Roy back on earth, those who may have suffered as a result of same. What I do propose is as before, that those of us of the light and higher-consciousness worlds should not forget the tenaciousness of physical life. With its many trials and tribulations that all souls here have gone through—God only knows. We hold that Cosmic-consciousness is and always will be progressive in its truest nature. That out of necessity, all souls must contend with the cause and effects of intelligence expressing itself and its inherent God-essence, on matter worlds like that of earth. The simple reason is apparent to all whose light of consciousness falls within the great spiritual matrix of soul development." Urge, I thought to myself—'you've lost me old man.' I'm sure Urge heard my thoughts and knew I couldn't speak for these other entities, souls and Angels here, but I was lost now to this heady language and concepts that Urge felt he had to expound upon—even at great risk to all of us here I'm sure. I mentally told Lord Nexus to 'zap him with some angel dust quick, before he condemns all of us with his excessive speaking.' Urge was still talking, not taking a damn breath, and just running his skills. "We all know that the final state of perfection, grace, and bliss is in returning to the state of oneness with the Godhead is it not?"

"And this journey of spiritual growth and salvation is only available to the masses of lost souls now manifest, as a result of their various life-experiences of exposure to matter world's duality of nature and its captivating illusions of good verses evil. It is through their growing spiritual understanding of Universal laws and principles, indeed apart of this cosmic system's plan for all life, that they gain spiritual growth, and ultimate salvation. With this being so—the only true impediment to a soul's ultimate resurrection and return home, is the negative and very real evil influences it is tempted by, and more often than not tainted by. The danger is the very real existence of the powerful and eternal dark forces ever so near to God's soul-life energy matrix. This then is the great obstacle to ultimate salvation for most unconscious misguided souls. Dark energy is ever present in abundance on and within the earth itself, and on all matter worlds occupied by young drifting wayward souls. It's long been the sole mission of the agents of Hell from the dark under-worlds to entice, entrap, and corrupt the essence of Godliness inherent in every soul-seed."

"Present company included here", (looking over at Lord Kokehead and his devilish minions). "Whoa Urge, what you thinking old man?" I mentally whispered over to him, "If you continue to play with fire, I know you know you'll get burned old dude! Hey, shit-we both could!" Sure enough Lord Kokhan jumped up and bellowed smoke and ash all over our shared table. I thought he was about to explode, so I prayed a quick prayer that he wouldn't! He turned towards the great translator as if he was really pissed off this time and said—"Excuse me Lord Translator and great Gods of Justice! If you continue to allow this fool to disrespect me, my God, and my honored hard won ranking amongst the League of Dark Angels and Inferno Law-givers of the manifest under-worlds! Then my God will be pissed and may have to come here to change things a bit! So I vehemently protest this great insult and lame-plea of excuses that we of the dark-side are totally responsible for the choices and grossly vulgar decisions that young ignorant souls make when they masquerade in human form destroying each other at will! Again I ask, what then are we to make of the so-called great gift of free-will given to all spirits at their birth? If this so-called holy court doesn't put an immediate stop to this foolishness and show me and my staff the real respect due the right-hand Emissary Advocate of the God Luciferious—then I will have to call on my God to intercede directly into these unjust affairs—hummph!"

"Then possibly the very heavens themselves may fall away to expose the true power and destruction, of a fiery Apocalypse in this Universe—or even here on this spirit plane of this great City of Light! Is it just me or does anyone else here believe that this cause, or struggle for procession of this one lowly soul-force. Could be enough to tip the scales of cosmic harmony and ruin the peace the forces of darkness and those of light have enjoyed for centuries within these holy halls of this great City of Light. So tread lightly you beings of light with little eyes! As it has been written in blood within the great books of wisdom—each soul ever created carries the great value of the seed of the Godhead. What if either side of the two sides of cosmic energy receives an unjust share of these so-called precious little jewels? Then surely the continued existence of life, of all cosmic activity of the Godhead itself could be jeopardized! Now may we please hear the words—the judgment, my royal ears representing the grand-presence of my Lord and Master, awaits from you people with little ears!" (still insulting us) he was pointing at Master Urge and me, and at the same time at the Gods of Justice and other Angels with his other paw (or hand). He stomped off back around the huge marble table obviously still pissed off at all that had taken place up to this point. The big translator looked as if he couldn't believed what he had just heard.

Did Lord Kokhan just threaten everybody here? Damn I was thinking, now what. Master Urge and his speeches had truly made Lord Kokhan crazy-mad. Lord Zulu asked Lord Nexus, as I asked Lord Urge—"Did that big ugly dragon Lord Kokehead actually threatened the Gods of Justice here, now—inside the this court!?" Whoa—damn, the shit was going to hit the fan now I just knew it! The Gods of Justice were communicating now amongst themselves—vibrating and humming louder then usual. The large translator was standing silently in front of the Orbs behind him, looking directly at Lord Kokhan, then his eyes started to glow a bright eerie yellow. He slowly begin to raise his large golden staff with an ever increasing glow at it's top matching the strange yellow light growing in his eyes. He brought his staff down hard and fast onto the marbled floor. It hit with a giant boom—then the room shook again, and everyone jumped in their seats! Slowly at first then more quickly, a large crack opened up in the floor where the big Angel's staff had struck, and it started moving towards our area! Growing bigger and wider until it reached our big levitating marble table. The table begin to crack a little—oh damn!

I couldn't move, I was frozen with fear, and remember saying—damn I told Master Urge to lighten up! Urge had floated quickly over closer to me when he saw what had just happened. Lord Zulu and Lord Nexus snatched my now paralyzed with fear body, up and out of the chair I felt glued too! They were holding my ass up (I'm sorry I mean spirit) on the other side of the court railing that had separated us a moment earlier. The big translator was speaking for the Gods of Justice now and everyone knew they each gave him a strong different kind of voice. He went from a deep sounding bass to a smooth-ass baritone to a mellow sounding soft tenor when he said with complete authority—"We have seen and heard enough Lord Advocate from the dark realms! Your behavior here today is inexcusable! You sir have no respect for these hallowed halls, by bringing the dead and near dead souls and other condemned ones into the hallways of this holy place without formal consent!" Next Orb-voice sounded—"You oh Dark Lord have shown complete disregard for the Great Translator, and the most-high consciousness of the Gods of Justice before you now! Both you and your foul associates have interrupted and continued to speak out of turn! You have continued to restrict the flow of spiritual love and healing throughout this court and great city—by attempting to bring chaos into the mist of spiritual harmony here!"

The third voice added—"Your display of the lack of proper court protocol again and again, here in this holy arena demonstrates to us who govern here and for all present that you are untrained for this! You and your dark crew Lord Emissary are a fraud of divine leadership. If your God—mentioning not his unholy name or power in this universe, sent you here to be the new Advocate for justice, spiritual balance, and cosmic harmony, he must be the biggest joker of evil manifest." The first voice returned—"Then he has failed you—as you have once again proven to us you have failed him, by being ill-prepared to follow the laws, and the great principles we espouse here! You Lord Kokhan have behaved like a simple messenger—a simple delivery boy with a big head, a undisciplined garbage man as you so willing accept this title, a evil-ego unchastised over ages, and centuries of sinful and wicked dealings!" The first deep voice continued—"We know you sir, we have your back-ground history. You are the great provocateur, the long used Lord of greed and dishonesty! You knew or should have known, there was no need for individual condemned souls to testify with self-serving, blame-placing, for the very choices they themselves made to create their sad but just conditions they still suffer under!" Again the second orb spoke through the translator's lips—"There can be no true justice made or given to any one under these haphazard and foul conditions here. You and your minions will be summararily dismissed and asked just once to leave this holy-court—yes, empty handed as of this soul's hearing!"

Then the third Orb spoke again, "Your pitiful petition and disrespectful cause against the split-soul Lee Roy and Lord Urge, will be judged a mistrial! We the most holy of God's sublime essence now find for the defense and command what is now deemed fair and expedient!" Lord Kokehead was standing now with his legs spread apart and giant paw on his hip—in a stance of defiance and shock. With short bursts of flames and smoke coming out of his large nostrils, he muttered mad grunts and groans, attempting to speak but couldn't do so. His other hand was grabbing at his own throat—I think! He obviously had been silenced by the court translator somehow, so all that were present could hear the surprising yet forceful disposition being handed down by the Holy Orbs of Justice. The great golden-skin court translator floated closer to where we were all bundled and huddled together. By now several other large gray and white robed court Angels had closed ranks around Lord Nexus, the Zulu, and me and Urge, with two more backing up the big translator. I knew it wasn't so much to protect me, but to show support for the translator. Then the translator spoke in his own voice—"You Lord Guardian Urge will hear and obey this holy edit now being rendered!"

"You should request your lower-self to rise and face the Holy Orbs of Justice. You, Angel Urge shall be reprimanded and be required to give-up your holy ranking and give back your wings to the League of Guardian Angels at once. You should have known that your fears of traveling into and through matter worlds, is unfounded and unacceptable for a spirit-entity of your class. It has caused you to lose faith in the grace and glory of the Universal Godhead. This lack of use of the powers made available to you—from this our merciful father to stay in direct physical and spiritual contact with your lesser-self Mister Lee Roy is indeed responsible for you and him being judged here today, which could have turned out much—much worse. You've been granted a holy mistrial my friend, which does not negate the accumulated sins or guilt you and little Lee Roy shall carry forth from this day forward. This just means you will not be deemed totally unworthy to reunite with him at some future time and place again. For now this incompatible spirit-union will be nullified temporarily for cause. Young spirit Lee Roy here will be given a spirit-pass for cause—a limited probationary existence to rise or fall on his own merits. This will be based on his future desires, spirit choices, and life actions during his next sojourn into matter school."

"You both may give praise and thanks for this miracle today of forgiveness and mercy that this honorable court's panel sees fit to grant you and him Lord Urge. But be advised and aware, if he fails to take advantage of God's grace, this merciful brush in time with the living love of the Godhead—then we will see you both again real soon. Know this, you two as one today are only a few feet away from falling into the pit of eternal separation and annilhalation! You both have been given only one half-day to report to the souls demarcation-deportation station of this great city. Do you accept this judgment without resentment or hesitation ex-angel Urge?" Urge responded sadly but quickly—"Yes oh Great Translator, but might I ask?" "You may." "Just how long shall we be apart and will we ever be allowed to return to this great city if I can re-earn my wings—I mean my status as a Guardian Angel or whole complete soul?""Yes you may Lord Urge once your rehabilitation and retraining is completed—perhapes over the passing of several lifetimes and with a renewed fearless spirit purpose, you may return if you so choose God's great mercy and grace." The tanslator turned and floated back towards the Holy Orbs. "One more question please (Urge asked)—in the interim, what of my young charge Lee Roy? Shall he be punished by soul suspended-animation, no longer to walk any path until I am cleansed and ready to lead him back into our trinity-state?"

"May be you haven't ben listening, young ex-Angel Urge—we three Lords of Justice all agree, (coming from the translator still speaking for the Holy Orbs with his back turned to us)—"that should be our holy decree, but his action of sacrifice for another soul, back in his old world—and his spiritual growth from his time spent here with you has given us pause. We three have decided he shall be required to repeat another existence in the same matter world he recently departed, as Hell sleeps nearby beside him. Hopefully to find away to balance out the negative karmic-influences his soul has acquired during this fifth time around. Master Lee Roy please stand! Be it known to you that usually a soul-force life-form such as yours, would have a limited say in this your continued spirit existence and judgment disposition. But to this day you haven't earned enough spiritual growth-points for us to even consider it. Do you young soul-force wish to appeal this ruling before you now—not that it would do you much good?" "Hell no!" I said without thinking, "Opps, no sir I don't" I corrected myself. Urge put a gentle hand up to my mouth—like a traffic cop directing me to stop and not talk, as he choose to speak now for me. "There will be no appeals Lord translator, we both are well pleased with the rulings and decisions of this wise and most holy tribunal. We only wish to offer up many prayers and tears of gratitude for this most miraculous outcome and the great mercy shown us here today!" The big translator said as he turned to float backwards towards the still levitating colored orbs—"miraculous indeed."

I sat down hard into my chair—truly exhausted, with only one question running rampant through my aching head—"What the hell just happened, whats up fo-real doe!? What does all this mean, (talking to no one in particular) what the hell just happened?" Lord Urge kneeled down in front of me and gently said in his most reassuring voice ever—"It's over Lee Roy—it's finally over, God is so great—thank you Jesus! It's like we caught a big break this time around young half-soul, thanks in part to Lord Kokhan's lack of self-control and disrespectful antics. It was like he was in such a hurry, and so hungry to get his hands on you again! Maybe it was me he truly wanted all along, perhaps for the Angel knowledge I posess that he would have tried to exploit to his own and his Master's advantage. Hell, I'm not truly sure myself of what went wrong—I mean right for us, word? Just kidding Blackman, Lee Roy don't-cha know it—we just dodged a serious spirit-bullet boy that could have meant our end! Truly God's great plans and principles for the life-forces he planted in this universe, are great beyond measure!" Lord Zulu and Nexus were shaking hands facing each other and jumping up and down singing like little kids—"God is great—God is great, always on time and never late!"

There was no mass celebratory clapping or singing by the other light entities, they were just quietly standing, shaking their heads in agreement, some praying, all waiting (I was told) for the translator to properly close the hearing and allow the Lords of Justice to rise and leave. I asked someone—"Hey what about Lord Kokehead?" As I was trying to look around our small group over at Lord Kokhan to see the last look on his big angry face. He was still standing on his side of the room near his dark-robed assistants cursing. I couldn't believe how calm and restrained he appeared except for the fire and smoke coming out of his large nostrils. Then I saw one of his gargoyle faced assistants was laying life-less at his feet, with the creature's neck still in Kokehead's left-hand—dead very dead! Urge said that had happened when Lord Kokhan was being chastised as he listened to the Lords of Justice's judgment condemning him instead of us! He finally could speak again (Lord Kokhan), having found his voice I guess. Every one else fail silent to listen—"Now that I have my voice back, thank you Oh Lords of Justice. I'd just like to say that I am shocked and totally disappointed in this great mockery of so-called spiritual justice! I truly don't give a damn about what this puppet court thinks about me! We were not assigned here to beg for our righteous share of miscreant souls!"

"I am of the Royal Dark Family and I'm proud of It. This place, this Universe, could not exist without the great counter point of darkness and evil to that of so-called grace or good and the cosmic-light! A very overly hyped source of light I might add! Keep in mind all that are witnesses to this travesty today, that the great darkness still exists everywhere, including within those spiritual-bodies that claim they belong to the light when its convient for them to do so! Hell itself and the great underworld exist for a reason, if this was not true—each wouldn't be so full of those lost spirits that sought to test the power of evil. Seeking to reward themselves from their damned state of self-created pain, suffering, and death! Now we all know why we have witnessed this hypocrisy of fair-play and a sham of soul judgment. Truly this fake-ass display of cosmic justice and spirit supremacy of good, of mercy, of love—always triumphanting over evil is the sickest form of self-deception and the greatest evil exhibited right here, and over there (pointing over to the now silent golden translator), and every damn where inside this perfidious cosmic comedy! Let it be written, that I—Lord Kokhan, the Imperial Emissary to Luciferious the Third himself protested this wicked abuse of universal power, as I now promise—I'll see Lord Urge and little Lee Roy again I'm sure—on my terms, on my turf, in my flaming-hot neighborhood!"

"Then we'll see if the Gods of Light, you so-called judges of spirits and souls will have the power or authority to save them, so be it! I am finished—so let it be known that I and my God don't make idle threats! So put that into your crack-pipes and smoke it over carefully! That which is done spiritually can be undone, and that which has been stolen will one day be found and returned to its lawful owner! I declare—Luciferious will have his great revenge, go ahead—write this shit down along with all the other bull-shit that has transpired here today! Oh cute little Lords of Justice—we are still most satisfied with our record here thus far. Let's see two-hundred and forty-eight wins with eighty-two give-backs and only three fucked-up mistrials! That's saying something for my Dark Master's power, it's hot! Hell, I don't care if I'm ever called upon again to come back here and play courthouse!" We all noticed that the big translator had slowly taken his time floating over towards Lord Kocain, I mean Kokhan, with his glowing staff now out in front of him. Lord Kokhan had tried his best to save face with his speech of defeat, and boy could he curse. He turned towards the dark side of the room and his minions and gave some kind of hand signal—which looked like a gang-sign to me. Which caused most of the dark visitors and shadow entitles, to quickly get up and move out the upper and lower level doors and exits on their side of the huge courtroom? They floated or flew en-masse in unison into the outer halls, not waiting for the great court translator to formally dismiss court—ending my turbulent, precarious soul hearing. Yes I believe it was finally over—thank God, thank Urge, thank God Almighty!

I think we all feared the great power of the court translator, and what he may have done if Lord Kokhan hadn't stopped protesting and cursing, while spitting large sparks of fire all over the room. I worried if this was the show-down part or the end throw-down of this spirit drama! The Great Translator was talking to Lord Kokhan as he slowly approached him and his now exiting minions and said — "It is time for you to leave us you vulgar emissary of the Dark Realms. You untrained, non-talented, empty of love spirit-priest. Say good night oh messenger-boy of Lucifer! Go tell your God and Master, that the Lords of Justice and all Angels of the Light — (the true warriors of God's power) speak as one voice! Tell him that his and your own time of evil influences and corruption on earth and all matter worlds is near its end! That he is right in only one respect — far too many of our young brother and sister souls are entrapped within your illusionary passions and pleasures of evil! Be gone foolish Devil, leave this holy place and spare us any more of your foul breath and evil stench. Say also to him — the dawning of a new era of the Godhead and spiritual freedom for all spirit-kind is close at hand. One day soon, the Heavenly Host will come for them, to free their tormented souls and bring them back into the light of their true spiritual oneness!"

"Let all who remain here today know that it is finished. This holy hearing is now over and this holy court is officially closed for the day! You may now leave this place oh Dark Emissary — go now if you value your tainted existence in the least! We shall pray for your un-safe return to whatever mental hell that spawned you and your staff." Lord Kokhan backed away cautiously from the approaching big Translator as he got closer to him, then turned and stomped down one of the ramps leading to the sub-exists I believe — never to be heard from again, we all hoped and prayed. The great translator and several court Angels had followed him to the exit, then turned and came back into the court. The translator gave one last holy command, as he moved back over to his spot near the Holy Orbs of Justice. "Attention all remaining angels, souls, entitles, and spirit life-forms. This court is closed until the arrival of a new Dark Advocate from the lower-realms is recieved, it shall be so ordered and posted. We all give thanks to the Holy Lords of Justice once again, as we accept that all is still in divine order and cosmic justice has again prevailed — peace." He then turned and faced us in my group and pointing to Lord Urge and me, he ended his protocol with — "Lord Urge and Mister Lee Roy shall report immediately to the north-wing. There to receive further directives and court seals for your default judgment and separate soul-force dispensation!"

"Go now and go with God, remembering his power of forgiveness, his essence of love." I will never forget those big yellow glowing eyes staring at me, intently, while he shook his big bronze finger at me — telling the little life-force left within me, "You lucked out this time little Lee Roy." Boy did

I know that, you think?! Like I said dear readers, don't hate the player, hate the spiritual game—I guess me and Urge are cut like that. Yeah, oh yeah, I get to go home—damn God is great! I felt like doing the jitt but didn't and only cried some tears of joy for myself and some of sadness for Master Urge. Urge looked at me and the others and simply said—"It is done, let us go—truly it's been a long day my friends. Again I—I mean we, Lee Roy and I, thank you both for your prayers and unforgettable support. We all left the court together through a rear door counting our many blessings. We were now headed towards the north-wing register's office and deportation staion. After our business was concluded there, we all gathered at our little rest spot near the great circular plaza at the center of the City. Urge had his right arm on my shoulder most of the way. While the Zulu and Nexus were talking about how great and good the love of God is, all day and all the time. Wow, we caught a holy break-word up!

They mentioned that God's grace and mercy never ceases to amaze them. Along with Urge they talked about how fortunate Urge and I had been, because they both thought it would have turned out much worst. Except that we received a little un-solicited help from King-Kong. They also shared how sad they were going to be while Urge would be away from them for a period of time, reschooling and retooling his Angel's skills. We stopped at our old rest-spot outdoor café and Urge felt it expedient to let them go, of course he was also sadden. They exchanged hugs and prayers, then took turns embracing me and each other as brothers do. They both felt compelled I think, to still give me more spiritual advice. I'll never forget what they told me that evening just before our final separation. "Little Lee Roy"—Lord Zulu said, "It was a pleasure to know you even though it was for only a short time. It shedded a new light on my friend Urge's truer nature. If you have felt his love, his great concern for his lower-self (me) as it was expressed this day in court with the sacrifice of his wings—it should instill in you forever the value that the Angels and Saints, and matter-world Over-souls have for even the smallest particles of spirit-consciousness. They know and now you do, that all of life is extremely important and valuable to the greater scheme of things. Each and every divine spark of consciousness must be fought for, must be protected and nurtured. You Mister Lee have received a gift here today beyond belief and you must treasure it young-lord in the making. Wherever you end up from this point forward, you should strive to make your light shine as bright as you can make it shine!"

"This is accomplished by growing your spirit consciousness, your ability to think righteously, and listening to that still small voice in your head—to make the best choices and decisions in life, in spirit, you possibly can ok?" Lord Nexus stepped in with—"Mister Lee Roy, what ever life form or continued existence the great spirit of the Godhead grants you this time around, has got to be a million times better then that which would have awaited you on the dark-side of our Universe. Therefore you have been blessed beyond reason. Always remember, that all—is truly spirit and that spirit is all, and that we both love you and say—one love litle brother, one love. Know that soul destruction is first caused by the unseen-power of spirit of the mental-self, creating and causing tempting indulgences and carnal desires to feed the false ego. You must strive to overcome your personal selfish ego-mind in order to come to know real selfless love, the unconditional love of God. Only then will you be able to share your love with others and to fully enjoy the love that they desire to give and share with you—understood? And please learn how to say no to drugs ok? I mean it, just say no! Love is all and all is love on the spiritual road. Know this Lee—when any soul-force chooses to intentionally hurt or cause pain and suffering towards others of its own kind in any form or fashion, even in it's thought activity—that soul condemns its own spirit-existence, a little more and more each time an evil thought or deed, a dishonest act, is committed towards other intelligent forms of consciousness. Know this Mister Lee, you have a lot of spirit-work to do on your self. So stop right now worrying about your main-man Lord Urge!"

"He'll do just fine with added time, becoming stronger and more fearless, and courageous before he re-connects with you, which I'm sure one day he will." I had to ask Urge—"Just how long will that be Lord Urge", who didn't answer me (who was sitting quietly in meditation I think), then I added before he could answer, "Cause I don't want to be anywhere to long again without my higher-self, my spiritual mentor and hero with me—you my Master Urge!" "He knows how you feel Lee", Lord Nexus added—"But his edit-decree from the court by the Gods of Justice is irreversible, and immediately binding for whatever length of time specified or conditions they have ordered. But take heart little brother, if Lord Urge works hard and studiously, he'll be back in wings and back with you in a cosmic second!" Lord Urge then raised his head, still appearing a little fatigued—ending a prayer of gratitude as he smiled at me, his lower-self. He said—"It is with much love and prayers for God's grace that I release now my two great friends and spiritual brothers from my presence, but not from my heart. Gentleman, Master Lee and I must be about our spirit business. I'll escort him to his departure portal, then I'll head straight back to the League of Guardian Angels."

"The sooner I get there—hopefully the sooner I'll be back, united with my dapper rapping hero here.""What?—(I asked him) what did you call me, your rapping hero?" "My rapping hero Lee Roy, cause I'd realized during court that you are a real hero, even to a small degree—a spiritual hero! You kept your composure and obeyed all the rules in court, and yes my friend—you've demonstrated that on a fateful day back on earth in prison—when your valued material life was given up for another, your friend Ike, so that his matter-world life may continue to exist above and beyond your own. You demonstrated that day that you understood the magnitude of the great Christ sacrifice. And thereby started the wheels turning that brought us together again—and that has never been easy for any life-force journeying through matter worlds without a whole lot of love and courage going on. Life conflicts arise because of the development of a soul's false personal ego, when spirit starts to masquerade as the false-self within a physical-body." I interrupted my higher-self, "Yoh Urge thank you again old man, listen—speaking of rapping, I never had a chance to finish giving my rap interpretations from all these notes I've been writing in this here dairy I'm never without. So since Lord Zulu and Nexus are still here and you for the moment, I'd be honored if you all will listen and tell me what you think before we all go our separate ways—Cool? Cool. So give me a minute ok, ok? (now searching my diary for the first part of my spirit-rap) I couldn't help it, and don't know exactly why I did it—I just felt I had to bust a sweet rhyme one more time.

I was excited, I was hyped—so glad just to still be alive I think. Besides my hero Urge had just called me a hero, cool—dat was so cool! So I said to my spiritual crew—"Let's do this, yoh Lord Zulu give me a deep bass beat—yoh Nexus we need a funky background swing, so come on dudes find your rhythm, be cool with it like this." Again I did a little jitt—jumping my shoulders up and down, then swung around all slow and cool like. Then started spitting all over the place using my mouth for my own beat-box, watching them all back up a few feet giving me space to bust a players dance move. I picked up my note-book rap right where I'd left off before—rapping it all again for the group. I re-did the first part, then broke into the chorus refrain, and sweetly into the second part—'You know in life you gotta get it right, to get through the pearly gates. If not then you'll get sent to hell or worse to get it straight. You know the trinities of mind, body, and soul—that's how it goes for our number one goal, before our tired old bodies fold. So check this rapper's delight. When I first awoke I seen this dude in a fifty-cent robe—I've never seen him before in life as I wondered where I was, because he was wearing all white and spoke so nice.'
'He said—so little brother you thought you had a good life, and now you must go forward and truly get it right. Your soul's in a tug of war with the dark ones and the Angels of the light. Your choices alone is what started this fight. So I stepped off to walk, just to avoid this talk—still feeling separated from my body, experiencing the blues, looked down at my feet, wasn't wearing no shoes. I studied my spirit move and it seemed like I flew from here to there. Who would have knew, this boy mister Lee Roy would one day float on air. I gotta admit that I played at being hard yawl, but really I was scared, really I begged—please Lord hear my prayers. So I speak now with an opened heart, cause my liberated soul was facing the dark. We began to embark on a mystical journey in this strange place of questions and wonders. Yes in life I tried to leave my mark, by becoming a friend to the forces of the dark. So will I make it to Heaven or will I make it to Hell. I'm counting my blessings as I asked myself well, then who do you serve? This older brother I now see in the light, who said his name was Master Urge, will he help me to get it right. He said my sins had to be purged, and added

he was my higher-consciousness. Having only my best interest in his heart, it was a new start. Then he added that when ever he talked, it would be best if I listened. Cause I could still go forward to face a fiery hell, or find myself living in an off-world pain filled cell. I felt like I kinda just left that place, but Urge spoke of an eternal death state. He said that the soul fire-works was the place that I didn't want to visit.'

'I started to shake like I was in a quake, from all these after death thoughts — that made my head ache. Making my soul feel like it was going to bust, when the last great evil I had to face was named by the Devil himself as Lord Kocainous. My main man Urge would speak words that would now ease my mind — most of the time. Telling me, my spirit-self must stay in line and I'll be just fine. I'm starting to realize and accept visions I've seen, visions of being condemned and my soul being cleaned, burning like bacon. I saw torture at the hands of Satan behind Hell's door. I may be already doomed in the sight of spiritual law, and need to worry no more. I needed to hear certain words, inspired by Master Urge as a gesture of his faith — a gesture of love, a story of fate. He said — be not afraid young soldier from the other side, my love and support for you shall never die. As he took me by the hand, and we started to walk, started to truly talk, and make our way to this great city of light — a place where evil has no might. A place where our united soul would be judged, two amongst many seeking justice amongst plenty. There were dragons, demons, and vicious killers chanting they would own my lost soul, by all of them screaming — "We love dope-dealers, don't care how young or old!'

'Hollering, shouting, chanting strange words, I started to get nervous, then I focused on my lessons from Angel Urge. When he gave his rebuttal — your most holies of holy, show us mercy in this cause against our young brother Lee. Give us another spiritual chance, and accept this as our humble plea. They said in unison, what will be — will be. Most of his life back then we know, was far from right — but while he was locked down he gave up his earthly life. For his friend called Ike, his earth-bound brother. In court Lord Urge was focused and confident. He was smooth and spoke with much passion and conviction, closed out his speech with a sacrificing petition. Some way some how a miracle was granted, our motion for mercy was a spiritual given — I felt joy and bliss, a real enormous happiness, more exciting then a kiss, being surrounded by a spiritual mist. Somehow I was released from my worries and my much troubled past, no more pain, no more grief, oh how I prayed that all this would last.' So I stopped rapping and asked them. Took time to catch my breath, and beaming with pride I said, "Whoa — thanks fellows, I think that's it. Now right here I would repeat the rap-refrain line again, but I wanted to know what you, my spiritual brothers and Urge thought?" Urge was just standing there looking proud and it appeared that he had liked it. "Mister Lee," Lord Nexus spoke up first—"Wow that was great son, quite poetic and well done. Talk about body language, I mean that little dance move and the crotch grabbing and all?"

"Whoa now" Lord Zulu said, while they both were clapping lightly for me. Urge added—"That was quite a sensation." Looking over at Zulu and Nexus he asked them—"Well my Angel brothers what did you really think?" Lord Zulu looked back at Urge then over to Lord Nexus and said to me, "You know Lee Roy you could have been a real rapping superstar player—I mean it! That was truly awesome, but we mustn't tarry, we gotta be about our angelic duties. So we bid both of you so long, adios, gotta go, and Allah be praised, keep on writing Lee ok." Lord Nexus didn't contribute anything else, they both just embraced Lord Urge one last time, as he promised them he'll see them both again real soon. As Lord Nexus and Zulu hurried away, I could vaguely see their angel wings slowly appearing and unfolding on their backs. I thought I could hear their parting whispers to each other, with Lord Nexus asking Lord Zulu—"Please pray tell me my brother, just what is a rapping superstar?" Lord Zulu answered him, "Hey I don't know! He seemed so proud of his poetry, couldn't you see that?" "So why then did you lie and tell him it was awesome, that he was great at it?" "Hey I didn't tell him it was awesome, I believe you did!" "What Zulu? You know what?" "What?" "I think we both just told our first lies, you think?" "Well what I think is that we should pray, so let us pray cool? Cool."

I turned and looked at Master Urge, who looked kind of sad, as we both watched them, such good friends take off and up, so graceful like. Urge said—"Lee you know what, I'm gonna miss those two powerful and righteous beings. I'll miss them as much I'm sure, as I'm going to miss you!" I said—"I know Urge, and the good thing is that once your rehab is over and you overcome your fear of earth, you'll come back and reunite again with me, and together we'll go find your friends cool?" "Yes—yes, you're right Lee Roy, since I've come to know again what it feels like to be reunited with my lower-self. I mean to once again exist as a whole soul-force, it has felt so good! I won't be gone to long I promise you, my love for you will stand beside that of the Christ-consciousness and together we'll be with you in spirit no matter where you are bound or found hence-forth. Come little brother—enough talk, besides I'm not good at long goodbyes—I got some one new I want you to meet before I go." We started walking like we had on many other occasions seeking mercy and justice which we found, and once again I felt a new experience coming on. Urge had his loving guiding hand on my shoulder, still reassuring me to trust him and never to be afraid again. As he talked of what he expected of me, he said—"Because I had created a miracle for another human being, and just once was all that was needed—I was then blessed to receive one. And we had received it back in the court of soul-judgment and dispensation in this great city of light. So it was time to make the best of our situation. I'll never forget how powerful Urge spoke to me, to my heart and soul's astral-mind, whatever—word.

His every word was burned into my spirit, my psyche, as I also felt this great mystical soul's dream-adventure was coming to its end. Lord Urge added—"Lee always remember that the power of love as expressed as the gift of life, is the greatest force there is. Remember also that each and every life-form is a self-contained spark or seed of the divine Godhead. It has immeasurable value and power from this our intelligent living universe. God has never wanted or created true life to extinguish itself—to end its eternal potential for reaching perfection, but to return to its eternal source, it's oneness with him. That's why he works so hard to nourish it, to heal it, and empower it—even though at times spirit life-forms seem so hell bent on feeding on themselves, and the great illusions of life. As opposed to sharing their energy to assist and help in feeding the life-force of other life-forms and the Godhead spirit that exsist around them. Remember I told you awhile back that whenever a soul achieves self-awareness (self-realization) after sleep-walking for ages—it experiences its first true light of consciousness. It then is held to a higher standard in its search for reunification with its Triune-self"

"A Soul seeks out its higher-self, its guardian over-soul, and finally its resurrection back into the source of its creation—God! Lee Roy it is and has always been our duty, and your spiritual destiny, to stay on the path towards enlightenment. Yes, yours and my own evolution into the perfect love expressed by this our living, breathing, universe as the loving, creative, oneness of God. Remember to pray daily, to meditate on questions of spirit, make good decisions, good choices before creating them firm. There is so much power in time spent communing with the holy spirit of the Godhead, for it will answer you and all your life questions. Remember to follow the Christ-pattern that has been given to us over and over again in the earth planes, and within all matter worlds since the beginning of times. Always practice this pattern of unconditional love and forgiveness towards others of your kind—humankind. Know that the Universal principles I've shared with you exist for your instruction, not your destruction, if adhered to and obeyed. They will set all souls free from sin and bring them untold bliss. The Ten Keys and other life-affirming universal principles found within all the holy books back on earth, (usually found in groups of ten) are a good place for you to start this time around young soul. Read the various holy scriptures and remember 'readers become leaders!"

"You can always manifest the joys of life, heath, wealth and happiness as a divine child of God by simply expecting the best, and making the attempt to do your best, to be the best representation of spirit you can be. Then the eternal flow of blessings and bliss will ultimately find you, and wrap you fully within the unified-field of God's protection and universal love. The one true source of our perfect expression of spiritual-life, you dig? Never ever forget young Lord in the making, it is only a hidden secret of a soul's constant evolving consciousness—that physcial-life is a simple illusion, that can be proven with deep meditation and purification of your mind and heart centers. Then you'll truly awaken to remember what is lost to many on earth now-a-days. That mankind, humankind is in actuality just little individualized pieces of God. Believing so little in themselves as human-beings and their spiritual-roots, that they embrace the old and false illusion of being separate from the Godhead. Being separated from their source and their own innate spiritual knowledge, they themselves actually impede the flow of cosmic energy into and out of themselves, their lives, their worlds. They reject the greatest known power in existence by rejecting the truth of who and what they really are!" Then I asked him, "What is it called again Lord Urge, that power you now speak of?" He smiled and simply said—"Love—Lee Roy, the power of cosmic love, the Godhead is love and love is the Godhead—the true source of all life, all health, all wealth and power!"

He also added—"The power of Creative Mind or God-mind as some celestial beings call it. Which is just another way of saying—your thinking creates your destiny, or your chosen beliefs become your throne, your faith becomes your power, your self-less love for or lack of same for others of your kind everywhere—becomes your pattern. Then when time and conditions are right, your very spoken words become your resurrection into the infinite one source—the great Godhead of all." We then heard the sound of a crowd of souls and entities gathering near the city's center. As we rounded a corner near the not-so-quiet commotion, we saw a huge bright light, hovering over a small crowd. It was floating about 10—12 feet above the marbled streets. It was an awesome sight, I mean truly mind blowing! With colored rays flashing about with sweet sparkles, and hanging, shimmering silk-like banners blowing all around and underneath this ball of light like from an unseen breeze. I could see this great Angel's face and I was surprised it was a female Angel—a women! A beautiful, levitating women, whose wings were snow white, quite large, and tipped with gold edges. She even wore a golden crown or tiara on her heavenly head. She was blessing and touching a few souls and other entities I think, gathering at her floating feet. She moved ever so slowly and so gracefully amongst them as they showered her with praise and adoration. Right then I had a flash back in mind to a movie I once saw as a kid called the Wizard of Oz and the scene where the good-witch showed up amongst the Munchkins in the land of Oz.

It was just like that but so much more! I couldn't move, I was stunned by this beautiful celestial creature. There was no other Angel or being in the city that I had seen that had even came close to her light and strong emanations of love and power. Then Urge spoke directly into my head, "She is the one I wanted you to meet Lee—she has power, she is power, for she is cosmic love itself!" I was like "Whoa look at her!" I saw her showering those that followed behind her and beneath her with rose or lotus petals as she whispered to all around her in a most beautiful voice that—"God is great—God is near, worship the Godhead and never fear. We are all one my children and all is love." Urge was now pushing me towards her saying—"I told you there was someone else I wanted you to meet, so please meet the Diamond Star!" This holy being touched down right in front of where we were standing. I was simply amazed and in awe of her most holy presence and light. She was dope, I mean awesome! Then she looked at me and smiled and nodded at Master Urge her approval of our approach.

Urge said softly, "Lee Roy meet her Holiness Diamond Star. She is the very first Arch-Angel here in the City of Light and the Over-Soul to this part of the Universe, so bow your head boy. I almost melted. Then Urge whispered into my mind, "Whatever you do or say—please don't lie to her, because she can read your heart Lee! Don't you dare embarrass me, or make me look bad in her holy presence—you hear me son, no matter what happens! She is the spiritual Over-soul and protector of this holy city and mountain. She is the royal link in the God-chain of powerful intelligences, of the Christ-consciousness class of beings that pervades this plane of spirit existence. Lee Roy she rules with absolute authority here and within every dimension in this part of the Universe. She knows all, sees all, and instructs all in the maintenance and operations of God's laws here. She is indeed the feminine aspect of the Cosmic-matrix expression of Christ himself, and yes she's here to meet you Lee! A lot of souls and spirit folks on earth have mistaken her over the ages, for the mother of Christ whenever she visited the earth. In fact she is the enigmatic-feminine principle or counter point of the Christ male pattern."

I hadn't said a word for what seemed like an eternity, when I noticed this Angel of Light was now floating just above Urge and me, and boy did she have a wonderful smile with a spiritual sparkle in her eyes. Urge had stopped talking to me and kneeled down slowly bowing his gray head low and respectively towards this Arch-Angel. Urge begin to softly pray out loud and I heard his words—"Praises to God Almighty, the source of Devine Love itself—we thank you for this very moment, your Holy presence. You feed us with your spiritual food and drink—of the body and blood of the Christos, and have given us this taste of your heavenly feast. We are indeed truly gratful and honored oh Diamond Star. As we pledge our inheritance to that kingdom where there is no death, neither sorrow, nor pain. We feel the fullness of joy in association with the Saints and Holy Beings, through the Brightstar, Jesus the Christ our Savior—Amen." "Wow, Urge—she's awesome!" She was indeed life itself, Cosmic love and power, and she spoke without ever moving her lips. I quickly found the strength to match Urge's—respectful prayerful position on the ground. Looking up I could see she was about six or seven feet tall, I wasn't sure cause I never did see her grounded. She was just floating there in the air watching us. She had two fingers of one hand held up like she was giving a gang sign or something (ok I know better) and her other hand gently draped across her small waist. Then I felt her voice inside my head—even within my heart, and it was a voice of pure love. "Good evening Master Urge and little spirit Lee Roy, (oh what a face, what a voice, and what a persona I thought) may all of Gods blessings be upon you both."

I held up my left hand to shield my eyes somewhat from her brilliance, and could see that she was truly beautiful. I was truly honored to meet such a creature and even more so that she would speak to me. My words must fail me in trying to describe all that I was feeling now. She spoke again, "I take it that all is well with you Lee Roy, and see that you have been in the very capable hands of Master Urge. I'm sorry to hear Angel Urge about the sacrifice of your wings, yet be not long in sorrow. For you Lord Urge have given and done so much good on other levels and for so many in the spiritual realms that your wings will be returned to you in short order I'm sure. Yes you have a spiritual power that is strong and well earned Lord Urge, and your young charge here has power as well." Urge said—"Yes—yes, I am more confident and blessed now and forever your Grace. It is a true pleasure and honor to be so near to you, that I truly thank God for his abundant love." She truly looked to us like a real white flame, floating slightly up and down in front of us. She reminded us her name was Diamond Star and that she travels all over this Universe healing, blessing, and intervening in cosmic spiritual matters. She didn't have to sell me on anything, I could feel the immense power she had and she said that I had power too. I knew she could raise the dead if she so desired. I knew she could walk on water if she chose to do so. Lord Urge was still kneeling when he sent me a short mental message.

"Yes Lee, she has only to speak the word and it becomes immediate and absolute—in any world, spirit or matter! Then Urge spoke directly to her—"Oh most Holy Diamond Star, indeed the very spirit of the Christ-consciousness, may I ask for your blessing for my young charge here as he goes forward into his next life. I worry not for my own life-force destiny, I only pray that all goes well for my little brother, until we can reconnect again in time to complete our journey home to the Godhead." Diamond star responded to Urge telling him—"Oh young Angel all is as it should be, your cup is full of God's love and mercy, as I grant you and your lower-self Mister Lee Roy safe passage whole and complete until all three of us meet again." Urge said, "Thank you your Holiness, then I shall be own my way now with my heart filled with unspeakable joy and bliss." He turned to look at me (one last time I felt) and added, "Lee just listen to everything she says, don't talk, don't rap, just listen and be grateful—please, ok? Always remember me, and our time spent together on this side of spiritual life. Know that I love you, like God loves all of his children, and that one day we will both see him again." I asked, "Wait Urge, when did we see God?!" I was stunned that Urge didn't answer my question, he just left me sorta hanging! "Now I must go, so wipe those tears from your eyes my mellow and go and do as Diamond Star directs"(I didn't know I was crying). "She will guide you and protect you from here on out. So stay out of trouble, and stay within the light son. Its truly been a pleasure young baller, I'll see you round the way, peace out dapper rapper." Urge finally stood up and said to the lady D-Star as he begin to fade out,—"By your leave most Holiest of Angels, I am now in transition for my time here is up, my job done—until God strenghtens my half-a-heart and speaks directly to me again, I bid you peace and farewell. I bid you cosmic grace and say Amen—wishing my eternal love upon you both." Urge bowed his head in reverence to her light, touched me lightly on the shoulder and begin slowly backing away from us. I could tell, I could feel it, Urge didn't really want to go. Not wanting to be separated from me once again his lower-self. He was holding his heart as he slowly faded completely away into the soft mystical light that surrounded all of us. "Oh God—please have mercy on him" I said. All I could think of

at that moment was that my friend my higher-self was now traveling alone
without his wings — because of me! My half-a-heart was more then heavy to
see him go, it was also hurting. Diamond Star spoke to me softly — "Wipe
away your tears young-spirit, you heard Lord Urge say you'll see him soon
again — it was promised and it will be so!"

"May I now offer you some friendly spiritual advice young soul known
as Lee Roy, before you too run out on me? First you should know that any
and all souls or life-forces that come into contact with me, being this close
see — will experience some kind of change, a transformation in their spiritual
molecular make-up, it never fails to happen but always for the better. I guess
you could call it a simple miracle or a divine-blessing of sorts. But that's not
what I truly wish to leave you with, please pay attention to these words now
young soul-force." I said quickly to her, "Yes, yes I will — please do Madam
Angel, give me your devine advice." I was trying hard to balance my joy
from being so near to her, and at the same time my sorrow from seeing Urge
leave. I finally came to realize just how much I loved him, and how much
I'll miss being apart of him again. He used to say to me that we never truly
miss our water until our well runs dry, and boy was I thirsty already for my
refreshing, uplifting higher-self. He also taught me that there were many
relationships and material things that mankind takes for granted because
they come to us so easily and usually with such a small price. Until we lose
or are deprived of those things, then we often realize — when it's too late, just
how precious they were to us. Just then I felt a gentle thump on my head or
in my mind, and the Diamond Star said — "Do I still have your attention Lee
Roy?" I quickly said, "Oh yes mame you do, I'm so sorry!"

Diamond-Star continued, "I feel your pain Lee Roy, like I feel the pain
of the smallest creature — believing itself all alone in this our cold yet loving
Universe. No soul or life-force is ever all alone. Know this young half-soul
and embrace this. You or any other soul-force anywhere, is never truly,
ever alone — understood? For the great omnipresent spirit of the Godhead
is everywhere within and without all living creatures, those with souls and
those without souls. Those in the physical-worlds, and those life-forms of
the spirit-worlds. Indeed we are all apart of the one true source, of the one
cosmic love, that forms life eternal. So have no fear my child, truly it has
never been a question of how long a soul shall live, but more the question
of how well it lives its many lives, throughout the Godhead's many visible
and invisible cosmic manifestations. See — if you never call on the great
provider and protector of souls, you limit your blessings and purposeful
existence anywhere you find yourself Lee Roy. Life-energy was created to be
lived fearlessly and abundantly at all times. Each and every soul, regardless
of its current disguise — has the unique ability to create this kind of life, an
abundant and happy life, even without selecting or choosing evil or sinful
ways to achieve it — your life is truly what you say it is!"

"Remember always Lee Roy its your choices from spirit-thought energy (the mental) that creates your desires, and your thinking and focusing on these (desires) in turn creates your actions, and the magnetic effects of your drive or actions eventually manifest according to your own designs. The key little Lee is to strive to make the best, the most beneficial choices you can make, with whatever consciousness (spiritual understanding) of the cosmic universal principle of cause and effect you have, wherever you find your spirit-self in life — in existence. That is all it takes to awaken unto your Triune-self (our trinity-state) and come to truly know that God lives within you. So Lee Roy enough of this holy chatter, if you so desire I'll escort you back to your resting place. Just a moment in time — it will be, before you can once again be put back on the path. But this time around you shall have my guidance and love to lead and protect you young soul, at least until your higher-self, Angel Urge returns to you."

Chap. 21   "Respect For The Feminine Spirit"

"Oh yes Lee before I forget—I need to enlighten you of a few more things young man-spirit if I may. So listen well ok?" With my head bowed I said, "Yes your Majesty, I hear and obey (trying to sound formal in my speech to this Holy Being)." I was still in awe of her holy presence. She began—"Throughout your many existences in and through matter worlds Lee, you have more often than not expressed your little soul-force as a male, a man-child, exhibiting the male polarity of the masculine nature of duality." I felt my mind slip a little and thought to myself, this is a bad time to lose my focus. "You have not yet gained the knowledge of the feminine side of the great illusion of spirit-duality within the physical expressions of matter. This is why you have way too little appreciation of the true nature and inherent greatness of a soul expressing itself as the female aspect of the great cosmic matrix. Hear and now learn little Lee. Most every soul has a choice in whatever sexual gender-aspect they will express in their multiple turns around the great wheel of incarnating into matter-worlds. There are many life lessons to be learned from both the male and female expressions of lost and misguided souls. Those that frequently return to the earth where you last touched down, before your journey into this astral-spirit realm, usually swing in between the male and female ego. Now I see that you are fatigued, so I'll come straight to my point little man-soul Lee. It is indeed a great honor to come to know and feel the strength of the female-matrix."

"Those souls that manifest as females on any given level of life expressions are often gifted beyond your awareness and even most times their own. They have been given great power to heal, to lead, to up-lift the very races or species that they bring forth into the world, through their own great sacrifices and long suffering spiritual act of procreation. Yes, even their powerfully cleansing tears helped to bring God's life-force (eons ago) into the fertile rivers of Africa on earth. They gave birth from celestrial bodies to the first civilizations of mankind on earth. You must always remember that without the feminine expression of spirit, the male expression can only come to know and feel half of its truest potentiality as spirit. So keep sacred and respectful the love and support, the sheer joy, beauty, and comfort that female souls bring to the male expression of spirit and to the spirit of earth. Learn to protect and cherish the soft, gentle, emotional natures of those that exist to make souls expressing as males, more whole and complete in their physically expressed lives."

"Within this our intelligent Universe Lee, it is accepted that what you call girls, mothers, and grand-mothers, the women-folk are indeed God's corporeal expressions of Diamonds and Pearls. Do you understand what I'm trying to teach you young spirit?" "Ughh—I think I do your holiness" (as I fought to keep my eye-lids open). "Ok Mr. Lee Roy, then it is time to prepare for the next leg of your journey. Know that God's great mercy and love—the truest love, has been shown to you young spirit, during these times of your visit into the spirit-realm. This love that I now speak of was once shared by a great soul of earth named Paul, with his spiritual followers called Corinthians. He said this love (God's love) is patient, hopeful, expecting, not a nagging kind of love. It is a love that's kind, not hurting with words. It is a love that's not conceited, self-centered, or ego-based. It is not a love that's selfish, nor does it keep a record of wrongs done . . . To conclude Lee, it was also a great female spirit back on Earth that spoke of this kind of love at her husband's funeral, Mrs. Reginald Lewis. Even I was touched when I heard her prayers on that sad day. She said, 'True love never gives up. Its faith, its hope, its patience endures. So my darling, (praying over her late great husband) you had it in your early life, and I tried to give it to you in our marriage. I have loved you without conditions, without reservations. My love for you will never end.' What an honour of love."

"Indeed, how beautiful her words. This love was with you in court Lee Roy, because I was present, yet invisible to your sight. Unseen to your eyes, even as I chose not to intervene, knowing that you were always in good hands my child. Indeed you had created a lot of bad and negative karmic-energy in your past lives—from so many bad choices and decisions. So know that any soul's ignorance of cosmic laws is no excuse my child, for any soul not to create better. Still you found away to create more life for another of your brothers, even at your limited stage of soul development. That took great courage and sacrificial love beyond mere mortal hope." I suddenly realized we were now out of the city and standing in a quite meadow outside the glass walls of the great City of Light, having no ideal of how I got there or how long me and this beautiful creature had been walking or floating since Urge had left us. It felt so safe—so peaceful being so near to her. She started to speak again and as Urge had requested of me, I listened to her every word intently. Truly this was the best part of this spiritual-dream or cosmic journey for me. She said—"Now it is only fair and just that you rest, and it is my celestial will that you little Lee should sleep now and pass on over. Go forward young soul-force by going back, to live a life expression that both you and I can be really proud of ok?"

"Because you—like other growing intelligent life-forms, have what it takes to ultimately achieve spiritual reunion with the Godhead again. Know that you need not die a physical death to be with your God idea, but only the death of the personal ego that your soul acquires during material existence. You must keep alive your search for understanding and spiritual knowledge, and keep the song of happiness and joy strong and deep within your heart. Know also little man that I will come and I will answer your calls, if in beseeching me or our Father God—your request is heart-felt and sincere. Rest now little one, close your eyes and sleep and revive. In your sleep you will find rejuvenation and resurrection. Sleep now you good looking man-soul, now you are a changed spirit. So you must go straight home, and know that you will do just fine. Please remember young soul, to be kind and loving to the females of your species that you will meet ok? They are always apart of you and you apart of them spiritually see, all is spirit and truly spirit is all. We are finished, it is done—go in peace and sleep now. Rustalalamba (so be it God's will)."

Even though I was feeling tired and quite sleepy I stood up from kneeling on my knees and was surprised to find myself all alone in a dimly lit room, with four blank white walls and a beautiful gray stone pedestal bed in the center of the room. There was no windows or doors, and I felt inwardly this was indeed some kind of spirit portal. The big beckoning bed looked so inviting, so comfortable, and I felt compelled to lie down upon it. I noticed there was no more Diamond Star, no Guardian Angels or spirit entities, no other sign or sense of any other soul-force in the room but my own. Truly I felt drawn to the oversized bed (or disguised spirit-portal). I then stood next to the edge of the giant bed, sleepy—very sleepy. I checked my mind for any negative thoughts at this moment and quickly reached for my spirit-dairy, and whipped out my magic pen. I felt a sudden need for speed because I wanted to capture this scene and all that transpired up till this moment, and what I still could remember had transpired on this side of midnight, before I fell off to sleep. So I knelt down on one knee with the other up to write on, and quickly scribbled down the end of my rap song. While still being pulled to get into this strange—uncertain bed beckoning me to sleep, within a white room with no doors or windows like I said. I wasn't afraid at all but I did feel tired and very sleepy now, so I had to write real fast. Again I don't know why I did it, all I knew was this rap must be blessed by the Godhead because rap itself has lasted so long as an urban art form—or maybe it's both, don't you think dear readers?

Well either that or God has a wicked sense of humor for young bloods rapping in the various hoods back on earth. Those still trying to make their own way out of the concrete jungles through music or rapping, or selling drugs or mugging each other. So I begin writing right after the chorus line of my Lee Roy's heavenly rap these words—'Some way—some how a real miracle was planted—our court room motion for mercy for us was granted. I felt joy and bliss, even enormous happiness. There was nothing more exciting than this, I was surrounded by a spiritual mist—I was relieved of all worries, all my troubles and pain. My constant fear and grief was replaced with a celestial peace. We had defeated the beast, peep this—I than felt a cluster of heat and saw a bright flash of blinding light. Her words sounded like distant thunder on a warm summers night. 'She was a pleasure to meet, a vision to greet. Speaking most holy-like, she said—'you've come a long way young soul to know love, mercy, and grace—yes I was present there thoughtout the whole proceeding, I was only unseen by you little brother, while the Gods of justice were leading. I know that I am a cosmic queen, to all souls it is love, healing, and joy I bring. Your Guardian Urge raised you up to this new spiritual level. You've grown quite mature compared to most lost souls young fellow. Most would have been truly condemned in the sight of their sins. But you and Urge somehow subdued all blame and found grace and mercy once again.'

I studied this white flame that surrounded a woman's frame, all mighty she came, showing us much love. She had accepted my shame than said, on earth I must remain, but I must now embrace a spiritual change. 'I had to wonder what this would be and I wondered only momentarily. I felt the change was acceptable to me, now a love filled being—all because I discovered love is supreme. A fragment of a whole, a particle of the cosmic fold—enigma to the mind, lost and found in a moment in time. The serpentine fires raising up my spine—setting me free to be, a new life for me—a new chapter and verse, more intriguing—more perfect than life at my earthly birth. I and my brother Urge had approached the great throne and thought it looked a lot like the great city of Rome. A great Angel looked me in the eyes for one last time, she who was of the cosmic life—a real part of my reformed mind. She sweetly told me, Mr. Lee it is time to go straight home. Go back little one and you'll do just find, with the passage of time, if you walk that fine line, between the wrong and the right, the darkness and the light. This is why you must go back—to get it right.'

'Than I fell into a deep sleep and slept even more—with my last parting vision, seeing Lord Urge smiling as he without me—walked through Heaven's door.' Wow I thought, my short sweet biographical (I think) rap prose is now complete. I've finished it—holler-holler! Somehow in some strange way, this hip-beat and rap song had been a security blanket for me. I had to write it when I did, cause I believed it was my last remaining memory of a past mad life of wickedness and evil deeds, in the foul dope-game back on earth. That now I'm having a hard time remembering all of the details, all the mad seasons and ghetto reasons—when I thought I was Mr. Big time—Mr. So-Fine, a money-getting dope dealer from the mean streets of Detroit. I finally laid back unafraid on this plane of spirit-life, this level of rest and change (on this big beckoning oval bed). Took in a big breath, feeling exhausted I sighed and fell backwards into the beckoning pillows and begin to pray—"Oh Father / Mother Godhead (the Supreme Universal Intelligence), holy be thy name—thy kingdom come (truth and love—the ultimate level of soul consciousness), thy will be done (eternal-matrix of spirit life). On earth as it is in heaven (the unseen cosmic spiritual unfolding). Give me this day my daily bread (a second chance at the spirit-dance and righteousness), as I forgive . . . (karmic law). Shoot, I just can't keep my eyes opened any longer. I feel so dam . . . sleepy," as I instinctively grabbed my crotch (bad habit, sorry yall), and rolled over on the big . . . soft bed . . . and—slept like a new-born baby, zzzzz . . . . 'Moma . . . where are you? zzzzz . . .'

Chap. 22   "Omega"

I awoke again this morning like I've done on many mornings past, questioning these strange and incessant dreams from my mind. I sat up in bed like I usually do, yawned, and fought the temptation to slide back under the warm covers. Which I would have done, except I didn't want to be late for school again. I knew I had to capture what I had just dreamed about, by writing it out in my personal dairy—which I usually hid under my mattress at night. I pushed the covers down and swung my legs out of bed still looking at them strangely. Then

I noticed my dairy was already out on the night-stand were I had left it the night before I guess. I reached over and touched it again as part of my morning ritual when waking up. As I sat up on my bed I noticed how small and ugly my night-gown was becoming. Then I stepped towards my mirrored dresser to check myself out as usual. Oh yeah I've been looking into this same mirror everyday, since I was big enough to climb onto a small chair and stand up there. Each time I would ask the same questions of myself. Who am I—or who are you, at my reflection in the mirror? Now I don't use the chair any more, while I'm standing there checking myself out. I still believe that God is not a practical joker, yet someone or something has played a cruel joke on me. I still wonder if this side of the mirror is the real world or could it be the other side that's truly real? Who was it that invented mirrors in the first damn place—I wondered?

I always notice how much I've grown up since those early days when I began to feel that something was wrong with me—wrong with my body. You see dear readers, every since I was six or seven years old I've felt like I was in someone else's body, whenever I spied my reflection in a mirror. This body continues to feel to me, like it was made for someone else. Not for me, this fifthteen year old girl named Lee Toya. I know that there is a strange and strong connection to these damn dreams I've had for as long as I can remember. As soon as I learned to write, I've felt compelled to write them down and save them for future study. I've written them down in detail in this here dairy of mine since my uncle Big Earl gave it to me as a birthday gift years ago. I guess he thought doing this would one day shed some light on why I still feel like I should've been born a boy, instead of a girl. Somebody, some where had fuc . . . -up! I know I'm a youngman whose found himself stuck in a little girl's body—damn, this ain't right! God why me, why? This shi—ain't funny! Shoot, I gotta get ready now.'

Just now my bedroom door swings open and in pops my little eleven year old bad-ass brother. He's shouting loudly at me—"Lee Toya, momma told me to wake you up miss strange fool, I see you're doing that mirror thing again huh El-sicko? Yoh my skinny older sister—you got some lose candy lying around girl?" I said to him, "Hell no runt—get out of my room now! I've told you to knock first if you ever had to come in here! Now get your little black-mailing behind out of here!" "Okaayy—(he shouted back) if that's the way you want it, no candy—no peace!" He screamed—"Mom, oh mother—Lee Toya is doing it again, I just caught her playing with her boobies again!" Damn that kid is getting on my last nerve, with his snitching little-ass! As he bounded down the stairs to save his threaten life, I heard my mother call out to me. "Lee Toya, get down here for breakfast honey—we need to talk!" I hollared back—"I'm going into the bathroom now mother." "Girl—don't—cha make me wait to long on you" she shot back. Because of that little tattle-tale useless brother of mine, I knew mom was bugging, and probably was preparing one of her loving little morality speeches for me—before I left for school. I washed my face, then my body (always feeling like some part of me was missing), brushed my teeth, and tied my hair back into a nappy pony-tail. I sprinkled on some baby powder, grabbed my perfume-spray and dashed towards the door, turned around and decided to finish getting dressed—opps. Damn school days, shoot, I can't wait for the week-end to get here!

Now in my fly denim Baby-Phat hook-up with fresh K-Swiss kicks I bounced down to the kitchen. I sat down at the small table in the kitchen nook to wolf down my breakfast and said—"Goood morning my sweet mother, please tell me just how much time would I get in jail for really jacking up an eleven year old rat? Oh I don't know for sure honey but, probably the same amount of time I'd get for hurting you real bad for hurting your little brother! He told me he saw you playing with yourself again—huh?" "That kid is a fool mom, when he burst into my room—I was just touching my, my breast. They seem to have grown bigger over night. You and dad wonder why I hate this body!" "Lee Toya, we've had this talk before young lady—I've told you many of times already that God doesn't make mistakes. If he put you into a little girl's body, then that's what he wants you to be." "Oh yeah, well please tell me about that thing called free-will mother-dearest, didn't I have a right to choose?" "Ok—you should love who you are—as you are, and be thankful for this family! Do you feel me Miss Lee?" "But momma, I've also told you many of times that somebody, somewhere, made a big mistake with me and this body!" "I'm still having those dreams again, you know—the ones I wrote about in my dairy?"

"No—I don't know exactly which dreams you're talking about, because you have so many and you won't let me read your private dairy—right?" "Yeah right—they're private dreams all right." "I know honey, so listen, you eat your eggs and grits before they get cold and I'll talk—ok? First, I'll talk to your father again about your on-going concerns, he seems to be accepting what I've shared with him already. But you need to seriously consider allowing yourself some counseling for this matter of your sexual orientation. Your father thinks like I do, that it may shed some light on what we can do while you're going through this sexual-identity crisis. Maybe you too should talk to your father again honey—you know I got-cha back ok?" "Mom I'm just not ready to go into these things again with dad—not yet!" "You know how traditionally male he is, I still think he's grieving over these past four or five years since he heard of how I felt about other girls. Hello—he's probably still grieving over the fact I wasn't born his first baby boy! Isn't that why he spoils that little brat brother of mine and kinda shuns me sometimes?" "Girl, all that foolishness stopped about five or six years ago after your little brother was born. Seriously Lee Toya—your father loves you very much and he stands behind your little strange tom-boyish ways." "See—that's what I'm talking about mom, I think he thinks that what I'm experiencing—what I'm going through right now will pass away as soon as I truly discover what girls really want from the boys. Whatever it is I don't want any from them!"

"Or what boys want from us girls he's talking about, I think I want it from other girls—not the boys, word up?" "Child hush your mouth, we will love you regardless!" "Mom I'm still attracted to other girls, but I haven't acted on those feelings yet!" "Ok—ok, too much information—no more talk now, we'll pick this conversation up this evening when you get in and have completed your homework—ok?" "Ok mom, I love you and I got to get to the bus on time—word!" "Lee Toya, remember the journey of life is itself a school—and I've learned that no matter how dark or depressing things can look in our little confusing and often times complicated lives, truly it's at the darkest moments when the stars (star light) above comes out. And the darkness always yields to the light baby-girl even star light. You my dear are my light, and your father's too—regardless of what any dreams or visions may be telling you at your young age ok?" "Ok got-cha mom, gotta go—I'm a little late now, besides there's only one other person that seems to understand what I'm going through. I'll call him when I get back". I rushed to open the front door to our middle-class house, in this so-called middle-class neighborhood—to dash to the bus stop two blocks away.

I heard mom call after me as I hit the sidewalk blazing—"Lee, so who is it you gonna call when you get home baby-girl?" Before I got to the end of the block I hollered back—"I'm going to call my wise and open-minded uncle, uncle Earl—your brother. Because he always knows what to say and do whenever I have a problem—cause he's cool like that." Mom shouted back standing in the door—"hummph! I'll see ya, wouldn't want to be ya." Yeah I thought to myself, as I boarded the school bus I'd almost missed. Still putting on my earphones hooked to my walkman-cd player in my back pack, I said to no one in particular—'I don't want to be me either. At least not with big boobs, lip stick, and nail polish, yicky stuff—girly stuff!' Damn, I thought as I sat down in the front of the bus like a proud Rosa Parks. I think I just might be a real fly gay be-atch, a real lesboe?! So what if I am, I know I'm still a divine child of God! That's all my dreams have been telling me, that everyone—everybody, even the strange and different ones amongst us are still a part of God. God has always expressed himself in many cultures and faces, genders and races. That's all that really matters—hello? I nodded off a little on the school bus while bouncing my head to the rap-tune by Eminim coming through my earphones—'will the real Slim-Shady, please stand up, please stand up.' Fuc—it, oops sorry. I needn't worry, I know God lives within me and even the confused haters of the world—word up! Look out ladies, Le'Toya is on the hunt—sheeit!

Epilogue—here are some additional notes from Lee Toya's dairy: Omega—the last letter of the Greek alphabet and the end to the beginning of Alpha. Here now in her own words is a few other thoughts and dialogue from Lee Toya's dreams that prompted the story 'Lee Roy's Heaven—Alpha to Omega'. Read and enjoy.

> "Because of the great illusionary nature of living on earth, with every soul caught up in physical material bodies—trying to understand and get it right (life and living it that is) and suffering under the weight of a false ego, that assumes that life revolves around itself. We as spiritual energy enjoy masquerading as human-beings who tend to become very selfish and small-minded people. Looking at each other every day and not noticing our sameness, only the false differences that truly don't exist. I'm sure that God is not always amused. There is too much self-hate, race-hate, fear, and lack of courage and honesty in our dealings with other human-beings. I believe it's because we perceive others to be so much different from ourselves then we really are. Even though we bleed the same blood, cry the same tears, share the same hopes and dreams of all people. Yet we can be as cruel and mean-spirited towards each other with vicious gossip, spreading malicious rumors, lies, and hating on our superficial differences. Totally oblivious as to the negative effects (short and long term) these backward and uncivilized attitudes will have on our own spiritual growth and destiny down the road. Karma is real—yes we will continue to reap that which we have sown in our lives, spiritually and otherwise—word up and grow-up peeps."

> "True spiritualized folks—the real givers and care-takers of our world see no color, or race, no age or sexual gender distinctions between the many

manifest life forms of spirit-energy. They seem to understand that even the lowly cock-roach has its place within the greater scheme of things. They see no rich or poor, no sick or perfect heatlh, they inwardly know that all are one, that spirit is all. And that all that is seen (and unseen) is spirit. They see this world as not existing without the good folk and the presumed bad, the Yin and Yang of many hearts, that daily gives and shares a cosmic love even on a small level. That true religion is always endowed with enormous compassion, tolerance, and acceptance. I once recalled reading a very potent phrase that more people need to hear, it read—'there is so much bad in he best of us, and so much good in the worst of us, that it hardly behooves any of us to talk negatively about the rest of us—word!"

> "Truly I believe what an old Angel once told me in my dreams. If ever I must choose to grow up with love or hate, happiness or anger—that I should choose both love and happiness every time. Because if I look for and search for these while growing up, in spite of a bumpy or ragged start, then I shall find them more and more manifesting within my life. He said seek and you shall find, knock and it (the door) shall be opened unto you, and ask and it shall be given to you."

"In other words—choose to know God first (seek his kingdom), choose to embrace his light over the darkness of our own self-created illusions, evil choices, and sinful actions. To experience the true freedom that only truth can bring to any suffering or blind spiritual being. I say,
I fear no evil (man-made or otherwise) because the Christ-consciousness (God's holy essence) within me is my eternal light—which the darkness can never prevail against. I am a divine child of god and shall live eternally with him always, and so will every one else in spirit."

>"We are all a tiny part (truly a magnificent part) of the great circle of life and death. Every human being may walk a different path to enlightenment and spiritual consciousness feeling all alone—not knowing or fully believing that the spiritual guardians are with each of us, all day, all the time. Even though they remain unseen to the limited eye—in most cases even their voices inside our heads go unheard—often unheeded. They too (the invisible guardians) like ourselves are indeed children of the light, the Universal Light of the Godhead. I know that God is love, and all life in this our grand and living Intelligent Universe is precious and needed. In truth there is only spirit, with many faces, speaking many languages, and dressed in many exterior forms. All species and all life truly originate from the same source—the living life energy and love of the Godhead. His light can be so blinding, and yet even harder to find—but once found, it becomes a healing, reawakening experience. A spiritual resurrection, a miracle of enormous grace, a rebirthing back into God's unified field of a loving infinite cosmic consciousness."

> "Again life and death are but two sides of the same cosmic spiritual-coin, a different level of spirit-consciousness for sure. The truest reality at any given time in the expression of life-force energy as a man or woman, a confused soul or enlightened individual, searching for spiritual knowledge and guidance in a world of matter—is this very moment in time! This moment is all we really have, all that is truly real, unbeknown to most—as a spirit-reality! Yesterday has gone forever, tomorrow is yet come—so this very moment in time' is all there really is see? . . . A single split-second in time awake—is a very special gift of consciousness, hence it's called 'the present'. Spend your moments in loving all others (at least trying to) and being opened to love. We can all live victoriously through the creative force of our own free-will saturated with Christ-like love. It's true, the spirit of God is real and lives within us all, even the lowly ants, Amen to that."

From Big Brother Earl: "Once again—if any readers of this story happens to cross paths with my little niece Lee Toya while in Detroit, please be patient with her, tolerant, and respectful—even loving towards her if you can. Because it's true, she is, was—and is again, a little mirror of who and what we all are I believe. I also believe she's been a straight-a-student since kindergarden and is very bright and enlightened for her age. I have always encouraged her to study world religions and spirituality. I personally believe she's really an old soul. You know, the ones that think and act way beyond their years of experience on earth. Yes I believe in her spiritual potentiality—might you the reader do the same? So stay true to your own spiritual adventure, because no one in a physical body on this earth, at present—is ever perfect, not even the Pope or the Dalai Lama."

"Until all of us (every soul) can get it right—life and living it that is. So untill we meet again, and again, and again if necessary, let us help God to increase the peace. Damn, now I'm sleepy—good night my beloved readers, and to whichever God you believe in, thank him or her for all life—One Love. Lee Toya and I (her uncle Big Brother Earl) says God bless you and your families . . . The good, the bad, the ugly, the beautiful, my own, your own, ours, them, theirs, those other folks—until these, our little life stories and humanity is finally one for-real-doe, sweet spiritual dreams—peace out family."

"Let us all (spiritual beings masquerading as human beings) dream a new dream. Let us dream of a world in which judgment is never again visited by one upon another, in which conditions are never again laid down before love is offered, and in which fear is never again seen as a means of respect. Let us dream of a world in which differences do not produce divisions, individual expression does not produce separation, and the greatness of the whole is reflected in the greatness of its parts." From the book series — 'Conversations with God' and 'Communion with God' by Neal D. Walsh — read them soon — O.M.G!

"Dear readers — thanks for your time, that's all the time it took . . . and so the story ends . . . for now. Read Lee Roy's Heaven — Alpha to Omega twice thank you. There is great wisdom and truth within these pages, believe it!

P.s. Question: "A brother can still dream can't he? Lets keep hope alive, no justice no peace, no bacon no grease, no God no love, no love no sex, no sex no children of God, back to our source, the alpha and omega, to return to forever, Billy Grahm Jr. — eat your heart out, ok I apoligize, writer's cramp u-know, let us all pray — Psalm 23. Jesus Christ Superstar — one love. Think people — it's not illegal yet! Oparah I'm coming my beloved Mississippian, sometimes u feel like a nut, sometimes u don't, pardon me, L-7 I'm out!"

— BigBro. Earl Roberts

Please enjoy deciphering and reading — A Sage's Lament — 1st, 2nd, & last puzzle-pages of this book, and send me your positive comments about Lee Roy's Heaven — Please order copies of this great fictional-spirit drama online for your family and friends. Yeah a brother got eat right?

The author — Big Brother Earl Roberts A.K.A.
Eddie Robinson II

Thanks Trafford Online Publishers

I WISH TO THANK ALL THE READERS OF MY FIRST BOOK FOR THEIR SUPPORT AND CRITICISM GOOD OR BAD, THANK YOU. FOR THOSE REQUESTING A (FREE-2-PAGE) SOLUTION-TRANSLATED COPY OF THE ENCRYPTED SHORT STORY—BOOK BONUS "A SAGE'S LAMENT", FIRST-2 AND LAST PAGE OF THIS BOOK. PLEASE SEND ANY POSITIVE COMMENTS AND A SELF-ADDRESSED ENVELOPE TO THE ADDRESS LISTED BELOW:

E.R.J. & ASSOC./ A SAGE'S LAMENT-L.R.H. AT HIBBARD COMPLEX— 8905 E. JEFFERSON AVE. Ste.# 503 OFFICE, DETROIT, MICH. 48214-4104 PLEASE ALLOW 3-4 WEEKS RETURN-DELIEVERY. P.S.—"GO EVERYONE TELL—THIS IS BOOK—A READ MUST—SURE FOR." BIG EARL BROTHER ROBERTS. WARNING, DON'T READ THIS BOOK IF YOU ARE HIGH, THANKS.

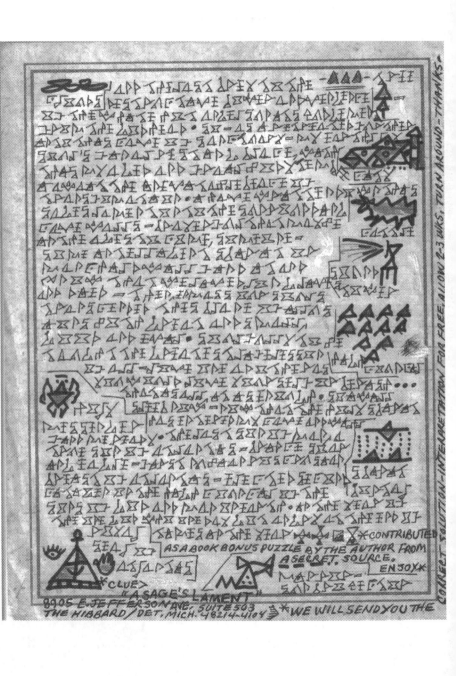

CLUE>
"A SAGE'S LAMENT"

CONTRIBUTED AS A BOOK BONUS PUZZLE BY THE AUTHOR FROM A SECR.FT. SOURCE.

ENJOY

8905 E. JEFFERSON AVE. SUITE 503
THE HIBBARD/DET. MICH. 48214-4104

WE WILL SEND YOU THE

COLLECT SOLUTION - INTERPRETATION FOR FREE. ALLOW 2-3 WKS, TURN AROUND - THANKS!